UNEXPECTED PASSION

Rose quietly approached the bed and stretched over it to steal a pillow from under his head. As she leaned over his chest, Trent groaned and rolled over, pinning half her arm under his head.

When Rose began to move her hand from under the pillow, Trent's arm came up and around her back, flattening her against his chest. Before she could utter more than a little gasp of surprise, she was swept under him and he was kissing her.

"Trent," she managed to say between kisses, "I'm sorry I woke you."

"Don't think of it."

"I only wanted a pillow."

"You can have the whole damn bed. Now be quiet and kiss me."

Rose's lips turned up slightly. "Are you sure you're not angry?"

"God, Rose, what would make you think that?" He moved his lips down her neck to the rise of her breast.

When he moved even lower, Rose tensed with anticipation. Her hands rested on his shoulders, his held her hips. But as he brushed light kisses over her stomach and down her thighs, if there was an inkling of protest left in her, it was quickly smothered by the suddenly overwhelming heat that raged inside . . .

ANN LYNN

PASSION'S CHASE

ZEBRA BOOKS
KENSINGTON PUBLISHING CORP.

For my sister, Nancy Lynn Harlow

ZEBRA BOOKS

are published by

Kensington Publishing Corp.
475 Park Avenue South
New York, NY 10016

First printing: August, 1992

Printed in the United States of America

Chapter 1

Not everyone would chance to navigate the deep ditches in Bailey Road on a rainy moonless night, so the route from London to Briar Hill was even more lonely when Rose and her father chose to travel. A heavy rain made lakes out of the ruts that potholed the main road, turning the journey into a hazardous venture.

Rose gripped the side of the coach as the vehicle lunged again to the left, its wheels dipping into a rut. Hardware jingled and leather creaked from the strain to keep the coach from tipping over. Another bump sent her off her seat and caused her bonnet to come sliding down over her eyes. Pushing the offending item away from her eyes, Rose grumbled. "This is a hellish reception, Father." She couldn't disguise her annoyance at being packed up and brought to England to spend a year with her staunch English aunt. Her father had threatened to send her to Briar Hill not less than a hundred times, but never did she actually think he would.

"And swearing, too," Roger Whitley said as if that were all the proof he needed to drop his incorrigible daughter in his sister-in-law's lap. Sadly, he had more reasons than that.

It troubled him to think that Rose was becoming as brazen as the Miller boys she kept company with. There had been little he could do to discourage her friendship with them until he had received his sister-in-law's invitation to spend a few weeks at Briar Hill. A few weeks! If Rose was to be groomed into a proper lady, she would need more time with her aunt than that. He had to swallow his own pride and admit that his wife's sister had been right all those years. Rose would grow up wild as an Indian, Stephanie had predicted when he'd taken his daughter from England to live with his family in New York and the woman was not too far from the truth. With only a mild-mannered housekeeper to keep an eye on her, Rose had grown a little wild. And he did spoil her, letting her grow up expecting to always have her way.

It may have been his prejudice, but at nineteen Rose wasn't just bold, she was beautiful, too. She had seemed to grow into a woman overnight. Never had his guilt for raising her in what Stephanie still referred to as the colonies been more evident than in the past six months, when Rose seemed to have changed from a tomboy into a woman of her own mind. If he could turn back the years and right his wrongs, he would stay in England if only to assure that Rose would grow to be as well-mannered as his dear wife had been.

If he could have seen into the future, he would have let Stephanie raise the child as she had offered. But instead he had packed up everything after Roseanna had died, and he'd settled far away from the sad memories. It was now all water under the bridge; immediate worries needed addressing, not past ones.

He hadn't worried half as much about Rose when she was little as he did now that she had blossomed and would be attracting every male within riding distance. Rose didn't know it yet, but she'd break hearts with her looks—her buttery hair, ivory skin and saucer-blue eyes that could stop one short. And her mouth, which was by far her most fetching feature—wide and full and, if she could keep it closed long enough, very kissable. A long sigh escaped him. Stephanie would have to be firmer with Rose than he had been.

Roger Whitley confessed aloud, "An English upbringing would have been better than letting you grow up in America. You've been left to clamber with no direction, like a wild rose."

"That's not true, Father. You've just been listening to Mrs. Ratchet and that tattletaling old maid, Miss Willard." Absently centering her bonnet again, Rose dared to argue, "I don't want to stay with Aunt Stephanie. She'll protect me like a baby."

"And well she should. You're her sister's child, and the very image of your mother. Except for the polish," he amended under his breath.

"I heard that. For heaven's sake, she'll have me sipping tea and curtsying up and down from dawn to dusk."

"And you'll be saying 'Thank you' and 'Excuse me' and not be using those dockside words you picked up from the Miller boys." He faced her and held her soft apple cheeks in his hands. "Honey, the men will soon be flocking at your feet. I only want the best for you."

7

"Well, I'll not be marrying any lords," she warned. "Aunt Stephanie's not going to stick 'Lady' in front of my name." Her voice softened when she realized how she was upsetting him. "I'm sorry. I know mother was an English lady. It just wouldn't feel comfortable to me, that's all."

Rose didn't want to sadden or disappoint her father, especially since she wouldn't be seeing him for a year. Rather than give cause to continue the argument, she focused on the rain-packed wind that whipped against her window. The gloomy weather reflected darkly in her eyes, deepening their dazzling blueness. She hated the storm clouds for making her sad. They brought with them the melancholy of her life—the death of her mother and now her separation from her father. "It's the angels crying over you, Rose," her nursemaid had said on the day the ground took her mother. Soon after, the storm clouds came again to carry them to America. It had even rained with a fanfare of thunder and lightning the night her Uncle George died; she'd felt the premonition of death as the dark clouds rolled over the sky and shrouded the sunshine of life. Since then, whenever a storm raked over the sky, fear began to rush through her veins and she knew something terrible was about to happen.

"Father, don't you think it would have been better to stay the night in London? I don't know how the coachman can see where he's going." She tried to look past the amber glow of the lamp.

Roger Whitley explained for the second time. "Your aunt expected us yesterday. I don't want her to worry more than she has to. She's anxious to get you under her wing. Don't look so glum. You'll like it at Briar Hill."

Rose sighed. It was the same argument, but no matter how much her father insisted and no matter how many reasons he gave as to how wonderful it would be, she still didn't want to spend a day, much less a year, with her aunt.

Rose squinted through the raindrops. "I wonder how far we've gone. We'll be on the road half the night at this pace."

Roger Whitley struggled up from his seat. "You're right. The man can do better."

"No! Father!" But Rose's plea was too late—he was already beating the window with the tip of his umbrella.

"I'm sorry if I distressed you, Father." She scrutinized her father's troubled face in the yellow coach light. "I will try to be civil to Aunt Stephanie. I'll watch my tongue. I'll have her wondering why you've put me in her care," she declared, trying to lighten her father's mood. He merely grunted and stared into the black polished glass of the coach window.

It didn't take Rose more than a minute to determine the real reason for her father's agitation, and it warmed her heart: he was truly concerned about her and didn't want them to be parted any more than she did. She also knew he'd have to suffer through her aunt's declarations that she'd have been the perfect lady had he not gone to the colonies. She didn't want to give her aunt cause to criticize her father. She really would try to be good, even if it killed her. She took her father's arm in hers and squeezed it.

"Will you be staying at Briar Hill long, Father?"

"No."

Rose's heart sank. "A week at least?" she asked. Roger turned his face away from the window

9

and looked softly at his daughter. "I'll be leaving no sooner."

"Good. Then you'll be here for . . ."

"For what, dear?"

"Nothing, father."

He knew the light in her eye meant she was up to something. "What is it, Rose?"

Rose's blue eyes widened to innocent saucers, and her gloved hands grasped her father's. "Lord Byron is visiting London." She could hardly contain her excitement at being in London at the same time as the popular poet. It was the only thing that seemed to make her arrival in England worthwhile.

His hands tore away from her grasp. "Do you know what he's doing? He's inciting revolution. I don't want you getting involved in this Greek Independence thing. It's too dangerous. Not to mention, if you breathe a word of it your aunt will swoon. She still holds a grudge against Americans for revolting against the king."

"Father, President Madison supports Greek Independence. How can you not be behind their efforts?"

Her father groaned. "You know that's not it. It's not a woman's affair, is all. Keep your opinions to yourself while you're here, missy." He smiled, giving her chin a nudge.

Suddenly, the coach lurched off to the side, throwing Rose into her father's lap. Before she could recover, it jumped a foot off the ground and then slammed down into a muddy ditch. When all motion stopped, the floor was a steep incline. Rose imagined their coach to be teetering on the edge of a ravine, ready to tumble end over end to the bottom of an unseen gorge. But instead, everything was quiet and steady.

"What is going on?" Roger Whitley blustered.

"You'd best come out here, sir," the coachman's voice quivered nervously.

Rose and her father exchanged alarmed looks.

"Stay quiet in here. I'll go see what he needs."

Trying to hear all that was being said, Rose leaned against the coach door. She could hear voices other than her father's and their driver's but in the moonless night found it difficult to see past the window glass. She leaned her full weight on the door and strained to catch every word of conversation.

"Put it right here. That's right, the ring on your finger, too," the dark voice demanded.

"We're being robbed!" Rose cried, her shocked voice muffled in her gloved hand. Before she could think of what to do next, the carriage door flung open. She tumbled out into the pitch black and landed with a splash into a muddy hole, taking the thieves off their guard long enough for her father to seize the second of confusion and turn it to his advantage.

Rose heard the ensuing riot from the puddle she sat in; however, the black night and the downpour masked the assailants beyond easy recognition. They were mere shadows moving around her father and the coachman as the two valiantly tried to defend themselves against the marauders.

Well-landed punches skidded against wet skin, mud sucked at the men's feet and hindered their movement, expletives flew and then a final slam of flesh against flesh sounded above the gentle dripping of rain, ending it all.

Weighted by her wet skirt, Rose struggled to get to her feet but was knocked back to the ground

11

when someone sailed into her. She heard her breath rush out of her in a scream laced with shock and indignation. By now her skirt had soaked up water and mud like a candlewick.

Rose looked around. There wasn't much she could see with the pouring rain running into her eyes. Two bodies stirred and groaned next to her. One was her father and the other she assumed, was the coachman. The horses were calm, held by one of the highwaymen. The leader, she guessed, sat perched on a huge horse and had a gun pointed directly at them. If there were others besides them, they were hidden in the soupy night.

"Stay where you are," the thief warned when Rose moved. "I don't want to harm you. Just collecting a little donation for the cause."

Roger raised a stilling hand to his daughter's arm. "Do as he says, Rose."

The thief reined his mount over to her, its big hooves slapping in the mud. He chuckled as if the whole affair was quite amusing and then, leaning over his horse, lowered a sack down to her. "You don't mind, do you, miss? Put it right here in the collection plate."

With the thief sitting so unbalanced on his mount, the sack dangling down in front of her nose was too tempting for Rose to ignore. With a sweet "Certainly," and a vindictive smile, she grabbed the bag with two hands and yanked as hard as she could. When she felt the line between herself and the thief slacken, she rolled aside. As she intended, the thief fell off his horse, a string of expletives following him into the muddy ditch.

Rose would have been on her feet had it not been for the soaked skirt that wrapped around her legs, but so hindered, she only managed to scramble a

12

couple of feet away before the angry highwayman pulled her up under his arm and pinned her against his hip. Deep laughter from his accomplice boxed her ears as she struggled to free herself from the thief's crushing hold. The light of the carriage lamp flashed off a gold locket that had fallen out from under her pelisse. The locket dangled temptingly from her throat.

"What have we here?" the thief asked, grabbing the locket with intent to rip it off her neck. It had opened in the struggle, revealing a miniature of her mother. The small painting made him pause, and then, as if he had touched a hot poker, the thief dropped the locket and put her on her feet, quick to catch her arms when she tried to thrash him. "Stay still," he ordered, "or I'll have to tie you up, and you wouldn't want that, now."

"Rose, for heaven's sake!" her father yelled.

"That's a good girl," the masked thief said approvingly. "You can keep your jewelry—if you behave—and we'll be on our way." He backed away from her as he talked, keeping a close eye on her in case she rushed toward him, and then swung up on his horse in one fluid movement. "Your donation to the cause is appreciated," he said with sincere politeness. In their hasty departure the thieves raised a blinding shower of mud and then disappeared into the murky night, ending the traveler's nightmare.

A low moan drew Rose's attention as soon as the thieves turned to leave. "Father, are you all right?"

"Ashamed to admit . . . a bit bruised, but I believe I'll live." He turned to the still man beside him. "We'll have to give our driver here a few more moments to get himself together. How are you, darling?"

13

"Muddy! Those despicable brigands! Well, at least they didn't take my locket for their cause."

"And I wonder what their cause might be," Roger grumbled, spitting mud from his mouth and wiping his hands on his pants. "Well, at least they'll be taking a few bumps and bruises of their own back with them," he concluded with satisfaction.

Rose straightened her soggy bonnet. Perhaps living with her aunt wasn't going to be so boring after all. She thought about the thief, his black silhouette and his voice, all the rest of the way to Briar Hill, while her father ranted and raved about how he'd find the thief out and see him hang from the gallows before he returned to America.

Rose indulged in the slim hope that the circumstances of the night would keep her father in England a little longer. Taking advantage of her father's outrage, she dared to ask, "Does this mean you'll be staying at Briar Hill indefinitely?"

Roger grimaced in the shadowy light. "It's not going to take long. Thieves are a greedy lot. He'll be working this road again, but next time he might just get caught."

Rose Whitley leaned her head against her father's shoulder and shivered.

"You're soaking wet, Rose! I hope you don't catch a chill before we get to Briar Hill."

When Stephanie Vanderhue's butler, Harold, opened the door on the two muddy callers, he was tempted to close it again quickly. It was Rose's quick explanation that numbed his good sense to turn the beggars away. "I would rather have stayed in London but father wouldn't hear of it so we've

14

traveled half the night in this horrid storm and if that wasn't bad enough we were robbed along the way—in case you're wondering. Is Aunt Stephanie here?"

With an arched brow, the butler looked to her father. "Please tell Lady Vanderhue Roger Whitley and her niece, Rose, have arrived."

The astonished servant stepped aside so as not to be muddied by Rose's cape as she whisked past him. Roger Whitley walked in after her, slapping his wet gloves, hat and cloak in the butler's hands.

The wide doors of the front entrance swung open to a dark paneled hall. Bright flowers and vines sprayed from a large urn which rested on a round marble-topped table. Visitors were greeted with the fragrance of a spring garden in full bloom. Triangles of marble polished to a satiny sheen spread out over the entranceway floor in a pattern of rose and green. Ornately framed paintings of family members graced the walls, and between the paintings lamps burned softly, warming the smileless visages. Not a happy face in the bunch, Rose thought dimly. One painting in particular caught her eye, a larger version of the miniature in her locket. A beautiful blond-haired woman with startling blue eyes drew her close. There was a sadness in the bare trace of a smile, as though her mother had tried to force herself to appear happy.

Rose's eyes swept up from the gallery of paintings to the balcony of Tudor oak that nearly circled the entranceway. "It certainly is more spacious than our home," she said as her eyes scanned the vaulted ceiling and trailed over the curved staircase. "She lives here all by herself?"

"Your cousin Philip pops in now and then I'm

told. And there are the servants."

"Of course."

Rose wasn't surprised or disappointed when she saw her aunt grace the top of the staircase; she hadn't had a set impression of her aunt's appearance, only of her personality. The heavyset woman was very elegant looking. She descended the staircase with the grace of a queen, the train of her deep, purple gown obediently flowing behind her. She wore her gray hair like a silver crown, all on top of her head in thick curls, and smiled down at them regally. Rose whispered to her father, "Is this when I curtsy?"

"It may well get you off on the right foot," he advised.

When Stephanie saw their condition, she gasped. "My heavens, what's happened?" She put her hands aside Rose's soggy bonnet and set it straight, clucking her tongue all the while.

"We had a little excitement on the road. Nothing to worry yourself over," Roger assured, then turned to introduce his daughter. "Stephanie, this is Rose." Rose did her best to appear regal and not stumble when she curtsied in her wet and muddied clothes.

Stephanie smiled. "My, how she's grown into a lady. I really can see Roseanna in her face, Roger."

"Yes, she's the image of her mother," he agreed rather uncomfortably, knowing that her appearance was all she had inherited from her mother.

Rose just smiled politely, not knowing what else to do and not wanting to disappoint her father at their first meeting by saying something she shouldn't.

Once the formal introductions were met, Stephanie turned a critical eye on Rose. It was the kind of look that made her feel like a problem to be tackled in the morning. And not to have her suspicions disappointed, she was hurried off upstairs for a bath and a good night's rest.

The following day, Roger Whitley had posted rewards all over London, but it seemed his efforts had been in vain. No one could identify the thief who for days after, brazenly continued to lighten the rich of their wallets and jewels for his cause. The thief never completely stripped his victims of their valuables and always remembered to thank the people for their generous donations in the name of Greek liberation. Roger doubted it was likely any of the so-called funds found its way to helping Greece loosen the hold of the Ottomans.

Rose delighted in the excitement of it all but was careful to heed her father's warning and not discuss the thief in front of her aunt. However, she did discuss him with her father, and thankfully he spoiled her with stimulating conversation.

"This is all Lord Byron's fault . . . stirring up the fanatics into thinking they can steal for freedom." Roger's fist punctuated his words, shaking the legs of the mahogany breakfast table and rattling teacups in their saucers.

"Well, at least the proceeds are going to a good cause. The thief isn't stealing for his own profit, or so it seems." Rose dodged her father's frosty look. Once the teacups settled, she dared to fill them. "He did leave my locket," she reminded him, remembering how the thief had paused with it in his hand, as if he recognized the painting in it.

"You sound as though you're defending him. Have you forgotten he absconded with my ring and all my money? I'll have to borrow money from your aunt for my passage home." Rose assumed silently that that was the real cause of his distress. "I wouldn't call his booty proceeds. Call it what it is—stolen property. And how do you know it's such a good cause? The world's at peace now. Why stir it up? Madison may have spoken up for Greek independence, but his views are not shared by everyone. Even the Holy Alliance is not ready to disturb the existing balance of power in the region."

"There are many who would like to see the Ottoman Empire weakened."

Roger Whitley held up the morning *Times* and stabbed it with his finger, drawing her attention to the bold headline. "Look here. Do you know what they're calling him? The Liberty Thief."

Rose watched her father's monocle pop like a cork and then bounce off his chest. She covered her smile with the rim of her teacup.

Roger looked at his daughter. "Humph! Liberty Thief! They're making a folk hero of the man who robbed your father."

Rose changed the subject to one of a lighter matter. "It was clever of Aunt Stephanie to have a masquerade. It's sure to be a success, don't you think?"

"I wonder if she'll lure the Liberty Thief. A thief," he mused, "would be well concealed at such a gathering."

"What's all this fuss about, Roger?" Stephanie asked as she swept into the room, the scent of her perfume well preceding her.

"Your party, to be precise."

"My party? Roger, it's a perfectly harmless affair arranged to introduce Rose. You're just upset

18

because Lord Byron will be here. He's a friend of Philip's and well regarded."

"Perhaps some of his less known supporters will also be here," he remarked, his voice rising disapprovingly.

"Really, Roger, I'd rather talk to Rose about what she's going to wear to the masquerade than worry about some thief," she said with a sparkle in her violet eyes.

Roger looked over his paper at Stephanie. "You're inviting the robbery of your friends. I dare say it will be a sparse party."

Chapter 2

Contrary to Roger Whitley's prediction, Stephanie Vanderhue's masquerade ball proved to be a huge success. The house was crowded with curious guests, all anxious to meet her niece from America.

Rose found herself on the arm of her gracious cousin, the marquess of Romwell, and was surprised and relieved that he wasn't as old and stuffy as his title had suggested he might be. She learned that he stayed with his aunt on occasion, but that he mostly enjoyed the freedom of his London town house. Since they were cousins he had insisted that she call him Philip.

Rose had to admire his appearance, for he was groomed to perfection. Every thread of russet-colored hair on his head was neatly tied back and fell in slight curls over the nape of his neck. The lines of his face were straight and would have given him a staunch look were it not for the mischievous curve of his lips and the gold sparkle in his brown eyes. The frock coat he wore was of a soft, satin-trimmed gold velvet, and his breeches were a coordinating buff color. The cravat at his neck was loosely tied over an unstarched collar in the style made popular by Lord Byron. He hid behind his mask whenever he whispered tidbits of gossip about those guests he had just introduced.

Philip moved smoothly and confidently through the throng of guests, keeping Rose possessively at his side. "There's your father and Aunt Stephanie," he whispered secretively. "Has she seen you yet?"

Rose wondered what had made him ask—until she noticed his gaze lower to her decolletage. "No."

"Then I rather think we should avoid her." He steered Rose away from her aunt. "Aunt Stephanie," he continued, "will run your life—if you let her."

"Is that why you stay in London?"

Philip smiled. "Certainly. But you don't have that option. She's not an early riser, though." He winked after giving her that information as if he knew she would use it deceitfully. "I know how you Americans like your freedom," he joked.

"And it seems you like yours," Rose countered with a sweet smile.

"I believe our aunt will have a time with you," he laughed. "Shall we see what Lord Byron's up to?" He extended his arm for her. Rose threaded her arm through the soft velvet and thought that if Philip visited often she might almost enjoy her stay at Briar Hill.

Lord Byron hardly had the undivided attention of the guests as he read his prose from the library. The main topic of discussion which was circulating the room in whispers, concerned theories as to the thief's identity—theories given authority by supporting evidence from those who felt lucky or, in Roger Whitley's case, unfortunate to have made his acquaintance.

The description of the thief was as varied as the characters who described him. His height ranged from tall to short; he was muscular and thin; he was polite but quick with the gun or knife he carried. Until that night when he had robbed Roger Whitley, he had jumped out from dark alleys to relieve gentlemen of their wallets and had silently plucked jewels from ladies' boudoirs. About the only aspect that could be agreed upon was that he only stole from those who did not show support for the Greek revolutionists. He only robbed the rich, and always during or after social gatherings.

Rose's bodice finally caught her aunt's eye. Stephanie excused herself from her guests and made her way to Rose and Philip. Once it was known Lady Vanderhue wanted to pass, the throng of guests parted like the Red Sea for Moses. Along the way she paused every few steps to chat politely, until she reached her niece.

"She's spotted you, Rose dear," Philip whispered in her ear.

"You look splendid, my darling," she complimented, holding Rose at arm's length and taking in her costume from head to foot. "I see Philip has taken care of the introductions." She gave her nephew a disapproving look.

Philip bowed slightly. "I think I'll see what Chloe's up to."

Despite Stephanie's smile Rose wasn't certain her sophisticated aunt approved of the gown that daringly revealed how much she had matured in the past year.

"You look like Aphrodite," Stephanie winked, tugging on the gold braided ribbon that circled above Rose's rib cage. She then added in a reprimanding tone, "I'm surprised your father let you out like this."

"Father didn't breathe an objecting word."

Stephanie narrowed her eye on Rose, clearly disapproving of the classical gown that negated a corset. It was popular in France to discard them in favor of sheer stockings, but this was England, where only the very bold would think of going out with next to nothing under their dresses. Rose stood still while her aunt's eyes brushed over the gown. A sheer white tunic fell over green-and-gold-trimmed cream silk, hinting at curves Stephanie would have preferred disguised under a less revealing gown. The sleeves puffed at Rose's shoulders and then tapered into a wristband of gauze that pleated at the back of her hands. "I doubt he saw beyond your shawl," Stephanie concluded.

Rose objected to her aunt's critical eye. "Maggie worked so hard on this costume." Her hand lightly touched the white-feathered and gold-sequined mask that hid most of her face. It had been a time-consuming work of art: pearls and flecks of gold were woven into a background of white feathers; gold braid trimmed the edges and cascaded into fringed tassels to brush her bare shoulders; and as a crown to it all, plumes of osprey feathers sprayed over the top of her golden curls.

"Maggie should have embellished the front of you with some of those feathers," her aunt grunted. "Whatever you do, don't bend over and stay away from tall men, particularly your father. Had I seen you, you never would have gotten by my eyes, young lady. Good gracious!"

Rose knew her aunt would have insisted on a

higher neckline, even for a masquerade ball. Before Stephanie fretted any more about the amount of skin exposed and sent her upstairs for another gown, Rose thought to veer the subject of their conversation away from her decolletage.

"Have you seen him yet?"

"Lord Byron, darling?"

"No, the Liberty Thief," Rose whispered.

"Shh." The prospect of the Liberty Thief's presence made Stephanie's nerve ends tingle. "Have you seen anyone who'd resemble the man?" she asked with alarm.

"No, not anyone who looked like the renegade I saw. But it was very dark," Rose reminded her. "Father would know better."

Despite her efforts, Rose's decolletage proved too distracting for her aunt to ignore. "Rose, we've got to do something with that dress! Follow me upstairs," she ordered briskly.

Rose sighed, rolled her eyes at Philip who stood aside watching them, and reluctantly trailed behind her aunt.

Stephanie led Rose up the curved staircase to the last room on the second floor. She stopped short in the doorway and gasped at the sight of an opened window.

"Florence must have been airing out this room," she said hopefully, rushing over to slam the window, but pausing to scan the shadows of the garden. Though it was a long drop down, Stephanie knew a true thief would go to any extreme for a fortune, even if it meant a turned ankle or a broken neck.

"What is it?" Rose watched wide-eyed as Stephanie pulled a small safe from behind a painting. She placed the box on the bed and unlocked it with a key pulled from her pocket. In her haste to inspect the contents of the safe, she flung back the lid, nearly tipping the box over, and exposed a treasure of jewels to Rose's surprised eye.

"Thank heavens, it's all here," she said, grateful she hadn't been robbed. She snapped the lid closed and turned the little key in the lock. "There, it's all safe now. I do wish they'd catch this thief so good people can sleep nights."

Before Rose could offer an optimistic word a cry traveled from the other end of the hall to Stephanie's room.

"Someone's stolen my mother's emerald brooch. Someone's taken my jewels!"

"The Liberty Thief," Rose gasped.

"It's Penelope," Lady Vanderhue gasped. She fell back on the bed in a dead faint.

Rose didn't know what to do first—go to the hysterical guest's aid or try to revive her aunt. She sat undecidedly on the edge of the bed and fanned her aunt with her mask.

There was a commotion of footsteps in the hall, and a tangle of confused questions. In the melee of panicky voices Rose recognized the cool calm of her cousin, Philip, as he tried to help the hysterical guest. "Now, Penelope . . . calm yourself."

"Where was the brooch?" another asked.

"Did you see anyone?" Philip wanted to know.

"Penelope!" a woman gasped.

"Get some salts. She's swooned."

Rose's hand quivered with excitement. The thief had struck. He was in the house, perhaps still mingling with the guests and secretly listening to their conversations while behind the protection of his mask. How did they know the Liberty Thief

26

would be a compatriot? Obviously he might not be. She had heard Lord and Lady James were supporters of the revolution, in which case the thief had made a terrible mistake.

Rose gently patted Stephanie's face. Her lashes fluttered over her rouged cheeks and then flickered opened. She sat up with Rose's help, clutching the gaudy brooch that sat on her heaving chest.

"Was it a dream? Tell me, Rose, it was a dream."

Chancing the woman would crash to the bed once again, Rose gulped and blurted the truth as she knew it from the bits of conversation she had heard.

"Lady James was robbed of her mother's emerald brooch while she slept off a headache in one of the rooms down the hall."

At the suggestion of a headache, Lady Vanderhue touched her own forehead. "Penelope and her headaches. What can one expect, sleeping around with a fortune pinned to one's bosom?" Stephanie squinted at an imaginary scene. "If she *was* sleeping!"

Rose was shocked at Lady Vanderhue's implied suspicion. "You don't think . . ."

"I do think—all the time. I wouldn't trust Penelope any more than I would the sultan of the Ottomans in a harem." The wrinkled lines in Stephanie's face softened when she saw Rose's puzzled look. "Now go, darling. Go downstairs before any more suspicion is raised. I'll lock the safe, and remember, don't whisper a word to anyone."

Rose promised to keep the scandal a secret and returned to the party, relieved that the diversion had at least saved her the embarrassment of having to change her gown. Her nerves, though, felt tight

27

as a bowstring. She couldn't help but look at each masked face as if the identity behind it was the Liberty Thief. She nearly jumped as high as the Tower of London when she felt a tap on her shoulder. She turned to face the snap of a Chinese fan.

"Meet your cousin Chloe," Philip said, smiling down at Rose. "She was almost as exasperating to Aunt Stephanie as you promise to be. But now she's a respectable married lady."

"It's a pleasure," Rose returned, exchanging a knowing glance with Philip, but keeping the upstairs robbery a secret between them.

"Philip's told me you're staying with Aunt Stephanie for a while."

"To get to know the rest of the family," Rose said quickly.

"And you will, if Philip has anything to do with it."

"Now, Chloe, I didn't breathe a word of family gossip."

"I'm sure." Her penetrating violet eyes turned to Rose. "Never mind a word he's said. Anything you want to know about family, I'll tell you."

Philip leaned over to whisper in Rose's ear, but loud enough for his sister to hear. "Don't believe a word she says. Besides, Chloe will soon be going back to her husband in France," he said, and his eyes sparkled devilishly.

Rose slipped off into the jungle of guests after Philip and Chloe had become steeped in conversation with another couple. She was happy to steal a moment to herself during which she would not have to make polite conversation with her aunt's friends.

Though the hour was late, the room was still

thick with people. Stephanie had managed to calm and silence Penelope and was mingling again as though nothing had happened to mar the evening. Her arm was clasped in Roger Whitley's, and from the look on her father's face Rose assumed he was enjoying himself despite the fact that he had admitted to her that her aunt's party promised to be a tedious ordeal for them both.

Escaping yet another conversation, Rose made her way to the punch table. A crystal bowl surrounded by a wreath of flowers sparkled like a ruby; cups circled the bowl, and the ladle rested unattended. Rose waited, as she should, for Harold to return to serve her, but the longer he took, the more ridiculous it seemed to wait when she was quite capable of filling her own cup. "To blazes with it," she mumbled, then lifted a crystal cup, unaware that she was being watched with guarded interest.

Rose's slender hand slipped around the glass ladle, and the curved handle settled in her palm. Before she could pour the punch into her cup, however, a wide, heavy hand covered hers. For an instant her eyes glittered in the green sparkle of a large emerald ring before her gaze moved over the masculine hand to a flounce of white silk beneath the dark cuff of a sleeve and then up a long arm to a pair of wide shoulders and an unnervingly hand-some smile. A cream cravat swathed his neck, and a black-pearl pin settled in the gathered silk at his throat. His face—except for the squarish jaw, straight mouth, and black eyes—was hidden behind a feathered mask depicting a raven.

Rose's eyes stalled on the gentleman's form. He certainly cut a fine figure in royal blue. A satin trimmed frock coat flared at his hips, and blue

29

breeches hugged his thick muscled legs, perhaps too tightly. He was solidly built, and although he wore the clothes of an aristocrat and possessed a certain grace and perfect mannerisms, there was something about him that alluded to a less-than-genteel life. Perhaps it was the sheer bulk of him— he was as wide as any man she'd ever seen, and taller than most—or the telling rough feel of his palm against the back of her hand. There was a firm, no-nonsense set to his jaw, and a challenging gleam in his slate-black eyes. Whatever it was, Rose was certainly intrigued.

"Would you like some punch?" he asked in a voice as smooth and warming as sherry. Rose realized her hand stiffly challenged his.

"Please," she said, and they emptied the ladle together without spilling a drop, a credit to his steady hand.

"Thank you," she said simply, feeling annoyed with how easily he had flustered her usual self-assurance.

"It's my pleasure to come to a beautiful lady's assistance."

Other than the straight line of his lips and his piercing eyes Rose couldn't see much of his face, but she was caught by the rich drawl of his speech. He wasn't one of her aunt's English friends—that was obvious. By his smooth, seductive drawl she knew he was American.

"I don't believe I know you," she said, hoping for a clue to his identity.

"Ah, but that is against Lady Vanderhue's rules. Not until midnight," his smooth voice teased as he put down her glass and swept her away on the lilting notes of a waltz.

Rose was caught in the mysterious stranger's

arms as he carried her in graceful strides over the ballroom floor. They made a striking couple, Rose in her flowing white gown and her partner a dark contrast. For a while there were no other guests as they moved in and out of the pale light sifting down over the ballroom from three large, candle-laden chandeliers.

Rose did not think to protest when he swept her into the garden and she found herself alone with a man whose name was unknown to her. She fell under the spell of violins singing softly to the night, their sweet song playing along a wave of fragrant spring air. Together they danced along the brick walk between budding red and white roses.

"Have you known Lady Vanderhue for long?" Rose asked, still curious about the man's identity.

"Long enough to wonder why I haven't seen you before tonight."

"I'm just visiting." For a year, she thought with dread, but then that did mean she'd have a year to become acquainted with this stranger. Rose was beginning to see her new home in a more positive light.

"Well then, I'm glad I decided to come tonight. Lady Vanderhue's parties are usually not . . . my cup of tea."

"What made you decide to come?" Rose wondered aloud.

"A masquerade ball intrigued me . . . and I already had a mask."

Rose stumbled over his smile, tangled her feet in his and would have completely embarrassed herself by falling had he not caught her in his arms. She leaned against him while he steadied her

31

and the night her father was robbed suddenly came back to her. This masked stranger seemed too tall and his voice was different. On the night of the robbery, however he could have been in disguise, and one of the thieves hadn't talked at all. Was she in the arms of one of the thieves? She paled at the thought of it.

"Are you all right, Miss Whitley?"

"You know my name?" That half smile again! How it managed to put her on the edge of trembling. Rose straightened, regaining her composure, and silently reprimanded herself for letting her imagination have the upper hand. Someone at the party had obviously pointed her out to him. "You have an unfair advantage, sir. What else do you know about me?" she asked, rather piqued at the game he played.

His eyes shone down at her like boot-black buttons as he led her over the walk. Rose was too aware of his hand wrapped around her waist and the warm touch of his fingers against hers to notice they were venturing further into the dark shadows of the garden.

"You're Mary Rose Whitley, Stephanie's niece, the daughter of Roger Whitley and Lady Rose-anna, born wealthy, raised American . . ."

Though charm wrapped around him like a satin cloak, it was not enough to soften her annoyance that all along he had known who she was, yet had pretended not to. His confidence, bordering on arrogance, stiffened her bottom lip. "Knowing that my cousin Philip is a veritable fountain of information, I assume he made my introduction without my presence. That's quite unfair and is considered very improper."

"Since you seem to know your cousin so well,

you also know there is nothing proper about him."

"There doesn't seem to be very much proper about you, either . . . Sir Raven," she said with a mocking tone.

Rose was caught off guard when his hands wrapped firmly around her arms and he lifted her up. Before she knew it, his mouth covered hers. She should have pushed him away right then but was held by the warm pressure of his lips moving over hers. His kiss was undeniably demanding and was not meant to gently seduce or tease a response from her lips; it was hot passion that melted her in his arms. His tongue forced past her lips and teeth; it flickered like a flame, spreading fire through her body. His hands ran down her side, measuring the curves under her gown before pulling her up against him in a tight embrace. Rose weakened under the heat of his lips, slowly responding to the new and curious sensation, cautiously answering his demand. The kiss turned gentle, and he slowly pulled away from her, smiling down into her eyes.

His finger traced her wet lips. "And it doesn't seem there's much proper about you, Miss Whitley."

Rose nearly shook from the inside out in the face of his audacity. She was so upset with his forwardness and then his criticism that her face burned hot under the disguising mask. She would have slapped the half smile from his lips if he weren't still holding her so tightly against him.

"I dare say you are taking too much for granted," she replied with the breath she captured.

"That could be, but I like the intrigue of not knowing what to expect, and if the rest of you is anything like your mouth—"

"You certainly hold yourself in high regard if you think there would be anything more!" she exclaimed, her exasperation inflating her words with disbelief.

His mouth broadened into a smile as he pulled her even more closely to his chest. "Dare we see if that's true, Miss Whitley?"

Rose could never resist a dare, a fact to which Jack and Robert would have attested. And though they had taught her how to play marbles and catch a ride on the back of a wagon without the driver being the wiser for it, they hadn't taught her everything.

She had known what they were up to when they would run off to the stable with Molly. She had caught the meaning of their exchanged grins and had noticed how disheveled Molly was after being with one of them. She had doubted they were playing marbles with her, though the rascals had sworn to it, for when she'd once threatened to spy on them the next time, they'd turned white as sheets. This stranger's dare made her wonder if Jack or Robert had enticed Molly into the stable in a similar way.

"Dare we?" she said, leaving the question open for him to wonder about; however, the flash in her eyes revealed that if he dared try again, he'd be met with more resistance than he could imagine. Rose pulled away from his hold and left him standing alone in the garden.

He laughed, plucked a white rose from its stem, twisted it in his fingers and then inhaled its sweet fragrance.

But much as she tried to ignore him, Rose could not keep her thoughts from returning to the raven-masked man. Her finger brushed against her lips, which still burned with the memory of his kiss. He had kindled a curious flame inside her and then dared her to forget it. Even with her strong resolve, she was finding that difficult to do. Twice she had almost asked Philip about him, but she'd caught the words that would betray her interest. Philip would certainly tell the stranger that she was asking about him, and she didn't want the scoundrel to know he intrigued her; yet she continued to look for him among the befeathered and bejeweled, hoping to find him just at the stroke of twelve when everyone threw their masks aside.

By midnight her aunt's guests were getting ready to reveal their identities. She found Chloe, standing close to her aunt on the arm of a new escort, and her father and Philip, but not the raven. It seemed he had mysteriously disappeared.

Chapter 3

"Stay away from her, Trent," Lady Vanderhue warned before Trent Jordan had even closed his office door behind her. Stephanie rigidly faced him, the buttons on her bodice straining against the stretched fabric with each heavy breath she took. She had made her way up the four flights of stairs in haste with Trent's murder on her mind. Her eyes narrowed on the handsomely cut figure. Not many women could resist the warm charm Trent Jordan possessed, and it was that charm in dangerous combination with his natural good looks that had caused more than one innocent girl to fall to her knees before him, only to crumble like the dry petals of a spent rose. Stephanie refused to let her niece fall victim to the same fate.

Stephanie knew Trent's weakness—a weakness for innocence. Though he was sometimes seen with women like Penelope, they served only as a mere convenience; his blood really simmered over someone as sweet and untouched as Rose. Stephanie ground her teeth. Rose posed an exciting challenge for Trent, one that would be hard for him to resist.

Trent extended his arm to the wing-backed chair opposite his desk. The late-afternoon sun stabbed through his emerald ring, shooting green beams of light through the room with each movement of his hand.

"Sit down, Stephanie," he said with smooth calmness coating his words.

Stephanie hesitated a moment, debating whether or not that move would give him an edge. "No, thank you. I prefer to stand. This is not a social call."

"Very well, then. You don't mind if *I* sit?" He settled himself comfortably before she could answer.

"Suit yourself, Trent."

Trent leaned back in the massive leather chair and settled his black eyes on Lady Vanderhue. She stood with her hands locked in front of her, her chin raised and jaw set firmly. Her eyes never wavered from his. She was as strong a woman as he had ever hoped to meet. It would be lucky for the men of the world if there was only one Stephanie Vanderhue. To run up against her protecting one of her own would be to invite a battle of the like he had seen others lose. If it wasn't for his friendship with Philip, Trent would have tossed her out politely; but then, if it wasn't for his friend's penchant for finding trouble, he wouldn't have such easy control over Stephanie.

"What brings you to London, Stephanie?" It always irritated her when he addressed her so informally, bringing her down off her royal throne to face him as an equal. By the way she squirmed, he knew that after all the years he'd known her his informal style was something she'd never get used to.

"My godchild, Mary Rose."

"She's quite a lovely girl."

"She *is* a lovely girl, and that's how I'd like her to stay. Leave her be, Trent. There are others you haven't sunk your teeth into yet."

Trent smiled. "You make me sound like a monster who devours young women. I promise not to sink my teeth into your godchild." He flashed a gleaming smile. "But I'm sure it's not my teeth you're worried about."

In truth, all Trent could think about was Rose—ever since the night she pulled Philip off his horse.

Philip had been aghast, and not just over the way she had neatly toppled him from his horse. "I've robbed my own relative," he had moaned into his tankard of ale. "When I saw Roseanna's face, I—"

"I told you this idea of yours was going to draw us into the muck," Trent had laughed despite the seriousness of the event.

"The gaming tables have not been kind, as well you know," Philip had said, defending his weakness, and had then reminded his friend, "Without funds, you won't be taking the Filiki Hetairia their supply of guns."

Trent knew that. They couldn't be "knights of freedom," as Philip called them, without funds, and all their victims could very well afford to contribute. Once they'd earned the distinguished title of the Liberty Thief, most of their victims began giving more than what was demanded just for the privilege of being robbed by the distinguished brigand. Philip had been finding it a satisfying occupation until the shock of meeting Rose Whitley had tightened his bootstraps.

Trent was smiling when Stephanie blustered,

"I'm not amused, as you seem to be. Rose is too young. She's naive and inexperienced."

How well Stephanie knew him. Rose's pure beauty, unblemished by experience, was enough to stir his loins. He ached to take her to his bed. It had been a long while since he'd tasted such eagerness on the lips of one so innocent. No matter how much Stephanie carried on, he had already made his decision: Rose was too precious, too exciting, to ignore, and too delectable to let slip through his fingers. Whether she was Stephanie's godchild or not, if she presented herself to him he would very well accommodate her.

"A woman has to gain experience from someone," Trent said, spreading his hands, "so why not the best?" He smiled, not taking himself too seriously but effectively infuriating Stephanie.

"You pompous, conceited fool. You're just like Philip, though I love him dearly."

"I'm glad to hear you love me, Stephanie."

Her glare debated his words. "You're a bad influence on my nephew and you'd be a worse one on Rose."

"Have you forgotten how many times I've bailed Philip out of trouble. All those times you came to me for a favor? I'd rather thought I was a good influence."

Stephanie knew when she didn't have an argument. "We're not talking about Philip."

"You're right. I'd rather discuss Rose."

"If you so much as touch that girl, I'll—"

Trent remained unflustered, but his voice was dangerously steady—the calm warning before the storm. "Don't threaten me, Stephanie. You have too much to lose yourself, and if you are thinking of standing in front of something I want, you will only serve to entice me with a greater challenge. Now let's stop this pointless conversation and get on with business. You didn't come to London just to discuss Rose. Now sit down," he said, the firmness of his voice an indication that he felt he had spent enough time debating an issue he considered dead.

Lady Vanderhue sat down with an audible huff, the arms of the chair hugging her ample body. From her bag she pulled a heavy sack and tossed it onto Trent's desk. The contents crashed and jingled against the wood. Trent poured gold and silver coins into a pile in front of him and sighed. "Again?"

"For Philip's gambling debt. You know he won't take the money from me."

"And I'm sure it irks you to ask a favor now," Trent said, annoying her with a grin. "Not good timing on Philip's part, is it? All right, I'll see that it's paid. He wouldn't like it if he knew his aunt was taking care of his debts, though. He wouldn't be happy if he knew I was, either," he added while scraping the coins off his desk. They dropped noisily into a metal box. Trent was tempted to ask to see Rose, wondering if permission might be granted, in light of his latest good deed. But he only smiled at the thought of it.

"There's something else." Stephanie, watching his expression warily, shifted uncomfortably in the tight-fitting chair.

"Another favor? My, you are running up your own debt."

"Never mind," she snapped and stood up to leave. Trent grabbed her arm.

"Sit down, Stephanie. I like having you in my debt," he teased. "What else?"

41

"The Liberty Thief. There's been a turn of events," she informed him. "It seems the thief has not been able to resist robbing even those who support the cause. He's become a common thief. Lady James was relieved of her mother's emerald last night, and no one's been a more generous supporter of Greek independence than Lord James."

Trent frowned, recalling the night before. It had been Philip's idea of humor to slip into the room while he and Pen were "involved." Trent had been certain she'd sense his distraction and see the shadow stepping around the room. At the time, he hadn't been quite as amused as Philip.

"I remember seeing the brooch," Stephanie said. "She had it pinned to her . . ."

Trent saw Stephanie smile smugly. It wasn't a friendly smile, but one that told him she knew why Penelope had removed the brooch.

"I convinced Penelope to be quiet about it," she continued. "The questions that would be asked might have proved embarrassing and difficult to explain to her husband." Stephanie smiled smugly at Trent, who returned her look with a mocking grin. "But I fear that this last thievery will encourage the thief more," Stephanie cried. "He's going to ruin all my affairs. No one dares to go out anymore."

"You certainly have a pressing problem, but I think you're overreacting," Trent said with a bite of sarcasm.

"You hear and see things . . . in your circle. Will you help us or not?"

Trent almost laughed out loud. Now Stephanie had him agreeing to investigate the crimes her nephew committed. If she only knew that at times he, too, rode along to make sure Philip didn't get caught. He played up to her concern. "You have a list of guests from last night?" he asked. Stephanie nodded. "Good. And your butler greeted everyone?"

"Of course, but everyone was masked. It would have been easy for the thief to circulate among the guests, and he had access to the upstairs." She paused. "There *was* a window open. He could have come in from the outside."

Philip was a scamp if there ever was one, Trent thought with amusement. "He still may be someone in your circle of friends. Someone who can come and go freely without fear of being suspect. He seems to have known who had donated to the cause and then picked out those who did not—at least in the beginning." Trent studied Stephanie's face—stubborn lines were set around her mouth, and her eyes held his as she waited for his reply. "This may cost you a favor in return," he warned with a smile.

Stephanie put her hand on the doorknob. "Find someone else besides Rose. I have my own plans for my sister's daughter. She's going to become a proper lady and marry into a good English family." The feathers in her bonnet shook with the determination she felt.

"Is that your plan—to marry her off so she'll be safe from my attentions? Well, you'd better marry her soon, then," he said, laughing at her look of dismay.

"I think I might just do that," she snapped.

Trent watched the bustle on her gown sway from her angry walk. Stephanie's mind was set as solid and determined as her figure. From experience Trent knew there would be no changing her mind.

However, what Stephanie was forgetting was that he could be just as bound and determined when it involved something he wanted as she.

"Stephanie," he called down the steps, "you know what's wrong with you? You don't have a trusting bone in your body."

"Humph! You just make sure you keep your desires away from Rose and everything will be fine between us."

Stephanie could hear his laughter behind the closed door. "The best thing that could happen to you, Trent," she huffed as she stepped down the stairs, "is to fall hopelessly in love. Oh, how I'd love to see the day a woman makes you helpless."

The next afternoon Roger Whitley and his daughter joined Lady Vanderhue in the garden for tea. The bite-sized cakes covered in fondant and garnished with candied violets were almost too beautiful to consider eating. The silver teapot shone, catching the reflection of bone china cups on its round side. Stephanie dismissed her maid, preferring to pour the tea herself. The three sat together at a square table covered with an embroidered linen cloth.

Stephanie and Roger talked, their voices muffled and lost to Rose, whose attention was focused on a white rose bush. All she could think about was the raven-masked man: his arms around her, his sultry voice, his warm and passionate kiss—and how he had infuriated her, slipping away without leaving a clue as to who he was. It seemed that not even Stephanie remembered seeing the man. Since that night the mysterious stranger was all Rose could think about.

"Aunt Stephanie," she blurted out, "did you ever discover anything more about the man with the raven mask? You promised to ask about him."

Stephanie's teacup stopped between the saucer and her mouth, and for a moment she lost her composure. Roger and Rose waited in silent wonder, for it was a rare moment when Stephanie couldn't come up with a quick answer.

"Rose dear, I've no idea. I think it's best you forget him. He probably didn't even have an invitation." She patted the back of Rose's hand.

"I'm sure he was a friend of Philip's," Rose insisted.

"Dear, I've told you—I simply have no idea." Stephanie firmly closed the matter with her blunt answer.

Roger looked from Rose's disappointed face to Stephanie, who shrugged her shoulders in answer to Roger's unspoken question.

"What is this about a raven?" he asked anyway.

"Nothing, dear, just someone Rose saw at the masquerade. Most likely someone who slipped by Harold."

"I danced with him and he was very charming," Rose said with a daring light in her eyes.

"Never mind charming," Stephanie said, distressed at her niece's interest in an unsuitable man such as Trent. "There's more to a good man than charm. It's the rogues who will leave your heart broken with their charm. Isn't that right, Roger?"

"Why didn't I know about this? Rose, you danced with this man?" Her father's eyes were wide with surprise.

"You were under the weather at the time," Stephanie said sharply, effectively ending the beginning of his round of questioning with that reminder.

Rose saw her father's face color at her aunt's strong hint that he had paid the punch bowl more attention than his daughter. She was ready to tell her aunt what for when her father intervened, handing her a cake.

"Try this one, Rose. It's quite sweet."

Stephanie looked from Rose to Roger and decided the time was right to make her proposal. "Rose, darling, would you take this tray back to the kitchen for more cakes?"

"But—" Rose was going to argue that the tray already had more than enough cakes, but she caught her father's warning look and spun around on her heel. "Certainly, Aunt Stephanie."

Suspicious that her aunt wanted her out of the way for a reason, Rose stayed close by but hidden behind the shrubs.

"What's Rose done now?" Roger asked.

"Nothing. She's been just an angel." Roger's brows shot up suspiciously. "Well, almost," Stephanie amended. "Rose has such a strong nature. I don't know where she gets it from."

"Must be her rebellious American side," Roger quipped with undetected sarcasm.

Stephanie was delighted to agree. "Yes, just as I thought! Briar Hill will be wonderful for her." She paused a long while, picking her words carefully before she spoke.

"Is there something else, Stephanie?" Roger asked, growing impatient while waiting for his sister-in-law to get to the point.

"Well, yes. I thought it would be a good idea if we started to look for a husband for Rose, possibly an English one."

46

"What!" exclaimed Rose, quickly clapping her hand over her mouth.

Roger Whitley could no longer sit. He got up and paced up and down the brick walk. Marriage wasn't something he had given thought to.

Stephanie's bosom rose with a deep sigh. "We'll just start planning, that's all, Roger. She is old enough, you know, and she's not getting younger." Stephanie was trying hard not to lose her temper at his indecision. "Roseanna would want the same thing," she reminded him.

Roger doused Rose's thin hope that he'd put an end to her aunt's notion when he didn't immediately reject the idea. He actually thought it over for less than a minute and then agreed! Her whole future was decided in less than a minute.

The silver tray Rose balanced dropped to the brick walk with a crash. Roger and Stephanie simultaneously raised their brows. A look of dread crossed Roger's face before he hurried after his daughter.

Rose ran all the way to the stables. When her father caught up with her, the groom had already saddled her horse. Roger reached for the bridle before Rose had a chance to mount.

"He insisted on putting a saddle on him even though I can very well ride without one," she cried, casting blame on the startled groom. "Blast! Even the grooms here are stuffed shirts." After that declaration she buried her face into her father's chest and sobbed.

Roger stroked his daughter's hair and let her cry out her anger. When she had calmed enough to hear him, he tried to explain.

"Rose, you're old enough to marry. It's not the worst thing. Your mother and I were very happy."

47

"I don't want Aunt Stephanie picking out my husband. No one arranged your marriage," she reminded him.

"Ours was rather unusual and quite a scandal!"

Rose, imagining it, smiled briefly through her tears.

Roger sighed. "Darling, this is difficult enough, so please try to be cooperative this time around. You're a young lady now, and we only want what's best for you. Your aunt truly loves you."

"All right," Rose agreed, and too quickly for her father to feel even a pinch of relief. "If I get to do the choosing."

Roger groaned. "Rose . . ." He smoothed away the leftover tears on her cheek. "I'll talk to your aunt. You'll have the year to make your choice. But," he warned, "from the men she approves of."

Chapter 4

The Liberty Thief was quiet for a few days, prompting Stephanie to throw a bon voyage party for Roger Whitley.

Rose paid special attention to her appearance, from the tips of her toes to the ribbons in her hair, just in case the raven-masked man showed up. However, she couldn't find him among the guests, and wondered if she would even recognize him without his mask. Despite her disappointment, there were plenty of men who rallied for her attention, something she had never before experienced. It was exhilarating, but the hopeful suitors failed to turn her thoughts from the raven.

"Just look at yourself," Chloe said when they were alone. She turned Rose to a mirror. "You're a beauty men will compete for. When you turn those blue eyes on a man, you are going to stop his heart. You can't be too particular with the man you choose. Someone rich and titled; someone who'll take care of you properly."

By chance Rose saw a quick reflection of Chloe's

sad eyes in the mirror.

"Does your husband take care of you, Chloe?"

Chloe recovered from a rare moment of undisclosed melancholy and laughed. "Of course. He keeps me very comfortable."

"But you don't see him very much."

"I like it that way. Now, let's go back to the party, I'm sure there's a line of men waiting to dance with you."

Chloe was right, and by the time the evening ended Rose was exhausted. She sat on the edge of her bed and let Lizzie remove her slippers. She fell back into the mattress, which folded around her like soft arms, coaxing her to lie still and surrender to sleep.

"Shall I prepare your bath, Miss Rose?" her maid asked.

"Oh, yes, please do."

While she soaked Rose thought of the raven. "We'll meet again, raven, and then we'll see who you really are," she said aloud.

"Rose?" Not wanting to draw the attention of her staff, Stephanie's voice was just loud enough to penetrate the closed door.

Rose jumped, splashing the water into a wave that flowed over the rim of her tub. "Yes, Aunt Stephanie?"

"Can I come in?"

"Of course," Rose answered with dread. Her aunt was surely going to review the long list of eligible suitors with her.

Stephanie slipped through the door and closed it softly behind her. She was regally dressed in an aqua robe run through with silver threads and her hair was twisted down her back in a long braid.

50

She sat down heavily in a chair, her face aged with concern.

"The Liberty Thief has struck again."

"When?" Rose exclaimed, her eyes wide.

"Tonight. Right here. My ruby hat pin is gone."

Rose was quiet for a moment until the reality of her aunt's news took hold. "Do you know what this means? The thief is someone who would not alarm us—a neighbor, a friend, someone we trust. He could even be one of the staff."

"Right here in my own house," Stephanie went on, her pale face colored with anger. "There will be an end to this. You're right, Rose. My suspicions are the same—the thief is one of us. He could be anyone and we must be careful."

"What will we do?"

"I know someone who can ferret the weasel out. Soon the Liberty Thief will be found and hanged." Once Stephanie became confident the thief would be stopped, her face relaxed into a smile and her normal rosy color returned.

"Who will find him?" Rose wondered.

"Trent Jordan," Stephanie divulged unwittingly.

"Trent Jordan?"

"Never mind. You're not to concern yourself with the man. He's an unscrupulous scoundrel, an American and an untamed one at that, but he's just the type who can sniff out a thief."

Rose was intrigued. "Is he a handsome scoundrel, at least?"

Stephanie's face became taut with concern. "What does that have to do with the price of tea?"

"I just wondered." Rose avoided her aunt's look by submerging herself in her bath. When she

51

reemerged, blinking away droplets of water from her lashes, her sight was blurry but her aunt was still clearly standing in front of her.

"By the look on your face he must be terribly handsome," Rose teased. "Will I get to meet Mr. Jordan? If he's going to find the Liberty Thief, he may want to question me about the night my father was robbed. After all, I did see the thief—somewhat."

Stephanie gasped. "I told you Trent Jordan was a scoundrel. Scoundrels only have selfish intentions when it comes to beautiful ladies."

"Like Chloe's husband?"

"Worse. Chloe's husband is only interested in spending her fortune. Trent Jordan's not interested in money."

Rose frowned. Her aunt wasn't making any sense, since every eligible man was interested in a wife who would bring him a hefty dowry. "What would Trent Jordan be interested in if not someone's fortune?"

"Oh, heavens, Rose! What indeed! Just forget his name. I'll find someone nice for you. Someone who'll be gentle and who will deny you nothing, like the young Lord Wesley."

Rose made an unpleasant face. She didn't want anyone choosing for her. "Lord Wesley did not interest me," she said flatly.

"Dear, what do you know? Your judgment of him is too hasty. One doesn't feel excitement right away—it takes time, nourishment, effort."

"Maybe, but the man in the raven mask excited me without much effort." Rose stretched out her arm for the towel her aunt offered. She stood and wrapped herself in its warm fluffiness.

Her mouth agape, Stephanie listened to the words she dreaded hearing.

"You may chastise me, Aunt Stephanie, and say that I'm ill-mannered, but I felt something right down to my toes when that mysterious man touched me. He only had to look at me to take my breath away."

Stephanie turned white. It was worse than she'd thought. Trent had already put his spell on her godchild. She couldn't delay planning for Rose's marriage any longer for fear Trent and Rose would meet again. She was sure Rose was ignorant of men and extremely vulnerable to Trent's type. It was time she spoke frankly to her niece.

"Rose dear, there's something you should know about men."

Rose had finished dressing and slipped under the bed cover. She leaned back against her pillows, folded her hands and waited with eyes so expectant that Stephanie almost lost all courage. She looked at her godchild's face, round as a moon, lips ripe for kissing, eyes too trusting—all too easy a prey for a worldly man as Trent. Stephanie was forced to admit it: Rose had lost the soft padding of childhood to the curves of womanhood. The girl was too curious and too bold for her own good.

Stephanie dreaded the moment. How she wished Roseanna were here to talk to her daughter. Roseanna would know just what to say, whereas Stephanie would rather lock Rose in the Tower of London until a suitable husband was found for her. Roger should have arranged something earlier; then Rose wouldn't be thinking of someone who would do more than "interest" her.

Stephanie sat on the edge of the feather mattress, her hand rubbing the throbbing pulse at her temple. "Rose . . ."

"Yes, Aunt Stephanie? You were going to tell me something of men." Rose tightened her smile.

"Yes . . . I just need to gather my thoughts a minute. It's a complicated subject—men. You see, they are . . . different from women."

Rose's eyes were shot full of amusement. Her poor aunt was having such a time of it. She leaned her chin into her hand. "I've always thought so, Aunt Stephanie. They're certainly much stronger," she added remembering how solid the raven's arms were and how weak she felt against the mysterious man's embrace.

"Exactly, dear, and more aggressive. Men like to have everything their way and will use their strength to obtain it—especially when it comes to women. You have to be very careful with men. If a man decides he wants you, darling, he'll just take you."

Rose thought to make it even more difficult for her aunt. She slowly blinked. "Really, Aunt Stephanie! Where?"

Her aunt was beside herself. She looked into her godchild's sweet face and fought for a way to make the words come easier. The struggle was apparent in the tight lines around her mouth. She expelled a great breath, looked to the ceiling and began again.

"An unscrupulous man might make you do something to jeopardize a good marriage." Stephanie paused for emphasis. "Such as holding you too close."

Rose thought of how close the raven had held

her in the garden, and her skin began to prickle as she remembered his hands around her waist and in her hair, his lips pressed to hers, her body against his, how hard he felt and how strong his arms were around her. There had been a wonderful magic in that moment, and that magic that still lingered and tempted her. She'd had a taste of something that made her hunger for more.

"An unscrupulous man," Stephanie continued, "would lure a woman away from chaperons and guardians."

Rose thought of the dark garden, the moonlight, the fragrance of sweet roses and the faint music singing only to her and the raven.

"An unscrupulous man would even dare to kiss a maiden such as yourself."

Rose's cheeks became pink with the memory of the raven's kiss, and her throat became dry with a thirst for more.

"Run away from a man who would dare suggest any of these things," her aunt advised. "For if you don't"—she shrugged as if it were also a mystery to her—"who knows what else he would try to do?"

"I can't imagine what else," Rose said in such wonder that Stephanie felt satisfied that she had sufficiently warned her godchild.

Stephanie kissed her cheek and patted her hand. "You would not want to know. Now go to sleep and let me worry about the Liberty Thief—I'm sure he will keep me awake all night."

"Good night, Aunt Stephanie." When her aunt closed the door behind her, Rose smothered her laughter with her pillow. She quickly straightened into a serious posture when the door opened again.

"And one more thing."

Rose was attentive. "Yes, Aunt Stephanie."

Stephanie looked at the puddle of water around the tub. "Do try not to splash so when you bathe—it's not ladylike." She softly closed the door behind her feeling confident that Rose was wary enough to look at men suspiciously, never suspecting that when Rose closed her eyes her dreams were sweetly touched with the things an unscrupulous man would dare.

The moon set and the sun rose high enough to stretch its arms through Rose's bedroom window. Opening her eyes to the warm embrace of morning sunlight, Rose jumped from her bed wondering why her maid had not wakened her as usual. She slipped out of her wrapper and struggled into her clothes—except for her corset, which she disdainfully kicked aside.

The sound of a carriage coming to a stop below her window caught Rose's attention. Looking down into the cobbled street, she saw a man emerge and rap on the front door with the silver tip of his cane. There wasn't much she could see but the top of his chapeau bras. After a moment, he disappeared into the house. Rose thought it was strange her aunt had not mentioned they were receiving a guest, but then Stephanie had been so upset the night before that she had probably forgotten to mention the visitor.

Rose met her maid face to face when she opened her bedroom door. The lightly freckled maid held a breakfast tray between her hands.

'I'm sorry I'm late, miss, but m'lady said to let

you sleep this morning." The petite girl set the tray on a mahogany tea table.

"It's all right, Lizzie. I'm not hungry. I'll just join my aunt for tea."

"Oh no, miss." Lizzie avoided Rose's eyes and looked down at her black boots. "M'lady said no one was to disturb her and the gentleman."

"I doubt that she meant me, Lizzie."

Lizzie looked as if she would cry. "Begging your pardon, miss, but she said 'especially Miss Rose'."

"Did she?" Rose's voice was filled with curious interest.

Lizzie's eye caught the discarded corset, and she was glad for the excuse it gave to divert Rose's thought of joining her aunt. "Oh, miss, I would have come up earlier. Let me help you finish dressing."

"I am done dressing."

Lizzie held the corset limply in her hand. "But . . ."

"I'm more comfortable without it. Besides, no one will know I'm so scandalously dressed, will they? Now tell me about my aunt's visitor. What's his name?" Rose picked at a piece of toast.

"I . . . I don't know, miss." The maid twisted her apron in her hands.

"He's the man who's going to catch the Liberty Thief," Rose said, taking another bite of her breakfast while she slid her feet into her slippers.

"Yes, miss, Lady Vanderhue said—" Lizzie clapped her hand over her mouth.

"The American, Trent Jordan."

Lizzie gasped. "Lady Vanderhue will discharge me!"

"No she won't, you're *my* maid. Now help me

57

with these top buttons, and I do need something done with my hair before I meet Mr. Jordan."

Lizzie's freckles nearly glowed through her pale skin. "Yes, miss."

Rose looked critically at the cascade of blonde hair that shimmered over her shoulders. "I look like a young girl," she said. "Put it up, Lizzie."

"But miss . . . your hair is lovely down, just running over your shoulders like that."

"It's styled like a child's," she said, handing her hairbrush to Lizzie.

After what seemed like a terribly long time to sit, Rose was surprised and delighted at what Lizzie had done to her hair. The new hairstyle made an amazing change in the way she felt, but there was still something not quite right. Rose set her eyes on her gown—it was too simple for a lady. Her aunt had promised to take her to London for new dresses.

"When did Lady Vanderhue say we were going to London?"

Lizzie puffed the bow at the back of Rose's gown. "Monday, miss. You look lovely, miss, and your aunt will be surprised to see you looking like such a lady. But if you don't mind me saying so, I don't think she'll be very happy about it."

Rose turned in front of the long mirror. "Maybe Chloe has some gowns she'd lend me."

Rose found Harold at the foot of the staircase polishing the banister to a satiny sheen.

"Good morning, Miss Rose."

"Good morning, Harold. Is Lady Vanderhue in the library?"

"Yes, miss, but she's left clear instructions not to be disturbed."

58

Her aunt's determination to keep Trent Jordan a secret piqued her interest even more. Obviously Stephanie considered him unscrupulous enough that she had gone to great pains to let Rose sleep through their morning meeting and to set Harold in the hall as a sentry.

Rose started for the library with Harold close behind. She had every intention of barging into the room and enjoying her aunt's surprise—until she saw Harold's face. He was looking at her with such a stern expression that it made her pause just outside the door. Harold had a talent for telling those above his station what he thought without using the words that would get him into trouble. She would wait for her aunt and the guest to finish their meeting. When the door opened she would just be stepping down the stairs, like a lady.

She turned on her heel before Harold could summon up a protesting look, climbed halfway up the stairs, then turned to face him again. With her own fierce look set on her face, she arranged her skirt and sat down on a step midway up the long staircase. She rested her elbow on her knee and her chin in her hand and was ready to wait until she heard the library door swing open.

Harold broke his silence and said in distress. "Miss Rose, why don't you run along and—"

"And play in the garden? Harold, I'm not a dim-witted child."

"This is a private meeting between Lady Vanderhue and Mr. Jordan. It's unladylike of you to be sitting there like a cat waiting to pounce on a mouse."

Harold, in Rose's mind, expressed his opinion too freely for a proper servant, and she was going

59

to remind him of that, but then the door opened. She heard her aunt's voice and quickly stood up, smoothing her gown and wrinkling her nose at Harold's disapproving frown before stepping down the stairs.

Stephanie passed through the doorway first and almost at once saw Rose descend the stairs. It was her first thought to push Trent back into the library, but it was too late. She could only stand and face Rose with Trent beside her.

Rose could not have looked more beautiful. Stephanie was sure her godchild had planned this chance meeing, and she cursed herself for being so foolish as to call Trent to the house. If it wasn't for her impatience to have something done about the Liberty Thief, Trent would not be looking as he did now at Rose poised on the staircase before them. Her muslin gown flowed over the steps like a waterfall as she stepped down to greet them with all the grace of a princess. The deep gauze ruff around her neck and the full-length sleeves that flared at her wrists in a soft ruffle made her aunt's irritation wane with approval.

"Aunt Stephanie, I did not realize you had a visitor this morning." Rose smiled sweetly at her aunt's guest. Not waiting for her speechless guardian to make an introduction, she dipped ever so elegantly in a low curtsy. Trent was entertained by her obvious effort to deflect her aunt's growing displeasure.

"You didn't tell me your niece was such a grown lady—and a beautiful one." Trent took Rose's hand and lingered over a kiss on the back of it, sending a tingle through her fingers and up her arm. As determined as she was to keep an air of cool sophistication, Rose felt a pink blush come to her cheeks.

"From your aunt's description I would have expected a child in braids to come skipping down those stairs."

Trent's words caused the hairs on the back of Stephanie's neck to rise. "Mr. Jordan—my godchild, Mary Rose Whitley."

"It's very nice to meet you, Mr. Jordan," Rose said, ignoring her aunt's reproving scowl and thinking how elegant and charming the American was despite her aunt's description of his scanty morals. While she admired his handsome face, she tried to place him, sensing she had met him before. "I feel we've met at another time, Mr. Jordan. Something about you is very familiar."

Stephanie bustled past Rose and Trent. "Let's not detain Mr. Jordan further, dear. I'm sure he's anxious to begin on the matter we discussed." Lady Vanderhue headed for the front door, expecting Trent to follow. When he did not she turned and glared at him. "Rose, Mr. Jordan has business to attend to. We wouldn't want to keep him with idle chitchat."

Hardly moved by Stephanie's nervous hints, Trent kept his eyes on Rose, who also seemed not to hear her aunt and did not acknowledge in any way that Stephanie was standing there. All Rose saw were eyes as dark and holding as pitch. To her they were the most intense eyes she'd ever seen; to Stephanie they were the eyes of a hungry predator. Stephanie grabbed Rose by the arm and pulled her away from Trent. His brow rose at the protective move and a wry smile crossed his lips.

"Good day, Mr. Jordan," she said in a tight

61

voice, then nodded to Harold. Harold held the door open for Trent. Trent seemed neither to notice nor to hear Stephanie, and coolly ignoring her irritation he let his eyes boldly linger over Rose. "I wouldn't think of rushing out after only an introduction."

Rose met Trent's appraising gaze. She did not try to hide her eyes meekly beneath her lashes or to curb the slight teasing smile that barely curved her lips. What she saw standing in front of her pleased her and she made no attempt to hide that fact. Trent Jordan was her idea of the perfect man— even if he was as unscrupulous as her aunt had claimed. He towered over her by a foot and looked even more massive in his black breeches and frock coat. His hair was black and full of soft waves that were caught at the nape of his neck by a satin ribbon.

Yet something about him was familiar—his eyes, perhaps. They were soul-searching eyes, eyes that could fathom the depths of her own and plunge to her very heart. He had the look of a pirate about him—sharp, dangerous and exciting. And he was American, not one of the proper suitors her aunt invited to Briar Hill to meet her. It was no wonder her aunt had chosen him to seek out the Liberty Thief.

"Perhaps you would join us for tea, Mr. Jordan," Rose dared to suggest.

Stephanie hurried a reply. "Mr. Jordan doesn't like tea, Rose, and there isn't any more coffee in the kitchen. Perhaps another time."

The tight smile on Trent's face dimpled his cheek. He wondered if the delectable Rose knew of her aunt's determination to keep them apart. He sensed it was not going to be an easy task by the rebellious light he detected in the niece's eyes. Stephanie's decision to make him taboo would only serve in his favor, for there was an obvious struggle beginning between the guardian and her angel. Rose was indeed going to be a most exciting conquest.

Trent lifted Rose's hand again and brought it to his lips. "Most surely, another time soon," he promised smoothly.

Chapter 5

Penelope leaned up on one elbow and gazed into Trent's distant and expressionless eyes. She had tried all her tricks to arouse him into taking her with his usual passion, but nothing she'd done had moved him. He was focused on something, and it was consuming all his energies. Whatever it was, Penelope was warming with hot jealousy.

His reputation warned her that one day he'd move on to another mistress, but she was determined not to let that happen. Penelope did everything to please Trent and did everything to discourage others from even thinking about him. Until now she had been successful.

Her hand slid possessively over Trent's bare torso and rested for a moment on his flat stomach. When he did not respond by wrapping her in his arms, she began to toy with the waistband of his breeches.

Trent sighed and rolled from her touch. "I'm sorry, Pen," he apologized, reaching for his shirt. "My business has preoccupied my thoughts."

Penelope's green eyes grew livid, but she dared not let her anger leave her tongue. "Why don't you let me help you forget your business?" She kneeled up behind him and ran her hands over his shoulders.

Trent stood up and moved away from her. He had already buttoned his shirt and was tucking it into his pants. Looking down at Penelope stretched across his bed made him doubt his sanity. Her dark hair fanned over his pillows, her breasts flowed over the top of a lace chemise temptingly enough and her lips pouted seductively. Here was a woman nearly pleading with him to mate with her, and all he could do was think of the pale, untouched Rose. The frustration infuriated him. The cherub Rose sat on one shoulder, the delectably bad Penelope on the other. Each whispered in his ear; each tempted him with promises that pulled him in two directions. He was listening to Rose more and more—she promised to be an exciting challenge.

Since the first night he saw Rose he was set upon with such a desire to have her that he could think of nothing else. He thought his green-eyed lover could make him forget her, but even the fiery Penelope could not erase Rose from his mind. Penelope only proved to him that he had to have the delicate Rose for his own.

It would not be easy plucking Rose from the garden when there was Stephanie to deal with first, and he would have to be careful not to frighten the unspoiled beauty. He'd have to make her want him and then trust him. Trent would not risk losing the prize by frightening her away. He would carefully tend Rose. Forgetting that Penelope was watching him intently, a smile teased at the corners of his mouth.

"You don't look very worried about business now.

66

Why don't you come back to bed?" she coaxed.

Trent bent down and kissed her forehead. It was not the kiss she had hoped for. "Go home to your husband now. I have much to do today."

"Are you seeing another?" Penelope's voice was harsh and suspicious. "I'm not a stupid woman. You'll not toss me aside lightly, Trent."

"There was never anything more between us than a need to indulge in mutual pleasure. There were no promises, Penelope. Of the many things you may accuse me, deceit is not one of them."

Penelope leaped off the bed like a wild cat. The fire in her eyes flashed madly, and a wounded cry ripped from her throat. "You will not discard me," she vowed, clawing his neck with her fingers.

Trent pulled her hands from him and restrained her arms behind her back. His free hand wound around her hair, and he pulled her head to him. His hot and angry breath against her neck gave due warning.

"Think before you threaten me, Penelope. Although your husband has his own mistress, he would not be so tolerant of his wife doing the same."

Penelope whimpered in pain, but Trent was not ready to release her until she realized her mistake.

"I'm sorry, Trent," she finally said, her voice empty of anger and filled with a tearful plea for his forgiveness.

Trent tossed her from him. He did not have patience for women who tried to tangle him in their web of guilt, threats and tears. He had been a prisoner of that web before and had vowed never again to let the wiles of a woman catch him unaware—he was always careful to keep his heart at a safe distance.

He threw her clothes to her. "Go to your husband, Pen," he said softly, knowing she was going to cry. Women's tears had little effect on him now, for he knew they were only a means to a desired end. He turned his back and closed the door on her sobs. She'd be happy in the arms of another in a week.

He had yet to meet a woman who did not harbor a selfish, conniving little heart beneath her breast. Penelope used her wiles well with the men she charmed. The fools were turned to mush by the pout of her lips and sway of her hips. He could make a list of the women like her, with his own mother topping it. He grimaced at the memory of discovering her in bed with another man. He'd promised himself then that he would never let a woman take control of his heart.

Trent hustled past his housekeeper on the way down the stairs and caught her puzzled look. "See Lady James out. I'll be back for dinner tonight," he said before leaving the house.

Mrs. Witherspoon nodded and continued up the stairs. She balled her hand into a fist and knocked lightly on the door to Trent's room. She had seen the same scene played out many times before: the self-pitying moan, the swollen, tear-filled eyes, the blame. She expected to be burdened again with the sorrowful tale of how Mr. Jordan had used an innocent woman for his own selfish pleasure. No matter. If there was a flood of tears, she could not feel sorry for Lady James, who had had her own designs on using Trent. She could not console a woman who deceived her husband.

Mrs. Witherspoon had kept her thoughts of Lady James private, but her expressions had become increasingly filled with caution and dread the longer the affair had continued. Now she sighed with relief that Lady James was leaving the house for good.

Trent didn't consciously think of where he was going—just that he needed a long walk to sort out everything that was on his mind. His affair with Penelope had come to an ungracious end, and his voyage to Greece looked questionable. Philip hadn't secured the shipment of guns yet, so the *Raven's* departure from its London berth was now delayed indefinitely. With the Greek rebellion becoming more of a reality, the Filiki Hetairia was stockpiling such shipments smuggled in from the free ports. Ramos, his contact in Greece, had come to rely on the *Raven's* periodic jaunts across the Mediterranean to supply his band of freedom fighters with the guns and ammunition they needed. Like his crew, Trent was becoming restless waiting for Philip to make his deals. In the meantime, Rose had promised to be a nice distraction, but Stephanie was stubbornly placing herself in front of him like a stone wall. Stephanie should have known better than to put someone that tantalizing out of his reach, he thought.

At first she had tried bribery, but when that had only amused him she'd resorted to using Philip. Philip had only halfheartedly tried to convince his friend not to pursue his American cousin. To Trent's amusement, Philip had wagered that with Rose, Trent had met his match. Trent grinned thinking about it. Stephanie would be paying up another one of her nephew's debts. It would serve her right for threatening to betroth Rose before he had time to court her.

Stephanie's main concern was to take her niece completely out of his reach. In anger he had threatened to make Rose his mistress, but Stephanie had laughed, claiming Rose was not like Penelope or Chloe. Once betrothed she would remain faithful, and not even Trent would be able to corrupt her values. Trent wasn't so sure. He had seen the flicker of desire in Rose's eyes. But he wanted Rose first. He wasn't going to wait for Stephanie to carry out her threat and rob him of that opportunity.

With the mystery of the Liberty Thief still buzzing through London, Trent had an excuse to call on Stephanie whenever he wanted. He would see Rose even if Stephanie didn't like it.

Trent ended his walk when he reached Philip's town house. From across the street he could see Stephanie's coach. He leaned against a lamppost and watched. He didn't have to wait long before Stephanie and Rose appeared. Rose was at her aunt's side and listening to the woman babble on as the two started up Philip's front steps. As was Stephanie's habit, her hands moved with her mouth while she looked at Rose and not where she was going. A careless step sent her sailing downward to a hard landing on her backside. In seconds she was heaped on the walk in a pile of tangled silk.

Rose scrambled after her aunt, her startled cry carrying across the street and turning every head within hearing. By the time Trent reached them, Rose had decently arranged her aunt's skirts and was kneeling on the ground beside her. Stephanie groaned—the only hint to Rose that she wasn't dead.

"Aunt Stephanie," she pleaded, patting her cheeks lightly.

70

"Get Dr. Wood." Trent's order sent the coachman running.

Stephanie's eyes fluttered open, and they were glazed with confusion when she looked into the faces staring down at her. She frowned with displeasure when she recognized Trent.

"Aunt Stephanie, you've had a fall. Mr. Jordan's here," Rose explained. "Do you need help getting up?"

Rather than be subjected to the humiliation of Trent Jordan picking her up off the sidewalk, Stephanie strained her aching muscles to lift her body. But even with her strong will she could barely move. She gruffly ordered Rose to get Philip's valet.

"Thomas can't lift you or carry you up those stairs by himself. You'll kill the man," Trent said, and then added with a teasing smile, "Besides, it'll be my pleasure."

Stephanie gritted her teeth more against the humiliation of being dependent on Trent and of giving him the opportunity to play the knight to the rescue before Rose's eyes than against the pain that shot through her leg.

"Can you hold on to my neck?"

"Of course I can—I'm not completely helpless," Stephanie snapped, making Trent smile even more.

The sweat beaded on Stephanie's forehead as she silently endured the pain of being moved. Trent frowned, knowing there was more to her pain than a bruised head.

When Philip's butler, Thomas, swung the front doors wide, he gasped at seeing her. "My Lord, my Lord, my Lord," he carried on fretfully.

"Do your praying later, Thomas," Trent said,

turning his head to avoid getting the feathery plume on Stephanie's bonnet in his mouth. "Help me get Lady Vanderhue to her room."

By now all the servants were huddled in the main hall, whispering to each other and shaking their heads. They parted into a receiving line when Trent walked toward them, their curious stares focused on Stephanie. Rose turned to see her aunt carried between Thomas and Trent. A purple bruise darkened her cheek, and her forehead was scraped to a painful red. She shivered from the shock that had set in.

"Go upstairs and prepare a room for Lady Vanderhue," Rose snapped the order to the nearest servant.

Trent heard the sharp tone of authority in Rose's voice and saw how she took charge of the staff. Rose suddenly became even more intriguing. There was more to the cherub-faced blond than beauty.

When Trent and Thomas got to Philip's room, the bed was turned down as Rose had ordered, and a fire had begun to warm the chamber. Once the hefty woman was settled comfortably, Thomas collapsed in a wide chair.

Rose saw the contained pain on her aunt's face and read the concern in Trent's eyes. She knew there was nothing more she could do until Dr. Wood arrived than make her aunt comfortable.

"Is there anything else I can do, Aunt Stephanie?"

"Yes, first get these men out of my bedroom, and then get me a bottle of sherry."

Thomas jumped from his seat. Rose didn't know if he was still red-faced from the exertion of helping Trent carry her aunt up a dozen steps or had just been terribly embarrassed. Trent didn't flinch. He casually walked over to the window and pulled aside the drape. Below, a hack and its driver waited at the curb.

"Dr. Wood's here," he announced in his ever-steady voice.

"Thank heaven," Rose breathed with relief.

"*You* thank heaven," grumbled Stephanie. "At this moment I can't see what *I* have to thank heaven for."

"You can be thankful you didn't break your neck or crack your thick skull," Dr. Wood declared from the doorway. "Your driver told me about your fall." He bustled past Rose and began to examine Stephanie with his eyes. "Now, let's see what you have managed to do."

Trent held his arm out for Rose. "Let's go downstairs and have that cup of tea," he offered.

Upon hearing that announcement, Stephanie struggled to sit up, only to have Dr. Wood push her down. "Now, you're not going to be an uncooperative patient. Stay still."

Rose and Trent were brought tea in the front parlor. Rose watched Trent as she sipped her tea. He stood by the long window, the light brightening his face as he stared out. His hands were locked behind his back while he waited with her for news from Dr. Wood.

For Rose it was an agonizing wait. She was guiltily torn between her concern for her aunt and her curiosity about the man before her. She couldn't help but be struck by something familiar about him and she found it hard to keep her eyes from appraising him whenever she thought he wasn't looking. He had taken off his waistcoat and folded it over the arm of a chair. Her aunt would

73

have been shocked that he'd made himself so comfortable in Rose's presence. Even though the room was as hot as hades, Stephanie wouldn't have felt one had an excuse to remove one's coat. It wasn't as though he was indecent, Rose told herself. He was wearing a shirt that merely suggested the muscular frame it covered, and it was neatly tucked into his trousers—trousers that hugged the shape of his legs. She felt her face warm and blamed the strong sun that poured through the windows.

Mr. Jordan certainly seemed to be nothing less than a gentleman. Though he seemed not to be too fond of her aunt, he'd cared enough to help her, and he insisted on staying until he knew of the seriousness of her condition. If he were truly the scoundrel her aunt had described, he wouldn't have offered his help.

Thomas rumbled his throat. "Mr. Jordan, Dr. Wood would like your assistance upstairs."

Rose jumped up from her seat and was ready to follow him.

"Stay here," Trent ordered so firmly that Rose automatically stopped. "Your aunt will be fine," he continued in a softer voice that eased away the argument she was ready to give. "I've known her a long time. She's too tough to let something like a fall keep her down for long."

Rose paced away her worry until a terrible shriek sent her flying up the stairs. She was met at the door by the solid broadness of Trent Jordan. She looked up at him, her face white from imagining the worst.

"Let me in," she demanded.

Trent stopped her from pushing past him. "Your aunt's asleep now."

Rose's eyes were wide with fright. "She's going to die," she announced with dread. All of a sudden the tears broke over her eyes and rushed down her cheeks. She'd known something terrible was destined to happen when last night's storm rolled over London.

It was out of reflex that Trent let his arms fall around her. His hands spread over her back and slowly slipped down along her curves to come to rest at her hips. Her warm softness pressed against his chest and made him heat with a sudden desire to have her. He held her away from him before he lost all sense of decency and seduced her right outside her sleeping aunt's bedroom. "She's not going to die," he assured her.

"How do you know?"

"She's too arrogant to let something like a broken ankle kill her." And, he thought, she certainly wouldn't die before making sure her niece was safe from him. "Her ankle had to be set and she fainted. But since she can't be moved, you'll be staying in London for a while."

Rose's eyes lingered on the strong hands that held her own. They were hands capable of strangling the life out of someone if they so wished, but they had touched her with gentleness. Her eye caught a sudden spark of green light. With so much happening she hadn't noticed it before. There was no mistaking that ring for anyone else's. The breath halted in Rose's throat; her knees threatened to unhinge. The night in the garden suddenly rushed back in the vivid colors of candlelight and red roses. She heard the violins and felt his warm body hugging hers. She was swept up again in a dizzying waltz and stumbled against him.

Trent caught her in his arms and, afraid she was ready to swoon, held her tight. Lines of concern furrowed his brow. "Are you all right?"

Rose wasn't in a hurry to leave his embrace. There was something very nice about being in Trent Jordan's strong arms. Reluctantly, she answered, "Yes, I . . . it's been a harrowing day." That was putting it mildly, she thought. First her aunt, then discovering her masked man.

"Philip has to be told. If you'd like, I'll break the news to him." Trent smiled. Philip would not be overjoyed to hear that his aunt had just become a long-term house guest.

Dr. Wood squeezed out of Stephanie's room. Cautiously, Trent released Rose. The doctor looked kindly on Rose. His long bushy whiskers and his rotund form put her in mind of a hedgehog. "Your aunt has a long recuperation ahead of her. I'm putting you in charge, although I do advise you to obtain some more servants. Knowing your aunt, she's going to wear them all out by the week's end. And get yourself some rest while you can. She'll be asleep most of the night, and will be fine until I stop in tomorrow," he promised. "I'll show myself out."

"You should get to bed," Trent said, making a move to follow in Dr. Wood's footsteps.

"Yes," Rose agreed, stopping him with the light touch of her hand on his sleeve. She didn't want him to leave yet and she hurried to think of a reason to keep him there longer. "I . . . where should I stay? Just arriving today, I'm not familiar with Philip's house. I don't know which room he would want me to stay in."

Trent looked down into her blue eyes. "There's a guest room down the hall."

Rose followed him. "So far away. What if Aunt Stephanie calls for me?"

"The servants will get you," he said, pushing the heavy door aside.

Rose scanned the small but inviting room. It was furnished simply. A high wardrobe graced one wall, a small dressing table was sandwiched between two windows, and a washstand holding a flowered bowl and pitcher was fit neatly in a corner. A small but adequate fireplace promised warmth. Eventually, Rose's eyes came around to the bed. She sat down on it to test its softness, unaware how much she tempted Trent's control.

"Dr. Wood said you should get some rest," he said, trying not to let the inviting look of her mouth shake his avowed resolve.

Rose searched his face. He looked at her so seriously. He wasn't at all like the tease he had been the night of the ball. Of course, he didn't suspect she knew. Rose smiled on the inside. Now it was her turn to do a little teasing.

"With all of today's excitement, I don't think I could sleep if I tried," she said, bouncing on the bed.

Trent clenched his hands behind his back. She was beautiful and so inviting.

Rose noted the muscles in his neck flinch. "Philip hadn't mentioned he had an American friend." Her smile flirted dangerously.

It would be impossible to carry on a conversation with her sitting on that bed, Trent swore to himself. He kneeled on one knee and gently lifted off her slippers. "Philip and I are old friends." He couldn't resist running his hand over her arch and around to her ankle.

A warm feeling rose up Rose's leg at his touch.

Despite her resolve to punish him for taunting her at the ball, she was finding it difficult to subdue her reactions to the feel of his hand on her skin.

"And I'm sure he will eventually mention it," Trent continued. "Now, you really need to try and rest." He put his arms under her and lifted her legs up onto the bed.

However, Rose wasn't going to let him leave so easily. She reached up and wrapped her arms around his neck.

They were not in the garden under the protection of night and masks—they were in her bedchamber. She shouldn't have been so forward as to provoke him, but she did. Without hesitation, he quickly brushed his lips against her forehead. He ran the back of his hand down the side of her soft cheek. Rose closed her eyes to the soothing stroke of his caress. "You're not at all like Aunt Stephanie said," she said in a near whisper.

A smile played at the corner of his mouth. "What did Aunt Stephanie say?"

"She said you were unscrupulous."

"Did she." He tapped her nose with his finger. "She said you were a child."

Her eyes flashed open. "Well, I'm not," she said indignantly.

"You are very young and I am unscrupulous," Trent warned.

"I don't believe that. If you were, then your kiss would have been . . . different." She looked into Trent's black eyes and was suddenly lost in their depths. "Kiss me again, Mr. Jordan, and not like you were my father."

Trent set his dark eyes on her. "You don't know what fate you are tempting," he warned. He held her head between his hands and covered her beautiful lips with his. He meant his kiss to be far from gentle this time. It was to warn her of the passion she tempted with such reckless abandon. His lips pressed hard against hers, claiming them with a demand that dared resistance. The full weight of his chest fell on her, holding her still to endure the full effect of a man's kiss.

The bold caress of his lips held everything that was taboo. It excited her and filled her body with uninhibited wanting for something that was forbidden and sweet. His lips were warm and firm and promising. He skillfully moved them over her mouth, setting a fire that swept over her. His kiss was restless and impatient, wanting more and soon demanding it. His tongue pushed against her lips, forcing them to open. He played in the soft, moist recesses of her mouth, teasing her tongue to join with his.

The heat that raced through her veins in the garden returned, rippling through her in a burning wave of desire. She held Trent closer, wanting the feeling to go on. He pressed against her, crushing her breasts against his chest. He nearly sucked the very breath from her as he proved how unscrupulous his kiss could be. When he reluctantly pulled away, she was sure she knew who her masked man was. She waited until her mind cleared, her nerves steadied and her breath returned.

"My, Aunt Stephanie was right. You are very unscrupulous. Do you always take advantage of young women in dark gardens, Mr. Jordan?"

He had fallen so neatly in her trap. It was all Trent could do not to laugh. He moved off the bed. "Only ones as beautiful as you, Miss Whitley."

79

Chapter 6

It was only a matter of time before Stephanie started to write out the wedding invitations, but before the ink was dry, Rose started to put an end to the idea.

"I don't need a husband!" Rose's voice was louder than she knew. If the shutters were open, her aunt was sure Rose had been heard in Trafalgar Square.

Stephanie sat still lest she topple the tea tray off her lap, but at the sight of her aunt's teeth gnawing at her bottom lip Rose knew she was agitated. Visitors were now coming in at a trickle, and Stephanie had run out of ways to amuse herself. Her newest project was to plan Rose's wedding from her bedside, and the selected groom was Lord Wesley. He had met Stephanie's criterion: he came from a solid English family. Anything else was immaterial.

Rose liked Lord Wesley as one would like a puppy, but her aunt had not yet been able to find someone who could stir something inside her. Watching the sun rise and set was more exciting than spending time with Lord Wesley. She would have much preferred her aunt invite the American, Trent Jordan, to supper. Lord Wesley was cool as ice, whereas with Trent . . . she could feel the heat of an ember radiate from his smile. He promised to be much more exciting than the Englishman, even if he was arrogant. But Lord Wesley was the son of her aunt's friend, and in Stephanie's eyes there was no better match.

"Lord Wesley has expressed an interest in courting you, and I've given him my permission," Stephanie continued, ignoring her niece's angry pacing as just another example of how her father had spoiled her into expecting to make her own decisions. "He's coming for supper tonight, and of course you'll be on your best behavior. Chloe and Philip will join you."

Rose felt better that Chloe would be there, but she still frowned.

"Don't look like that, Rose. It wrinkles up your face and is quite unattractive. This isn't going to be a long courtship, so please make the best of it." Stephanie's last words came near to pleading. Her niece was as stubborn as her father.

"Lord Wesley is not the man I want to marry," Rose said for the tenth time that morning. "Father promised I could decide."

"And that I approve your choice. However, as of yet you haven't settled on anyone, and you don't have time to wait until you fall in love." Stephanie laughed at the absurdity of that idea. "And as for your father's promise—he's not here."

"Don't you think Father should at least know? He would want to approve of my future husband." Rose thought to stall her aunt's idea for as long as she could.

"I've already sent word to your father that I've

found a suitable husband for you as we had discussed before he left. He will approve of Lord Wesley even if you don't. He'll be returning to London in two months. That should give you enough time to get to know Lord Wesley."

That was that. Aunt Stephanie was determined. Before Rose knew it the dressmaker would be unrolling bolts of lace and silk all over the place. She wouldn't be surprised if the invitations were already ordered. She fled from her aunt's room in a blur of tears.

The afternoon wore away faster than Rose would have liked. If she could have jammed up the clock, she would have. Despite Lizzie's words of encouragement, she dressed for supper with little enthusiasm. Rose was still teary-eyed when Chloe came to her room.

Chloe looked wonderful in a scandalously revealing lavender gown; it was a complement to her violet eyes and soft brown hair. Her coloring made Rose think of how her aunt must have looked in her younger years before too many puddings had settled on her hips.

"You chose quite a . . . nice dress." Chloe didn't sound or look very excited with Rose's choice. "You know it *is* after dark—you can bare some of your shoulders." Chloe draped herself comfortably over the bed while she waited for Rose to finish dressing.

Rose glanced at Chloe's reflection in her mirror while she fastened her earrings. Good God, Chloe was flowing over the top of her gown.

"Well, Lord Wesley will like your modesty," Chloe said, absently twirling a long brown curl around her finger.

Rose turned around and faced her cousin. "You

83

mean this dress will please him?" Rose hoped her dull choice would somehow make her less desirable in Lord Wesley's eyes.

"Lord Wesley would not like a flashy wife. He's not at all like Philip."

Rose began to get curious about Lord Wesley. "What else wouldn't he like?"

"If you're out to please Lord Wesley, then be demure. Don't talk too much and especially don't touch on the more masculine subjects. Keep your distance and wear that dress."

Rose took one of her new gowns from her wardrobe, the one she had secretly convinced the dressmaker to alter. She laid the shimmery blue gown on the bed next to Chloe, a smile touching her lips. She was feeling better about seeing Lord Wesley already.

"Help me with these buttons."

Chloe kneeled up on the bed and began unbuttoning Rose's dress. "What are you up to? Has Aunt Stephanie seen this dress?" she asked, watching Rose wiggle into the blue gown.

"Button me up, Chloe. By the time supper's over, Lord Wesley will be looking for a new wife."

"He may decide he likes what he sees, and if I may say so, there's a lot of you to see. He is quite taken with you," Chloe added with second thoughts. "Not to cast a cloud over your evening, Rose, but you'd better start thinking of someone you like well enough to marry if Lord Wesley doesn't meet your approval. Aunt Stephanie is bent on the idea."

"I'm not marrying Lord Wesley. I'd sooner marry that American friend of Philip's."

"Trent Jordan?" Chloe laughed. "You can't be

serious. Well, if you are, it won't matter. Trent wouldn't think of asking you or anyone to be his wife. With an idea like that, no wonder Aunt Stephanie is in such a hurry to marry you."

Exhausted, after a seemingly endless evening with the straight-laced Lord Wesley, Rose went right to bed without looking in on her aunt. Her aunt would surely want to know how well the evening had gone, and Rose didn't think they'd view its "success" in quite the same light. Rose smiled when she thought of how shocked the man was when she dared to discuss politics. Apparently he didn't approve of ladies delving into those areas.

However, Rose wasn't going to avoid her aunt so easily. Hours later she was awakened from a sound sleep by a shrill scream. She threw back the covers and, not wasting time with slippers and a robe, raced to her aunt's room, navigating in the pitch dark and keeping to the center of the hall where she knew she'd be safe from furniture legs and floor vases. She passed Philip's room—another few yards and she'd make her aunt's bedroom without tripping over anything. Another loud scream sent her heart jumping to her throat. A flash of lightning and a clap of thunder got her running even faster down the dark hallway that never seemed to end.

Once in her aunt's bedchamber, she found a lamp and brought it to life. Her aunt was sitting up in bed, wide-eyed and in a terrible sweat.

"What is it, Aunt Stephanie?" Rose asked breathlessly.

"Someone was in here."

Rose looked around the room. Everything seemed in order. "Are you sure you weren't having a dream?"

"I know someone was in here—I heard him. Dear Lord! What shall we do?"

"Maybe it was the shadows." Rose tried to sound hopeful but looked nervously at the sky fluctuating from dark to light with intermittent flashes of light. "You know how lightning makes the shadows move," she offered in an unconvincing tone; Rose shared her aunt's feeling that someone could very well be prowling about the house.

"I'm not one to imagine things. Now, have a look downstairs."

"Aunt Stephanie," Rose began calmly. "You thought someone had stolen your ruby hat pin at home and then we found it the next day. Every little noise is not the Liberty Thief." Her aunt's expression became hard as stone. "All right," Rose agreed weakly and added, "It could be Philip coming in. Will you be all right for a minute?"

Stephanie pulled a little pistol from under her nightclothes and held it between her shaking hands. "You're a brave child, Rose. Bring me a sherry from the kitchen." Rose nodded. "For heaven's sake, take the candlestick and don't hesitate to use it."

Rose held a lamp in one hand and the silver candlestick in the other. Even though she suspected her aunt was only dreaming, she slowly ventured down the stairs, checking each shadow as she went. Despite her doubts that anyone else was in the house, she began to imagine things; her nerves tensed and her legs stiffened with each step that drew her into the darkness. If the storm was not enough to put her on edge, her fears that a prowler was going to pop out at her were gnawing her nerves to a frazzle. Her hand clutched the candlestick. She dearly hoped Philip wouldn't startle her in the dark, for she'd probably crown him.

Rose checked each of the downstairs rooms. In a flash of lightning the whole parlor was lit as bright as day. Every dark corner a prowler could hide in was uncovered for a second, and in that second she could have sworn she saw a man stiffly standing next to a long length of drapery on one side of the front window. The room was dark again, thrown into shadow from the soft light of her lamp. Rose froze where she was until a second flash of lightning exposed the room and confirmed that she had just imagined the figure of a man. "I'm getting as paranoid as my aunt," she said to herself.

Rose couldn't stop her heart from pounding as loud as thunder or steady her shaking knees no matter how much she tried to convince herself that the shadows were only playing tricks on her eyes. She didn't want to believe someone was actually sneaking around in the house. She satisfied herself that her aunt had only been dreaming, and she left the parlor for the kitchen.

Fear of the Liberty Thief coupled with her helpless confinement to bed had Stephanie's nerves overwrought with worry; it was no wonder the poor woman heard and saw things. Rose looked in the cabinets for the sherry her aunt wanted, and she couldn't deny her own nerves could use a little calming.

She placed the lamp and candlestick on the table and pushed a stool over to the closet where the cook kept Philip's supply of spirits. She then lifted the hem of her wrapper off her bare feet and climbed up on the stool. The bottles clanked as she shifted them around until she found the one she wanted. Grabbing it by its neck, she lifted her wrapper and was just about to climb down when the back door slammed open. A gust of rain-filled wind swept over the floor, touching its path with cold, wet fingers and sending a chill right up her legs. Rose would have fallen off the stool then had she not been so frozen with fright; she would have screamed, too, had her heart not been stuck in her throat. But all she managed to do was stare wide-eyed at the two dripping-wet and less-than-sober-looking men in the doorway.

When she recovered from her initial fright, she realized that Philip was standing next to Trent and grinning like a cat coming back from a night's prowl. The men smelled of drink, and their spirits could be described as nothing less than jolly. Rose didn't see any humor in her situation—she was mortified to be discovered in such a compromising position when she was only doing a good deed for her aunt.

"Raiding the pantry, Miss Whitley?" Trent said smoothly, a crooked grin curving his mouth. His eyes raked over her from head to foot, reminding her of the picture she presented: a woman standing high on a stool, gripping a bottle of sherry in one hand and hiking her wrapper up past her ankles with the other. She quickly dropped her hem.

"Aunt Stephanie thought she heard someone in the house, so I came down to investigate," she began to explain to Philip, doing her best to ignore Trent.

At least Philip looked like he believed her, but Trent simply seemed amused at her story. "Find anything?" he asked, his eyes on the bottle in her hand.

"Mr. Jordan, I don't need to give you an explanation," she replied testily. She then beseeched her cousin's support. "Philip, you know how your aunt likes a glass of sherry every now and then to calm her nerves."

"You were on your way up, then?" Philip took the bottle from her hand and helped her down. He filled the two glasses with sherry and handed her one, then tucked the bottle under his arm and grabbed the stem of the second glass. "I'll take it up to her. You enjoy your sherry," he said with a wink, leaving her alone with Trent.

Rose's cheeks were infused with color. Philip was as bad as Trent. But her annoyance with Philip disappeared when she looked at Trent. He was blocking the only way out of the kitchen with his wide body, summing her up with such an unguarded look that she blushed from head to toe.

"I've seen women in less than their nightgowns before," he admitted coolly.

If he thought that was going to make her feel more at ease, it didn't. He only reminded her that he had noticed how scantily she was dressed, and from his satisfied smile she'd bet he had noticed a lot. She wasn't going to let him make her feel as though she were naked, and she wasn't going to let him think she had done something wrong, either.

"Mr. Jordan," she began in as calm a voice as she could master given the circumstances, "it isn't your house or your place to make a judgment. I was helping my aunt. She heard a noise and I investigated. She asked me to bring up some sherry. I was about to when you happened by. And if I *had* wanted a glass myself, well, that would

89

have been my business. If I had wanted to come down here stark naked, that would have been my prerogative, too." She put the glass of sherry to her lips.

"Well, I wish you would have . . . come down naked," he declared wickedly.

The fire of the liquid burning down her throat took Rose off guard. She sputtered, completely shattering the seriousness of her speech. She looked at his eyes, which were still dancing with the teasing he had done and the promise of more if she stayed. Rose decided not to stay. Not because of his taunting, which she could handle, but because of the dangerous feeling that sparked around them. A fire began to smolder inside her whenever they were together. She was always sure of herself, except when she was with Trent. It frightened her that a man would have such an effect on her that she couldn't think sensibly in his presence.

Rose had to somehow get past Trent to escape the kitchen, and he didn't look like he intended to move from the doorway. As ungentlemanly as he was, he would make her slip by him. She tried to calm her pounding heart and keep her voice strong.

"Mr. Jordan, I think we've covered the subject as to why you discovered me in the kitchen at this late hour."

"Early hour. The sun's nearly up."

"Regardless, I'm going back to bed now, so if you'll excuse me."

"Certainly, Miss Whitley." He moved slightly, just enough so she had room to squeeze by.

Rose held her annoyance at bay. The rogue was going to make her slide by him after all, as if it wasn't bad enough she'd been caught in her nightgown. Regardless, she slipped between Trent and the doorjamb and would have succeeded if he hadn't leaned in and pressed her against the frame of the doorway. If that wasn't enough, he put his hands on either side of her, blocking her way past him.

She thought she'd swoon when his long hardness leaned into her. Every part of his warm body pressed firmly into her: the wide chest that crushed the breath from her lungs, the hips that pinned her firmly in place, the buttons on his breeches that dug into her stomach. His muscular thighs were placed boldly astride her legs, insuring she stayed where she was—pinned neatly between him and the door frame.

It certainly wasn't proper for her, in her nightgown, to be so close to a man and to feel every part of him rub against her, but it sent the most wonderful heat through her body. She wasn't anxious to move away from him; however, she was afraid if he didn't put his arms around her soon, her legs would melt from under her.

"Can you find your room, Miss Whitley?" he asked with a tease in his smile.

"I can find it easily, Mr. Jordan," she said less than convincingly. Her head was in such a spin, and she wondered if she could make her way to the stairs much less her room. To steady herself, she placed her palms on his shoulders, which were wide and solid under her hands. She avoided his eyes, which would be her complete undoing. Instead, she focused on the center of his chest, but that didn't make her heartbeat any slower.

Trent lifted her chin and looked down at her. "Are you sure?"

"No," she answered breathlessly. How could

she be sure of anything with the heat of his body searing through her thin wrapper?

He bent down and covered her mouth with his. Rose felt her knees give. He wrapped her up in his arms and carried her up the stairs, his lips never leaving hers.

Chapter 7

They were cloaked in the dusky light of dawn.
The house had not yet come to life; Philip was
snoozing off the drink from the night before, and
Stephanie hopefully had sipped enough sherry to
put herself into a good sleep. A curtain of secrecy
fell around them.

Trent laid Rose on the bed, and his mouth
captured hers in a kiss that made her forget
everything that was right and everything that was
wrong. When the warmth of his lips met hers, he
set loose her reckless nature and she returned his
kisses without demur. Her willing response was
enough to quell any sense of caution he might
have had when he'd brought her to her bed. Her
arms still clung around his neck, and when he
tried to break the kiss he felt a small resistance.
Leaning back, he looked upon her. His eyes moved
over every curve the thin shift clung to, from her
shoulders, over the hard points of her breasts that
swelled against the fabric, to where it fell between
her legs.

Rose felt Trent's eyes on her and wondered if it
was the sherry she'd downed so quickly or his gaze

that warmed every part of her.

Reaching out to her, his hand brushed against her cheek, then trailed along her neck and over her shoulder. He coaxed her back to him and she felt the warmth of his chest against hers. In her faint moment of indecision he leaned down to kiss her. Rose's lips touched his in a cautious kiss. She felt his free hand graze her ankle and move up her leg, inching the hem of her shift over the curve of her calves, her knees and thighs, slowly revealing her soft skin to his appreciating touch.

His mouth played with hers ever so gently. He was very skillful in his way of persuasion, taking her lips in his, flicking his tongue over them, teasing with his teeth, whispering her name so softly. So skilled, so mesmerizing was he that she didn't protest when his hands continued up her side and moved her shift higher. She knew that what she let him do was wrong, but it was terribly exciting. Even so, she felt a glimmer of caution. It wasn't too late to stop him; her hand rested on his. She quelled its movement and debated weakly against right and wrong while her body prickled with the most wonderful sensations. Her heart pounded in her ears, beat at her temples and throbbed in her middle. Her skin was on fire with the heat that continued to rage from his touch.

Reluctantly Trent's mouth left hers and he stood back from her, his eyes glowing with a warm light.

Rose's head was spinning when Trent left her bed. At first, she thought he was leaving her room—as he should. By letting him into her bedchamber she had truly gone too far. She was dangerously attracted to this rogue of a man.

To her surprise he unbuckled his belt. A

paralyzing panic gripped her. He had misunderstood how far she was willing to let his kisses go. In her shock she couldn't push a protesting word past the knot in her throat.

Rose's unbelieving eyes watched his fingers work the buckle loose. She should save herself, she thought and jump off the bed now. She should have stopped him before this, but he had tempted her most ruling trait—her reckless curiosity. That curiosity had now brought her dangerously to the edge of no return.

Trent had unleashed feelings that she had no idea she possessed. The passion his hand coaxed forth with such tender care surprised her. She was overcome by the sudden tumultuous upheaval of emotions that rose up like a tidal wave and hovered above her. As Trent came closer, she gripped his shoulders. Something was going to crash down on her and she wasn't sure what.

"Rose," Trent said softly, trying to peel away her fingers. "You don't have to be so tense. I'm not going to hurt you."

"I'm not tense," she disputed, even though a muscle painfully knotted in her calf. Almost grateful for the distraction, she reached down to massage her leg.

Trent saw her and moved her hand aside, replacing it with his own. "Then why does your leg feel as hard as a rock?"

"Trent, this is too much. You have to leave. Aunt Stephanie will . . . oh God, I never meant to—"

"Lie down," he ordered in a throaty whisper. Ignoring her stammering protests, he gently pushed her down into the mattress. "I won't do anything you don't want."

Rose eyed him apprehensively.

"I swear."

Rose rolled over to her side and then lay flat on her stomach, her eyes clamped shut, her body stiff.

Trent's hands moved to ease away her tenseness. He massaged the knot out of her calf, then worked his way over her thighs, kneading out all the tightness and warming her wherever he touched. He moved his hands up her back and over her shoulders and arms, squeezing and caressing until she felt her body melt into the feather mattress.

She moaned with pure pleasure. "I see why my aunt warned me of you. I could very well seek this kind of attention every time I see you."

"You will," he promised.

"You are so sure?"

"I am very sure," he said, pressing a kiss on her neck. His lips moved to her ear, where his teeth lightly nibbled. Rose felt his warm breath brush against her skin and softly gasped with the shock of pleasure that raced down her side to her toes.

Rose knew it was wrong to let him touch her, to let him feel every part of her, to let him explore all the curves of her body. But she could never resist a challenge, and she let him massage her freely and stir feelings that seemed to paralyze every rational thought her conscience threw at her. It wasn't a playful dare—she wasn't stealing an apple from a barrel in Hodge's General Store. This was far more dangerous. At the most, Hank Hodge would tell her father and she'd suffer through a tongue-lashing and promise not to do it again. But this—this was different: it was more intriguing, more daring and certainly more dangerous. It was more thrilling than stealing apples.

Another warning weakly tried to push in front

of the promise of more to come, but it was quickly consumed by the warm contentment she felt. Indeed, Trent had her under his spell. There was nothing that could be done to stop the feelings that ruled her good sense. She didn't want him to leave her; she wanted him to continue his sweet seduction forever. She'd worry about consequences later, when she could think more clearly. For now, she would let him mesmerize her with his touch. She drifted away on a cloud of sweet contentment, dreaming of how wonderful Trent made her feel.

By the time Trent had reduced Rose to soft clay, every muscle in his body was strained to its limit. His eyes burned with her nakedness glowing through the thin wrapper, and his hands were filled with her soft, warm skin; he had explored every aspect of the terrain he had plotted to conquer and now was ready to take what he had prepared.

Trent settled down next to Rose. His side brushed against her side, his leg touched hers. Almost cautiously, he smoothed his hand down her back and over the soft mound of her derriere. He methodically caressed her smooth skin.

"Rose," he whispered, "you are beautiful. In all your sweet innocence, you are beautiful beyond compare."

Trent carefully lay down next to Rose. Leaning up on one elbow, he smoothed his hand over her hair. "Rose?" He looked over her. Long, sandy lashes rested against the blush of her cheeks; it was the first time any woman had fallen asleep on him. Trent leaned back, rested his head on the pillow next to Rose and closed his eyes. It was very late, he told himself, pulling off his breeches. He fell asleep nursing a slightly bruised ego.

* * *

The sun tried to shine through the drawn curtains of Rose's room. Perhaps if it could have penetrated the heavy drapes, they wouldn't have been wakened by Stephanie's bell.

"What's that noise?" Trent asked, his voice muffled against her soft shoulder.

The bell tinkled lightly, then became more frantic. Rose turned to look at Trent and gasped at the sight of him. "What are you doing here?" She leaped off the bed as his arm came around her. The bell rang again.

"Aunt Stephanie's bell," Rose said, as she searched for her robe. Finally finding it in the wardrobe, she snatched it up and wiggled her arms into it. "My God, what are you doing here? What time is it?" She ran to the window and pulled aside the drape and groaned. It had to be nearly noon.

She looked again at Trent in her bed. He leaned up on an elbow and greeted her upset nonchalantly. Seeing him in all his glory without a shred of modesty about him made her blush to a beet red. The remembrance of what had happened between them came flooding back. How could she? Her father was right, he should have held her with a tighter rein, then none of this would have happened. She eyed Trent suspiciously. "Did anything . . . did we . . ." Her eyes couldn't help but stray to his long, lean body stretched across her bed.

Trent laughed as a high color rose in her cheeks. "You were delightful. Every part of you, in fact."

Rose suspected and hoped he was only teasing her. "I don't remember anything other than you . . . Tell me the truth, Trent Jordan!"

Trent sighed, grabbing his breeches from the floor. "You're as pure as an angel. You fell asleep."

Relief surged through Rose. "Thank heavens."

"You can thank my upstanding morals, my dear," he said, pulling on his boots.

"Your morals! How am I going to explain all of this. You spent the night in my bed."

The bell rang again, this time impatiently. Rose became frantic. "You can't stay here," she said in a panic. "Good God, I've got a man in my bed," she said as though she still couldn't believe it. "Aunt Stephanie is going to have an absolute fit if she finds out."

Trent laughed. "Not unless you plan on telling her. It isn't like she can come walking in."

"Tell her?" Rose moaned. "All she'll have to do is look at my guilty face." Rose checked the mirror: she was bright as a cherry. "Oh God, what a fix. I've been in messes before, but this takes the cake."

She turned and looked at him accusingly. At least he had pulled on his breeches. She didn't have to face that naked part of him. Instead all she saw was his chest—smooth and tanned and bare. She'd wait until he was completely dressed; she couldn't talk to him standing there half-naked. She went to the wash basin and splashed cold water on her hot face.

He came up behind her and wrapped his arms around her middle. His hands lightly brushed over her breasts. Rose peeled away his hands and turned around to face him. She slammed right against his chest. He lifted her up off her feet and unexpectantly covered her mouth with his in a very hard and familiar kiss. She pushed her hands against

99

his chest and sputtered, "I would not be in this predicament if—"

"If you had had the good sense to wear your robe down to the kitchen," he said, casually reminding her of her nightclothes. "Then I wouldn't have been so tempted by the form of you peeking through. It was quite a fetching sight."

Rose glared up at him. "I wasn't trying to appear fetching. No one else was home. I didn't think you'd come barging in with Philip. Philip!" she groaned. "Philip is home. He's going to think—"

"Of course. He's a grown man and subject to the same wicked thoughts as us all. He'd have taken you to your bed himself if you weren't cousins."

Rose raised her hand to slap him. He'd expected her to swing at him, so he effortlessly caught her wrist and held it. The bell rang, reminding them her aunt was still calling.

"You'd better go see what she wants before she sends in one of the servants. Wouldn't they be—"

"You just shut up."

Trent grinned. "Your aunt does need to work on that mouth. What comes out of it, that is. I'll take care of the rest."

"No you won't, Mr. Jordan," she said with more determination laced in her voice than she actually felt. His laughter followed her down the hall. She stopped short for a second. It was the same deep chuckle she'd heard the night she'd pulled one of the thieves from his horse. She doubted it could be the same and shrugged it off. Facing her aunt was, at the moment, a more serious concern than matching a man's laugh to a possible thief-in-the-night. God, she hoped Trent would show himself out before she got back.

100

Rose's knees shook from her rattled nerves as she stood at the foot of her aunt's bed. Her aunt liked to make people wait and wonder what she was going to say before she actually said anything, and this time that annoying habit made Rose so nervous she had to cross her legs to keep her knees from knocking. She was sure her aunt knew everything that had happened just from her red face. It was also possible that one of the servants knew Trent had stayed the night and had already told all.

"How did you sleep, Rose?" her aunt asked.

If Rose were weakhearted, she would have confessed right then. But she'd been on the spot before and knew not to breathe an incriminating word before solid evidence was presented and there was no possible way out of the jam.

"As a matter of fact, Aunt Stephanie, since you are inquiring, I didn't sleep well at all."

"I thought as much," her aunt said gruffly.

Rose began to wonder how she knew. She was either going to send her back to her father in disgrace or insist Trent marry her.

"I wouldn't have slept well myself," Stephanie continued, "had it not been for the two glasses of sherry Philip made me drink. You poor dear, you must have been a bundle of nerves just worrying about the thief all because of my alarm."

All of a sudden Rose felt as light as a feather. An audible sigh of relief escaped her. "That was good of Philip to see to your rest," she agreed, but thought, "The wretched devil was insuring that Trent had an uninterrupted morning and probably warned the servants not to disturb her."

"It turns out it was nothing, just my jittery nerves. I do wish Trent would find out something.

Maybe he'll have some news for me today. You must make yourself presentable, dear. There's no telling when Mr. Jordan will arrive, and it wouldn't do to be caught in your nightclothes."

Rose felt her body go numb with a rush of tingles. If her aunt was expecting him, he was most likely still in her room.

Chapter 8

Rose entered her room with trepidation. Peering around the door, she was relieved to find that Trent had already gone. She quickly bathed and dressed, and on her way down the stairs she met Philip on his way up. He was grinning like a gargoyle, which, at the moment, was as horrid as she thought him to be. His sparkling eyes told her that he knew Trent had spent the dark morning hours in her room. At the next affair, she imagined, her name would be included in his tabloid of family gossip.

"Rose, sweet cousin, where have you been all morning?"

She stared down her nose at him and in her most regal voice warned, "Don't taunt me, Philip. I'm not like the tame ladies you're used to. I wouldn't think twice about punching you in the stomach after last night." That managed to erase his smug smile, but after the shock of her threat wore off, he followed her back down the stairs, chuckling behind her.

"I told Trent he'd meet his match in you. I bet that you'd have him wrapped around your finger in less than a week, but he—"

That piqued her interest and fueled her temper. She swung around and faced him. "You made a wager? You and Trent made a wager as to who was going to . . . You two scoundrels! Well, let me make a wager with you, Philip. What did he bet?"

"Now, Rose, I shouldn't have been so open-mouthed. Ladies don't make wagers. It isn't proper."

Rose growled, "Now you sound like your aunt. I'm not a lady. I've played in the streets of New York, I've wrestled with boys, climbed trees and done other things that would cause your aunt to swoon." She looked him straight in the eye. "Now, what did Trent Jordan wager?"

"Rose, you don't really want to know . . ." She looked ready to crown him. "That he'd have you by the week's end." He rambled over the words in one breath, obviously hoping she wouldn't hear them if he said them fast enough. The color in his cheeks deepened.

Rose looked thoughtful. "Really?"

Philip looked warily at the plotting expression on her face. Her smile was filled with mischief. "I'll bet in a month's time Mr. Jordan will be asking my aunt for my hand in marriage."

Philip doubled over with laughter. Rose scowled at him. "You'd best save your good humor for the day you'll be paying up. The end of the month, Philip, I'll be coming to collect."

"In your wedding gown, I presume?" His face was red with glee.

"In my wedding gown."

"Not to cast a shadow over your sunshine, Rose, but Trent would never ask you or anyone to the altar. And even if he was so touched, Aunt

Stephanie would never consent. She still has hopes of making a lady out of you." He looked at her suspiciously, "Unless you do something as low as telling Aunt Stephanie—"

"I could, but that would be too easy and it wouldn't really give him much of a sporting chance. He'll ask—and without any prodding from Aunt Stephanie or anyone else," she warned.

"Hell's bells, Rose, you are a rebel."

A smile still split Philip's face when Thomas showed Trent in. Trent stood at the bottom of the stairway, looking up at them curiously. Philip sobered quickly, but Rose kept her sweet smile and continued on down the steps, stopping next to Trent.

"How nice to see you again, Mr. Jordan. Sleep well?" she inquired. She could kick the scoundrel in the shin for using her in a wager.

Trent returned her false smile. "Quite well. And you, Miss Whitley?"

Philip interrupted their exchange. "I'll just be on my way. Say good afternoon to my aunt for me," he said to Trent, then nodded to Rose and quickly departed.

Rose could feel the sparks fly between them. Whether it was the anger she felt at the moment or the same heat that flared every other time Trent got close to her, she didn't know. But she felt it coming slowly, wrapping around her and then stripping away all her defenses. He was handsome and charming in his arrogant way, and he fired her up like no one else ever did. When he wanted to, he could seduce her with his eyes alone. It was sinful that he could make her do anything with a look and a touch. Just recalling his touch sent shivers through her. How well he must have known his effect on her; how well he used it. However, she wasn't so enthralled with him not to notice that she had her own ways of affecting his calm. Now she was going to put what she learned to use. At least she was going to enjoy putting him on his knees and then telling him about her wager with Philip.

"You look well rested," Trent noted with a tease in his voice. "Did your aunt guess?"

She knew he was going to come around to it. "No, Philip was quite the gentleman and made sure I wasn't disturbed by the staff."

"That was considerate of him. I'll have to remember to return the favor." The corner of his mouth curved up in a slight smile.

Rose glared at his back as he climbed up the stairs to her aunt's room. How she had wanted to slap the grin off his face. A reaction like that wouldn't do if she was going to pull him down to his knees. She'd have to keep her temper and be ever so charming, but not so agreeable that he'd be suspicious. A smile came to her lips thinking about it.

Her eyes followed his broad back until he disappeared around the top of the staircase. If she was going to be able to wrap him around her ring finger, she'd have to know everything about him— starting with why her aunt wanted to see him. She looked about for Thomas and then tiptoed back up the stairs.

Rose listened at her aunt's door. It wasn't closed all the way, so she could see Trent through the scant opening. He was standing at the foot of her aunt's bed, his hands clasped behind his back.

"I don't have a clue. Now, you really should try to get some rest today," Trent advised her aunt.

106

"Rest! Not until the brigand is caught."

"You're letting every little sound in the house alarm you. No one was here last night except Philip and Rose," he assured her.

Rose pressed her lips together. Philip and Rose indeed!

"When will you be leaving?" Stephanie asked.

"Ah, we're getting to the real reason behind this summons," Trent said with a grin. "You are quite transparent, Stephanie."

Stephanie's fingers gripped the end of the blanket thrown over her legs. She suspected Rose was still enamored of Trent. The silly child couldn't even see how wonderful a man Lord Wesley was or even know how lucky she was that he'd shown any serious interest in her. Stephanie wouldn't be able to successfully make a good match for her wild niece if the vision of Trent was still appearing before Rose's eyes.

Stephanie couldn't keep as close an eye on Rose as she had hoped now that she was confined to her bed. Keeping her safe would be a lot easier with Trent out of the way. Philip had mentioned that he was almost ready to sail east, and as far as she was concerned, the sooner the better.

"You're that anxious to be rid of me, are you?" he teased, making her expression shrivel with a sour look. "You're not worried I'd get in the tangle of web you're spinning around Lord Wesley and Rose, are you? I promise you—I won't interfere. He can marry her . . . as long as I can kiss the bride," he added with a wink.

"That's precisely why you're not good for her," Stephanie grumbled. "You're too much like her— wild and undisciplined. Rose needs an influence like Lord Wesley. Someone who can calm her

107

down. The two of you together would wreak havoc. If you insist on pursuing Rose, be prepared to battle with me."

Trent leaned over to place a kiss on her forehead. "You're quite right about one thing—she does lack discipline. I'm afraid she'd be a poor influence on me."

"You're impossible!"

Something in the crack of the door had caught Trent's eye, and he was anxious to discover who was gaining an earful of information. He gave Stephanie a wink that set her cheeks aflame and parted with a swiftness meant to catch the spy off guard.

Rose hadn't expected Trent to dash out of the room the way he did. He was at the door in two long strides and she was caught before she could get away. There was nothing to do except wait for him to pull her into her aunt's room for a reprimand. Instead, he held her arm and closed the door behind him.

He looked sternly into her eyes, holding them with such magnetism she was helpless to turn away. He stood so close to her she could feel the heat of his body, but her feet remained rooted to the floor. She wished he'd say something to break the thick silence. It seemed like a very long time before he was ready to acknowledge her ill manners. She guessed he first wanted to make her feel as uncomfortable as he could by touching her all over with his disapproving look. When her senses came back to her, Rose made a move to leave, but Trent anticipating this, held her tighter.

"No questions?"

Rose tried to look as though she couldn't

imagine what he could mean. "Let go of my arm," she demanded.

Trent ignored her and pulled her down the stairs behind him. Rose was forced to step quickly.

"Mr. Jordan," she protested indignantly, "explain yourself. This is most ungentlemanly behavior."

Trent's steps didn't falter. He just chuckled, pulling her along, past Philip and on to the front door. "And listening at your aunt's door is quite unladylike. That would make us the ideal pair, though your aunt would beg to differ. She thinks we'd wreak havoc," he laughed heartily.

Trent turned to Philip, who was grinning at the sight of his cousin struggling against Trent's hold. A woman trying to be free of him was an unusual sight. "Mind if I borrow your carriage?"

"Be my guest." Philip's chuckle made Rose even more angry.

She wasn't going to make it easy for him when he began to shove her into the carriage. She dug her heels into the walk, but that was useless since he effortlessly lifted her up and onto the seat. She quickly slid as far to the other side as she could and was ready to escape by the opposite door when he clamped his hand around her wrist. He slammed the door and the carriage jolted forward.

She sat across from him, glaring at his face. "Wait till my aunt hears of this," she threatened.

"You're not really going to tell your aunt you were listening at the door, are you?" He smiled knowing she wouldn't.

"Are you kidnapping me, Mr. Jordan?" she asked coolly.

He put his hands behind his neck and leaned back against the black leather seat. He was so satisfied with himself that Rose could have screamed right then.

"I thought we'd have a picnic lunch," he announced, surprising her and almost disarming her anger.

"You certainly are spontaneous," she exclaimed, and then added warily, "Or did you plan this?"

"I've planned on being alone with you since the first night I saw you. Today, the opportunity presented itself."

Her cheeks flamed as she thought about how he had caught her at her aunt's door. "What you must think. I wasn't really—" She'd meant to deny eavesdropping but was quickly interrupted.

"You were."

She straightened her back. This could ruin her afternoon if they didn't settle the issue. He didn't have any proof she was listening. She could have been on her way to her room for all he knew.

"Maybe, but—"

"'Maybe' is not even close to the truth. You were listening."

Rose was getting annoyed. The man wasn't going to let her say a word unless she admitted to it, and he was beginning to agitate her even more with his persistent smile. Nevertheless, she rather liked his smile. It was less than perfect, a little crooked at one corner, but it managed to distract her thoughts, and that was really quite annoying.

"All right! I suppose I was listening at the door and it was quite ill-mannered."

He leaned over to her. "Now what I'm wondering is why."

Rose felt the heat rise in her face. "I don't have to tell you anything," she said stubbornly.

"Yes you do or it's back to your aunt, and *then*

110

you'll have a lot of explaining to do."

"You wouldn't dare." His smile told her he would.

Rose thought it over. It wouldn't be the first time she'd have to tell a convincing lie, only she knew this time it would be very difficult. She had lost her calm when he'd set his dark eyes upon her. Wherever his gaze traveled, he lit a fire that raced over her in an uncontrolled fury, burning and licking with erotic pleasure. When his look made her tingle in places that made her squirm in her seat, the fire leaped to her cheeks in a telling blush.

"I didn't intend on eavesdropping," she began. By his sly smile she knew he didn't believe her. "But I was tempted to stop on my way to my room," she continued.

"You don't have to pass your aunt's room to get to yours. But do go on. You're entertaining, at least."

Rose gritted her teeth, but she swore at him anyway. "You can go to . . . the devil."

His laugh burned her ears. "Did your father tell your aunt to stock up on smelling salts before you arrived?"

Rose had to smile, despite her irritation. She had managed to fool everyone in her life with a good tale and a sweet smile or a temper tantrum, but Trent . . . he was going to be a challenge to get around. Her smile turned to light laughter. She really did like Trent Jordan.

The carriage hit a pothole, throwing Rose into Trent's arms. Her eyes met his, and all of a sudden she was drawn into his gaze. She felt as helpless as if she had fallen into a bottomless well. Rose lowered her lashes and saw only his lips. Nervously, she traced her own lips with the tip of her tongue, unaware of that action's effect on the man who held her.

It wasn't enough that she was thrown into his lap, but did Rose have to tempt him so by drawing attention to her lush lips? Full and ripe and sweet as berries, Trent agonized. He remembered the night before, when they were rich with the sherry she had quickly downed. He knew she felt the attraction warm between them. Trent cupped his hand behind her head, threading his fingers in her hair, and coaxed her closer. He doubted she'd resist as he moved his lips to hers. The tip of his tongue traced the line between Rose's lips and verily they parted, accepting the sweet seduction. His arm drew a circle around her waist, holding her soft body against his.

"You have a lovely mouth," he said between kisses.

"Really?" Rose was surprised. She'd always thought her mouth to be too wide and she opened it to tell him so, but just as she did he clamped his right over it.

Like a heavy stone, Rose fell right to the bottom of the pond. Into his arms she willingly sank, heedless to all her aunt's warnings. His kiss was most delicious, and she didn't at all mind her indulgence. The tips of his fingers lightly brushed over her back and the wonderful feelings he was so good at evoking came rushing over her in a warm wave.

Trent knew Rose was completely intoxicated and curiously fascinated by the new feelings he aroused in her, and he knew she would not resist his next advance. He was hard-pressed to continue, but he separated his lips from hers and gently ran a final trail of light kisses over her cheek. He looked down at the soft trusting face that rested on his shoulder and felt a tinge of guilt twist his conscience. He had used his charm on many an unsuspecting woman, but this time his wager with Philip had made him feel dastardly.

Rose was going to put up a fuss when he left London. And if she ever found out about the wager, she'd likely chase him all the way to Greece just to give him a piece of her mind. He smiled imagining it. It was wrong to trick her. She wasn't like the rest of them; she was more honest with men. She hadn't learned to use her soft curves to get what she wanted. Rose would never think of it.

Chapter 9

Rose planned on sweeping Trent right off his feet. It was going to be easier than she thought, since he had shown her that he had as much trouble resisting her as she had in avoiding the stirring effects of his kisses. Carrying her off into the country was his idea and she was sure he had his motives, but it was her intention to turn them to her advantage. She'd try to remember everything her aunt had told her. As much as he provoked her ire with the wager he made with Philip, she would strive to be demure, the perfect lady. She would sit well away from him, as propriety dictated, and she would insist on gentlemanly behavior.

They stopped at his town house, a looming, ivy-covered limestone with shuttered windows opened to the afternoon breezes. They were greeted at the door by a matron who smelled of freshly baked bread and cinnamon.

"Mrs. Witherspoon, this is Rose Whitley. We'll be leaving for a picnic lunch as soon as you can pack the hamper." Trent didn't waste words on a lengthy introduction, giving Rose the impression he didn't want the woman to get to know her too well. Mrs. Witherspoon gave her a measured look and then disappeared into the kitchen to prepare their lunch.

The inside of the house was dark in spite of the long front windows and high white ceilings and smelled completely masculine. Rose could not detect a sweet fragrance—only bee's wax, leather and the hint of baking bread. There were no vases filled with flowers; instead, leather bound books were stacked in all manner of ways—vertical, horizontal—and one still lay opened on a desk. Two portraits in heavy oval frames hung on either side of the fireplace. Rose could detect a resemblance to Trent in the determined set of the gentleman's jaw and in the slight smile of the woman.

Rose grew curious about the mysterious Mr. Jordan. "Your parents?"

"My grandparents—staunch supporters of freedom, traitors to the crown. I come from a long line of rebel-rousers, I'm afraid."

"Then you're also an advocate of freedom," she said, beginning to pry cautiously.

Trent's smile told her he knew in what direction her questions headed. "Most definitely, especially my own. I'm in full agreement with Lord Byron on that issue—people should be free to choose their own course in life."

"Is that why you're living here instead of with your family?"

"I didn't know that I had mentioned family, but since you're so interested—my father and younger brothers maintain a plantation in Virginia."

Rose was given enough background to arouse her curiosity; however, her questions would have

116

to wait, for the door leading to the kitchen suddenly swung open from the forceful thrust of Mrs. Witherspoon's hip. The housekeeper's arms were full, carrying the basket she had packed. Trent took it from her arms, lifted one end of the linen cloth that covered it and frowned at her.

"I thought cider would be more refreshing," she offered.

"The cellar has been stocked," Trent reminded her.

"Yes, sir." Mrs. Witherspoon hurried away, returning minutes later with a bottle of wine, which she tucked under the cover of the hamper.

Rose sensed an underlying tension between Mrs. Witherspoon and Trent. The looks they exchanged could not be misunderstood—Mrs. Witherspoon did not approve of their unchaperoned picnic. The woman's upset changed Rose's mind. She was not going out alone with Trent. It wasn't proper, and if she was going to entice him into proposing marriage, she would have to follow all the rules of courtship. Trent *would* take her on a picnic—properly chaperoned.

He held the hamper and waited at the door. "Rose," he called. He expected her to follow him compliantly and without a word; what he *didn't* expect was to hear her invite Mrs. Witherspoon to accompany them.

All the tight lines left the housekeeper's face and were replaced by an approving smile. "Certainly, Miss Whitley. I'll be a minute."

Rose was afraid to turn and look at Trent. She sensed the steady glare of his eyes behind her and knew he was annoyed. She had ruined his plans to take her out into the country alone. There was no doubt in Rose's mind that it would have been a very romantic afternoon. Just thinking of the touch of his hands grazing against her skin made the flame inside her flare. As much as she tried to tell herself she could resist him, she wasn't completely sure.

In the tight confines of the carriage, Mrs. Witherspoon sat next to Rose, and Trent sat across from them. His disgruntled look didn't seem to affect his housekeeper's happy mood one bit, but it left Rose squirming in her seat since it was mostly directed at her. He obviously felt manipulated, and for someone who was used to giving orders and having them followed, it was a bitter tonic to swallow. If Rose was reading his expression well enough, she knew it was not something he'd let slide. He was not going to forgive her for appeasing Mrs. Witherspoon.

By the time the landscape was rolling past in one green wave after another, Mrs. Witherspoon had learned everything there was to know about Rose. She always began her questions with "I hope you don't mind my asking, but . . ." Talking helped Rose keep her mind off Trent—he looked like he wanted to strangle her.

"I remember when Lady Roseanna married your father." Mrs. Witherspoon's face wrinkled at the strain of calling forth an old memory. "It was quite a scandal. Her father was very upset she'd married an American. He wouldn't speak to her after that—not even when he was on his deathbed. It clear broke her heart. She died after that. I suppose that's when your father packed you up and left for the colonies. I'm surprised he brought you back." Mrs. Witherspoon took her hand in a friendly gesture. "Your aunt must be proud of you. You're a good girl."

Trent stretched his legs out in front of him, bridging the distance between himself and Rose. Rose tried to move her leg away from the suggestive stroking of the tip of his boot.

"I'm glad to see that you've found yourself a nice girl, Mr. Jordan," Mrs. Witherspoon said with final approval.

Fragrant air rushed through the open carriage windows and brought to Rose the scent of Trent, a blend of exotic spice as sultry and warm as summer. Rose dared to look at him, in the scant moment when Mrs. Witherspoon wasn't talking. He still glared at her, perhaps thinking of the afternoon he had to spend chaperoned, something she didn't imagine he tolerated often—if he ever did. She couldn't help but feel a little nervous that he was going to find a way around it.

When Rose stepped down from the carriage, her feet sank into a thick green carpet of grass. The beauty of the countryside unfolded before her eyes. Fruit trees were frothy with pale pink blossoms, and birds sang their joyous ode to spring under a canopy of a blue sky. Flowers graced the base of a stone wall that snaked over the hills, rising and falling with the terrain. A stream cut a natural border between the two estates they trespassed. Birds crossed their path, chirping their alarm at the trespassers.

"Are you sure the owner won't mind?" she asked.

"Yes," Trent answered flatly, ending her inquiry. But still, she worried that trespassing would be looked upon unfavorably.

The coachman stayed with the carriage while Trent looked for a place to spread out their blanket. Rose pointed out a few nice spots to

Trent, but her suggestions were put aside. He chose to climb to the top of a hill, where a copse of trees huddled in ruffles of pink and white blossoms. Though tempted, Rose didn't complain about the uphill hike. It was obvious Trent had a reason for his preference: he was likely hoping Mrs. Witherspoon would fall so far behind that he'd have Rose alone for a moment and be able to voice some of the anger he had so far kept a cap on. Rose knew he was angry, and he didn't have to *say* anything to get that point across—his body radiated with the heat of his ire. He seemed to be letting off some of that steam in his determined walk.

They came to where a stone wall stretched across their path, and it was then that Rose had to say something. Mrs. Witherspoon was far behind, trying valiantly to keep up, the heavy hamper in her hands; Rose had hung somewhere between the woman and Trent.

Trent rested on the wall, waiting for her to catch up. He didn't look so angry anymore; in fact, he almost looked triumphant—and that annoyed Rose.

"Mr. Jordan, what do you think you're up to? You're exhausting Mrs. Witherspoon."

"I hope she's not too tired to climb this wall," he said with a hopeful smile. "There's a favorite spot of mine over there."

Rose followed his arm. "Over there" looked like a distance of another mile to her. She pressed her lips in a tight line. "You go ahead. We'll meet you there tomorrow." She spun around and bounced down the hill, his vindictive chuckle ringing in her ears.

Mrs. Witherspoon looked doubtful at the stone

120

boundary. "Oh dear, I don't think I'm going to be able to climb over this very decently."

"There isn't anyone around to see, if you should happen to show an ankle," Rose assured. "Now, please try. I'll help you." Rose took the hamper and set it on the top of the wall. "I'll get over it first." Without knowing Trent watched her from a distance, Rose pulled her skirt up and climbed over the wall, exposing more than an ankle in the process. In less than a second she had scaled the three-foot wall. It was not difficult; she'd scaled higher fences than that chasing after Jack and Robert. "See how easy that was?"

"For you, dear. If you don't mind my saying so, I've a suspicion you've led a tomboy childhood," she said, her look too discerning.

Rose smoothed her skirt, realizing that a real lady would never have done such a thing. She should have objected to Trent's outrageous insistence that they climb mountains and scale walls to keep up with him. If she didn't try harder to curb her wild ways, she was surely going to disappoint her father. He expected a changed girl when he returned. She sighed. "What should I do, Mrs. Witherspoon?"

"You go on ahead and tell Mr. Jordan that he has to come back here. I can't—I just *won't* climb over a wall—and that's that!"

Rose smiled weakly and looked over to Trent. He was a distance away and had already made himself comfortable on the blanket he'd spread out. "All right," she agreed, "I'm sure the gentleman in him will see your point." Rose continued up the hill, worrying about the scoundrel awaiting her.

Trent lay under an umbrella of crab apple trees.

121

He had removed his waistcoat and cravat, and had unbuttoned his shirt enough to expose a distracting, tan wedge of skin below his throat. He had pulled off his boots and stretched his long muscled legs across the length of the blanket. Rose's knees went weak at how much man lay beneath her feet. He leaned up on one elbow and looked up at her.

"Where's Mrs. Witherspoon?"

He seemed surprised, but Rose knew better. "You knew very well she wasn't going to climb over that wall. You're going to have to go back and find a spot on the other side."

"Mrs. Witherspoon was not invited by me, if I recall. If she can't get over the wall, she'll have to picnic by herself."

"You can't mean that! I'm not telling her that. You can relay that message yourself!" Trent sat up and pulled on his boots. "What are you doing?"

"As you suggested, I'll tell Mrs. Witherspoon myself."

Rose watched him leave, shocked that he would actually do as he threatened. There was even some doubt that he would, but that dispersed completely when she saw him lift the hamper from the wall and climb back up the hill.

"I can't believe you wouldn't help that poor woman over the wall," she said, horrified at his triumphant grin as he set the hamper on the blanket. Nervously Rose turned to look for Mrs. Witherspoon asking, "Where did she go?"

Trent smiled some more. "Back to the carriage for a nap, I'd expect."

"You sent her back to the carriage?" Rose asked with alarm.

"She insisted on it."

She eyed him suspiciously. "I don't believe she

122

would leave me alone with you that easily."

"She said, after I swore to behave myself, that if you could climb a wall like that, you could very well handle any impolite advances." His smile promised he'd test the housekeeper's theory. He settled on the blanket with a long, satisfied sigh. "And she'll be sure to get an accounting from you. Now, are you going to sit down, or stand and eat?"

Rose folded her legs under her and sat as far away from him as she could without sitting on the grass.

Trent unpacked the lunch Mrs. Witherspoon had prepared for them and laid out a smorgasbord of cold meat, cheese, strawberries, bread and jam. He unwrapped two wine glasses and balanced them on level ground then gripped the neck of the wine bottle and squeaked the cork from its channel. Like a fountain, the wine gurgled and sparkled as it tumbled into the glasses. Crystal clinked when he touched his glass to hers in an elegant salute.

Rose held her glass still while Trent drank. She watched the wine pass his lips, and she watched the muscles in his neck move with each swallow as he emptied his glass. Her gaze slipped to the hollow of his throat and the triangle of skin exposed by his unbuttoned shirt. She liked watching him. He caught her gaze before she could divert her eyes, and Rose felt the warmth of a blush sweep her cheeks.

"Is something wrong with the wine?" he asked.

"No," she said hastily, gulping the drink too quickly and then sputtering it all over. Trent reached out to slap her back. When he was done saving her from choking, she felt like she'd been rolled over by a pair of wagon wheels. So much for trying to be the proper lady.

"Thank you. Some bubbles got stuck in my throat," she explained, knowing that next time she'd be sure not to look at him and drink at the same time.

"Bubbles will do that on occasion—get stuck in your throat." She flushed. Now he was making fun of her. "Try sipping the wine," he suggested, smiling at her faint expression.

She sipped her wine slowly, trying not to look his way, but even with her eyes diverted she could feel him taking her in with his gaze. It took a few minutes, but she finally dared to peek at him from under her lashes. He was stretched out casually, occasionally picking at the food on his plate.

"Hungry?" He began to put a little of everything on her plate before she could tell him that her appetite was not quite there yet. Nor would it ever be, with him staring at her as though she were the entrée.

Trent affected her like no one else could. Lord Wesley had tried, and so had some of her aunt's other hopeful prospects, but none had the magic charm of Trent Jordan. She found she liked being with him, even though he took her appetite away and made her breathless. When she watched him intently preparing her plate, she found herself measuring his worth as a husband. As quickly as the thought emerged, she pushed it aside, but it merely resurfaced each time she looked at him. Of course she was being silly; it was only a wager. She had no intention of marrying him, even when he did ask.

Rose ate as much as she could, considering the circumstances, then helped him repack the hamper with what little food was left. Mrs. Witherspoon had packed them a lunch that would have fed half a dozen people, and Trent had neatly devoured nearly all of it. Not that it mattered; she wasn't hungry anyway.

But she did enjoy strawberries and Rose smiled, for she had promised herself Trent would be eating from her hand. She put the basket of berries in her lap. When Trent reached for the basket, she pulled it out of his reach. Their smiles met.

The effect of too much champagne made her brave enough to tease him, as she held the best of the bunch out to him. It was so large she'd have to take two bites to finish it. When Trent moved to take it from her, she quickly put it between her teeth. There was a sparkle of fun in her eyes. He paused, smiled, and was quick to take up her dare. He moved closer; she stayed painfully still. He leaned forward and slowly nibbled at the fruit until his lips met hers in a sweet lingering kiss. He ran his tongue over her stained mouth, licking the sticky juice from her lips until, finally tasting the sweetness inside, he leaned into her, pushing her down onto the blanket.

A traitor to her promise, Rose surrendered immediately. Her hair had fallen loose from its pins and she would be hard-pressed to find them later, but she liked the feel of his hands in her hair too much to worry about how wild she looked.

Trent moved his kiss from her lips to her earlobe and then slid his mouth down the column of her neck. He ventured further, first drawing kisses along the ridge of her collarbone and then lower to the soft rise of her breasts. Rose's fingers tangled in his dark hair, pulling out the ribbon that secured it neatly at the back of his neck, and she curled a lock of it around her finger. She pushed aside his shirt, wanting to run her hands over the smooth expanse

125

of his shoulders. He rolled her over and settled his weight on her. She felt the demanding power of his body pressed against her hips, and at once caution leaped to stand between them.

"Trent," she began to protest, but his mouth covered hers, hungry and wet, telling of the need that quickened his heartbeat and hardened his longing. She struggled for a moment beneath him, then weakened, setting aside all propriety even as she felt the hem of her skirt shift up past her knee.

He found the tie of her pantalettes and pulled the ribbon free. Her stomach quivered at the brush of his fingers against her skin. The desire that mounted inside her grew as he slowly peeled aside her clothes.

All thoughts of caution were quickly consumed by the fire that now surged through her veins. There was nothing that could be done to stop the feelings that ruled her good sense. She wanted to know what lay beyond the wildfire that whipped around her heart. For now consequences didn't matter. Rose was used to getting what she wanted and she wanted Trent.

Rose slipped her hands under his shirt, pushing it back over his wide shoulders and down his strong arms. She ran her hands over his expanse of chest and brought him closer to her.

Trent covered her with his body. With a light touch, he smoothed his hand down her middle and cupped the soft mound between her legs. He ran his finger along a mouth he had yet to kiss and found her to be wet with desire. Her legs opened and he probed further into the velvet valley of her womanhood. He was inside her, teasing her arousal, bringing her close to madness.

Trent paused only to shed his clothes. In the

bright sunshine his shadow fell over Rose. When he gazed down at her, she saw the flames burning in his eyes. With a gentle nudge of his knee he moved her legs apart. He slipped into her and she gasped with the shock of being filled with him.

Rose felt an unexpected moment of pain stab at the previous pleasure that had ruled her. She would have willed him to stop then, but he moved in and out, smoothing away the pain and replacing it with a pleasurable heat that warmed her insides until she was sure she glowed from the joy of it. Her own body responded, moving to meet his, sliding against him, enjoying the common rhythm of their bodies joined in heated passion.

She wrapped her legs around him and felt Trent delve deeper into the center of her being. She felt as though she folded around him in the most exciting of all embraces. The sounds of pleasure he made, his voice in her ears telling her how wonderful she felt, his warm breath on her neck, all made her throb even more in the place that he filled. He buried his face in her neck and stroked her insides until she groaned with unbearable pleasure. Possessed and driven by a greedy desire, their lovemaking flared and burst into a shower of sparks that fell around them and consumed them in a blaze of flames.

Trent rolled lazily off her, pulling her with him until she lay on top of him. Rose looked down at him, smiling into his very satisfied face. Her eyes were bright as stars, her cheeks rosy, and her hair swept over his shoulders and chest like the flutter of an angel's wing. Trent looked up at her and became lost in the blue of her eyes. They were like patches of blue sky, their depth endless. A flurry of white petals fell over them like snow. Rose tenderly tickled his face with light kisses. She placed them over his forehead, down the straight line of his nose and over his cheeks, and then teased his lips with kisses light as a feather's touch. He brushed aside her hair and moved his mouth over her neck to her earlobe. The sound of his kiss and the flicker of his warm, wet tongue made her whimper and fall victim to a new onslaught of tingles that raced and jumped from one place to the next. She felt cold and hot at the same time. He moved his hands over her buttocks and pressed her into his arousal.

"I don't think I could ever have enough of you," he whispered in her ear.

A new shockwave rolled through Rose. She was frighteningly willing to let him have her again. A voice inside her called, and she trembled, pushed him away and released herself from his arms. She'd planned on making *him* love *her*. She hadn't expected to fall in love with him herself.

Chapter 10

Mrs. Witherspoon glared at Trent from the corner of his study. She was still upset with him for ordering her back to the carriage so he could have the afternoon alone with Rose. He didn't care about a lady's reputation as much as he should; but the older woman was hopeful for he didn't have the same satisfied look on his face that usually earmarked a successful outing with a young lady. In fact, he looked a little strained. Worry lines waved over his forehead as he stared down at the opened book on his desk, yet it still didn't excuse the fact that he acted ungentlemanly. After all, the girl was Lady Vanderhue's niece.

She noticed that he was so absorbed in thought that he'd failed to move on to the next page. She began to worry that something had gone wrong the day of the picnic. Rose had been very quiet in the carriage; she hadn't said a word the whole trip back. Of course, Mrs. Witherspoon understood why Rose had been upset: as a chaperon, the older woman shouldn't have left the pair alone, even if it *had* meant scaling a stone wall. Mrs. Witherspoon, incensed, whipped the dust off the bookshelves with her rag, causing Trent to raise his eyes curiously from his book. She paid him no mind and continued to vent her exasperation with this man whom—despite his ways—she dearly loved. He just couldn't help himself, of that she was certain. Pretty things were too much for him to ignore, and his weakness inevitably led first to selfishness and then to such guilt that he began bestowing on the young ladies every imaginable gift but that one they really wanted—his heart. The housekeeper liked Rose and didn't want to see her discarded like an old cloak. She beat the dust up into a cloud that finally tickled Trent's nose to a loud sneeze. She was startled by the noise and stopped whipping around the cloth.

"Mrs. Witherspoon," Trent began carefully, so as not to insult her good intentions to keep his home neat, "do you have to do the study now?" And then, more vexed, he asked, "Or are you beating my library to death for some reason other than to cause me discomfort?"

"That would certainly not be my intention, Mr. Jordan."

"Well, then what *is* your intention?" Trent closed his book, not even aware of its title. He had grabbed it because it was near and provided a good place to hide his thoughts, but by Mrs. Witherspoon's look he deemed his ploy unsuccessful.

Since the picnic he hadn't been able to still his thoughts of Rose. He saw her yellow hair lifting in the breeze, her lips stained and sweet with strawberries, and her eyes so beautiful they rivaled the sky on the clearest day. He couldn't deny that he'd been successful in seducing her; but he hadn't expected to be so captured by her reckless beauty that his feelings would begin to venture beyond physical attraction. It confused him and scared him. He wanted Rose, but when he felt his emotions coming into play, he wanted to run away from her. Trent was afraid of nothing except when it came to becoming attached to a woman. It was then that he began to consider retreat.

Mrs. Witherspoon put her hands on her hips, as she often did when she thought Trent would give her an argument. It was her way of warning him that she had no intention of backing down, no matter how much he hollered. "I think you should marry the girl."

Trent's mouth nearly dropped with surprise. Were his feelings so obvious? The woman was more than a servant to him, but still she stepped way beyond her bounds. "I appreciate your concern for the young lady's reputation, Mrs. Witherspoon, but one unchaperoned afternoon does not constitute the need for marriage."

She held the dust rag on her hip like a whip, her face as red as he'd ever seen it. "Her aunt would think so," she said bluntly, her mouth a grim line.

It wasn't like Mrs. Witherspoon to voice her opinion on his behavior. He'd received many a look but never a lecturing word. What disturbed him most was that he knew she was right—Rose deserved better. He cared enough about the girl to think of her as special and to feel guilty about his selfish acquisition of her innocence. Stephanie was at least offering her the chance to marry respectably, even if it was to the meek Lord Wesley. The thought of being obligated to marry her himself had never entered his mind. The solution to his problem seemed simple enough:

Philip had sent him word that the shipment of guns was ready, so there was no better time than now to make his voyage to Greece. When he returned, Rose would have married and forgotten him.

Rose was having lunch with Philip. She was glad she had found him enjoying his cook's fresh bread when she had come downstairs looking for him. Lately he had been making his presence as scarce as had Trent, whom she hadn't seen in three days. If she was going to convince him to propose to her, it was going to be difficult if he never came to visit. Her pride couldn't accept losing the bet to Philip. He'd probably boast of it to Trent and they'd both have a good laugh at her expense. Philip knew where he was, she was sure of that. And by the way Philip was avoiding her, she knew he was guilty of something. Perhaps he had already told Trent of their wager; perhaps that was why she hadn't seen Trent. She stopped buttering her bread and turned her eyes on Philip until he felt her stare and looked at her. He raised his brow quizzically.

"Did you tell him?" she asked in an accusing tone.

"I don't know what you're talking about," he answered innocently.

Rose slapped down her knife. "Why hasn't Trent been around?"

"Don't get all huffy, Rose," he said defensively. "He would have told you, but—" Philip groaned as a blue fire began to flicker in her eyes. "Now don't get upset with me. I told him to tell you, but . . . you know how he doesn't want to answer to women."

"No, I don't know. Tell me what it is, Philip, and don't think to lie to me, because I'll march right down the street to his house and ask him myself."

Philip chuckled nervously. "I believe you would, dear, but he's not at home. He left this morning for Greece."

Rose felt like she was going to slip off the chair and slide right under the table. He couldn't have left. He hadn't mentioned he was leaving London. Surely he would have said something.

"I suppose you won't win the wager," Philip said lightly.

Despair was suddenly replaced with disbelief and then hot anger. She jumped up, startling Philip to his feet.

"I don't believe you. You're just saying he left to win the wager. I'm going to see for myself if he's gone or not." Rose knocked her chair to the floor in her haste to leave. Philip raced her to the front door.

"Rose, wait. I tried to tell you he would never ask to marry you. Trent looks at marriage like the anchor on his ship." Rose whipped her shawl around her shoulders, and the end of it caught Philip in his face. "You can't go out alone."

"I know—it wouldn't be proper," she snapped, slamming the door behind her. Philip quickly opened it again and called out to her. "Rose, let him go."

"For whose sake, Philip? Yours or mine?"

Philip watched in despair as Rose ran out of the house and climbed into his carriage.

*   *   *

Rose's hand trembled when she reached for the brass knocker on the door of Trent's town house. A lady just didn't call on a gentleman. If Stephanie found out, she would probably have Rose locked up until the wedding day. And Rose's father— well, thank God he was across the Atlantic. She didn't even know what she was going to say to Trent's surprised face when he saw her. In the carriage she had tied a tight knot in her shawl trying to come up with a sensible reason for calling: she was out for a ride and just happened by; she wanted to thank him for showing her the English countryside; she was calling on Mrs. Witherspoon. Her explanations mounted, but none came close to what she knew as the truth: she missed him.

It seemed an interminable wait before the door finally opened, and when it did Rose was speechless. Mrs. Witherspoon waited. An uncomfortable silence hung between them. Rose stumbled a little and then managed to faintly voice her excuse—as unbelievable as it was. "Lady Vanderhue sent me by to . . . to ask Mr. Jordan if . . ." Mrs. Witherspoon waited patiently while Rose fumbled around for the right words. "If Mr. Jordan would please come to the house. She had a question for him. I believe it's about her nephew. She's worried about where Philip's been nights, and since they're such good friends, she thought Mr. Jordan might know."

Mrs. Witherspoon wondered why the girl would go to such lengths to explain why she needed Mr. Jordan when it certainly was none of the housekeeper's business why Lady Vanderhue would want to see him. "I'm sorry I can't help you, Miss Whitley," she said pleasantly, "but Mr.

Jordan is not here."

"When he comes in, then, would you please give him my aunt's message?" Rose prayed she'd say yes.

Mrs. Witherspoon sighed. She hoped the child wasn't going to get upset. "Tell Lady Vanderhue Mr. Jordan has left for Greece. The *Raven* was to set sail today."

Rose felt her heart fall to her stomach. It was impossible. He wouldn't leave her so suddenly, not without telling her. He must have known. One just didn't decide on the spur of the moment to sail off to Greece. It would make him the scoundrel her aunt had warned her about. She looked at Mrs. Witherspoon for a better explanation, but one was not forthcoming.

Mrs. Witherspoon saw how pale Rose had turned. "Why don't you come in and sit for a moment."

"Yes," she said faintly, letting the housekeeper take her arm. Rose sunk down into the soft velvet pillows of a settee.

After a few moments Mrs. Witherspoon handed her a cup of tea and sat down next to the girl. It was obvious that Rose had come to see Trent, and if that gentleman had walked into the room at that moment, his housekeeper would have personally strangled him. How could he have let the poor child think she had a claim to him? Mrs. Witherspoon knew very well he could not have resisted Rose—and he was used to having whatever he set his mind to. He was not a bad man, just an untrusting one, though at the moment it would be hard to convince Rose of that. And, he was a frightened man. Anyone who thought he knew Trent would certainly laugh at that claim. But

135

Mrs. Witherspoon knew him better than anyone. Trent Jordan was terribly afraid of falling in love, and never had she seen him run away from anyone like he had run away from Rose.

"When will he return?" Rose asked.

"Sometimes Mr. Jordan is away for months. It would be best if you forgot him." Her advice was offered in vain.

Rose stood up. "That's what he'd like. I'm not going to forget him, and I'm not going to wait until he returns, either. Thank you for the tea."

Mrs. Witherspoon was beside herself. "It wouldn't be like a lady to chase a gentleman."

"He's already accused me of not being a lady, so I doubt I'd disappoint him, and at the moment I certainly wouldn't be calling him a gentleman."

Mrs. Witherspoon could not argue with the last part of Rose's statement; acting like a gentleman was not one of Trent's known habits.

Rose hurried to her carriage, intent on finding the *Raven* before it set sail. Mrs. Witherspoon called her back. "Wait! Mr. Jordan said to give this to you—*after* he'd left." She dropped a gold ring into her hand.

"Father's ring! The one the Liberty Thief . . ." She searched the woman's face. "Where did he . . . what was he doing with it?"

"I don't have a clue. He just said to hold it for you."

Now there were two questions in Rose's mind: why had Trent left London, seemingly in a hurry, and where had he gotten her father's ring? There was a lot of suspicion building up in her thoughts about Trent Jordan. He seemed to be close by

136

whenever the Liberty Thief struck—at the masquerade ball, in Philip's house—and now the ring was suddenly in his possession. Rose wasn't going to wait months for the answers. Trent would answer to her even if she had to chase him halfway across the globe.

Chapter 11

Rose looked up at the tall-masted ships that rocked like a long row of cradles. As if sensing her indecision, the driver pointed his whip to the topmast of one of the vessels where the shadow of a raven flapped against a white background of canvas.

"Is that the one you're looking for?"

Rose thanked him for his help and headed out towards the ship. The driver was right: it was getting late. The sun glowed like a fireball but in minutes would extinguish itself in the black sea. With trepidation, she started up the ramp that bridged the gap between land and sea. Under her feet the waves chopped against the dock and splashed up to the ramp. Rose didn't look, for it scared her enough to think that between her and two inches of plank waited deep sea.

A thundering of footsteps over the ramp made her stop short. A man holding a lantern rushed past her. He stopped suddenly, turned and looked back at her, raising the lamp up so it shone on her face. The lantern not only threw its light on Rose but also brightened the man holding it. He was a short fellow, but his muscular arms and shoulders looked as if they were meant for a taller sort. His hair was bright orange, and his face was fuzzy as a peach. He was weatherworn, wrinkled in more places than Rose thought possible. She was sure he had lived more on the water than on land, and the freckles on his arms further attested to that summation.

"What could I do for ye?" the seaman asked once he had measured her up with narrow, hazel eyes.

"I'm looking for Mr. Jordan. This is his ship?"

"It is, but he wouldna be interested in ye right now. He's a mite busy."

"It won't take long."

The seaman laughed as if she'd said something funny. He was a strange sort, putting her in mind of a leprechaun—and one with a brogue at that!

"I'm sure wi' a lass as bonnie-looking as ye, it wouldna. All right, follow me up quick. If the captain inna pleased, the splash as ye hit the water wi' tell."

Rose glanced back at her carriage, her resolve to challenge Trent faltering at the seaman's comment.

"Well, are ye coming or na?" he asked, not even looking to see if she was behind him.

Rose hurried before the path of light that spread behind him was too far ahead to do her any good.

"Watch yer step," he warned after she tripped over a pile of coiled rope.

The seaman showed Rose to Trent's cabin. "Ye wait here and I'll get the captain," he said, leaving the door wide open. "And dunna be touching any of the captain's belongings. He likes everything the way it is."

While she waited, Rose rehearsed what she'd say

140

to Trent. She wanted to know what he was doing with her father's ring. The last time her father wore it was the night they were robbed by highwaymen. But what she yearned to know most of all was why he was leaving London without telling her.

Rose checked the sky for the tenth time. If Trent didn't show up soon, she'd be searching for another carriage to take her home. Just when she'd decided to look for him herself, the ship suddenly moved and the floor of the cabin pitched, slamming the cabin door shut with a vengeance. Rose jumped and dashed for the door. She grabbed its handle and turned, pulled and jiggled, but for the life of her she couldn't budge the jammed door. What luck! The swelled wood had locked her in Trent's cabin. Now, for sure, she was going to be stranded without a carriage. Rose resorted to banging her fist against the door and finally to screaming, but no one above seemed to be aware of her predicament.

It was going to be a long while before Rose could put her feet on solid ground again. The *Raven* was well out to sea by the time the seaman, Peach, remembered her, and even then it took the sight of her asleep in the captain's chair to fully jog the first mate's memory.

After the *Raven* was underway and the harried time of setting sail was over, the seaman had come below for a last check. On his return, he'd stopped to light the lamp in his captain's cabin, and it was then that he saw Rose bathed in the amber lamplight, her head nesting in her arms on the captain's desk. His heart stopped, and his head immediately began to pound with a surge of panic. What was he to do with her?

Trent would not be pleased to have this extra passenger on board, and Peach didn't think his captain would be too understanding. And what of the lass? Did she know they were far out to sea? Possibly it was her plan all along. Peach ran his hand through his hair and took a hard gulp. He had to hide her before his captain discovered his blunder. Maybe he could keep her hidden until they made port. He didn't really believe that, but it made him feel better to imagine the possibility.

The captain was in a chipper mood. Everything had gone as planned except for the delivery of the guns. But even that delay was tempered by good weather. They glided over a sea as smooth as Peach had ever seen. His captain was content at the helm and would stay on there until the next bell.

When London had disappeared behind them, Peach had seen the tension ease out of his captain's body. It was as if Trent had left all his troubles there. Maybe now was a good time to tell him about the lass, while things were still going smoothly, for a better opportunity might not soon present itself. He closed the door and tiptoed across the cabin floor.

Peach leaned over Rose and studied her face. She looked just like a china doll. Her skin was a creamy bisque, and her cheeks were brushed with just the right amount of color. He guessed her eyes would be blue. He brushed his hand gently over her angel-soft hair. She was pretty. Maybe Trent wouldn't be so displeased after all. Peach stopped his admiring gaze and wrinkled up his face. He hoped she wasn't the loud type. Trent would really be displeased if he had a hysterical woman to deal with. Holding up one hand to clap over her mouth in case she screamed, Peach cautiously tapped on her shoulder.

Rose opened her eyes and then slowly blinked. He was right: they were blue as bachelor buttons.

"Lass, ye fell asleep in the captain's chair," Peach explained, still ready with his hand.

Rose looked around the room and back to Peach. "Has Trent been here to see me?" she asked, still a little foggy.

"The captain? Not yet, but he will be soon," Peach worried aloud.

Rose got up to stretch. "How long have I been asleep?"

"I wouldna know that, lass."

Rose looked sharply at Peach. "How long have I been here, then?"

"A good twenty miles." Peach answered so quickly, Rose had to ask him to repeat himself.

"Twenty miles!" she gasped, running to the window.

Peach scrambled after her, making shushing sounds and crossing his lips with his finger.

"Twenty miles," Rose wailed, resting her forehead against the cool glass.

Peach tried to console her before she got too excited. "It's not so terrible as ye think."

"My driver has left and now I'm floating out to sea," Rose moaned.

"It's not that bad," Peach repeated, nervously patting her shoulder.

Rose produced a handkerchief and buried her face in it. Peach looked on the miserable girl and was smacked with blame. It was all his fault she was stranded on the *Raven*, and with each passing minute she became even more distanced from her home. There wasn't anything he could do about it but try to make her see the brighter side, and it was going to be a task lighting that candle in the wind. He rubbed his fuzzy chin between his thumb and forefinger. He tried to say something positive. "You'll get used ta it."

Rose spun around, catching Peach off guard. "Get used to it! Oh no, Trent Jordan is not going to take me on a boat ride. He is going to turn this—"

"Ship, lass. The *Raven's* a ship." Peach helped her with the correct terminology. Trent wouldn't want her referring to the *Raven* as anything less.

"He's going to turn this around and take me back to London. After he's answered a few of my questions," she added.

Rose started towards the door, but Peach cut quickly in front of her and threw himself spread-eagle against it. "The captain's not gonna do that, lass. He wouldna even like ye asking, never mind telling."

Rose wished the man would move out of her way. Trent would certainly take her home if she asked him to.

"What is your name?" Rose asked as calmly as she could.

"Peach. I'm called Peach."

The name certainly described him, Rose thought. "I'm Mary Rose Whitley, and I know Mr. Jordan would take me home if I asked him to."

"Where's that, lass?"

Peach's mouth dropped a foot when she told him. Now that he really looked at the girl, he wondered how he could have made the misjudgment. She was a lady, not a harlot. She had a respectable reason for wanting to see the captain, but whatever it was, he would bet the stone of Dunmore Castle would burn before Trent would turn the *Raven* back.

"If you don't mind, Mr. Peach," Rose said, pointing to the door, "I'd like to see the captain now. I have some important questions to ask him."

The seaman stretched his lips into a worried smile. "Just Peach. I'll see if the captain's free ta see ye." Peach thought his best tactic would be to humor her until he could think of a way to break the news to Trent, but Rose persisted.

"I'm not waiting any longer," Rose insisted. "All that got me was twenty miles out to sea. Heavens, I could be halfway to Greece before your captain finds the time to see me." Rose scrutinized Peach's face. "Why hasn't Mr. Jordan come down here?"

Peach flattened his body against the door.

"Did you tell him I was here?" At his weak smile Rose's voice climbed an octave. "You didn't tell him, did you?"

Once again, Peach tried to make light of the situation. "It's not that bad, lass," he said, though he couldn't think of one reason to support his positive outlook.

"Don't deny you forgot about me. I can see it in your color. The last thing Mr. Jordan would do would be to knowingly sail off with me aboard."

It was the way Rose said it that made Peach uncomfortably sure that she was what Trent left behind in London. He thought of how relieved his captain had looked when London was at his back. It was worse than he thought. What Trent was fleeing was right here in his cabin and Peach had put her there. Feeling a sudden need to sit down, he slid to the floor and sat at Rose's feet.

Rose crouched to look at him. "Are you all right?"

"Lass," Peach said numbly, "the captain will ship us both back ta London—in a dinghy."

Rose patted him on the shoulder. "No, he won't. When you explain to Mr. Jordan that you forgot, he'll have to understand." At least she hoped he would.

"He was shouting orders left and right, from stem ta stern. We dinna expect ta be setting sail till morning since we had been delayed all day, but the Thames cleared and—"

"He'll understand all of that. He'll see how easy it was for you to forget. You know," Rose said with concern, "something should be done with this door. It sticks terribly. If it hadn't slammed shut and got stuck, I would have been able to get myself out of here and wouldn't be on my way to Greece right now. But of course, that will all be changed when you talk to Mr. Jordan."

Peach couldn't believe his ears. She not only wanted him to tell the captain they had a lady aboard—the very one he was sailing away from— but also to complain about a tight door. He wasn't about to put his neck in a noose just yet. Lady or not, the lass was going to have to stay hidden for a while. He hoped she'd take the news calmly.

"Lass, it wouldna be the best time ta bring up the subject of sticky doors or turning the *Raven* about. The captain's as dark as the moors on a moonless night, if ye know what I mean." Peach sincerely hoped she did. "Might I suggest we wait just a wee bit? So I might prepare him. It might give him a start ta see ye, not expecting ye," Peach choked, grabbing her hand and pulling her up with him before she could think to disagree.

"There's another cabin for guests. Not as spacious, but a place ta hang yer hammock. You can wait in there—just for a wee bit," he promised.

Peach showed Rose to the other cabin—or closet. The bed was a hammock simply hung from two hooks. A small sea chest underneath the hammock doubled as a seat. Rose felt claustrophobic as soon as she entered the windowless room.

Peach began to close the door, squeezing her in. "I'll come for ye in the morning."

"In the morning!" Rose exclaimed as the door closed.

"Ye get some sleep," said Peach. "Ye'll need it for the long day ahead." So would he, he sighed, ignoring the pounding of her fist against the door.

An hour later Peach passed his captain. From the tune Trent whistled and way he sauntered to his cabin, Peach could tell he was still in a good mood. Peach debated whether or not to tell him of their guest, until he heard his name bellowed.

"Peach!"

"Aye, Captain," the seaman answered, hurrying to see what his captain wanted.

Trent's cabin was as much a surprise to Peach as it was to his captain, for he had been too busy fretting over Rose to notice the carefully rolled charts, the unwrinkled bed and the general lack of clutter. While she'd waited, the lass had even put away his clothes.

Trent looked down at Peach, his brows knit together in a good frown. "Just because we didn't have enough time to engage a cabin boy doesn't mean you're supposed to worry over me like a wife."

"I guess I got carried away wi' meself. Captain, at risk of sounding mothering, would ye be wanting something sent from the galley? Bones made a fine stew. It would still be warming in the pot."

Trent grinned. "I'm agreeable to that."

Peach left for the galley hoping his captain would be just as agreeable when he found out about Rose.

Trent stretched out his legs. He'd been trying to concentrate on his charts, once he'd found them, but his eyes kept wandering to the side drawer of his desk. He opened it again and took out a tapestry reticule. He rubbed his thumb over two delicate does grazing under a tree. It was an expensive purse for a trollop.

Now that his anger had dissipated, he was getting impatient waiting for Peach to return.

There was not a harder working or more loyal member of his crew that Peach MacCory. He could well captain the *Raven* himself, and it was that reason alone which prevented Trent from sailing without him. If the poor man had a vice, it was his great heart, which had gotten him stewed in many a pudding when it came to the fairer sex. Trent hoped the man didn't intend on hiding the girl for the whole voyage. That would mean he'd have to drag her from her hiding place himself. He wondered what she looked like. For Peach's sake he hoped she was attractive and hardy enough to survive on biscuits.

Trent grinned to himself. He never would have thought of Peach needing a woman so bad that he'd take on such a risk. While he waited, he thought of ways to keep her busy so she wouldn't be a distraction to Peach and the crew. She'd be sorry she had convinced the seaman to stow her aboard after she'd washed and dried and shined the *Raven* from stem to stern. By nightfall the woman would be so exhausted, that all she'd be able to manage would be sleep, and that would serve up a measure of bitter tonic for Peach to swallow.

Trent answered the tap on his cabin door. His face tightened into a stern expression but his eyes laughed when Peach entered holding a bowl of Bones's soup. He held the reticule in his hand and waited for the seaman to notice.

Peach's eyes popped when he saw it. He bolstered himself against the anger that was sure to come. Once his captain got over his initial displeasure, he'd most likely have the lass swear by his rules and keep hidden in her cabin. Peach drew a long breath.

"I've done a fool thing, Captain."

"It wouldn't be the first time now, would it?" Trent kept his grin to himself. "Go on, Peach. I'd like to hear it."

"There was this lass—and I thought—well, she was a pretty sight and—"

"And she attracted your attention."

"She did, sir."

Trent let go of the smile he had held back. "You'd like to talk about the fool thing you did."

"I see no other way about it."

"Then go ahead," Trent encouraged, dangling the tapestry reticule from his finger.

Peach hadn't expected such a calm response. If the situation wasn't bad enough, it was compounded by the fact that Trent already knew of his deceit. The swinging purse didn't make the words of his tale come much easier, but after a shaky beginning he came to his story's end.

149

"The girl is waiting to see me? To ask me to take her back to London!"

Peach nodded. Trent paced back and forth, slowly swinging the reticule around his finger, and began to issue stern orders. "She'll be your charge until we get to Athens. She can stay in that cabin if she likes, for I won't have her wandering around my ship bewitching the men. She'll keep the galley clean—Bones could use the help—and make sure she keeps her complaints to herself. She'll scrub the deck and clean fish if I ask her."

Peach looked even more distressed than before. "I canna ask a lady ta . . . clean fish."

"You're right. You'll *tell* her to clean the damn things." Only Peach would refer to her type as a lady. "And be strong about it or she'll be leading you around like a dog on a rope," he added.

"Aye, Captain," Peach said faintly. He supposed there were worse fates for the lass, but it would pain him to see her ruin her pretty hands on account of his failed memory.

Trent wasn't going to chance Peach softening up on him. He faced him with his legs astride and his fists balled on his hips, and he sighed heavily. "Send her in. I'll tell her myself."

Chapter 12

Trent felt like he had been hit with an anchor. He had been expecting a street waif and instead was presented with Rose. This complicated his plan considerably; he wouldn't have to worry so much about the crew's distraction; it was now his own that concerned him. He had not been away long enough for his mind and body to forget the pleasure Rose could give him.

She had planned this. Somehow she had fooled Peach into bringing her aboard. She had proved herself to be as conniving as Penelope. He was used to making the choices, but with Rose he uncomfortably felt like the chosen. He looked behind her for Peach, but the seaman had wisely disappeared.

Rose summed up Trent's reaction as he stood there in the center of his cabin, her reticule dangling at his hip, the strap clenched tightly in his fist. She then focused her attention on what he was wearing. His attire certainly was more casual than it had been in London. Dark gray trousers hugged his calves and thighs, clearly defining the shape of his muscles. A white lawn shirt, casually opened at his neck, revealed a wedge of tan skin; the shirt narrowed into the waistband of his breeches and was secured there by a wide belt from which a sword hung. His sleeves billowed softly to his wrists, where her eyes came back to the strap of her reticule wrapped around his wide hand.

"I see you've found my reticule." Rose wondered if he had looked inside and found her father's ring.

Trent recovered from his shock. He closed his mouth and held her reticule out to her, then stepped over to his desk. He leaned on his hands and talked to her in a low, steady voice that seemed to come up from the pit of his stomach. "You have a lot to explain."

"*I* have a lot to explain! I'm not the one fleeing London."

"Close the door, Rose," he said with strained patience.

Rose was hesitant about doing that and about getting too close to him. "The door sticks," she said weakly.

"What?"

"The door gets stuck. If you don't mind, I'd rather not get locked in here until you're in a better mood."

Trent couldn't believe her. She was an uninvited passenger on his ship and was complaining about his door and his mood. He strolled past her and over to the door and kicked it shut with his foot.

Rose flinched at the vibrating slam. She watched him walk calmly back to his desk and sit in his chair. He locked his hands together, keeping them restrained.

"You're very perceptive to notice that at the present time I am not in the best of moods. And as for the door, it's swelled like my temper."

152

Rose grew increasingly indignant with his tone. "Well, if your door didn't swell, I'd be in London and we wouldn't be here talking about your temper," Rose retorted, feeling her own anger heat her cheeks.

"What am I supposed to do with you?" Trent thought aloud. He wasn't seeking an answer from Rose, but he got one.

"Take me back to London."

"What?" he laughed, and then frowned. "Can you swim?"

Rose thought his question peculiar. "What would that matter?"

"Because that is the only way you'd be getting back to London."

When Rose overcame her shock, she gritted her teeth and her whole body tensed—it was as though she were preparing for battle. He was more like the man her aunt and Chloe had warned her of—crass, amoral, loveless and unscrupulous. He was the biggest mistake she had made in her life, though, she had to admit, he certainly was a handsome mistake.

People lived with their poor choices all the time, she rationalized. She looked at his unpleasant scowl and wondered if she could learn to live with that. Decidedly she was going to have to make the best of it. Maybe it was only a temporary setback in his personality; after all, she was an unexpected guest. The same romantic who had kidnapped her for a picnic and with whom she'd danced an entrancing waltz had to be somewhere behind all that grisliness. She was going to find him if it took her the entire voyage. Rose threw back her shoulders.

"Seeing as I can't swim and you're so determined to be contrary—"

"Contrary? Would you mind telling me what you mean by that?"

"Why, contrary to gentlemanly behavior. A gentleman would apologize for my inconvenience and take me home; an unscrupulous one would not. A gentleman would not suggest I swim for it. A gentleman would not kick a door shut and . . ."

Trent was slowly rising up from his seat. He walked around Rose, stopping behind her. She stared at her feet and continued in a faint voice. "A gentleman would not shout at a lady, either." She felt his hands close around her arms, and she stumbled over her words. "A . . . a gentleman would have known how . . . how upsetting it was for a lady to wonder why he'd suddenly left London after . . ." She bit off her words.

Rose didn't dare turn around to look at him. Feeling the heat of his eyes against her back was enough to make her knees quake and her face heat with something other than anger.

She wanted to hear him say how much he had missed her. But instead, he preached. "You would have done well to listen to your aunt rather than to follow me. Furthermore, a lady would not have arranged to have a gentleman put her to bed."

Rose caught her breath. How dare he insinuate she had seduced him?

"A lady would not stow away on a ship," he continued. "A lady would not have gone on a picnic unchaperoned, and a lady would not have lifted her skirts—"

"Stop it!" Rose was shocked by his audacity.

Trent chuckled. "It's all right for the kettle to call the pot black."

"Our motives were altogether different."

"Really? You mean you didn't intend to lift your skirts?"

"I certainly did not!" Rose felt like hitting him. "You think it was my intention to seduce you? That it was my intention to chase after you! Well, believe me, it was not. It wasn't *my* suggestion to send Mrs. Witherspoon away," she flatly reminded him. With as much hauteur as she could assemble, Rose aimed to make him feel as loathsome as she currently considered him to be. Pulling her father's ring from her reticule, she added, "I came aboard your ship only to thank you for this." As she'd expected, that effectively silenced him.

Rose wasn't going to wait to be dismissed. She was going to let herself out—*if* she could open the door. Trying not to make a comic spectacle out of herself, she took the handle in both hands and pulled with every fiber of her strength. The door wouldn't open on the first, second or third try. Even with her shoulder braced against the door-jamb, she couldn't budge the thing.

Trent watched Rose's intent struggle with the door. He hadn't paid much attention at first, and he was still mulling over her last words.

Rose whipped around, her chest rising with each labored breath. "I told you this door sticks."

Trent came over to the door and leaned his shoulder against it; he then looked down at her, his arms folded over his chest. "I still haven't decided what I'm going to do with you."

Trent's heart began to beat wildly as several possibilities came to mind. Even when he was furious with her, she had a way of changing that anger into a different kind of passion. His finger traced the ridge of her nose.

"You need a place to sleep."

155

"Peach showed me the small room across the way," Rose said, wary of where their conversation headed.

"Did he tell you it was *his* cabin?" Trent locked his hands behind his back and walked over to the bed. Rose's gaze naturally followed him and then settled on the bed behind him. Her eyes suddenly widened with understanding.

"On such a large boat, I'm sure there's another cabin."

"*Ship*. And there's no other room that you could sleep in or would want to."

"Oh no, Trent Jordan. Not after you practically accused me of . . . I'll not share your cabin even if it is the last one on board. I'm sure Peach wouldn't mind giving up his hammock!"

She might have regretted giving up his big, soft bed to hang like a bat in a belfry, but in her present mood she'd sleep in a fishnet before risking one night in Trent's cabin.

Trent sauntered back to her and opened the door effortlessly. "You don't have to worry about me. I won't bother you," he said in parting before he shut the door again.

Rose caught the door too late. She kicked at the bottom of it. He meant to lock her in his cabin. She looked over at the bed. Not for a minute had she believed he was going to leave her alone, and not for a minute had she honestly wanted him to. All she wanted was to be in his gentle embrace. She didn't want to feel the tension in his arms when he held her. She wanted him to smile at her and to be glad she was with him. She wanted him to tell her—but why was she thinking this way? He had never wanted her. He'd used her to win a bet with Philip, and as long as he refused to return to

London, she was going to make him regret his lowly wager. When she wasn't so angry, she'd make him want her; she'd have him proposing on his knees, and then she'd have the satisfaction of tossing him aside just as heartlessly as he'd done to her. She hoped they'd return to London within a month.

Good God! She'd forgotten about Aunt Stephanie!

Trent didn't return to his cabin for days. When he wasn't standing at the helm, he was shouting orders or inventing menial jobs just to keep himself busy. His gruffness rubbed off on the crew, and before long everyone was walking around grumbling without a clue as to why—except for Peach.

Peach was the only one who remained quiet. He alone understood the reason behind his captain's behavior, although, neither one of them mentioned her name. Peach wondered if Rose would have simply starved to death if he hadn't taken it upon himself to bring her meals. He'd even brought her clothes and had one of the boys bring pails of water for her baths. It took some searching, but he did manage to find a pair of breeches small enough that they didn't fall down around her ankles. With her hair tied back simply in a black ribbon, and wearing a baggy white shirt and breeches tightened with a long length of rope, she could have almost passed for a cabin boy. Almost. The breeches were snug over hips too round for a boy's, and the cut of the shirt dipped low, revealing enough of her feminine qualities to erase any doubt that she was a woman.

157

Trent slept in the widow's nest. The large hammock swung out over the water, giving him the privacy he needed. Waves lapped underneath him, and stars blinked over him as they popped out of the black sky. Everything was quiet. It was the time of day he dreaded. When his hands and mind were idle, he began to think of Rose. Trent clasped his hands behind his neck and looked up into the starry night. He thought of Rose sleeping peacefully in his bed, her eyes closed, her lashes resting on her pink cheeks, her lips puckered in sleep, and her pale hair falling over her shoulders. Every night he was tempted to go to her, and every night he resisted the temptation only because he was too exhausted to climb out of the widow's nest. He fell asleep thinking of Rose and awoke at dawn determined once again not to give her a single thought. When he needed something in his cabin, he sent Peach to get it. Except for the evening he couldn't find Peach.

Trent needed his sextant and it was on his desk. Wanting to keep Rose's presence a secret stopped him from sending anyone else for the instrument. After an hour of grumbling, he stiffened himself up and ventured below where he stood at his door a good ten minutes before pushing it open. As he had hoped, Rose was asleep. The reason for his being there completely flew from his mind when he set his eyes upon her. She was as he envisioned and more. His eyes traveled the length of her, following every curve the thin blanket clung to. He dared to get close enough to see the rise of her chest every time she took a breath, the gentle arch of her brows, the sweep of her lashes, the soft curve of her lips. With a slight tremble in his hand, he lifted the blanket from her.

Trent was surprised to see Rose dressed only in breeches, especially ones that fit her hips so snugly. His eyes swept longingly over her bare back. He ached to smooth his hand over her skin and pull the ribbon from her hair, releasing her lovely locks, allowing them to fall freely through his fingers. He moved back from her, not trusting what would happen if she opened her eyes. He knew it would be an invitation to take her in his arms and do everything he had dreamed of for the past nights he'd spent alone in the widow's nest. She'd object weakly at first, but he would coax her into giving into his desire completely. Trent would have her if he wanted; he *always* took what he wanted. But it was different with Rose. Having Rose somehow stirred in him a feeling of being conquered rather than being the conqueror. The thought was disturbing enough to remind him of why he returned to his cabin. He gripped the cold sextant in his hand and fled the room.

Trent was in such a hurry he crashed into Peach. "Watch where you're going. And where have you been for the past hour?" he growled.

Peach hated to admit it, but he could think of no better excuse as to why his captain couldn't summon him. "I've been asleep in the dinghy, sir."

Trent frowned. "If I can make do with three hours sleep, I don't see why you can't function on six without having to hide in the dinghy."

Peach dared to argue, for Trent had to be made to listen to reason before he pushed his crew to the edge. "I've been making do wi' less than that and so has the crew. Yer pushing the men too hard. They think yer possessed by the devil."

"Let them think it."

There was nothing worse than a man possessed by a woman, Peach thought, but he didn't dare suggest it out loud. He noticed the sextant the captain strangled in his hand. "I see ye've been in yer cabin."

Trent's look challenged Peach to say anymore. "I forgot my charts. Make yourself useful and get them. I'll be waiting for them, so don't get distracted."

"Aye, sir," Peach promised.

In no time Peach was standing in front of Trent with the rolled charts in his hand. He stayed to watch Trent measure the angle of three stars that hung just above the horizon and carefully record their earthly positions.

The way Trent drove them all, they were going to arrive in Athens in record time. Peach guessed they'd conclude their business without delay and return to London swiftly. To the seaman's way of thinking, if Trent was so afraid of being tempted by a woman that she could drive him like a whipped horse, he must be in love with her and not know it. The thought of Trent in love was so funny that it made him laugh out loud.

Chapter 13

It wasn't the usual mutiny. Trent's men were more loyal than they would appear when they locked him in his cabin with Rose. They had conferred with Peach before deciding it would be best for everyone if Trent finally faced Rose. It was obvious to them all that their captain was fatally in love with the lady and that he was going to work them all to death if he didn't admit to it soon.

Trent would never go willingly to Rose. Peach thought they could get him good and drunk and when he passed out they could stuff him in his cabin, but Trent wouldn't stop issuing orders long enough for anyone to make the suggestion of opening the rum barrel. Paddy was the cautious one, thinking it best to wait for the captain to fall asleep and then tie and gag him, but after it got too dark to see past their elbows the crew was ready to go with Paul's plan. Paul simply suggested they knock him out and drag him to his cabin.

When Peach drew the short straw he was tempted to make another suggestion, but the looks of the men told him they weren't in the mood to hear one more plan. They were all exhausted and in dire need of rest. With a little prodding, Peach sneaked up behind Trent, raised the oar from the dinghy and whacked him over the head.

"Could ya find somethin' big enough to hit him with?" Paul laughed.

"He didn't want to take any chances of missin'," Paddy declared.

"We'd better all hope the plan works. If the lass canna tame his disposition we're all gonna hang," Peach worried.

Three of the men quietly carried Trent to his cabin and propped him in his chair, his head resting on his desk next to a jug of cider and a good supply of biscuits and salted meat. The crew didn't want to chance opening the door for at least a few days. They all smiled to see Rose asleep in Trent's bunk.

"Aren't they in for a surprise," Paddy chuckled.

It was pitch black in the cabin when Rose was awakened by a low growl coming from the center of the room. At first she thought she was dreaming, but when she realized the sound was coming from inside the room instead of inside her head, she stiffened with fright. How would an animal get in Trent's cabin? The window! Something had gotten in through the window. Heaven only knew what kind of animal it was. She held her breath and listened. Her wide eyes tried to see something, but it was too dark. She heard the terrible noise again; this time it was louder. She clapped her hand over her mouth. The beast grew in her imagination. Suppose it was one of those sea things with long arms. Her heart beat in her throat. If she could stay quiet, maybe it wouldn't be able to find her.

She didn't even want to breathe let alone scream, but imagining long slimy tentacles slithering over the floor and getting closer while she lay as still as a rabbit was too much. Many a rabbit had met its doom that way.

Rose scrambled from her bed with her blanket wrapped around her and beat the door all the while she screamed. There wasn't a chance she couldn't be heard all the way to the main deck. Then why was Peach taking so long when his cabin was only across the hall? Someone *had* to hear her.

Someone did. Trent groaned even louder when he lifted his head from his desk with Rose's scream throbbing in his skull. Alerted to danger, Trent stood up, knocked over his chair and set off another round of screams.

"Rose," he said gripping the edge of his desk.

"Trent? What are you doing in here?" Rose could have cried with relief. "I thought—"

Trent moaned again and cautiously touched the spot on his head that hurt the most. "This is *my* cabin," he reminded her. "And I have a right to be here when I want. Do you have to scream so loud?"

"I wanted someone to hear me."

"The *world* heard you. Don't talk now," he said in a strained whisper.

Rose felt her way to the desk. "Trent, are you all right?" she whispered.

"Someone hit me." Trent's voice was a mix of disbelief, rage and agony.

Trent brushed against her on his way to the

163

door. He was going to find out just who had hit him. From all the swearing and the eventual administration of a few good kicks, Rose assumed Trent was having difficulty getting the door opened.

"It must have swelled," she said.

"Hell, it's locked. Something's happened to the *Raven*. What did you hear, Rose?"

"Nothing, only you groaning. You scared the life out of me." As if she wasn't edgy enough, he had to come in her room and make god-awful noises in the dark.

Trent tried the door again, but it wouldn't budge.

Summoned by Rose's screams, Peach talked through the locked door. "Are you all right, lass?"

"Peach! What the hell's going on? Open the door," Trent demanded.

"Donna worry, Captain, the *Raven*'s sailing smooth. The men had enough. They was afraid ye'd kill em before ye killed yerself. They figure ye gotta work out what's between ye and the lass."

"Peach, I'm ordering you to open this door."

"I canna do it, Captain."

"You're talking mutiny." There was only silence to answer him. "Damnation! Peach!"

Rose pulled the blanket up to her chin. The crew had taken over the ship and had locked its captain in his cabin—with her. "What does Peach mean? Work *what* out?" she asked.

"Damned if I know," Trent grumbled settling on his bed. "But I'm not going to lose any sleep over it tonight. I'll need my strength to strangle them all one by one, beginning with Peach."

Rose heard the bed give under his weight and nearly jumped at the sound of his boots being thrown into a corner. Her heart began to pound when she heard the rustle of clothing and she realized that Trent had slipped out of his shirt as well as the rest of his clothes. She suddenly remembered how naked she was beneath the blanket and began a frantic search in the dark for her clothes.

"What are you doing, Rose?"

"I'm looking for my . . ." She couldn't tell him she was looking for her clothes. "Since when are you interested in what I'm doing?" she snapped back after she stubbed her toe on the leg of the desk.

"Since I'm trying to sleep off this headache, I'd like some quiet."

Rose rubbed her foot. "This desk is in the wrong place."

"Now you're going to complain about my furniture?"

Rose found the chair and sat in it. "It's in the middle of the room!"

"You're just accident prone," he grumbled.

Rose wished he could see her grin. "I'm not the one with a bump on my head." Just think of something to say to that, she thought.

As long as Rose remained quiet, Trent didn't have anything else to say. He'd let his guard down, something he'd never done before. He hadn't even noticed the men were discontent. There had to have been signs that would have warned him of a mutiny, but he hadn't noticed them. *Why* did Peach say they had done it? He fell to sleep while he thought of the answer.

Rose was awake before Trent; in fact, she had been awake most of the night listening to his restless sleep. She heard him breathe and move between the sheets as he stretched each muscle in his body. And she heard the threats muffled into the pillow he gripped.

She pitied the men who had shanghaied him for what his subconscious was vowing to do to them. It was strange justice that he would be locked in his cabin just like she was. Peach had said something about working things out with her. Maybe they wanted Trent to take her back to London. What else could it be? She was sure they didn't want a woman aboard. There was some kind of superstition about women on ships, especially in light of the cargo buried in the *Raven*'s hold. If Trent didn't do something, they might decide to get rid of her themselves.

Rose bathed at the washstand and dressed while Trent slept. Afraid the dampness coming in through the window might settle on him, she carefully covered him with a sheet and then settled back in the chair.

She must have drifted back to sleep, because when she awoke, the darkest part of night was over and the gray light of morning was beginning to creep over the windowsill. The sun tried to burn through the fog, casting a soft light into the cabin.

From a safe distance away Rose watched Trent with unguarded eyes. The stubble of a beard had begun to shade his face, and his hair fell in thick black slices to his bare shoulders. Lashes as thick as a chimney sweep's broom lay on his cheeks. How different he looked from the first time she'd seen him; how smooth and chivalrous he'd been the night of the masquerade. In his rugged state he was no less disappointing. Trent was a fascinating man and she wanted to know everything about him, but first they had to settle whatever it was the crew wanted them to settle.

Trent stirred and stretched under the sheet; it fell aside, slipping over the top of his waist and between his legs, exposing all the fine muscle of his torso and the taut, twisted fibers of his legs and arms. His eyes slowly opened and settled on her. Rose was caught drinking in the sight of him, and she flushed to a pink hue when she realized he was staring back.

Trent sat up. His hand went to the back of his head.

"How's your head?" Rose asked, turning her eyes away from his bare chest.

Trent tossed the sheet completely aside, unconcerned that he was exposing every male part of himself in her presence. Rose caught her breath and quickly diverted her eyes. "It's still a remembrance."

He gathered up his hair and neatly tied it back, then walked over to the washstand. Rose tried to keep her eyes sedately diverted but was still tempted to sneak a peek at Trent bathing. Her eyes followed the streams of water dripping over and around his tanned pectorals. Her heart missed a beat or two and her cheeks colored. Her blush became even brighter when Trent noticed her.

"You'd better get used to the sight of me. I think Peach is serious about keeping us locked in here together. It seems he's trying to prove a point of some kind. Have any idea?"

Rose backed away from him so fast she nearly

fell over the chair. "I have absolutely no idea, except that the crew is not happy."

"That we can agree upon."

"They probably think you should take me back to London," she suggested.

Trent had a good chuckle at that. "Not after coming this far."

"Then why would they lock you up?" Rose was finding it very hard to concentrate while her face burned and her heart pounded furiously.

Trent looked at Rose in the most peculiar way, the way Harold's cat looked upon an unwary bird before pouncing on it. Rose decided she didn't like his look. It made her heart race, her ears pound and her body break out in a cold sweat. She wanted to run, but there was nowhere to run to except around the desk. It was the only shield she could put between herself and Trent. Anticipating something, she put the desk between them.

Trent dried his hands with the towel and then slipped into the breeches he swiped from the floor. She almost breathed aloud a sigh of relief. "I remember Peach saying to settle it between us."

Trent walked over to Rose, but she kept the desk between them. For having been hit over the head and locked in his cabin, he was frighteningly calm. "I was thinking while you were watching me." Rose tried to appear as if she didn't know he had noticed that, but she felt the telling, red-hot color return to her cheeks. "Their suggestion probably wouldn't be a bad idea. I've been rather tense."

At the moment, Rose would have bet he wasn't as tense as she was. She moved steadily around the desk, keeping a close eye on his hands as he followed her. "Perhaps some sherry would help," she suggested with a sly smile. At the moment she could use some herself. "Aunt Stephanie would order it whenever she was tense. It would put her right to sleep—for hours."

"They already put me to sleep. The crew put us together with something else in mind. They think you could relax me." They were certainly on the wrong course, he thought. Rose *relax* him! Whenever he was near her he felt as if it was his first time with a woman. Just the sight of her constricted his breathing.

Rose was slow to catch on to how she could relax the *Raven*'s captain. "Now, how could I . . . Oh! The devils!"

Trent pulled a clean shirt from his trunk and put it on, buttoning it up while he talked. "Don't worry, Rose, it's not my intention to ravish you. On the contrary, I'm inclined to stay away from you for as long as we're together. You may continue to sleep in my bed. I'll take the chair."

Hearing him so casually dismiss her—when just looking at him was making her feel like an overwound timepiece—was disheartening. He calmly tucked his shirt into his tight breeches and sat down at his desk. The knock on his head hadn't affected his appetite. He put a handful of biscuit in his mouth and rinsed it all down with a swig of cider. Trent thought it odd for Rose to stand there without voicing her opinion. "The arrangements are agreeable to you?"

Rose was still admiring the breeches that fit his hips as well as her kid gloves fit her hands. "Of course." Her answer was quick. "How long do you think they'll keep us—you—locked up?"

"For the rest of their lives if they're smart."
Trent grinned at her straight face and added, "But
I don't think I could be a gentleman for that
long—in case you're wondering."

"I wasn't," she lied. "I didn't think you'd be
anything less." Positive thinking was the best
approach in such situations.

Trent smiled at her confidence. "I am a man,
Rose, and you certainly are a woman."

Rose flushed. He didn't have to point out the
particulars. She was very well aware he was a man.

Now that he was forced to face Rose, Trent was
in the best disposition he had been in since they
had left London. He wouldn't admit it to anyone,
but his crew had been right. He had been a slave
master while trying not to think of Rose and it
hadn't done anyone any good. He thought of how
horrible he'd been not only to his men but to Rose.
He'd never given her a chance to explain herself
and had cruelly inflicted his frustrations on her.
An apology was due, but he had to be careful not to
give her the impression that he'd softened. His face
turned stern.

"Stowing away on a ship is a serious crime," he
began. "But I judged you guilty before hearing
your explanation to its full extent. I don't want to
spend any more time as a prisoner on my own ship
than I have to. The sooner we get this discussion
over with, the sooner we can reconcile the
differences between us." Trent waited a minute.
"Well?"

"Was that an apology?"

"*I* didn't commit the crime." Trent's voice was
louder than he intended. He looked at the door and
wondered if Peach had his ear against it yet.

170

Leaning forward, he asked, "Don't you think *you* should begin the apologies?"

Rose almost choked. *He* wanted an apology when *he* had made such an underhanded bet with Philip. She was tempted to tell him she knew of his little wager, but forced herself to wait until she had him on his knees begging for her hand; it would certainly be sweeter then. "I only wanted to thank you for my father's ring and ask you how you came by it. And, I told you I got locked in here because of that sticky door. When Peach finally remembered me, the *Raven* had already set sail. I'm not going to apologize for something that wasn't my fault."

Trent returned to her reason for boarding the *Raven*. "So you came all the way to the dock and boarded the *Raven* just to thank me for your father's ring?"

Rose nodded, then added, "And to ask how you came by it."

"I appreciate your good manners, but I would have preferred you staying with your aunt. How I came by your father's ring is not important. You have it now." Trent never expected to be facing Rose while she held her father's ring in her hand. He'd thought he'd be far away from her by the time her thoughts began to fill with accusation. Now he saw the blame in her eyes and had to address it honestly. "I didn't take it from your father, if that's what you've been thinking."

Rose remembered that there had been more than one thief. "But you were there," she ventured to guess. "You know who the Liberty Thief is."

Trent laughed. "You certainly have clear suspicions. Yes, I know who he is, and you certainly muddied him up."

"I don't see any humor in it. Who's the other brigand?" Even though Rose pressed her lips tight, she couldn't suppress a smile when she thought of how neatly she toppled the thief from his horse.

"Come on, Rose. Isn't knowing of my thievery enough?"

"No, I want to know who robbed my father and how you're involved."

"So you can see your cousin hang, and perhaps me, too?"

Rose's face went stark white. "Philip? Philip was the one who—?" She put her hand over her mouth, not to cry out, as Trent thought, but to stifle the giggles that tickled her throat when she thought of Philip sitting in the mud.

"Rose, he isn't bad. Hell, *we're* not bad. We're working to free people from tyrants. Except for with your father and a few greedy noblemen, our proceeds are donated to us quite willingly. Some have even felt slighted that we *didn't* rob them," he laughed. "And they're the ones who would most like to see us hang."

Rose managed to collect her senses. What Philip and Trent were doing was a serious crime. She frowned. "What are you doing with all of this wealth you 'collect'?"

"We purchase supplies in London for the Greek resistance, then the *Raven* transports it all to Athens where a friend of mine will see to its distribution."

"Then you bring food and clothing and—"

Trent rushed to end her thought. "Medicines. Only it is dangerous. The Ottomans don't look too kindly on anyone helping the Greeks these days.

172

So when we arrive in Athens, you are to keep out of sight."

"I can't see why they'd object to anyone feeding or clothing people. It just doesn't make—"

Trent balled his hand into a fist and pounded on the door until he got attention. It was Peach who timidly answered.

"Are ye all right, lass?"

Trent grumbled loudly before Rose could answer. "She's well. You'd best worry about someone else."

"Aye . . . I'm sorry about yer head, Captain. Is it swelled much?"

"It's not me you need to concern yourself with. It's your own skin that's in danger of being turned inside out if you don't unlock this door."

There was a long pause.

"Peach, open this door."

Peach left laughing after he told them he'd be back in the morning. Rose turned to Trent and shrugged. His chin rested in his hand while he looked at her. He tried to stay angry, but the look on her face made him smile.

"What is he finding so amusing?"

Trent couldn't very well tell her how well Peach knew him, that the old seaman could see right through him like clear glass. Peach knew Trent wanted Rose and that his captain was denying himself to the point of making everyone else on board miserable.

But Peach would never understand why Trent avoided Rose. Life was simple to Peach; if you wanted something, you took it. Trent had lived by that philosophy all his life until he met Rose. With Rose, he was afraid he would get more than

173

what he bargained for.

"Our predicament, or rather my own, seems to have lightened his days. Don't be overly concerned. These little insurrections happen all the time. I know my men. Once they begin to argue amongst themselves, one of them will release me. Until then, we'll just have to make the best of being in . . . close quarters."

"I suppose we will," Rose said slowly, caught on the emphasis that had been in his voice when he'd said 'close quarters.' "It *would* be an opportunity to get to know each other better. I don't see that there's much else to do to bide our time other than talking."

Rose's voice settled in Trent's ears and that was as far as her words went. He tried not to think of how he'd rather bide his time as he found his thoughts wandering to what he deemed forbidden territory. But he wasn't going to be very successful keeping a distance between himself and Rose when every other thought turned to the taste of her kisses. He found looking at her sitting there on the edge of his bed very distracting. He almost had to sit on his hands to stop from pulling her into his lap. At the end of his internment he was sure to hang Peach.

Keeping Rose talking wasn't hard, and for lack of anything else to do, Trent listened. He learned why she was such an independent. Without brothers and sisters to confide in, and with a father absent more than not, she'd sought the friendship of two ruffians. He wanted to tell her she was fortunate they were protective of her, but he just listened. He thought she'd go hoarse before she ran out of things to talk about, and he even toyed with the idea of kissing her lips shut but quickly brought his thoughts back to reality, reminding himself that that would lead to what he was trying to avoid. He was going to return Rose in time for her wedding and he wasn't planning on being the groom.

"Aren't you hungry?" Trent asked, finally finding a place to break in. Rose took the biscuit he offered. "There aren't any glasses. Do you mind?" Trent held the jug of cider out to her.

She lifted the jug to her lips and wrinkled her nose at the biting taste of it. The cider was not the kind of cider Rose was used to and the biscuits already had weevils, but being a guest, and knowing how sensitive Trent was about her other criticisms of his ship, she wasn't going to complain about the food or drink. She just picked out the worms and gulped down the fermented cider.

While Trent watched, with more patience than he thought he owned, Rose made a mound of biscuit crumbs on his desk.

"Go ahead," Rose said, squinting at a piece of biscuit. "Tell me about you. I'm a captivated audience."

"Do you have to do that?"

Rose looked up at him and could see that he was concerned about the mess on his desk. "Don't worry, I'll clean it up. What did you say you were bringing to Greece?"

"I didn't say. What are you doing? Just eat the damn biscuit."

Rose didn't understand that it wasn't the crumbs that bothered him but the strain of being so close to her. "I'm not eating the little things inside, if you don't mind."

"I do mind. We've only come with so much food. They're not going to kill anyone, but starvation will."

"Well, you eat the rest if it concerns you so much."

"It does concern me. I'm the captain and the food supply is my responsibility. I'll not have shortages because you have an aversion for . . . 'little things.'"

"When it's little things in my food, I certainly do have an aversion. Since last I've checked, I don't have feathers. I'm not eating bugs!"

"We're not on a picnic."

Rose found herself shouting back, "*That* you certainly don't have to remind me of!"

"No wonder your father handed you over to Stephanie."

She braced her hands on her hips. "And what's that supposed to mean?"

"I'm only thinking about what you've admitted—running around with Jack and what's his name, when you were old enough to—"

"To what? What are you insinuating? They were gentlemen."

Rose and Trent stood face to face. Their day's confinement had been more of a strain than either of them realized. Their voices were loud enough to travel out the window and up to the main deck, yanking at the ear of every seaman. The crew stopped what they were doing and listened intently to every word that sailed up to them.

"What's she sayin'?" Paddy asked Peach, his gnarled fingers still entwined in the net he was fixing.

176

"She's complainin' about the biscuits." Peach's cheeks ripened with a smile, giving definition to his name.

Paul leaned his ear over the side of the *Raven* and called back over his shoulder, "She's said she ain't noticed anyone callin' him Captain lately."

They all took a deep breath and waited for the next round.

Chapter 14

She had a point, and as disturbing as it was, there was a sharp ring of undeniable truth to it. His men had mutinied.

With his noble intentions, he had worn his nerves thin and had driven his crew over the edge. He thought he could ignore Rose as long as she was out of sight, but just knowing she was close at hand caused his unsatiated desires to flare up into a bad temper. When his crew had jailed him with the object of his frustration, whether they knew the rhyme or reason for his self-denial, they'd do what they thought would set his disposition right. He could only imagine how many of them had already placed their bets on how long it would take to get their old captain back.

What was she thinking of when she came aboard? he asked himself. Now she was traveling alone with him, and like a cannon ball her reputation would sink with any excuse at attempting to explain how innocently it had happened. A stuck door! Stephanie would certainly believe that one. At this moment London Town was probably having a field day with the scandal. And what was he thinking of by denying his lust for her? Even if he did manage to resist Rose from London to Athens and back, no one would believe it. But keeping his talons out of Rose proved to be more of a challenge than he had first thought it would, and he was fast becoming weary of it. No one would expect him to do anything less than take her to his bed, and he wanted to; he just didn't want her to misinterpret how he felt. He didn't love her, and he was going to have to set her straight on that issue. Once that was understood, it would be smooth sailing, so to say.

There was another reason for his tenseness, for Trent realized the delivery of guns and ammunition to Ramos would be complicated with Rose aboard. The Filiki Hetairia was still a secret revolutionary group, gathering strength before making its presence known. Ramos knew and trusted the *Raven*'s crew but certainly wouldn't like the notion that this time a stranger traveled with them. Somehow Rose would have to be kept a secret.

It would have been so much simpler had Rose not come aboard. She was supposed to be safe in London, attending her aunt's parties and meeting respectably titled marriage prospects. She was supposed to have been safely married by the time he returned to London; then he could have had her all he liked without dreading the suggestion of tying the knot himself. If they had not already been in the channel, he would have turned the *Raven* around and set Rose back on the quay. Like no other woman, she had managed to complicate his life beyond belief.

Now that he had convinced himself that his noble idea of saving Rose's reputation was all in vain, the girl never looked more ravishing. He watched her while she swept the crumbs of biscuit off his desk and into her cupped hand. She wore her dress now, but he thought of how she looked in the tight breeches Peach had managed to scrounge up. He rather liked the look. Her derriere fit well into the seat, nothing like the way they bagged when young Sean wore them. They followed the shape of her thighs to just above her knees, and from there tight stockings defined the rest of her shapely legs. Peach most likely thought she'd be less noticeable dressed as a boy, but unless a man was half-dead, the disguise wouldn't last for a moment.

Rose could feel Trent's eyes on her while she tidied up his desk. She knew he reclined on the bed, and knowing he had nothing on beneath the sheet covering him, she tried not to look his way. The man had most likely exhausted himself over the issue of how to properly eat a biscuit. Or, he might have had second thoughts as to who was going to get the bed that night. Well, no matter what the reason, she wasn't going to eat a weevil to save her life, and when he had mentioned it might just come down to that, she'd said she'd rather die. Of course, he had said that would be fine with him. Then why was he looking at her like that? He was supposed to be angry with her, but instead he looked rather pleased with himself.

After tossing the last of the crumbs out the window, she was tempted to glance his way. Just let him make one more remark about biscuits. Turning away from him, she stood in front of the windows and pulled the bodice of her dress away from her damp skin. Why was he so blasted calm when she was still hot as a muffin in a tin?

The sun was getting ready to once again plunge into the depths of the sea. For now, the cabin was bathed in a soothing orange light that filtered through the mullion windows. Where the glass beveled, colors shot across the room, touching here and there with shades of purple, blue and yellow. A fresh breeze touched the side of her face, gently teasing stray threads of yellow hair and calming the tightness she felt in her shoulders. She would have loved to ease herself into a cool bath, but the chance of getting water from the galley was less than slim.

The rustle of bed linen reminded her that she no longer had the same privacy as before, so a full bath wasn't likely until the crew forgave their captain for whatever were his sins. Until then, she'd have to make do with a sponge bath. She glanced at the washbasin wistfully. Privacy was going to further test Trent's manners. However, he *had* complied when she needed to use the commode, and she had done the same for him, not that she would have done anything different. Living in such close proximity certainly had its tense moments.

Rose walked over to the washstand, unbuttoned her sleeves, then pushed them up to her elbows. He was still watching her when she ran the sponge up her arms. Did the trickle of water over her skin make her flesh rise, or was it the intensity of Trent's look that gave her goose bumps? She splashed water onto her hot face. She guessed he wasn't going to turn his head unless she said something. True to the form he'd been in that day, he would wait for her to ask for privacy.

"If it's all right with you," she said tersely, "I'd like to bathe the rest of me."

"Don't let me stop you."

Rose pressed her lips together and turned her eyes on his grin. "I've always thought there was something of a gentleman in you, even when my aunt warned me of—"

Trent sighed and closed his eyes. "Go ahead and spare me your aunt's wise words. I won't look." He opened one eye and smiled in his crooked way. "I promise."

"Both eyes."

She was tempted to make him double-swear to it, but he seemed agreeable enough and she didn't want to press her luck by irritating him. Nevertheless, she turned her back to him when she slipped her dress over her head. "I'll tell you when I'm decent," she said, looking over her shoulder to make sure he still had both eyes closed.

"Don't worry, I'm likely to fall asleep."

Said the wolf to the lamb, she thought.

Trent tried to keep his eyes closed, he really did, but the trickling sound of water as she squeezed out the sponge proved to be torturous. He opened his eyes just a crack. He hadn't lied; they still were *technically* closed.

The mellow softness of the vision before him took his breath away so unexpectedly that he nearly gasped. Even at Philip's town house he hadn't seen her so ravishing. She was bathed in amber light and standing before him, stripped of everything but the scanty lace undergarments that barely covered the essentials. Rose was a tempting vision with the setting sun shining through her hair and touching her skin everywhere he wanted to. His eyes followed her hand as it slid the sponge up her leg from her ankle to the curve behind her knee and then all the way to—

183

"Trent?"

Quickly closing his eyes, he answered more sharply than he meant to. "Yes." The strain of having this half-clothed beauty standing almost within his reach and not being able to touch her was something no man should have to submit himself to.

Catching the clip in his voice, Rose turned to look at him. Satisfied his eyes were still closed, she continued with her bath. "I don't mind if you have the bed tonight—it is your bed—but would you mind lending me a pillow for the chair?"

"Certainly," he choked. There was no way she was going to sleep in the chair that night, but he'd tell her that bit of news later. His eyes cautiously opened so slightly that if she turned and looked at him, he doubted she'd notice.

Rose was confident he'd kept his word, so she slipped out of the rest of her clothes. Trent felt himself fully swell with desire. His eyes opened wide so as not to miss a single detail of her lovely form. Peach was nothing less than a saint to have shown him the error of his ways.

The glow of the lamp shone over her, bathing her wet skin in a shimmery amber light. She rubbed the sponge over her shoulder and squeezed it, sending a small stream of water down her back. Trent followed the wet trail from her shoulder, down her back and around the curve of her derriere. It took all of his control to stay in his bed when he watched the sponge return to slide between her legs.

"Trent?" His eyes snapped shut. "Trent, are you asleep already?" Rose looked over her shoulder and smiled. He certainly looked innocent in his sleep, nothing like he had earlier when he'd

184

seemed ready to throttle her for making crumbs out of the ship's fare. She grabbed a towel from under the washstand and rubbed herself dry. "I was going to ask if you'd mind if I slept in your robe . . . but since you're already asleep . . ." She took the robe from the hook over the washbasin and wrapped it around her body, loosely knotting the tie. That she was naked underneath the thin silk robe didn't worry her. Trent had already proved he could be trusted, and there was no sense in wrinkling her clothes by sleeping in them.

After brushing her hair, she tiptoed over to the bed to get a pillow, stopping just short to admire the sleeping captain. He was the most perfect man she'd ever seen. From the first night she'd seen him, when only his mouth and eyes were visible, he had taken her breath away. Now, looking down at his whole face—the straight nose, the squarish jaw, the slightly sunburned cheeks, the crook of a smile—she trembled. He was comfortably asleep under the bedcover now, so the rest of him was hidden from her admiring eyes. She was thankful for that, since just his face and strong arms made her cheeks burn.

To Rose's distress, the second pillow was neatly tucked under Trent's head. She wouldn't dare wake him, for who knew what kind of a mood he'd be in after being woken up? Well, given his reputation, she had to admit to herself there were some who knew, but she didn't want to chance discovering his habit herself after having had a taste of his temper that afternoon. She supposed she could do without for one night.

Under a shade of lashes, Trent watched Rose settle into the desk chair—or rather, try to make a bed out of the hard piece of furniture. She pulled

185

her knees up to her chin and rested her head on them; then she straightened out her legs and laid her head on the desk; then she laid across the chair, nestling her head into her shoulder. The third position made him wonder when she would make another attempt for the pillow. He certainly hoped she would; otherwise he'd be obliged to get her himself. But he was not disappointed. Rose couldn't bear the hard chair another minute.

She quietly approached the bed then stretched over it to steal a pillow from under his head. She leaned over his chest, her left arm reaching behind his neck to tug gently at the pillow while her right hand slipped under his head to ease the pillow out. Her robe gaped, releasing two round breasts that came temptingly close to his face. Trent groaned and rolled over, pinning half her arm under his head.

Rose nearly panicked. She was stuck up to her elbow, and if she moved she'd surely wake him. She clutched the gaping robe closed with her other hand and tried to calm herself with reason. If he wakes I'll just explain that I tried not to disturb him and that I couldn't sleep without something just a little softer than an oak chair. He'll understand. What am I worrying for? He probably won't even wake up. No, he wouldn't understand. It would just be another irritating fault he would add to her tally.

When Rose moved her hand under the pillow, Trent's arm came up and around her back, flattening her against his chest. Before she could utter more than a little gasp of surprise, she was swept under him and he was kissing her. At the moment his lips touched hers, the indignant protest she thought to muster dissipated. Her arms

186

came up and around his neck. God, she'd almost forgotten how sinful his kisses were.

His hands, his very wide, exploring hands, moved down her sides to her waist and the flare of her hips, then slipped under the bottom of her robe and pushed it up to her middle, rendering her naked beneath him. Rose felt his skin warm against hers. Lord, she'd forgotten *he* was naked, too!

Pressed down as she was, into the soft bed, she was not in the best position to protest his undress or the fact that he had slipped the robe from her in one swift movement. She had wanted him—she'd even come to the *Raven* for him—but now that everything she dared to imagine was happening, she was taken aback by the suddenness of it all.

"Trent," she managed to say between kisses, "I'm sorry I woke you."

"Don't think of it."

"I only wanted a pillow."

"You can have the whole damn bed. Now be quiet and kiss me."

Rose's lips turned up slightly. "Are you sure you're not angry?"

"God, Rose, what would make you think that?" He moved his lips down her neck to the rise of her breast.

"Well, being locked up in your cabin . . ."

"Peach is a capable first mate."

Rose quivered when the trail of his kisses reached her stomach. "The biscuits . . ."

"You can eat biscuits any way you please."

When he moved even lower, Rose tensed with anticipation. Her hands rested on his shoulders, his held her hips.

Trent was relieved when Rose finally quieted

187

down. He eased her fears with a tender seduction, brushing light kisses over her stomach and down her thighs. He parted her legs gently, meeting only a tinge of resistance. Once his hand slipped over the proof of her longing and showed her what further pleasure he promised, Rose squirmed with impatience. Her hips moved of their own accord, sliding against his slow and gentle caress.

She closed her eyes and moaned with the sensuous stroking he imposed on her most sensitive parts. If there was an inkling of protest left in her, it was smothered by the overwhelming heat that throbbed in her middle.

When Trent was sure Rose was hot with desire, he drew his tongue over the tingling part of her. She throbbed with a passion that was on the brink of exploding. She was ready for him now and no amount of pain could pierce through the pleasurable sensations that numbed where he meant to thrust his manhood.

Trent moved up over her, his chest against her chest, his arms pinned against her side. Her legs naturally parted; she opened her heart to him and he took it. Rose closed her eyes in ecstasy as he probed deeper into her hot center. She writhed in the flames of passion that raged inside her. She embraced his full desire with a moan of pleasure.

Trent nibbled her ear, then held her head in his hands, kissing her fully.

They soared like gulls on a current of wind, sailing together above the clouds on a journey that brought them close to heaven. Higher and higher they climbed, coming to paradise together in a burst of light that warmed their hearts and promised to brighten their days forever.

When Trent moved inside her, euphoria swelled

a little more with each stroke, until, like a bubble, it burst and fell in sparkling glory. A sigh left her lips, joining his own cry of gratification when he finally appeased his long-awaiting desire.

Trent held Rose in his arms, not wanting to roll away from her now that he was satisfied. It was somewhat disturbing that he still wanted to hold her close. What was it about Rose that made him want her like no other woman? His hand gently stroked her side while he pondered that question. Contrary to what he felt, he should still be furious with her for following him and causing mayhem on his ship, but all he could think of was kissing her. She wasn't the most perfect woman he'd ever been with. Though he found everything about her enticing, her mouth was too big for her delicate features, she talked too much and was opinionated beyond belief. He smiled at that. There was one wonderful way to close Rose's mouth, and the more she talked, the more he could exercise that technique.

Chapter 15

Paul wasn't keen on letting Trent out of his cabin so soon.

"How do you know they worked things out? Just because it's been quiet in there don't mean anything. He could have killed her."

"It hasna been *that* quiet." Peach's cheeks turned orange.

Paddy laughed and slapped his knee. "He probably don't want to come out no more. I say, let him stay where he's happy."

"A day or two at least," another in the group suggested.

When it came to a vote, the crew decided to let their captain and Rose spend a little more time together. They solved the problem of getting food and water to them by lowering the provisions down through the cabin's open windows by rope. No one wanted to chance opening the door until they were positive that the captain had come to his senses.

Rose rested her cheek on Trent's warm chest while she casually brushed her hand over his shoulder. Trent hadn't confessed to loving her but had admitted to wanting her, and that was one step closer to what she desired. He grabbed her hand and kissed her palm. His warm lips against the center of her hand stirred something inside Rose that made her want him. Sliding over his chest, she teased him with light kisses; her lips touched his cheeks, the ridge of his nose, his eyes, his forehead, tickling like a feather, making him laugh and shiver at the same time.

"Come here, you sea witch," Trent growled, pulling her tightly against him so she could feel every hard part of his body under her. Cupping his hands under her soft bottom, he kissed her firmly. "The men were right to lock me in here with you."

"Are you going to tell them that?"

"I'll give them hell for it. They should have presented their grievances to me."

"Would you have listened?"

"Perhaps," Trent said, kissing behind her ear. "It was getting more difficult not to think of you, knowing you were so close. You should have stayed in London," he added between kisses.

Rose frowned and sat up next to him. Trent reached up and ran his hand over the curve of her breast. "You're as perfect as a Greek statue."

Her change in mood didn't affect him; he didn't even notice, which perturbed her more.

"You're sorry I'm here, then?"

His hands measured every inch of her, running down her sides and around the curve of her hips to the fleshy part of her thighs. He impatiently pulled her back down to him.

"Trent . . ." He *would* have preferred she'd stayed home. It was as effective as throwing sand on a fire. He coaxed a kiss from her lips. She kissed him back, but her lips lacked the passion he

TO GET YOUR
4 FREE BOOKS
MAIL THE COUPON BELOW.

FREE BOOK CERTIFICATE

Heartfire Romance

GET 4 FREE BOOKS

Yes! I want to subscribe to Zebra's HEARTFIRE HOME SUBSCRIPTION SERVICE. Please send me my 4 FREE books. Then each month I'll receive the four newest Heartfire Romances as soon as they are published to preview Free for ten days. If I decide to keep them I'll pay the special discounted price of just $3.50 each; a total of $14.00. This is a savings of $3.00 off the regular publishers price. There are no shipping, handling or other hidden charges. There is no minimum number of books to buy and I may cancel this subscription at any time. In any case the 4 FREE Books are mine to keep regardless.

NAME

ADDRESS

CITY _____ STATE _____ ZIP

TELEPHONE

SIGNATURE

(If under 18 parent or guardian must sign)
Terms and prices subject to change.
Orders subject to acceptance.

HF-104

GET 4 FREE BOOKS

HEARTFIRE HOME SUBSCRIPTION
SERVICE
P.O. BOX 5214
120 BRIGHTON ROAD
CLIFTON, NEW JERSEY 07015

wanted. "Would you really have wanted me to stay in London?"

Trent sighed, rolling to his back. He wished he could take back those words. Avoiding her eyes, he stared at the ceiling. "I don't love you, Rose. Just because I want you . . . like this . . . doesn't mean I love you." Trent waited for her to cry but she didn't.

Rose sat up. "That's good."

He propped himself up on his elbow and looked at her with unshielded astonishment. "It is?"

"Yes. You're being honest. Only someone unscrupulous would have professed his love to me right now. When you tell me you love me, I know you'll be telling the truth."

Rose might not have thought him to be a scoundrel, but she certainly had a knack for making him feel like one. His hand rested idly on her hip while he pondered her last sentence. He wasn't planning on falling in love, and he didn't want her to count on it.

The sound of cannon fire brought Trent and Rose immediately to their feet. Trent jumped into his breeches, swearing all the while. Rose grabbed her own clothes and dressed with the same urgency.

"What is it?" she asked, panicked by his alarm.

Before Trent could answer, the door to his cabin flew open and slammed against the trunk behind it.

One of the men—Rose remembered seeing him but didn't know him by name—stood in the doorway with his sword drawn. There was a look of excitement on his face, as though a long-awaited moment had finally arrived. The event later proved to be one she'd never forget.

"She's here!" Paddy exclaimed, handing Trent his sword. "The *Black Orchid* is back for revenge, and her sails are as full as a woman's bustle."

Trent grabbed Rose with his arm and addressed her brusquely. "Stay in here and don't make a sound, especially if we're boarded. Angel wouldn't expect you to be here."

"Who's Angel?"

"The most villainous pirate a man would ever want to meet," Paddy said. "But *you* don't need to worry none, it's *Trent's* heart this one would like to cut out. But then," Paddy eyed Rose from head to foot—"I don't think you'd please Angel much either."

Trent glared at the seaman.

Another volley of cannon fire thundered through the ship, and Rose felt the floor tremble under her feet. She gripped the nearest body.

"That was ours," Paddy explained, prying her fingers off his forearm.

"Thank you for making that clear," Rose tried not to look worried when the two men rushed away, closing the door behind them.

She ventured to the window and cautiously looked out onto the expanse of blue ocean. Framed in the panels of glass was the most beautiful but most sinister looking ship Rose had ever seen. Clouds of black sails made it difficult to sight as the menace slipped almost unseen through the water. It was usually a surprise when the *Black Orchid* was finally close enough to be noticed; then it was its cannon fire that alerted others to its dangerous presence.

Rose felt faint when she saw the white skull and

crossbones gleam down from the mainmast. She was a ship fitted for battle. Heavy cannons trimmed her sides, and her sleek lines assured the speed needed to outrun an enemy. The recurrent explosions nearly knocked Rose off her feet. When they hit close to the *Raven* water rose up in fountains and splashed against the window. The *Raven* shook in response, sending its volleys to the *Black Orchid*. In a short while, there was a pounding scramble of feet above and a chorus of shouts. Smoke from the cannon fire formed a thick cloud around the two ships, making it impossible to see anything more than occasional pieces of sky and explosions of light flashing through the smoke. Rose prayed that Trent could stave off the attack, but she feared that the *Black Orchid* had claimed too much of an advantage through surprise.

As if in answer to her prayers, the cannons suddenly became quiet. It was an eerie silence that stalked through the gray cloud of smoke. Rose didn't trust such calm; it made her worry more than the deluge of cannon fire. She strained to hear something that would clue her to the status of the *Raven*. Shortly, she heard the sound of footsteps approach the cabin. She remembered Paddy's warning of the terrible pirate, Angel, and hid under the bed.

The door was pushed open and from her low vantage point she could see two black boots stride over to Trent's desk. The leather boots were covered with an elaborate swirled design, and the toes were tipped in pure silver. They were not boots any of Trent's men would own. They were fancy Spanish boots that clicked like castanets when the pirate walked. Out of the corner of her eye Rose caught the ruffle of her petticoat peeking out from her hiding place and quickly pulled it back. She calmed herself, remembering that Trent had said the pirate wouldn't expect to find her there.

The pirate pulled out the chair, scraping its legs over the wood floor, and then settled in it. Rose heard his feet thump up on Trent's desk. He was apparently making himself comfortable while he waited. Waited for what? Rose's heart began to thump. What if Trent was dead and the pirates had killed his crew as well? She was so scared, she didn't think she could stay quiet for much longer unless she fainted. She battled unsuccessfully to expel Chloe's gruesome pirate stories, which had chosen that moment to come back to her.

The day certainly could not get any bleaker. At least that's what Rose thought until Trent was led into the room. There were two pairs of booted feet on either side of him, and Rose made a good guess that his hands were tied behind his back. When the black booted pirate saw Trent, he stood up.

"He's trussed good, Angel, but we'll be outside the door if you need us," Rose heard one of them gruffly announce.

"Don't torture him to death, Captain. Save some for later," the other said, laughing sadistically.

Rose shrunk as far under the bed as she could. The pirate meant to torture Trent and she was helpless to save him. Knowing she could not silently endure his screams of agony, she tried to think of something to do. No situation was hopeless, her father had often told her.

Trent spoke and confirmed Rose's fear that the *Raven* had been overtaken by the *Black Orchid*. "You've won this time, Angel. Now we're even."

Rose watched the black boots tap slowly across the floor toward Trent. Their silver points flashed like daggers; the sharp tip of his drawn sword skewered the floor at Trent's feet. The pirate came just short of stepping on Trent's toes. Rose knew the two must be face to face.

"I haven't won until it's over, Captain Jordan," the pirate said in a breathy voice.

Good God, the pirate was a woman!

Chapter 16

It wasn't the first time Trent had encountered her; apparently they had jousted with each other before. The fact that Angel was a woman didn't make Rose feel much better, especially since Trent was held captive and Rose was stuck under the bed. She knew she couldn't stay there for the duration of their captivity, not with the biggest cockroach she'd ever seen staring at her.

"You still owe me for the last time." Angel's voice was low and creamy, not high-pitched and irritating like some women Rose knew.

"I thought I paid for that in canvas—*yards* of black canvas, if you remember." Trent reminded Angel that he already made amends for the last time he damaged her ship.

"You would be uncouth enough to remind me. I suppose I shouldn't have attacked an old friend, but I couldn't resist the fun," Angel laughed. "You're getting careless. Were you asleep at the helm?" she asked in a more serious tone.

Rose was afraid Angel might be as beautiful as she sounded. Sliding closer to the end of the bed, she dared risk peeking out from under it. Since

Angel's back was to her, Rose slid out of her hiding place far enough to get a good look at the pirate. Lying on her stomach, Rose gazed up at the lean woman.

If there had been any fat on Angel, her clothes wouldn't have concealed an ounce of it. Tight black breeches accentuated her shapely thighs, and soft leather boots hugged her calves like a pair of gloves. At her hip she wore a sword that was sheathed in the same pure silver that tipped her boots. Long, black hair curled wildly down her back, covering most of the white silk blouse softly gathered at her waist. She was as hard looking as Rose imagined a woman pirate could be, but there were still gentle aspects that could be detected in her voice when she spoke to Trent. Rose decidedly didn't like those soft womanly tones and hoped when Angel turned around her face would be ruddy like Peach's and scarred like a pickle barrel.

"I can always count on you to keep me awake," Trent said, smiling at Angel. "You can untie me now. As you said, you've won this round."

"Oh no," Angel parried, with the little tease in her voice that began to grate on Rose's patience. "I don't trust you. How do I know that as soon as I let my guard down you won't capture me?" Angel teased the buttons on his shirt. "Besides, it's more fun having you tied up and at my mercy."

"Rumors in London say you lack that quality when it comes to men."

"You don't believe them?" Anyone who didn't know Angel would think she was genuinely hurt. "Just last week I let a knock-kneed lord get away in his skiff when I should have let him sink with his ship. You wouldn't believe the names he called me—and after I spared his life!" she exclaimed with an incredulous huff.

"I also heard you're going to marry the earl of Hatfield. Settling down, are you?"

When Angel smiled at Trent, all the hard lines in her face softened. It would have been easy to mistake her for a princess; it was hard to imagine she was a ruthless pirate. "The wedding is in a month and I've promised to kill him with sweetness."

"I wouldn't doubt it. The man's in his eighties."

"He's a dear and he loves me," she said defensively.

"I believe he does. Do you plan on keeping it a secret that you capture and tie up men for fun, or does he like that sort of thing?"

Angel's laugh was deep and warming. "All right, as long as you've cried uncle, I'll cut you loose. You have agreed to defeat?"

Trent glanced over Angel's shoulder and saw Rose creep out from under the bed. There was obviously no stopping whatever fool thing she had in mind. Fearful his attention would give Rose away, he tried not to watch her and concentrated on Angel.

"You've bested me this time," Trent said in surrender.

Angel was gloating so much over her conquest, her usual sixth sense for danger was dulled. Rose silently made it to Trent's desk, where Angel had laid her broad-brimmed hat and pistol. Rose couldn't believe her luck. She wrapped both hands around the ivory handle and steadied the gun at the pirate's back.

"Untie him now," Rose ordered, praying the pirate took her seriously.

Angel assumed correctly that the pistol she had

left on the desk was pointed at her back. She exchanged a half smile with Trent. "You always have an ace hidden somewhere, don't you?"

"You'd better do as she says, Angel. She's bound to hit one of us if that pistol goes off."

Angel did as Rose asked, but Rose didn't like the way she went about untying Trent—slowly, very slowly.

The pirate didn't move except to wrap her arms around Trent's waist. She pressed her body against his as she reached for the rope around his wrists. Rose shifted from one foot to the other. It seemed to her that it took Angel much longer than it should have to loosen a few knots. Finally she was finished and Trent was free.

Without a pause, Trent quickly grasped the pirate's wrists in one hand and relieved her of her sword, then reached down and pulled the dagger from the top of her boot.

"I wouldn't want to make a mistake and overlook this," he said, tossing the sharp weapon over to Rose. "You can put the pistol down now."

Rose was gaping at Angel's beauty, a fatal mistake many a seaman had made. As fair as she was, Angel was dark. Thick, black hair fell over her shoulders, and her lashes were so dark her eyes looked like chunks of coal. Her features were perfect, as if carved from stone, and despite the time she spent at sea, her skin was barely tanned. At first, Angel glared at Rose, but then her look turned to amusement when she realized the whole scene. "How curious of you, Trent, to keep a woman under your bed instead of in it." Ignoring her comment, he pushed her out of his cabin.

"Rose," Trent repeated, "put the pistol down."

202

Rose dropped the pistol at his shouted command.

"I do believe she had no idea how to use it," Angel said.

"That isn't true. I'm quite a shot," Rose returned.

That comment gained Trent's attention. Rose ignored his grim look. "I always hit my target," she said.

Trent tightened his hold around Angel's wrists, and although he spoke to the pirate, he glared at Rose. "You're going back to your ship."

Angel sighed. "Men are such sore losers."

"You seem not to have noticed your hands are the ones bound." Trent pushed Angel out of his cabin and turned to Rose, "Bring her weapons if you can carry them."

Rose mumbled to herself while she gathered up Angel's sword, dagger and pistol. Trent was acting as if it was her fault his ship had been attacked by pirates. Granted, it hadn't been a smooth journey, but it wasn't her fault his crew mutinied. He could blame his own sour disposition for that.

Her arms full, Rose put the pirate's plumed hat on her head and followed Trent to the main deck. There were plenty of stares to greet them. Most of the men settled their eyes on Rose. Angel's men released the *Raven*'s crew at her signal and backed away.

Angel wasn't a new menace to Trent's men, she was an old acquaintance—a devil of a woman who periodically challenged them with her war games. The crew knew Angel's looks were deceiving, for she was as dangerous as any pirate that prowled the Mediterranean Sea. Whenever she looked at a man, she rendered him senseless with her black

203

eyes and innocent face. Trickery was not beneath her; she'd capture a man and his ship any way she could. To stand at the tip of Angel's sword was the ultimate humiliation. It was lucky for the crew of the *Raven* that she liked Trent and only meant to tease him with her cannons and swordsmanship. She was never serious in her attacks against the *Raven*. But the men feared that finding another woman on board would change her playful games to the more deadly type she engaged in with other ships. Apprehension lined their faces as they regarded the two women.

Peach needed to talk to Trent before the captain made a serious error in judging the nature of women.

"Careless, Peach." Angel clucked her tongue and winked as she passed him. "I was up on your lee side before you saw me."

Peach flushed with embarrassment. "Captain, canna have a word wi' ye?"

"I'd like to see Angel back to the *Black Orchid* before we have any more mishaps."

"It's what I'd like ta speak ta ye about." Angel's steady smile began to make his Scottish blood boil. "That black-hearted—" The rest of his mumbling was cut short by a castrating look from Angel.

Trent leaned over and whispered to Rose. "Keep your distance from her. She'd be better named for Satan."

Trent kept a wary eye on Angel and Rose while he listened to Peach.

"Do ye think it wise ta send her off in such a hurry?" Peach asked, glancing nervously at Angel.

"She accomplished what she intended."

"True, she showed us up this time."

Trent rested his hands on his hips. "She showed

204

you up. I was below. Remember?"

"It's that what worries me. Angel's feelings might be a wee hurt, seeing Rose an all."

"She's betrothed to the earl of Hatfield."

Peach's brows rose up in surprise. "The earl?"

"She says he loves her."

Peach laughed. "The earl of Hatfield? Does he know she's more devil than angel?"

"I doubt she told him of her . . . other side."

Rose clutched Angel's weapons in her arms and waited next to the pirate until Trent returned. She watched Angel out of the corner of her eye, but the pirate didn't attempt to hide her bold perusal of Rose.

Angel leaned over to Rose. She smelled distinctively of exotic oils. "Trent hasn't properly introduced us. In the heat of our battles, he forgets he's a gentleman. I'm Angel, soon to be Lady Sinclair."

After seeing a woman pirate, Rose hadn't thought anything else could surprise her—until now. A woman pirate with high aspirations! Her guarded interest shifted to a bold summary of the pirate. "Are you planning on holding the earl at sword point?"

Angel laughed. "I'm the most well-behaved woman you'd ever want to meet on land, but when the sea's beneath my feet, my heart and spirit are as free as the wind."

It figured Rose was lucky enough to encounter the woman at sea. "You'll not be free for long if you're caught attacking other ships."

"I'll not be caught. There isn't a seaman alive who can catch the *Black Orchid*." Angel looked behind them and gloated over her ship like a proud mother. No one would deny it was a beautiful sight. Outlined against a violet sky, as though penned in ink, the *Black Orchid* starkly waited for its proud mistress. Rose followed Angel's eyes from the *Black Orchid* to Trent. "It was Trent's idea to fit her with black sails."

"How clever of him to help you like that."

"Well, it's been mutual. I've saved *his* neck on occasion, too. With what he carries in his hold, it's no wonder he's still in business."

Rose's interest sharpened. "What business is that?"

"You don't know? He smuggles guns for the resistance."

"Guns! Trent is a smuggler!"

"It isn't all tea and china down below. He hides them in the center of crates filled with china or cotton or whatever." Angel shrugged. "I've tried to convince him to do something for profit. If one is going to put one's head on a block, it might as well be for something more than a heartfelt thank you."

Rose glanced over to Trent. Noticing her interest, Angel gushed. "He's a handsome devil, isn't he?" Her eyes lingered over Trent.

"Are you in love with him?" Rose blurted.

Angel looked at her with undisguised pity. "You poor darling. I hope you haven't gotten too attached to the man." Rose looked away from Angel's sharp look. "I see. Too late already. Well, don't worry. I have no claims on Trent Jordan, even though his men might think so. Did you see them check their pistols when they saw the both of us?" She smiled wickedly. "I do believe they fear my vengeance—or possibly yours? I could have some fun with that."

"Please don't take this the wrong way, but I

think I've had enough of a sample to get the idea of the kind of fun you mean, and if it's all right with you, I'd rather not be aboard."

Angel seemed not to hear Rose. She was concentrating on Peach and Trent. "I'd wager they'll have their captain convinced to keep me aboard till morning."

Rose looked in their direction and then back to the beautiful pirate. "I'd wager you're back on your ship in less than an hour."

"And what could you have to wager that I'd be interested in? If it's jewels or gold, I have more than I need."

"It's something more valuable to you: my silence." Angel stopped smiling. Rose fought the impulse to move further away from her and forced herself to look at Angel with as much insolence as she felt. "I doubt the earl of Hatfield would intentionally marry a pirate."

Angel glared at Rose with a look hot enough to make her sweat. "I could drown you like a new born kitten if I so choose, and yet you dare to threaten me?" Rose resisted cringing and unexpectedly won the pirate's admiration. "Well, I like you. I think you just might be plucky enough to anchor the rake."

Even with what she took as a compliment, Rose still heeded Trent's warning and kept a watchful eye on the pirate. Not for a moment would she let her guard down with this woman.

When Trent returned and read the dueling faces of the two women, he made up his mind then that there was no way he would risk having the both of them on his ship at the same time. He braced his legs against the roll of the deck and in carefully measured words addressed the two ladies.

"You know how I feel about women on my ship or any ship." His last words were delivered to Angel. She answered his opinion with a demure smile. Trent scowled at her patronizing expression. "I hope the earl of Hatfield knows what he's in for."

"Oh, he does, but I wonder if *you* know what awaits you." Trent looked quizzical.

Rose admired Angel's rebelliousness and applauded it with a smile.

Trent was disquieted by their comradeship. In a matter of minutes the two women seemed to have become allies. He'd known there was a reason he didn't want to leave them alone together. He sent a furious glance in Peach's direction. The seaman ducked his captain's look and returned his attention to the rope he was splicing.

Trent returned to the matter at hand. "I could hang you both for crimes at sea if it so pleased me."

Angel prodded his temper. "Well, do it, then, if it pleases you. We wouldn't want preferential treatment because we're women."

Rose grimaced, wishing Angel wouldn't have included her in the generous offering of their necks. She thought to remind Trent of a few particulars before he included her in the same breath with the pirate.

"Excuse me, if I may—"

"You may not," Trent shouted.

Rose bristled. He was certainly quick with his temper, but that wasn't going to deter her in the least from continuing with what she had to say. "I didn't have anything to do with Angel's crimes, and I've never heard that getting locked in the captain's cabin was a crime punishable by hanging. Unless, of course, you're blaming me for distracting you, thus giving the pirates the advantage of surprise. But that wasn't my fault either. If you remember, it was your own men who—"

"Peach!" Trent shouted. The pulsing veins in Trent's neck were telling. His voice cracked like a whip. He turned to Angel, whose lips had already parted. "Don't interrupt me while I'm feeling gracious. You're free to leave with your men—this time—as long as you promise to return to England and your betrothed without further mischief."

Peach was at Trent's heels, still holding one of the end rope he had been repairing. He realized his error when Rose's eyes widened at the rope in his hands.

Trent handed Angel her weapons and then whipped the pirate's hat from Rose's head and plopped it down over the pirate's eyes. "Gather up her men. Angel is returning to the *Black Orchid*."

"Aye, Captain."

"And see Rose below." Trent reached down and lifted Angel into his arms.

Peach drew a long breath when he saw Rose raise an eyebrow to that move. "Come wi' me quick, lass."

With Rose at the end of his arm, Peach communicated Trent's order to see the pirates off. "Dinna ye hear me, mon?" The men nodded. "Why is it the most intelligent mon are struck dume by a mere lassie?"

Rose didn't hear him. She was keeping her eyes on Trent helping Angel back to her ship. "And he asked me if I could swim!" she said. The two ships were still close together; clawing grapnels narrowed the distance to make hopping ships less perilous. Angel possessed the strong grace of a feline, effortlessly leaping to the *Black Orchid*.

"I wouldna take it to heart, lass. The captain's a good mon. He wouldna let ye swim. He dunna want any harm coming to ye."

"She has her own men to see to her safety."

"Aye, she does. I wouldna doubt they'd follow her through the flames of hell to meet the devil himself."

When Angel and her crew were once again aboard the *Black Orchid*, the ships pulled apart putting a black expanse of sea between them.

Without warning, a cannon belched loudly, sending a cloud of smoke up from the *Raven*.

"What was that?" Rose asked.

"The *Black Orchid* will have a limp in her walk just to assure she dunna come after the *Raven* again. The captain's not taking a chance she'll be sneaking up on us in the middle of the night ta do more mischief. I'd like ta see the mon who calms *that* storm," Peach added, throwing a glance back at Angel. He took Rose's arm. "Come on, we best get below before the captain gets back. We all have explaining ta do when he does."

Chapter 17

With the cat-o'-nine-tails clutched in his hand, Trent was a hard figure to ignore. His crew lined up in front of him, their faces grimly set. Hardly a man dared even breathe.

Most hadn't even known the *Raven* carried a whip until Trent had produced the thing right after returning from the *Black Orchid*. Paul wondered if the pirate, Angel, hadn't slipped it to him. Such an action would have been character-istic of her twisted sense of humor. His eyes shifted for a moment to the *Black Orchid*. The wench was probably having a hearty laugh at the rail.

"Women!" Paul whispered in quiet revolt. "It's all because of them."

"Aye," Paddy agreed. "We're between this one and that one." He nodded to the pirate ship.

"Something's come over the captain. He would have never let a wench—"

"Shh!"

Impatiently tapping the coiled leather in his hand, Trent glared at the two men until they felt his eyes on them. They ended their discourse at once and straightened to attention.

From their faces Trent could tell his crew honestly regretted their mutiny, but that fact still couldn't excuse the action. As captain, he was expected and obliged to deliver punishment for the crime even if the men thought they had had his best interests in mind. They had risked the *Raven* and all aboard with their good intentions. If the pirate who had attacked them had been someone other than Angel, the day could very well have ended differently. Instead of facing the lash they might be dead. From the depressed air about him Trent surmised agreement to his unspoken sentiments was unanimous.

"May the man who had the brilliant idea of imprisoning me in my cabin—and thus encouraged mutiny, promoted disorder and endangered this ship—step forward and stand the gaff for what he's done."

Following that order there was a very uncomfortable silence. All eyes were riveted on the lash. Trent wasn't really going to flay the skin off any one member of his crew, there wasn't a bad one in the lot. He was simply using the whip to successfully illustrate the severity of their crime. But that didn't mean a punishment wasn't due someone, and Trent meant to find out who the culprit was who had suggested his interment with Rose and then deal with him personally. As for the crew, they would begin to suffer the embarrassment of having been outwitted by Angel as soon as they sailed down the Thames, for Angel and her crew would likely reach London with the news before the *Raven* did.

Trent wasn't going to wait around all day for the guilty one to come clean. He knew it was going to take a deal of discussion and prompting before

212

someone was encouraged to step forward. "Very well, you have until the next bell. I'll be in my cabin if you should decide before then."

Now *that* was a puzzle if there ever was one. The same captain who wanted a hide to tan for locking him up with a fetching wench was voluntarily lengthening his sentence. The men had the good sense to hide their chagrin until he was below decks.

"What do you make of that?"

"I think he's gone loony, if you ask me."

Peach took offense at the disparaging remarks. "Whatever ye think he'll be wanting a mon below decks before the next watch. Now, who'll the brave mon be?"

All eyes converged on the Scot.

The window in Trent's cabin provided an almost panoramic view of a very wide expanse of sea. Rose felt her stomach flutter at the thought of all that water and nothing solid for miles around. However, the flip of her insides was more likely the result of watching Trent help Angel back to the *Black Orchid*. The pirate had wrapped her arms around his neck; it was a wonder Angel didn't pull him back over to the *Black Orchid* with her.

At long last, the sultry ship sailed away from the *Raven*. Its black sails hardly made a rustle in the gentle wind and soon blended into the darkening horizon; but even when she was almost out of sight, Rose couldn't keep her thoughts from returning to Angel.

Pirates! Trent was a pirate himself to dally with the likes of her. Angel didn't exactly appear to be the helpless type, and gentleman that he was, Trent just *had* to help her to her ship—yet he'd practically offered Rose a boost over the rail so she could swim back to London Town! How she had ever noticed anything in him that came close to being gentlemanly she'd never know. He dabbled in thievery, smuggled guns and associated himself with pirates. Her aunt was right, Trent *was* a scoundrel. It would be best if she listened to those more experienced and kept her distance.

Rose's pique was interrupted by a sound at the cabin door. She had done what she was told, put herself in Trent's cabin, and only because Peach had nearly pleaded. But she wasn't going to share it with that scoundrel any longer. If she could help it, she wasn't going to lay eyes on him for the rest of the voyage.

"Rose, open the door." Blast, it was him, the gentleman scoundrel, the knave of hearts. "Rose!" And impatient, if his shout was any indicator.

She thought that if she didn't answer he might go away, but the angry pounding attested that he wouldn't.

"I'm sorry, I'm indisposed at the moment," she answered with as much dignity as she could muster. She thought she heard a growl through the door.

"If you don't open this door now, Rose, I shall be disposed to break it down."

Given his temper, she believed he would, so reluctantly she snapped the bolt aside. She'd expected the scowl but hadn't thought her eyes would be greeted by what he had wrapped in his hand: a long length of rope.

He walked right past her and tossed the heavy coil onto his desk. Like her stomach, it landed with a thud. He meant to hang her after all. "What's that for?"

He looked at the coil, smiled wickedly and then picked it up. She had to ask and now she was probably going to get a demonstration. Why did she doubt he meant to hang clothes on it?

"This? Why this is a cat-o'-nine-tails—a lash, a whip, an instrument of discipline. It's used to scourge, flog, thrash and flay the skin off a man's back, and is most effective when used aboard ships to maintain order. Yet, in my lifetime at sea, I've only had to use it once. I'd almost forgotten where I'd put it," he said, running the tails through his fingers.

Rose wished he *had* forgotten where he'd placed it. Her worst thoughts were confirmed; this was no gentleman standing in front of her. He meant to whip someone for his bad day, if he hadn't already. And if he hadn't, then . . . She took a step back from him, her intention plain: she was going to run like hell if he took one more step towards her.

"Where are you going?"

"I thought you might want to be alone."

"You should have thought of that before putting a foot on the *Raven*. I was looking forward to an uneventful trip."

That was it. Now he blamed her for the pirate attack, or rather the embarrassment of being caught by a woman with his pants down, so to say. She was getting rather tired of all this blame, and the edge in her voice showed it. "It wasn't *my* doing Angel paid you a visit. It seems to me you rather enjoyed the reunion."

Her eyes moved to the whip. He let the coil slip through his hand and watched it slowly unwrap like a long, deadly snake.

215

"Enjoyed it! She could have sunk my ship!" His voice snapped like the crack of a whip, but Rose wasn't going to be intimidated—even if he was, at the moment, running the lashes through his hand.

"And I suppose that would have been my fault, too. And how can you think I'd believe that crock of nonsense?" she added indignantly. After all, she wasn't *that* naive. "She meant to *board* the *Raven*, not *sink* it. And for what reason? I'm wondering. Certainly not for your cargo. No, she certainly wasn't interested in anything way down in the hold. She intended to come straight here, which . . . Why are you locking that door?" Good God, he was going to whip her now, if not for almost sinking his ship then for her sassy mouth. And, she inferred from his tilted smile, he planned on enjoying it.

"If you take one more step . . ." He took more than a step. "Put a hand . . ." He put more than a hand on her—he wrapped the cat-o'-nine-tails right around her waist and flattened her against him. "Trent if—" His mouth was on her now, working its way up her shoulder.

"What was that last warning?" he asked between nibbles and kisses.

"If you should ever so much as look at that woman again, I'll sink your ship myself." After that admonishment, Rose began to sink herself right into his embrace.

She wrapped her arms around his neck. She should have resisted him—she meant to, she really did. If he hadn't kissed her quite like that, or held her quite so snugly, maybe she would have. Instead, she molded her body to his.

He kissed the top of her head.

"You mentioned Angel . . ."

"Must we talk about her?"

At the risk of completely annoying her, he did anyway. "You thought she might not be interested in the holds of my ship."

"I didn't think her type would have a particular interest in English bone china."

"China?"

She blinked innocently. "That *is* what you're carrying?"

Trent narrowed his eyes on her.

"Don't you know what's in your own hold?"

"Of course I know—crates of flintlocks," he said irritably, giving her backside a pinch. He then came more to the point. "I'd like to know how you know?"

"Because, your Angel told me. We had quite a talk." Rose wiggled to free herself, but his arms were like an iron casing around her.

"Is that so? What else did dear Angel tell you?"

"That pirating would be a whole lot safer. Trent, you're a gun smuggler! If you're caught, you'll be hung."

"I don't plan on getting caught."

"Angel says she's saved your hide on more than one occasion."

Trent laughed heartily. "She *would* say that. Fact is, I've done her the honor more times than I can remember."

Rose's cheeks flushed with jealousy. "You'd make quite a pair of bookends. Let me go."

Trent felt a smile start to show itself and knew that would top off her ire. "You're not jealous, are you?"

Rose was startled that he suspected she cared that much for him, and distressed that he had seen through her anger. "I'm certainly not," she said, slipping from his arms. "Why are you risking your life shipping contraband to a place so far away from home?"

Trent answered her seriously. "Others don't enjoy the same freedoms as we do. You pretty much do what you like." He grinned at her frown. "I'm investing in the spread of freedom. The success of the Greek resistance depends on help from the west. Some, like myself, carry the weapons of freedom to them. Others have enlisted in the Filiki Hetairia and are helping to organize and train small militias to battle the Ottoman Empire. A revolution is brewing that will return democracy to Greece, and there are those who want to be part of that history. It would be safer to sit in my parlor and debate the rights of Greece, but would it do Greece any good?"

Rose felt a little guilty, remembering her own praises for Greek freedom and then her initial feeling of disapproval when she found out that Trent was a gun smuggler. She felt a new admiration for Trent. He was doing something about freeing a people, and smuggling guns seemed safer than actually enlisting and doing the fighting.

There was a faint, almost timid knock on the door.

"Maybe that's Angel come to rescue me," Trent teased, gathering Rose up in his arms and covering her mouth with his.

There was silence outside the door, the intruder likely questioning his timing.

"It's me. Peach."

"What is it, Peach?"

There was a measurable span of silence this time when the seaman heard his captain's voice.

218

"Have you forgotten what you've come down here for?"

"No, sir," Peach answered his captain.

"Then am I to guess your reason for interrupting?"

"I've come for the lash, sir."

Trent straightened, his face somber. He'd almost forgotten. He let go of Rose and gathered the whip from where he had dropped it.

"What are you doing? You're not intending on using that?" Rose asked.

He gave her a sound warning before opening the door. "Don't interfere with ship's business, Rose." And then he confirmed her worst fear, "And I intend to use it."

Trent held the lash out to Peach, who looked at it as though it would bite him on its own.

"Well, take it."

"I wouldna be the one ta do the whipping, sir. It was I who locked ye in wi' the lass. It's me, the guilty one yer looking at."

"Hell and damnation, I never would have figured it. I'm not going to whip my own first mate."

"Thank God for that," Rose said.

Peach looked so relieved, Rose thought he was going to melt on the floor. But the relief was short-lived, for Trent's brows met in a frown.

"There'll have to be some sort of punishment. One just can't go locking up his captain whenever he gets . . ."

"Lecherous," Rose said, finishing his thought.

Trent's only admission that he heard her was a quick sideward glance that warned her to still her tongue. But Rose was enjoying Peach's dilemma too much not to participate. At the moment, she wasn't feeling very sympathetic towards Peach's plight. He hadn't helped *her* situation at all. "Perhaps he can start making amends by filling up this tub. I certainly could use a nice, deep bath while you're thinking of retribution."

Trent grinned. Rose had offered him a solution. It would take Peach more than an hour to carry pails of fresh water from the galley to his cabin. "You heard the lady. She wants a bath."

Chapter 18

Piraeus, Port of Athens

Ramos greeted Trent with a bear hug and a buss on each cheek that would have been cause enough to send any other man who tried the same sliding across the tavern's floor on his ass. Ramos's exuberance, thankfully, was something Trent only had to suffer on occasion—the occasion when the *Raven* sailed into Piraeus with contraband for the Filiki Hetairia. Not that Trent would risk insulting his friend—the peasant was half the size of Mount Olympus.

Despite Ramos's intimidating size, he was more heart than brawn, a fact conveyed by the full smile creasing the leathery skin around his eyes and by the light that danced in them. He sported a full beard as black as the woolly locks of hair that curled at his neck just above the collar of his muslin shirt. At their meeting, he carried no weapons that were visible. It wasn't often that he needed to, for not many were insane enough to cross the giant Greek, despite his generally complacent nature.

What would rile Ramos most and set him off was a Greek who obeyed the Ottoman soldiers who ran over his homeland. While it appeared to outsiders that he accepted the tyrants from the Ottoman Empire, Trent knew that those appearances were deceiving. Spokes were being put in the wheel of revolution, a wheel that was getting ready to roll over the occupied land of ancient democracy.

Ramos had captured Trent's sensitivity for a cause that had as its battle cry "Liberty or death!" For an American, there was not a nobler cause. Like other Europeans and Americans, Trent joined the Filiki Hetairia in secret ceremony. He became a klepht of the Peloponnese—half brigand, half patriot. He sailed the *Raven* to Piraeus, port of Athens, unloaded his disguised cargo, moved on to India, then back to London with a shipment of tea and silk. He made the trip twice a year, strengthening the Filiki Hetairia with each voyage.

While the *Raven* was being unloaded, Trent and Ramos watched from a table outside the tavern. The Greek's wary eyeing of the quay alerted Trent to a flash of silver light coming from the belt of an Ottoman soldier.

"There are only a few, but enough to cause trouble if they should start to question the contents of your cargo," Ramos said, keeping his eyes on the soldier now conversing with one of the crew. "And these days they have been doing a lot of questioning."

Trent leaned back in his chair. "Let them open them, they won't find anything. Only fine English china is being unloaded. You can come later tonight . . . for dinner." Trent and the patriot exchanged understanding smiles.

Even though Trent seemed to have reassured Ramos, he noted a tightness in the Greek's face. "You're causing a stir in Europe." Trent didn't mean Ramos personally but the Filiki Hetairia; the group had grown in numbers and was beginning to worry the neighboring powers. Their raids coming down from the rocky hills were increasing in frequency. From Ramos's sly smile, Trent knew the patriot had stepped up his own local campaign. But while the Filiki Hetairia had its strength in numbers, it lost that advantage in organization. In a hushed voice, he advised the patriot. "Stop being so damned individual and organize the Filiki Hetairia into one army. Then Prince Metternich and Czar Alexander will have to listen to you in earnest. The Czar, I've heard, has yet to be convinced your bantering with the Ottomans at the present time is in his best interest."

"Psh, leaders without backbone," Ramos spat with undisguised disgust. "There will be war, with or without the Holy Alliance." His eyes narrowed. "I hope you have brought me something that will echo the hills with our war cry."

It wasn't exactly the cry Trent or Ramos had in mind, but it was a cry that echoed against the hills and turned both their heads to the quay. Trent had leaped over the foot-tall wall of rock that fenced the front of the tavern and was halfway to the dock by the time Ramos had pushed back his seat. The panicky scream quickly drew a curious crowd.

*   *   *

Rose had jumped into the harbor. It had been the only way she could think of to distract the soldiers who were bent on opening the crates pulled up from the *Raven*'s hold, but she hadn't thought she'd sink to the bottom so fast and then nearly drown before someone pulled her out.

While she sputtered and thrashed below the surface, she vaguely remembered what had given her the courage to do such a foolhardy thing. She hadn't had to do much to convince herself that Trent's life would be in peril if the real contents of the crates were discovered by the Ottomans as the cargo was being unloaded in the light of day. She couldn't believe Trent had been so careless, no, so audacious, as to set the contraband right in front of them when he wouldn't even be there to see what was happening. He had left Peach to oversee the unloading while he dallied in a pub—to "relax after a harrowing voyage" was the way he'd put it.

She had watched the unloading from the rail. The sight of the soldiers poking around the crates and parcels being laid on the quay, and the soldiers obvious intent to pry off the lids of barrels, had made her worry about what they'd do to Trent if they were to find what was hidden behind the china. They'd likely shoot him or maybe hang him, but in either case he'd be dead as a stone.

She would never have considered jumping overboard had it not been for the harsh order given to split open the crates for inspection. Nothing short of shooting the soldier would have guaranteed distracting him from his harassment. She had checked the water that hugged the bow of the

224

Raven; it was clear as glass. How deep could it be if one could see rocks at the bottom? she'd asked herself. After having taken the plunge, Rose could answer that it was very deep.

Not knowing how to swim was a minor detail that didn't fit into Rose's plan, so she hadn't given it much thought until she'd felt herself break the water. Her scream on the way down had turned to a gurgle. Panic now took control of her limbs, and by sheer luck all the kicking and floundering of her legs and arms was what brought her back to the surface long enough to take a gulp of air before sinking again. Just when she thought one of the stones at the bottom of the harbor had her name on it, a hand gripped her arm and pulled her up to the surface.

Soon she was gasping for air and spitting out what she swore was half the sea and listening to the muffled voices hovering over her. From the sound of them, her near suicide had caused enough of a stir to make everyone within sight and earshot of the *Raven*'s berth forget about what lay on the quay. Relieved at that, she surrendered to a veil of unconsciousness that gently fell over her.

"I dunno why the lassie would get so close ta the rail, as afraid of the water she is. She gave us a bonnie good fright."

"I'd agree with you there, since not a one of you had the sense to jump in after her," Trent growled at the assemblage of curious soldiers and sailors who had not yet regained their color.

Ramos watched it all with his dark brown eyes. Trent, soaked as a sponge, was kneeling on the quay, holding the girl in his arms as carefully as if she were a half-drowned kitten, and directing his

225

unreasonable anger at all those around for not moving fast enough, when his crew had all they could do just to get out of his way. A helpless worry warred over the captain's face as he pounded the water from her lungs and checked her pallor. It was plain to Ramos that whoever the girl was, she had quite affected his old friend. She was very pretty; even drenched to the skin she was a fetching sight. The true test of how much she had affected Trent, however, would be known when Marguerite heard the *Raven* was in port.

"Who is this mermaid who has caused such a calamity?" Ramos asked with more than a little curiosity.

Trent lifted the limp bundle that was the reason for his distress and grunted. "She's more of a barnacle in my side than a mermaid."

Ramos grinned at Trent's back and then exploded into an unappreciated, hearty rumble of laughter. "I know just what you mean, old friend."

"No you don't," Trent tossed back, and then said for emphasis, "You really have no idea."

Trent watched the color return to Rose's cheeks and lips and felt relief rush out of him like a tide. What in God's name had possessed her to get so close to the side that she'd fall overboard in the calmest of weather? He couldn't wait to ask her, and it was a damned inconvenience she was still out cold. In the meantime he'd get some answers from his crew, if any of them had noticed her. It was his mistake not to lock her in his cabin—a mistake he wasn't going to repeat.

He dropped his bundle on his bed. Her hair was dark with water, lying in long slices over her

226

shoulders; her lashes spiked over her cheeks; the natural color of her lips beckoned. His imagination was led astray by the wet clothes that clung to every curve, detailing the fullness of her breasts and the tightness of her nipples under the damp cambric dress. It even clung to her legs, defining her figure from her hips to her ankles. Trent groaned and began to strip away the wet clothes, tossing them into a pile on the floor.

Rose opened her eyes to see Trent leaning over her, industriously buffing her skin to a rosy hue. She propped herself up on her elbows and turned a bright red to see that she was stark naked. She grabbed the end of the towel and pulled it up to her chin, but before she could fire a protest, he whipped the towel from her hand and tousled her hair up into it.

"Now that you're awake you can tell me what in God's name you were doing so close to the rail to risk falling over? Did someone run into you? I want his name."

Rose had no doubt from the way he roughened up her hair that he was annoyed with the latest calamity aboard the *Raven*. She hadn't had time to think of a good enough excuse as to why such a thing would happen. She couldn't very well tell him the real reason, that she was trying to distract the soldiers so they wouldn't find the guns, that she had been desperate to save his neck. But what exactly could she tell him? He knew she was afraid of getting anywhere near the rail. She thought of pretending she had lost her memory—then she wouldn't have to say another word. He might just believe that. Maybe she could say she'd bumped her head on a rock. But before she could say anything at all—he did.

"Don't think to tell me you don't know."

Rose was insulted at that accusation. How dare he accuse her of making up something, even if she *was* considering it. "Of course I know," she replied defensively. "No one ran into me. I slipped on the wet deck and went flying. The next thing I knew, I was in the water."

He smiled at her annoyance. Her explanation made sense enough. The deck could be as slippery as ice when wet, and with the slippers she wore . . . He noted her feet were bare. "Well, then that explains it. Be more careful when you take walks. You could have drowned. You're lucky you only lost your slippers."

Rose glanced down at her feet. "So I did," she said weakly, remembering she had had the grand idea of removing them before jumping ship. With luck, she'd find them before Trent did.

Trent reached to lift a strand of hair from her shoulder. "You look even more fetching wet."

He leaned his body into hers, pushing her back into the soft bed. Rose felt the coarseness of his shirt rub against her skin. His eyes met hers and chased away whatever chill remained. His lips warmed hers with a tender, loving kiss.

Right then Rose almost told him that she had fallen hopelessly in love with him. It seemed like the right time. She had almost gathered up enough courage to admit her love to him when a tap at the door interrupted the moment.

Trent tucked the quilted blanket under her chin and, satisfied every bit of her was covered except her face, opened the door.

As her luck would have it, Peach stood in the

doorway holding two completely dry slippers in his hand.

"I found these on the deck, Captain. I thought the lassie might be wanting them."

Trent looked over his shoulder at Rose, holding the slippers up for her to see. "Thank you, Peach. I'm sure Rose is just delighted you found her *dry* slippers up on the deck. Aren't you, Rose?"

Now *this* was going to be hard to explain. She couldn't very well tell him that she had taken off her slippers before jumping because she hadn't wanted to ruin them—that would be confessing to a lie. This was a fine kettle of fish, as Bones would say, only at the moment she was *in* the kettle *with* the fish. Rose sunk further under the blanket until she was nearly hidden. She heard the door shut, not so softly, and then felt the bed sink under his weight.

"There's no use hiding. I'm going to stay right here until you explain why these slippers were sitting pretty up on deck while you were floundering in the harbor."

"There's a good reason," she said from under the blanket.

"I'm up for a good tale." He pulled the blanket down. Rose sat up and looked at the slippers in his lap.

"When I went up for a stroll I noticed the deck was wet, so I removed my slippers. If they got wet, they'd be ruined, and since I don't have another pair, I didn't want them to get . . ." Trent frowned. "All right, I honestly don't see the point . . . really, Trent." Blast, he could see through anything that wasn't the truth. "I took them off before I jumped over the side. I didn't want them ru—"

"You jumped? You *jumped* into the water?"

"You don't have to repeat yourself, I can hear you perfectly fine. As I told you, I did it for a very good reason. The soldiers were going to open the crates. Then they would find the guns behind the china. I didn't want the soldiers to shoot you. It was the only way I could think of to distract them."

"By doing something stupid! You could have thought of something less dangerous. For God's sake, Rose, you can't swim!"

"It didn't seem important at the time. Actually I did think you'd be a little quicker with the rescue."

"Quicker! I had to jump a wall, run down a hill. I nearly broke my neck over a boulder, crashed through a dozen men who were frozen with panic, jumped into the water . . . Quicker! I wish you were thinking in less noble terms. You risked your pretty neck for nothing. There aren't any guns in those crates, only English china."

"But—"

"There was only china packed in those crates, Rosie dear, but thank you for your trouble just the same."

Rosie dear! He was deliberately being condescending. She folded her arms over her chest and glowered. "I hope you're very careful with this smuggling business, because next time I certainly will not lift a finger to help you."

She was doing it again. She was making him feel like a scoundrel. Her eyes were beginning to get glassy. As tough as she looked, he feared a waterfall of tears would spill from them at any moment. "I'm sorry." He couldn't believe his own ears. Was that him apologizing? Thank God, no one else was around to hear it. "I don't need a woman trying to save me every time a little difficulty arises. I can take care of myself," he said more gruffly.

Rose nodded and threw her arms around his neck. The tears he'd feared were coming did, right down his neck and over his shoulder. Damnation!

Chapter 19

"Turn around." By way of explanation, Madame Hortense motioned with her finger. Rose found the light French flavor of the dressmaker-madame's words charming, not an impediment to communication. Yet, Hortense made motions about everything, regardless of how many times in the past hour Rose had assured her she understood every word, except for the French ones Hortense threw in every now and then when English momentarily escaped her.

Rose also understood clearly that Hortense was more than a dressmaker. Trent described her as being a mother of sorts, since Hortense had six girls living with her whom she affectionately referred to as her daughters. Their names rolled off of her tongue: "Monique, Mary, Mona, Michelle, Monica and Marguerite. If Captain Jordan doesn't keep you too busy"—she winked, causing Rose to blush red—"come see them. They adore visitors from faraway places."

With interest, Rose noticed Trent's eyes leave the ledger he labored over, to look sharply at Hortense.

"Oui, I know, I babble so," she said quickly, and then added in her singsong voice, "Turn this way around." She turned Rose so her back was to Trent.

Hortense and her girls lived in a two-story whitewashed house overlooking the harbor. Its windows were dressed on either side with gray shutters, and sheer curtains blew in and out over the balconies, waving to arriving seamen. Often the girls leaned over the railings, watching the ships arrive and depart. Their flashy clothes, a contrast to the usual black garb worn by most women there, blazed like bright flowers against the bleached white building. Rose knew that half the crew of the *Raven* had already paid their respects to Hortense's daughters.

It was the seventh daughter's dress Hortense was altering to fit Rose's figure. As the story went, Marie, despite her many warnings, fell in love with a pirate. The girl sailed off with the rascal, leaving an empty bed in the house and many a disappointed seaman in her wake. From all the tucks Hortense made in the scarlet silk dress, Rose conjured a vision of a girl much more endowed than herself.

"What do you think?" Hortense asked, standing back to admire the fit.

Trent looked up skeptically. Rose looked hopeful. If she had to stand and turn one more time, she was going to tear the thing off, but the look on Trent's face suggested he might do the same. Trent's gaze went right to the decolletage.

"Can't you do something about the—collar?"

"What collar?" Hortense looked perplexed.

"Precisely. Can't you *add* a collar?"

Hortense understood, even if Trent didn't. He

234

wanted to save this one only for himself. "Well, some ribbons perhaps . . . here and here. I'll see what I can do."

"A lot of ribbons," Trent went on to insist. "Ramos will be dining with us tonight."

"Ah, I see." Hortense smiled at Rose. "Now, ma chère, you are finished. Within the hour, I bring your dress. And I will see about some slippers for you. Your own must be as wet as the rest of your clothes." Hortense folded the gown over her arm.

"She managed to keep her feet dry," Trent commented grimly, without looking up from his work.

Hortense looked to them both. Sensitive to whatever it was being shared between them, she refrained from asking the question she had ready and only wondered why the girl's clothes would be soaked and not her slippers.

As promised, an hour later Hortense returned with Rose's new gown and insisted on dressing her herself. "Voilà, Marie never looked so beautiful as this one, oui?"

Trent frowned slightly. Rose guessed he didn't approve of Hortense's halfhearted effort to conceal the cut of the bodice. It still dipped daringly low, with ribbons added more at the sleeves than where Trent thought they were needed. With a show of concern, Hortense yanked the front up and shrugged. "There was just so much I could do without ruining the lines of the dress."

Trent was firm in his answer. "Rose has a shawl. She can use it."

It was Rose's turn to frown. She certainly wasn't going to let this man tell her how she could dress. "I think it's lovely, thank you. If I get chilly, I can use my shawl."

Departing, Hortense predicted, "With that man's hot eyes on you, chilly is not what you'll be."

When they were alone again, Trent wrapped Rose in his arms. "She could have been referring to Ramos."

Rose looked up into his eyes. "I dare to differ. If anyone has hot eyes, it's you."

Trent pressed his mouth on hers in a long, lingering kiss. His hands gathered up the silk of her dress until they slipped under all the fabric. There he found the round softness of her derriere and pulled her hard against him.

Rose broke away from his kiss. "Hortense was right. It *is* warm in here."

"I'd say hot." His mouth buried kisses into the soft mounds of skin so abundantly available above the scant neckline; his tender affections inched it further off her shoulders so it fell nearly to her waist. He lifted her in his arms, his mouth not leaving hers, and brought her to his bed.

"Captain." At the moment, Peach's voice penetrating the door was not a welcome sound.

"Damnation, the man has a knack for timing," Trent complained. "What is it?"

"Ramos has arrived."

Trent groaned. "Show him to the dining room and tell him I'll be a few minutes."

"A few minutes?" Rose wondered at that.

Trent was already helping her off with her dress. "Ramos is a patient man." He smiled slyly.

More than a few minutes later, Trent stuffed Rose's shawl in her hand and led her to a luxuriously paneled dining room. Her eyes widened with surprise at the room she had thought was a mere broom closet. Cabinets built into one

236

wall sparkled with china and crystal. Ornate lanterns glowed against the walls, shedding a soft light over the mahogany paneling. The banquet table, large enough to seat eight, ran the length of the room. It was set with candles, silver, and gold-rimmed china. Their glasses were filled with wine, and a fare worthy of royalty was spread down the table on platters and in bowls. A panel of windows aglitter with reflected light lined the back wall.

Ramos rose from his chair when they entered the room, his head nearly grazing the low ceiling.

"Sorry to keep you waiting," Trent apologized. "May I present Rose Whitley."

"The mermaid who risked her life like a true patriot. Ramos Natairos, if you are ever in need," he smiled approvingly, ignoring the hard look of Trent's eyes as he pulled Rose away from him.

"You know how the deck gets when wet," Trent added.

"Slippery as a fish. I'd imagine," Ramos chuckled. When Rose sat so did Ramos, and without so much as taking one eye off her. His bold admiration had not gone unnoticed.

"If you're cold, Rose, don't hesitate to put on your shawl," Trent hinted. "After this afternoon, I wouldn't want you to catch a chill."

"Cold?" Ramos boomed. "It's hot as hades in here."

"I agree with . . ."

"Call me Ramos," the Greek said to Rose, his mouth already full of food.

Rose continued despite Trent's disapproving look. "Ramos. It *is* rather warm."

Trent bounded from his seat. All eyes followed him to the wall of windows. "Then let's get some air in here," he announced, pushing each one open.

Rose felt the sudden rush of a sea breeze sweep through the room, tickling the table candles into quivering lights. It was more air than they needed and probably would chill her bones and their dinner before they had a chance to sample their cook's diligent efforts.

She almost laughed aloud when Ramos beheld Trent with astonishment. He truly didn't know what was wrong with the captain, but shrugged it off and continued to devour everything on his plate. With the constant flow of cool air and the speed with which Ramos ate his meal, he was surely the only one who had enjoyed a hot supper. Trent ate diligently. Rose, however, too affected by how concerned Trent was that another man had found her interesting enough to allow his eyes to linger over her, merely stirred her food around on her plate.

She found herself smiling inside. Then the doubts returned. Of course he cared for her—he showed her that at least three times a day—but was he on the way to loving her? Of that she wasn't sure, and she wondered if she'd ever be sure of him before they returned to London.

"So," Ramos continued, looking right at Rose, "how is it you've become interested in Greek liberation?"

"Quite by accident," Trent remarked, looking up from his plate.

Rose ignored his silent warning. "I've enjoyed the freedoms my ancestors fought for. A king and a sultan are much the same as far as tyrants go."

"Yes," Ramos agreed, his voice muffled with food. "It is the American and French revolutions that inspire us to seek our freedom from Mahmud. Sadly, they are holding back their support of our small efforts to stop the march of the Ottoman army through our country. Every day I see more and more soldiers. If Czar Alexander and Prince Metternich would help us—"

"Then there would be a great war involving the Holy Alliance," Trent explained. "And the small clashes in the hills would explode into large battles, with Greek independence not being the only issue. Prince Metternich wishes to expand Austrian interests eastward, thus threatening the czar's interests in the region. Great Britain wants a strong Ottoman Empire; otherwise, the czar will become too strong. The czar does not want to see Austria or the Ottomans gaining any strength. No one wants to be the first to make a move and that is what Mahmud is banking on."

Ramos shook his fork in the air. "I will predict that in less than a year what Rigas Pheraios began in 1798 will come to be. All Balkan people will rise against Mahmud II and his empire, with or without the princes, kings and czars." Ramos leaned back and grinned. "We have those like Captain Jordan who have joined the Filiki Hetairia since its conception in Odessa. They are patriots of Greece. We have yet to induct a woman."

Trent cleared his throat. "Rose is rebellious for sure, but not interested."

Rose's eyes glittered in the candlelight. "I can answer for myself, thank you." She turned to Ramos, "I would be honored to be a patriot of Greece. As long as I am in Greece and I can be of help—"

"Thank you, dear lady, but please, no more

jumping into the sea." Ramos laughed heartily at Trent's grim face.

By dessert, Trent got his way. The damp breeze cooled Rose's skin enough for her to suffer his smug grin when she wrapped her shawl around her shoulders and knotted it over her bosom.

"Delicious," Ramos commented, smacking his lips. He happened to be looking at Rose when he said it, provoking a black look from Trent. He leaned back, his rotund stomach attesting to how much of the meal he had eaten.

"It's an improvement over biscuits and weevils." Rose teased the scowl from Trent's brow.

"Then fill up. It will very well be biscuits and weevils for the last leg of the trip," Trent advised.

"I'll save you the weevils, thank you."

Ramos watched their exchange with interest. "You will be going your usual route, no?" Ramos questioned Trent.

"The usual, to make the trip profitable and keep it above suspicion. The demand for silk and tea in England is ever growing."

Rose would have liked to stay for the after-supper conversation, but Ramos's stretching hinted he was getting fidgety waiting for something. She was given the impression her presence was delaying the reason for his being on the *Raven* that night. She suspected Ramos was Trent's contact and that he had something to do with the guns and ammunition the *Raven* carried. Far be it for her to hold up the exchange; in fact, she couldn't wait until it was over and done with, for only then could she breathe easy when the Ottoman soldiers passed the *Raven*.

When Rose stood up, the two men did likewise. "I hope you'll excuse me. I'm getting rather

240

sleepy." She smiled sweetly at the Greek, noticing how Trent tensed. "It was nice to have supper with you."

"It was all my honor. The captain has my envy to have such a beautiful mistress."

Rose drew a breath. His mistress! Of course she would appear to be just that. Hortense had assumed the same, but at least she had had the discretion not to mention it. They all knew she wasn't his wife; she shared his cabin and his bed, but somehow she never considered herself to be . . . that. She wasn't his mistress . . . she was . . . blast it all, she wasn't going to be just a mistress. She couldn't have looked more insulted than if he had just said she looked like his goat.

Ramos couldn't have been more confused by her consternation. "Are you all right? Did something not agree with you?" He looked to Trent for help but got merely a shrug; Trent didn't know what had put Rose into a tiff, either. Ramos tried unsuccessfully to take his foot from his mouth. "Perhaps it was the fish?"

Rose couldn't open her mouth to say a word lest she burst into tears or outrage. Not wanting to show a display of either one, she opted to rush out of the dining room in a flash of red silk, leaving two men totally confounded as to her sudden departure.

"Was it something I said?" Ramos asked, the concern on his face almost comical in contrast to his rough look.

"I think it might have been, but one never knows with women and none's confused me more than that one. We'd both be looking at the bottom of a bottle if we spent too much time dwelling on it."

Nonetheless, Ramos speculated on the reason. "She's spent too much time aboard the *Raven*. No doubt she needs a change. Come to my village when this is done, It will be our last celebration before the rocks begin to slide from under our feet. Take her to Athens—that will make her happy. And for you"—his eyes sparked—"Marguerite's been asking. You will see her?"

"No, I'm not staying in Piraeus long."

"Ah, not long, eh?" Ramos said thoughtfully. "Then let's get this business over with so we may begin to slaughter the lambs."

Chapter 20

It was poor timing that on the night the Filiki Hetairia chose to unload the shipment of guns and ammunition, the dock was lit by a full moon.

Ramos was right to be concerned with the unloading of the *Raven's* cargo. Mahmud II had sent more soldiers from Constantinople to smother the bands of revolutionists that seemed to grow by day in strength and number. The resistance, made of churchmen, peasants and chieftains, was successful in preventing the Ottoman invasion from gaining a strong foothold in Greece, but the Filiki Hetairia was only a fragmented army, and without unity the more experienced Ottomans would eventually take the golden country.

Mahmud worried that Czar Alexander would be encouraged by the fighting bands and come to Greece's aid, using this as encouragement to take Constantinople. Mahmud hoped the Holy Alliance would keep the czar in his own country until he could stop the Filiki Hetairia. The sultan knew shipments of guns were arriving from the west aboard ships sympathetic to Greece's freedom and so had ordered a concentration of soldiers at the ports and around the hills close by.

Hassan al-Hassan was one of those soldiers who had been sent to Piraeus with orders to keep watch on the ships that sailed in and out of the port. For weeks, crates and barrels were opened for inspection. Not one gun was found. But every day he heard fire from the hills around Piraeus. Somehow the Filiki Hetairia was being supplied.

Hassan began to think nothing was coming through the port. What smuggler would risk unloading his ship right under Mahmud's eyes? So he concentrated the bulk of his men on the inlets away from port, where a ship could anchor and send its tenders full of contraband to the beach. There, his men would overcome the brigands and confiscate their shipment before it made its way into the hills and into the hands of the resistance. Even with that strategy, Hassan was unsuccessful in catching the smugglers who seemed to slip by his guards and disappear into the hills.

When the *Raven* made port, Hassan's instincts sharpened. Its captain was friendly with the big Greek, Ramos, a man already on his list of suspects. All in Piraeus seemed to know Captain Jordan. The *Raven's* visits were made often enough for the captain to have made many friends. One friend in particular interested Hassan: Marguerite.

Hassan looked down from the second-floor window. The moon cast Piraeus in a pale light and turned the sea a color reminding him of polished gun metal. At the late hour, all was quiet aboard the ships. Too quiet, he thought.

Marguerite wove her arms around Hassan's sides. She wondered why he was so interested in what was happening *outside* her bedroom. Trying to bring his attention back to her, she brought her hands up over his chest. Marguerite liked the feel of the silk Hassan wore. He had promised her bolts of exotic fabrics from the markets of Constantinople. He promised cloth woven with threads of gold, rare oils for her skin, and trinkets of gold to wear on her arms and around her neck if she would help him. Marguerite followed Hassan's gaze down to the quay, where ships were black outlines against the silver sky. For a price, he had promised her the moon.

"Tell me again what you know of Captain Jordan," Hassan asked without acknowledging the impatient touch that ran over his chest.

Hortense had warned her daughters not to talk to the soldiers. If they jeopardized Greece in any way, they would not be welcome in her house, and Marguerite did not want to lose her home. Hortense told them all that if the soldiers wanted to they could sell them to sultans in Turkey. They would be nothing better than chickens in a henhouse scrambling around for one rooster. Hortense threatened to sell them to the soldiers first if they ever helped them. It was only the Filiki Hetairia that protected the women from that fate. Marguerite didn't relish the idea of having to share a man with a hundred different women and she did respect Hortense's threats. Marguerite laid her cheek against Hassan's cool shirt.

"Captain Jordan is American. He comes to Piraeus every six months."

"What does he bring?"

"Sometimes cotton, rum." Marguerite smiled, remembering. "And dresses, bonnets and perfume from France."

"Hmm, and this time china."

Marguerite slipped her fingers into the waistband of his breeches. "Why are you paying him so much attention? Don't you like Marguerite?" she pouted.

Hassan turned his back on the opened window and wrapped his arms around Marguerite. Her painted lips were pursed into a pout; her lush mane of fiery hair swirled in curls around her shoulders. "I like Marguerite very much. I would like to make you a wealthy woman. You don't always want to be working for Hortense, do you?"

Marguerite was greedy but cautious. She still did not want to do anything that would harm Trent, even though he had that woman aboard his ship.

Hassan knew people well and he knew women best of all. He could see through Marguerite's mask of innocence. Hassan knew she was raging with jealousy over the woman who had fallen into the harbor. Marguerite had no doubt seen the way Captain Jordan had run to her rescue. He would eventually convince her to tell him more about the American, even if it took half the night.

"He won't come to you," Hassan announced softly in her ear.

Marguerite pushed away from his chest and looked into his black eyes. For a second she knew she had let her guard down. She had given Hassan a glimpse at her feelings. "Who are you talking about?"

"The captain of the *Raven*. You have been waiting for him to come to you, but he is occupied with a new love. And he has brought her from America to dangle in front of your nose."

Marguerite had to get away from Hassan. His perception chilled her. Knowing she would return to him, Hassan let her go easily.

Marguerite felt his eyes follow her with the concentration of a predator as she paced at the foot of her bed. Why couldn't he get on with the reason why he was with her? He wanted her, not Trent. Marguerite stared into the candles set on her dressing table. Her eyes flickered and burned in the trembling light while she thought of all Hassan had told her. Trent holding the fair-haired woman in his arms on the quay simmered in her head. Why hadn't he come to see her? Trent always came to see her when he was in Piraeus.

As if reading Marguerite's thoughts, Hassan drove a knife into her feminine pride. "He won't come to you this time. He's with her aboard the *Raven*. In his cabin, most likely. Why would he go through all the trouble of leaving the comfort of his bed to walk up the stairs to your room?"

Hassan put his arms around her shoulders and felt her tremble. He felt her resolve to protect Captain Jordan begin to weaken. Lowering his lips to her shoulder, he brushed them lightly over her skin. He pushed Marguerite into the cluster of pillows scattered over her bed and lay next to her. His hand toyed with the lace trim at the sleeves of her blouse. "It is time to move on, wouldn't you say? What else does Captain Jordan bring to Greece?"

Trent and Ramos struggled with a crate packed with guns, bringing it up from the hold and resting it on the deck.

"Zeus, it's as bright as midafternoon out here,"

247

Ramos swore. "What I would not give for some cloud cover."

"Hortense promised to care for Hassan's men," Trent assured him.

"Ah, yes. And what of their leader, Hassan?"

"Hortense says he has an eye for Marguerite. She will keep him occupied—all night."

Ramos looked troubled. "Marguerite. You should have humored her a little and paid her a visit. You don't think she is going to notice you have ignored her existence? You are a man who knows how to live dangerously."

"She'll recover. My worry now is not Marguerite—it's getting the rest of this loaded before sunrise. Your men will be hard-pressed to hide twenty crates of guns and ammunition before the light of day."

"Then we had better hurry," Ramos said, lifting a smaller crate to his shoulder.

Trent's crew and Ramos's men moved in and out of the shadows, transporting their goods from the *Raven* down into a small fleet of dinghies. The crates were lowered over the stern and down into waiting hands. They were nestled into the bottom of boats and covered with mounds of heavy fishing nets. The patriots silently slid over the harbor, heading for shadows that would conceal them as they traveled the rock-laden shore. They would unload the contraband further down, far away from Piraeus, where others waited on the beach with wagons. Once loaded, the donkey carts would begin a perilous journey into the hills, where most of the weapons would be hidden in caves.

Rose was awakened by the scraping sound of crates being moved over the deck. She lay in Trent's bed, safe and comfortable, thinking of how he risked his life for the dream of a free Greece. She knew he would be furious if she set one foot out of his cabin. It was understood that she would stay below. Curiosity getting the best of her, Rose slipped out of bed. Her bare feet padded softly against the floor to the mullioned windows. Looking out, she was surprised to see a small boat easing away from the *Raven*. It had to belong to the resistance. If there were soldiers out tonight, they would see everything. Rose was torn between wanting to obey Trent and stay in the cabin and wanting to venture above—just to see how soon they'd be finished with their business. The sooner the forbidden cargo was unloaded, the sooner she could lay to rest her fear that something would go awry before the night's end. Once the guns were out of the *Raven's* hold and in the hands of the Filiki Hetairia, Trent would be safe and they could return to London.

With good intentions, Rose climbed back into bed and tried to settle comfortably beneath the pile of blankets. She wrapped them around her ears so as not to be tempted by the sounds of activity that kept calling her. At the sound of a loud crash and scrambling of feet, Rose flipped back the blankets and began to dress. Something was wrong. She wrapped her shawl around her shoulders and hurried up the stairs imagining the worst had happened. As soon as she was on deck, she saw the reason for the loud noise: a barrel had fallen and split, spilling pellets of lead all over the deck. Men were on their knees, hurrying to pick up the pieces before they rolled away.

Rose looked for Trent, and when she didn't see him she picked up a mop that had been thrown into a clutter of sacks and began to push the pellets into a pile. The crew appreciated her help, casting her an occasional smile as they scooped up ammunition in makeshift dustpans.

When Trent returned to check the disaster site, he found Rose sweeping and his men on their knees like plebeians before their queen. He came up behind Rose, grabbed her arm and pulled her down to the deck. Rose gasped in surprise.

"What are you doing up here? I thought I told you to stay below."

"I did, but I was concerned when I heard the crash. I only came up to see if everyone was all right."

"That's my job. Now, go back to the cabin."

Rose didn't care for his tone. In a harsh whisper she answered him, "You know, I'm getting tired of being ordered around. I can help here."

"Everyone on this ship has to listen to my orders, including you. Now, get below."

"Why won't you let me help?" Rose persisted.

"Because it's too dangerous."

"It's not any safer down there."

"Are you going to persist to argue?"

"Yes. I'm on board. I'm guilty by association. If anything happens I'll hang as sure as you will, so why not let me risk my life for something? I'd hate to be executed just for sitting on your bed."

"She's right, Trent. Let her finish here and keep watch. We don't have to spare a man to stand guard. She can keep her eye on Hortense's house." Ramos's voice came out of the shadows. Rose found him standing against a mast. Like most of his men, he was dressed in black from his neck to his boots. If it hadn't been for the moonlight reflected off his face and the belt buckle at his waist, Rose would not have seen him.

Trent sighed. Rose noticed it was a sound he made before he was about to let her have her way. She didn't dare look pleased but inwardly thanked the Greek for giving her a chance to do something for the Filiki Hetairia.

Trent admitted to himself that it wasn't a bad idea. No one was going to leave Hortense's house, and Rose would feel happy she was doing something to help them. He wouldn't have to worry about her because he knew she'd be hidden in one spot, keeping watch for the rest of the night.

Trent sounded reluctant. "Under one condition: that you obey your captain's orders just like any member of my crew." Rose nodded and let the beginning of a smile curve her lips. "Keep low and in the shadows while you are cleaning up this mess. When you're finished here, stand right over there and don't move from that spot. Keep your eyes sharp for any soldiers."

When Trent left Rose on her knees to sweep up the remaining lead pellets, he was sure she would be safe. Never would he have guessed that a soldier would stray from the arms of one of Hortense's daughters for a breath of fresh air.

Trent had failed to mention what she was to do if she spied a soldier. He only told her to keep watch. Rose stayed hidden and kept her eye on the man leaning in the doorway of the house. The light from inside shone behind him, making him look all the more dark and sinister. His gaze was on nothing in particular. He seemed just to be staring out to sea. Rose felt her body tense and her stomach become a tight knot in her center as she waited for the soldier to make a move. She hoped and prayed he would go back inside. Behind her she could hear oars fold into the water. The slapping sound was magnified by her rising fear that the soldier would hear the boats and the creaking of rope and pulley as the guns were lowered from the *Raven*. How much longer would it take? It seemed like time was standing still for the Filiki Hetairia. Rose glanced behind her. "Hurry," she whispered.

As Rose feared, something caught the soldier's attention. His relaxed stance became alert and now he looked out over the pier with interest. Rose could only imagine he saw what she saw: crates and barrels scraping the side of the *Raven* on the way down to the tenders, and the small boats sliding away on a moonlit path. She looked up at the sky and wished for a cloud to cover the revealing light that betrayed the secret unloading of weapons, and then turned her gaze back to the soldier, who now was taking steps toward the quay. He was getting closer, obviously wanting to better see what had caught his attention. Lord, what was she to do? Rose thought to run for Trent, but by then the soldier was almost upon them. Why hadn't Trent left her a way to signal him?

The man came so close Rose could no longer tell where he was, but a sense of impending danger grabbed her. Rose's heart leaped to her throat. Dear Lord, she thought, he going to board the *Raven*, Rose crouched down and gathered as much of her skirt in her lap as she could. There was no time to warn Trent. She couldn't let the soldier come aboard. He'd soon alert the rest of his group. She thought of what might happen then.

Rose's eyes searched the deck for some kind of weapon, anything she could use to detain the man. She couldn't let him sound an alarm. Every soldier would be running out of Hortense's house then. A wooden mallet lay on the deck a few yards from where she crouched. Rose crawled across the rough planking, scraping her knees raw. When her fingers curled around its handle, she felt helpless and more positive that maybe she could stop the soldier from discovering the exchange of weapons.

Rose moved to a position from which she hoped to surprise the intruder. She would hide behind the mast until he was slightly beyond her and then, if her petrified legs would move, she'd clobber him with the mallet.

Rose waited, hardly breathing, her blood pumping through her veins furiously. She was stiff with fright as she heard each footstep get progressively closer to where she stood. She closed her eyes and said a quick prayer. Now was not the time to fall apart, not when Trent's life and the lives of all the men aboard depended on her keeping her head. The soldier was so close now she could smell the rose scent of the woman he had been with. A few more steps and he would pass by her. He stopped, with the mast between them. Rose held her breath and waited for him to continue. The soldier watched and listened, his dark eyes scanning the shadows, and when he was satisfied it was safe to go on, he slowly stepped past Rose.

Rose was rooted to the spot. For the life of her, she couldn't move; she was paralyzed with fear. Her eyes riveted on a long sword that swung at his side with each step he made. What if she should miss? What if she didn't hit him hard enough? The soldier continued, slowly moving to where he would discover Trent. In another moment he would be too far for her to reach him without immediate discovery. At the last second, Rose

253

leaped at him and brought the mallet down on the back of his skull.

Rose stepped back and waited for him to fall, but he didn't. He had been moving forward, so she had merely grazed his head with the mallet. But before he could gather his senses, she lowered another blow to his head. This time he did fall. The soldier slumped to her feet.

Rose felt like she was going to collapse right next to him. Her knees began to quake so badly she had to run to keep from shaking apart. She ran right over the deck and kept going until she found Trent. Rose leaped into Trent's arms and clung to him for dear life. Immediately, without wasting time with questions a half-dozen men hurried around the ship.

Rose took comfort in the safety of Trent's arms. They were strong and warm with life. She didn't want him to ever let her go.

"Rose, what happened?"

Rose didn't think she could answer. Her mouth felt as though it was stuffed with cotton. Finally she whispered, "I killed him."

"Who?"

"The soldier who boarded the *Raven*."

"Just one?"

Rose looked up at him incredulously. "Isn't one enough!"

"Shh," he tried to calm her so he could make sense of her babble. "Were there others, Rose? I have to know if any other soldiers came aboard."

"Just him. He came from the house. I think he saw the tenders." Rose lifted her watery eyes to Trent. "We have to leave here, tonight, before the soldiers come."

"Did you see if he alerted the others?"

"No. He was the only one."

Trent's men returned in a thunder of footsteps. "There's only the one we found, Captain, and Rose took care of him. He won't be waking up till noon tomorrow, I'd expect." Paddy made the announcement with great bravado in his voice as he grinned at Rose.

"He's not dead. Oh, thank God."

"I'd say too bad. A dead man can't talk," Ramos said, coming up behind Paddy and the other men. A cold shiver shimmied up Rose's spine. "What shall we do with him?"

Trent smoothed his hand over Rose's back. "Paddy, take Rose to my cabin and pour her a glass of wine."

The back of Trent's shirt was twisted in Rose's fingers. From the looks of her, Paddy thought he would have to remove his captain's shirt to do as he was bid. Trent planted a reassuring kiss on Rose's forehead. "I won't be long, I promise."

"What are you going to do with him?"

"Well, that's for me to decide when I see what kind of damage you've done. I may have to put him out of his misery like a lame horse."

Rose looked up to Trent. "You're making light of this."

"No, but I can't do anything about the man until I see him. You know we can't let him go. He's seen a great deal and he could have all of us in irons by tomorrow. Now please, Rose, leave the rest to us."

Rose was too shaken to argue anymore. Trent was right—the man was a danger to them all. She had to trust that Trent would do what he thought was best to protect those on his ship and the Filiki Hetairia. She let Paddy take her below.

Trent groaned when he saw the soldier lying on the deck, his arms and legs now tied in case he came to.

"That was my reaction," Ramos said. "Your lady has downed Hassan al-Hassan. I thought Marguerite was entertaining him."

"Maybe he saw something from the window."

"Humph! I wouldn't be looking out windows if I was with Marguerite. I told you she was a dangerous one." Then Ramos laughed. "Isn't it funny that Rose was the one to spoil his evening? Now what do we do with him? If we kill him, there will be even more soldiers sent to Piraeus."

"And if we don't, he will make trouble for us. He did not get very far. How much could he have seen? Certainly not faces. He has no proof other than what he thinks he saw in the dark after a night of drinking—"

"I don't smell any drink on him. What are you saying?"

"That we don't kill him."

"Are you crazy!"

"We douse him with rum and send him back to Marguerite. She tells him he drank heavily and fell, hitting his head on her night table."

"Ahh, I see. I will take care of Marguerite, too. If she likes that lovely neck of hers, she will convince Hassan that he never left her room."

Chapter 21

The day was perfect for sailing. A bright sun broke over the horizon and spilled pieces of golden light into the harbor. Gulls screeched and soared high into a sky that could get no bluer; not a cloud interrupted its color. There was a playful breeze about, lifting the scarlet ruffle around the rim of Rose's parasol. It was enough of a current to get the *Raven* underway, but Trent insisted on waiting for a stronger wind.

If it wasn't for her vivid memories of last night's close brush with the Ottoman soldier, Rose would have been glad for the delay. Trent was going to show her the countryside on their way to Ramos's village. With the whisper of revolution in everyone's ear, and the uncertainty that the soldier would not return, Rose thought remaining in Piraeus longer than necessary was brazen and foolish.

Ramos was as much a tempter of fate as Trent. He insisted on giving his friend a send-off and had invited everyone he knew in Piraeus to celebrate last night's victory. Even Hortense and her daughters would be there.

Rose curiously looked up at the top windows of the white structure as she and Trent rattled alongside it in the borrowed donkey cart. At a closer look, the house was less of a villa than it had seemed from the *Raven's* berth. The window frames rested, perilously, on stones once cemented with mortar that had long since crumbled and fallen to the ground, leaving holes as big as a man's fist between the rock. The wooden rail of the stretch of balcony looked as though one strong gust of wind would rip it away. Contrasting with all the disrepair of the outside, fine lace curtains gently waved in and out of the open windows. So silent was the house; it seemed no one was about. Amused, Trent noticed her intent interest.

"The girls are sleeping. No doubt they had a late night."

Rose flushed and quickly looked away from the house. Trent offended her more by laughing aloud. Of *course* they wouldn't be up so early in the morning—She wasn't a dolt. She glared at Trent when he wasn't looking and then settled her eyes on the gray-black back of the donkey. It wasn't as if she didn't know by now that Hortense was more than a seamstress and that her daughters really weren't related. Just the same, Rose was curious as to what it looked like beyond the front door and windows. If the lace curtains and the luxuriousness of her scarlet dress was any clue, the inside of Madame Hortense's abode would have to look like a palace.

Thinking of Hortense made her sullen with the memory of Ramos's rude insinuation that she was Trent's mistress and the fact that Trent hadn't even disputed it. Certainly before he made any introductions, this would have to be cleared up.

258

She didn't know quite how to broach the subject with Trent but thought if she brooded long enough he was sure to notice. At least then she might be able to gather up the courage to mention it.

The donkey cart followed an ancient earth-and-stone road into the mostly sparse countryside. Interlacing mountains and the island-studded Aegean Sea basked in golden sunlight; flocks of sheep and goats grazed on the velvety pastures of the small plains, their bleating discord pairing with the tinkle of an occasional bell. Ground-hugging shrubs grew randomly between the rocks and cracks in the road; a wind-twisted tree surprised her every now and then; bright orange poppies and white anemones spattered the fields like confetti. It was a festive sight, crowned by the silver dome of a church winking from between distant hills, disclosing the location of Ramos's hamlet.

Trent would have been content to continue as tour guide if it wasn't for the stiff silence Rose carried like a cross. He'd thought she'd be thrilled with the prospect of leaving the *Raven*, but, then, he'd failed to notice she was still upset from Hassan's surprise visit. He had tried to no avail to convince her the danger was over. The cargo was now in the hands of the resistance and Hassan had survived the blow she'd landed on his head, having spent a peaceful night with Marguerite. Despite his assurances, Rose insisted on returning to London and had to be practically dragged from his cabin. Now she was annoyed she hadn't gotten her way and sat sullen beside him.

Trent tried to focus on the road ahead and could have managed to keep Rose from his thoughts if the soft sleeve of her dress didn't tease his arm every time either one of them moved; if the silk strands of her hair didn't brush against his cheek whenever the wind blew, if the scent of her didn't stand apart from the field flowers; alas, acute awareness was forced by the confines of the cart. Trent had all he could do not to pull her into his lap. He became so preoccupied with the thought of her firm sweet thigh pressed against his that it was a good thing the donkey knew where they were headed or they would have long ago driven off the rocky cliff.

The journey was uphill and the ride so bumpy Rose thought every bone in her body and every tooth in her mouth would soon be rattled loose. It was a relief when Trent tugged on the reins and brought the donkey to rest at the edge of a copse of cypress. Little did she know that it was even more of a relief for Trent to momentarily end the torturous ride.

He jumped from the cart and stretched out the stiffness in his back. "You can stay sitting there on your sore derriere if you'd like," he grouched. "We've got a ways to go before we reach the hamlet and I only stop once to rest the animal. There's enough privacy in the grove if you need it." And with that he walked off, leaving her to fend for herself.

His bluntness didn't put her in a better mood and neither did his lack of manners. He just reminded her that he was the same man who told her she could swim home. "See if I care if the Ottomans shoot you," she grumbled to herself, and taking him at his word, she climbed from the cart and, careful not to catch the fine material of her dress on anything, looked for a secluded spot among the olive trees.

Not far into the thicket, she stumbled across an array of white columns downed like trees in a forest. They lay at angles to each other, partially hidden by grass and partly marred by patches of moss. Remnants of a temple or promenade, they were sad echoes of a time lost in the past. Her hand ran over a column, her fingers settling in the vertical groves; it was cool and smooth with age. She was quite lost in the wonder of her discovery when she heard Trent calling her name. She hurried, making the best of nature's facilities, and was just straightening her skirt when she looked up and saw Trent standing by a column, his back to her.

"How long have you been there?"

"Not long." He grinned at her standing there with her hands still gripping her dress. "I thought you got lost."

To his surprise she was smiling. "You were worried?"

"No." Her frown returned. "I knew I'd find you. Let's go before Ramos eats all the food."

The hamlet of Ilithyia was tucked in a valley. Limestone buildings stood brightly against a background of terraced hills; the ranges of Parnes, Pentelicon and Hymettus rose behind them. They followed a narrow earth-and-stone road that ran down the center of the hamlet. Hens and goats scattered in front of the donkey cart, and women huddled like a flock of crows stopped to stare at the handsome couple in the cart. Rose felt uncomfortably out of place in her red silk dress and parasol, but she was sure to be made more comfortable when Hortense and her daughters arrived in their own bright finery.

"Perhaps I should have worn something more

261

sedate," she whispered to Trent. "Not that I had a wardrobe to choose from," she rambled, as was her habit when she felt edgy, "but my own dress would have certainly been less flashy than this scarlet dress of Maria's. Good God," she gasped, "if they think I'm one of Hortense's—"

"You look perfect," he assured.

When Ramos saw them, he left the men he was talking to and trotted over to the cart. It was too late now to discuss her introduction. She could only hope that Trent caught the idea that she did not want to be looked upon as one of Hortense's daughters and from that he should deduce she would frown upon being considered a mistress of any sort.

The Greek embraced Trent with his usual exuberance, a foreign show of affection between men that first startled and then amused Rose when she saw Trent's I-dare-you-to-make-a-comment look.

Trent helped Rose from the cart before Ramos had a chance to extend an offer.

"Welcome to my village," Ramos said, throwing his arm over the town, encompassing the white buildings, the silver-domed church and the terraced fields behind them.

"It's beautiful," Rose complimented, keeping an eye on Trent as he unhitched the donkey.

"It does well for us. Come, you will meet my family."

Now was her chance to speak on the subject of introductions—if she could keep up with his long strides. "Ramos," she said loud enough to slow his steps. She thought she'd start simply. "My name is Mary Rose Whitley—"

"Yes, I remember. Rose, like the flower."

"Yes, and I'm not . . ." He looked intent on understanding what she was saying. Lord, how was she going to say it with him hanging on her every word? "I'm not one of Hortense's daughters." There, he should get the idea without her actually having to say she wasn't Trent's mistress, or anyone's mistress for that matter. She was startled by a thunder of laughter.

"Of course, I know that. You came on the *Raven*, I remember. You are from London. You are the angel who came to our rescue."

Well that was a relief. He didn't mention that she was also Trent's mistress.

"You are Captain Jordan's woman."

He couldn't think that she was his wife. "Ramos, Captain Jordan hasn't asked me to be his . . . his . . ." She stumbled painfully through her explanation.

Ramos's eyes lit up with understanding. So, his old friend hadn't asked her to be his mistress yet. That explained why she had suddenly turned cold the night the three dined together. "No need to say more," he consoled her discreetly. "I understand completely."

"Thank goodness." Rose breathed a sigh of relief. The day was going to go better than planned.

The day was a disaster. Rose spent most of it surrounded by the womenfolk watching Trent huddled in with the men. It seemed they were to remain on separate ends of the town, having their own celebrations. Actually, the men were doing more of the celebrating while the women made sure there was plenty of food available. Rose didn't think she'd feel glad to see Hortense and her daughters arrive, but she was. They rode in on

263

donkeys, arriving in the village like a flock of exotic birds. Bright feathers adorned their bonnets, and parasols—each of a different color and each matching a dress of the same hue—shaded their faces. The women of the village hardly acknowledged their presence, but the men could almost be heard sucking in their breath at the sight of Hortense and her entourage. Instead of joining the other women, as Rose did, the ladies immediately mingled with the men, and to Rose's horror one boldly attached herself to Trent. Rose latched her eyes on the daughter in emerald green and gritted her teeth when the woman wrapped her arm around his.

Ramos noticed everything in his town, so it did not escape him that Rose was staring with deadly intent at Marguerite's familiarity with his friend, or that Trent flinched at her touch. It was natural for Marguerite to expect an affectionate squeeze—she hadn't seen Trent for six months. When he didn't provide one, she pressed on, running her hand right up the front of his shirt. Rose turned white and then red at that, then turned her back to the pair before she could see Trent firmly remove both of Marguerite's hands. It was getting interesting to watch, but seeing his friend caught between two women was not something Ramos could enjoy for long. But what could he do? He would not suggest Marguerite join the other women, for Rose, if the violent type, might cut her throat. And if Marguerite stayed standing next to Trent for much longer, she was apt to drag him away to the nearest room. But what business was it of his? Only a meddling fool would get caught up in something like this. He was a meddler but not a fool.

Marguerite was beautiful, from her flaming hair to her cool green eyes, but she wasn't Rose. When Marguerite's touch did less to his male sensitivities than what Rose could do with a mere look, Trent realized that Rose had inched her way under his skin. Marguerite would understand; she didn't expect faithfulness—just a good time. When he explained, she'd be disappointed but she'd bounce right back.

"Good to see you, Maggie."

"I couldn't wait to see you," she said, closing the slight space between them. "Six months is a long time. You know, I wouldn't mind leaving with you this time."

"You're getting right to the point."

"I don't want to wait any more. Take me back to London with you."

"You know Hortense wouldn't like that. Besides, I don't like getting attached."

"I haven't forgotten that, but I thought I'd try," she added brightly. Marguerite's eyes followed Trent's to the huddle of women opposite them.

"Who's the scarlet lady?"

Ramos thought it was time to meddle. "That's Rose. She's come on the *Raven*."

Marguerite looked sharply at Trent. "You're carrying passengers now? That would explain it." She watched Rose closely. "I doubt you could stay away from her for all that long, but I am surprised you haven't tired of her by now."

"Maggie . . ." Trent began, but she put her finger over his lips.

"I'll be here when you get . . . bored."

Marguerite exited with grace, leaving Trent grateful and Ramos eying her suspiciously.

"I don't trust her, friend. No woman takes

265

rejection that well," Ramos warned, following Marguerite's walk with his eyes.

"No, she knows the old Trent Jordan. I would have gone back to her."

"Well, when she learns about the new Trent Jordan, I hope you are back on the *Raven* and far away from her reach. She'll cut your heart out." Ramos's sharp eyes converged on Trent. "What is the new man going to do?"

"I'm going to ask Rose to marry me."

"Marry! Zeus, are you crazy? Why do such a thing when she would be happy to be your mistress?" Ramos could not believe what he was hearing. Being so closely confined with the same woman for so long at sea had addled Trent's brain. Ramos thought of a way to help his friend.

"I have it figured. Last night, she was not feeling good, not because of something she ate but because she was not your mistress and I thought she was. How could I have not seen it? Even today she made mention of it."

"She did?"

Ramos became animated, "Yes, yes! Ask her to be your mistress. It makes more sense, no?"

Trent thought a moment. Ramos was right; why marry when it wasn't necessary? His eyes found Rose. She was talking with Hortense and two of her daughters.

"And," Hortense continued, "the Turks had not a care in their heads other than my lovely daughters. They were so . . . busy, the revolution could have started and they wouldn't have known."

"Or cared," Michelle giggled.

"So, Trent and Ramos were able to unload the cargo quite safely," Rose said, wondering to herself why one soldier had wandered from Hortense's house.

"Without stirring a bit of suspicion. They were done with it before my daughters were," Hortense laughed. Then her face drooped with a serious thought. "I hope they didn't enjoy my girls too much. You know how they like to keep their women to themselves in those harems."

It was somewhat of a relief to Rose that the Ottomans had not had a clue that guns and ammunition were being unloaded right under them and that the daughter in green had been kept too busy to have anything to do with Trent. And according to Hortense, the soldiers would be battling the effects of too much wine to care much about what came into and went out of Piraeus, at least until they returned that night. And Trent was sure the soldier she clobbered would blame his aching head on overindulgence. Then why was a worry still nagging her? Rose stretched her neck to check on the whereabouts of the green silk. At least Trent was not near her.

Hortense caught Rose's interest. "Don't concern yourself with Marguerite. Al-Hassan will be waiting for her tonight."

Rose lifted her chin. "Even if he isn't, there wouldn't be a chance she'd step foot on the *Raven* . . . or that Trent would have a desire to see her."

Hortense was amused. Marguerite might not wait for the night. "It is hard for a man to resist Marguerite when she has herself set on him, and she has been waiting for your captain for six months."

"We'll see."

Rose thought nothing suspicious of the young

Greek who introduced himself to her when Hortense left to chat with a man who had been vying for her attention. She hadn't noticed his eyes had noted her with interest long before he had approached her or that Trent had already noted the boy's hope of turning conversation into something more.

Rose was delighted to talk with someone other than Hortense and her daughters. His English was limited, but she listened attentively while he talked of ancient Greece, of battles won and lost. There was no doubt that when it was time, a gun would be in his hand and he would fight to return his beloved land to its past glory as a country of democracy. He pointed to where Athens lay just beyond the hills and told her of how it glowed white in the moonlight.

Trent wasn't going to let the conversation take its course, not when the young man's face was painted with such hope. He approached them, his shadow falling over the flat stones in the road. Marguerite saw him too, observing that he seemed in too much of a hurry to join his scarlet lady. Ramos watched all three: Marguerite was distraught, Rose was smiling at the boy, and Trent was taking even longer strides to reach them.

Trent didn't give the boy time to object. He grabbed Rose by the arm and swept her away on her toes into the nearest building—the church.

"What are you doing?" Rose whispered her outrage in the cool darkness of the empty church.

"Can't you tell when you're being rescued?" Trent said lightly, amused at the rise of his jealousy over a mere seventeen-year-old boy.

Rose was not amused at his handling and shook out of his hold. "Rescued? I wasn't in any kind of danger. What's gotten into you? You nearly scared him half to death, coming up on him like a charging bull. All we were doing was talking."

"It's a start."

"Oh, good God, a start to what?"

"To more serious talk."

"Oh, I do understand now. Like the talk you and that . . . Hortense's daughter were having?"

"Marguerite? You would have rescued me from her," he teased, pulling her up against his chest and blessing her with a long, almost reverent kiss. "I want you with me, Rose, always."

It didn't take much coaxing for Rose to return his kiss. She melted into his arms and let him pull her down into the quiet and peace of the church pew. The scent of wax and incense annointed her hair and clothes. She looked up from the bench she lay on, over Trent's shoulder to the vaulted ceiling; heaven looked down on them—he wanted her for his own.

"I'll always be yours," Rose pledged softly.

"You'll have the best house in London," he promised. "And whatever you like—clothes, jewels . . ."

Rose pushed her hands against his chest and struggled out from under him. He couldn't have meant *she'd* have the best house; he must have meant to say *they'd* have the best house. He couldn't be asking her to be his *mistress;* he meant his *wife.*

Rose's reaction was not what he expected. She must have been overwhelmed by the good news—nothing his kisses couldn't fix. Instead of complying, Rose dodged his attempt.

"You'll be living with me?" Rose checked.

"Of course, when I'm in London. And with you

there, I intend on staying in London more often."

Rose felt her face warm and knew it must have rivaled the scarlet of her dress. She barely steadied her voice enough to ask her next question. "Are you asking me to be your mistress?"

Trent smiled. Rose hoped she was worrying for nothing and that he was going to tell her how silly she was to assume such a thing, but he didn't. Right there in a holy place he came right out with it.

No sooner had Trent clarified his offer than Rose jumped back from him. "How could you? And in a church, no less."

Trent was perplexed. Hadn't Ramos said it was exactly what she wanted to hear? "I thought . . . Where are you going?"

"Home," she flew back at him as she marched in red anger down the aisle and out of the church. "Even if I have to swim."

Chapter 22

Rose was enough to drive a man to his knees in prayer. It was a position in which Trent found himself after she fled the church. He found it hard to believe that he was kneeling there alone, feeling very much jilted by a woman he had just offered his life to. He propped his elbows on the back of a pew and rested his head against his folded hands while he thought about how he had gotten as far as asking Rose to be his mistress. Perhaps he should have prefaced his question with how much he had tortured himself before admitting he wanted their relationship to last longer than the voyage from London and back. Had she understood how big a step it was for him, maybe her response would have been different. Regardless, she was insulted by his proposal and was likely swimming home. Only she couldn't swim. Damnation, he'd have to chase after her before she did herself harm.

Rose was near drowning in tears when she fled past Hortense and her daughters. Marguerite's green eyes sharpened with interest and she made a move to investigate the church, but Hortense caught her arm and issued a reminder, "You're busy tonight. Leave him alone."

At the moment, Rose wouldn't have cared if Marguerite took Trent up on his offer. She was sorely tempted to tell her she could have him with her blessings, but despite her hurt she couldn't say it. Instead, she hurried past the women, scattered a flock of geese in her path and retreated from the hamlet. She didn't give a thought to where she was going, just that she needed to leave him and stew in some self-pity for a while. She couldn't help but think she'd come a long way for nothing—Trent hadn't fallen in love with her. Oh, he wanted her, she was sure of that, but he didn't want to marry her. Chloe was right, her Aunt Stephanie was right, and Philip: Trent would sail right out of her life, just as everyone she had ever cared about had.

Running and crying at the same time was draining. Too tired to go on, she rested against a boulder. Through the sparse planting of trees she could see bright shards of the Aegean Sea flashing like scattered pieces of mirror. It was quiet except for her sniffles. She took a lace-edged hankie from her sleeve and dried her face. It was time to pull herself together.

The last person she wanted to see was Trent. But she was not to be spared even that humiliation. She could smell the spicy scent he wore as he came up behind her. For him to come upon her so soon, the whole village must have pointed out the way she'd gone. That he cared enough to follow her didn't matter. She didn't turn around to look at him, either.

When Trent walked in front of her, she turned her back to him. She was not going to risk changing her mind about giving up on him by looking on his handsome face.

"Rose, I'm sorry I offended you but . . . Hell! What in tarnation am I apologizing for? Turn around, Rose." He grasped her shoulders in his hands and forced her to face him. "I complimented you . . . in my own way. I like being with you, that's all. I didn't think asking you to be my mistress would be so damn offensive. After all, it hasn't seemed to be disagreeable to you so far."

Rose removed his hands from her shoulders and stood up to face him. "It is disagreeable. I want you to get me passage on another ship back to London."

Trent stiffened. "You'll go back on the ship you came on or you can very well swim, and might I remind you what happened the last time you tried that?" He grabbed her arm and pulled her along with him.

He dragged her all the way back to the hamlet and, under curious stares, hitched the donkey to its cart and sat Rose in it. He left her just long enough to bid his farewells and then climbed up next to her and slapped the donkey to life with an olive branch. The cart rattled along, but not in the direction they had come. It irked Rose to talk to him, even if it meant asking a reasonable question, such as where they were going. She kept her stubborn reticence for a good mile before she broke her silence.

"Where are you going?"

"Same place you are, darling," he said without rancor or a hint of sarcasm.

Her own tone was not as agreeable. "And where am I going, if I may so ask?"

"You may ask but I'm not telling you. It's a surprise."

My, he was being annoyingly coy. She could just

imagine what he was planning. Another picnic? However charming he was, but it wasn't going to work this time. She had made up her mind that she was finished chasing the scoundrel, even if his hand on her knee shot shivers up her spine. She took the hand that moved to her thigh and ceremoniously removed it. He grinned over at her, not in the least discouraged.

Rose didn't have to wait much longer for the bumpy ride through the hills to end and Trent's surprise to reveal itself. Beyond the mountain pass, the remains of a city gleamed through cypress trees. Colossal blocks and fallen columns spread about them. An ancient stone road led to the toppled remains of Athens. It rose from the plain of Attica, cradled by the ranges of Parnes, Pentelicon and Hymettus. A fleeting purple light reflected off Mount Hymettus and cast the colors of sunset over the Acropolis.

Trent stopped the donkey cart to take time to quietly admire the white city. A soundless awe dropped between them. Here was where the child of civilization was given birth; here rested the reason for revolution.

They had taken the donkey cart as far as the strewn blocks of marble would allow, then walked the rest of the way through the crumbling passageway of the Propylaea. Trent held her hand as she stepped carefully around and over parts of the fallen city. There was no need for words. Rose watched him silently retreat to a time when Athens was the jewel of civilization. Through his eyes she saw how wonderful it must have been before man and weather had wreaked havoc on the glorious temples. Now they were the toppled shrines of an era of enlightenment and would have been forgotten had it not been for those, like Trent and Ramos's band of patriots, who fought to keep the flame alive.

Trent pointed to the crest of a hill. "Over there, above the city, stood a bronze of Athena Promachus, the goddess who led their battles. Her helmet and spear of gold could be seen by sailors rounding Cape Sounion. She was a beacon of light on moonlit nights."

As they walked further into the city, she listened, submerged in guilt over her long pout, while he shared the history of these holy places, describing them so well she could almost imagine how they looked in their day of glory.

"The temple of Erechtheum was built in the fifth century B.C. for Athena and her son, Erechtheus. On the right of it is the porch of maidens. Don't let all of this white deceive you, then it was painted brilliantly, at least that's the popular theory. And over there . . ."

Trent didn't have to point out the Parthenon, for Rose was already dumbstruck by its rows of massive columns. It dominated the Acropolis, a stark, white monument gleaming against the purple hills and deep blue sky. An anxious moon as round as a discus showed faintly behind the temple, reminding her the daylight hours were fading. No matter. Trent continued his narration seeming not to be concerned with what they'd do among the dark remains of the Acropolis. She was sure he had thought of it, and that made her wonder even while he talked.

"The Parthenon was built to honor the virginal Athena, the patron deity of Athens. It was lavished with sculptures, most of which have been removed by Lord Elgin. When we get back to London, I'll

275

show them to you."

His last comment was taken as a subtle clue that he still meant to have her as his mistress. "When we get back to London . . ." she started, but he was way ahead of her, climbing over blocks of marble ruins up to the steps of the Parthenon. When he was too far to hear another word, she had no choice but to follow him. Lifting up her impeding skirt, she hurried to make her point before the moment was lost.

"Trent," she found herself shouting at his back. "You'll have to take someone else to see Lord Elgin's treasures. Once we return, I don't want to continue as we have."

He was ignoring her, she was sure of it. With her echo thrown back from the hills, he had to have heard her twice. "Honestly," she mumbled, continuing ahead around the maze of marble and rock. She stubbed her toe at least once and tripped several times before she reached the foot of the temple. She lifted her skirt and looked down at her slippers.

"My slippers are ruined."

"I'll buy you a hundred more when we get to London. In every color you can think of." He stood at the entrance to the temple and looked down at her. He looked so sure of himself, his hand propped against a column, striking a pose that made her determination falter for a moment. A light breeze blew through his black hair and softly billowed his white shirt. He was handsome and everything she had always dreamed of right down to the knots of muscles in his calves. But she was sure of herself, too; she wasn't going to be his mistress and that was that.

"Your slippers may be ruined, but you have

lovely ankles," he teased.

She dropped her skirt, flattened her hands on her hips and glared up at him. "You're as thick as one of these marble blocks. I'm not going to be your mistress."

"Come up here, Rose. I want you to see the inside."

When she didn't move at his command, he came down to assist her up what remained of the marble steps.

"Did you hear what I said?" Rose asked him.

"I heard you," he said, unaffected by her repudiation. "Watch your step."

"Well, I'm glad we understand each other." Rose waited for a reply.

He pulled her inside and pointed up to the architrave above the columns. It was worth the climb. A continuous sculptured frieze encircled the cella. In awe, Rose admired the spirited movement of horsemen as they traveled through the ages. When she looked down again, her eyes met Trent's, and as determined as she was, it was impossible to turn them away from him.

"According to ancient writers, an immense ivory-and-gold statue of Athena stood in the cella," he said, inching his arm around her waist.

"How do you know all this?" Rose asked, squirming against his constricting hold. He wasn't making it easy for her to establish how serious she was about not seeing him again.

"I'm not risking my life for fortune, Rose."

Standing in the ruins of the Parthenon, surrounded by echoes of Athena's horsemen riding to defend her people, Rose felt very proud of him. She wanted her aunt to know that he wasn't the scoundrel she thought him to be. Even though he had asked her to be his mistress, he wasn't completely without morals. The lives of people were important to him. She wanted to throw her arms around his neck and kiss him. It was hard not to lose herself in the dark draw of his eyes, and it was nearly impossible not to answer the smile that captured his lips. Still, she managed to muster up enough sense to leave his arms and put some distance between them before she lost all of her resolve.

Surprisingly, he let her go, but she hadn't taken more than a few steps when he stopped her with three words spoken in barely a whisper. "I love you."

She couldn't take another breath; her heart didn't strike another beat. She stood as still as the columns that fenced them inside the Parthenon.

"I love you, Rose," he repeated in a husky voice that wrapped around her and warmed her from the inside out.

She smiled warily. He was making progress. He not only wanted her, he admitted to loving her, too. It didn't feel like she had imagined back in London when she'd made the wager with Philip. She hadn't imagined her heart would pound and her blood would rush hot in her veins, yet she kept from running into his arms. There was an agonizing pause. If he thought love made a difference, it didn't. She wasn't going to be his mistress.

She turned to face him and it was her downfall. Her words didn't sound convincing even to her own ears. "My father will be in London expecting a wedding, not the news that I've become your mistress. It won't do, Trent, no matter how much you relish your freedom."

His warm smile drew her in, closing the distance between them as much as the slow steps he took toward her. "I've come to know that my freedom would be a lonely state of affairs without you." He grinned his lopsided smile, which she was finding more and more endearing. "Strange things come to mind when one is on his knees. If you will not be my mistress, will you marry me, then?"

She was ready to say no—the word was on the tip of her tongue. She had bolstered herself up to accept that a marriage proposal was not forthcoming. Was she even sure she had heard correctly? She had been warned: Trent Jordan was not the type to marry.

"Haven't I done it right?" He kneeled before her and held her hand in his. "Mary Rose Whitley, will you do me the honor of becoming my bride?"

Rose felt her eyes fill with hot tears, and her throat suddenly got so tight it hurt. It was just what she wanted; what she had planned for and had vowed to refuse. She had brought him to his knees. "I'm not quite sure if you've done it right," she said in a voice mingled with happy sobs. "I think you should have asked Aunt Stephanie first."

"It's not her I want to marry."

Rose laughed at that. "Oh God, Trent, can you imagine?" Then her expression switched from amusement to worry. "She would swoon on the spot. Aunt Stephanie would never give her consent. I'm sorry to say, she doesn't like you much. But father . . . Oh, but he's so influenced by her. Yet, with a little—"

"Rose, are you going to keep me on my knees forever? This marble floor is not the softest . . .

Will you marry me?"

"Yes, yes, yes. Get up and—"

Rose didn't have to tell him to kiss her. Before she could take a breath for her next word, his lips sealed hers in a kiss that was impossible to return without wanting more. She didn't even think to object when his hands slid over the smooth silk of her gown, drawing her firmly against the long, hard length of his body. Right through the thin fabric she could feel his warm touch spread through her.

"Be careful," she mumbled between kisses when she felt his fingers begin to work at the long row of buttons. "Hortense would hate to have to sew them back on."

"As much as it will pain me, I'll try. After we're married you'll have to find another way to fasten your gowns or we'll have to employ someone just for sewing on buttons. I think I prefer the latter idea," he added with a devilish smile.

True to his word, he was so painstakingly careful it seemed to take him forever to undo each button. Goose bumps raced to the top of her head as, one by one, each silk-covered button fell away and the fabric parted, exposing her skin to a cool breath of night air. Through the soft, loving sounds of tender kisses touching her shoulders, she vaguely heard the quiet rustle of her gown falling to her feet in a red puddle.

Unnoticed by the lovers, dusk had fallen around them, throwing the Acropolis against a deep blue sky; a milky white moon spilled its light over the marble ruins. The darker the sky became, the brighter the Parthenon glowed in the grand splash of moonlight.

Still heady from his proposal, Rose leaned

against a pillar lest her shaky legs crumble beneath her. Trent stepped back to admire the vision cast in the pearly light of the full moon.

While his eyes brushed over every inch of her, Trent removed his shirt. This time, Rose did not turn away—she enjoyed the sight of him. With a long, languid look she traced every curve of every muscle in his arms and chest. He stepped out of the rest of his clothes, revealing to her downcast eyes just how much he desired her. She felt faint. Polyclitus could not have sculpted a more perfect male form. Trent was Apollo in the flesh: in the humid air, his black locks tightly curled over his head and neck; his arms and legs were lean muscle, warm with the passion flowing through his veins; his eyes were bright with life; his breath was warm and sweet.

Rose reached out and, with a light, teasing touch, moved her hands over his chest and down the tight length of his torso. When she paused, he took one hand in his and guided it further. With curiosity and daring, she wrapped her fingers around him and felt the blood of his heart rush and pulse through his veins. She moved her body between his legs and stroked the part that made him a man. A moan of pleasure coming up from his throat urged her to continue the sweet torture.

When he could stand no more, he pressed the full weight of his body against hers, bracing her between the cool column and his warm chest. He hurried kisses over her face and then settled on her lips in a long, captivating kiss that foretold the explosive passion inside him.

She felt his hands come around her hips and cup under her buttocks. With ease, he lifted her off the floor. While her hands rested on his shoulders, his

281

mouth trailed along the curve of her throat down to the soft rise of her breasts as they pillowed softly against his chest. He loosened his hold and let her slide down the length of him to finally meet his throbbing arousal.

Rose instinctively wrapped her legs around his waist and dropped her hips just low enough to allow him entry. Putting his hands under her thighs, he pushed the tip of his manhood between her legs. A carnal moan slowly rose from his throat as he slipped into her warm embrace. He filled the cavern inside her, joining them with the love they had pledged. Driven by the growing intensity of his longing, his quick and powerful thrusts brought them over the edge of fulfillment in a shared burst of euphoria that drained every ounce of their strength.

Rose's legs slid down over his hips, and her feet touched the cool marble floor as she slowly came down to earth. Trent crossed his arms around her back and rested his hands on her derriere. She laid her head on his chest; the chase was over. She had won his heart.

Chapter 23

Rose lay in Trent's lap, his arms wrapped around her to ward off the chill that lingered in the marble ruins. Her head rested against his chest.

"You make a comfortable bed," she said, turning her smile up to his face.

Trent pressed his lips against her forehead in a endearing kiss. "This marble column does not make a soft pillow," he said, shifting his weight to a more comfortable position.

"Are you complaining about the accommodations?" she teased. "Surely the view makes up for such trivial matters as soft mattresses. Look over there, where the stars seem to gather around the mountain peak like a crown. And look how the moonlight is trapped in the ruins, each piece of marble is glowing with light."

Trent nuzzled his face in her hair, inhaling her sweet fragrance. "The view cannot compare with the company. I know Ramos can find us a nice, soft bed at the village and it's still light enough to travel."

Rose didn't want to return to the village for fear the spell would be broken. For a while longer she wanted to marvel at the white city—beautiful, even though scattered about in pieces—and the mountains that tried to protect it from great odds. And for at least a few more hours she wanted to keep Trent all to herself.

Rose turned around in Trent's lap, kneeled astride his hips and wrapped her arms about his neck. Trent's hands spanned her waist. "Tell me again," Rose said for the tenth time that evening.

Trent smiled; it was coming easier now. "I love you."

"And?"

"And I will marry you, first chance I get."

Rose nearly strangled him with a hug.

The quiet night was spoiled by a whistle that flew past them. Trent ducked instinctively and, taking Rose by surprise, rolled with her to the floor of the Parthenon. More shots broke the silent night, sailing through the Acropolis from an unknown direction.

"What was that?" Rose whispered.

"Soldiers. Perhaps they know more about last night than we thought."

Rose ducked as another volley of gunfire sang through the Parthenon. "I knew we should have left right away."

"But then we wouldn't have shared the night here."

"We may end our lives here!"

Trent led Rose down the crumbled steps of the Parthenon. They ducked behind toppled pieces of columns as they made their way out of the lighted city and into the dark mountainside, getting as far away as they could from the exchange of gunfire between the resistance and the Turks. Rose expected to be hit every time she heard the snap of gunfire. Trent held her hand and led her through the low brush that sprouted from between the rocks. Once Trent felt they were far enough away from the skirmish, they stopped. Squatting behind a boulder, they looked down on the Acropolis. Trent evaluated their position while Rose watched the bright fire of gunshots light the night like fireflies. It was all they saw and heard.

"It's not safe to travel back to the village now. There may be soldiers on the road," Trent said, his eyes fixed on the ancient city. "There are lots of caves in the mountains. We might be able to find a good hiding place for the rest of the night and then get the wagon in the morning."

Rose gripped Trent's hand. She let him pull her through the dark, trusting his instinct to find them shelter from the fighting. She thought her dress was going to be torn to shreds by the branches that caught the delicate fabric. Her arms stung with scratches, and her feet were sore from climbing over rocks and stumbling into holes. They climbed higher, hoping they would find a cave before being discovered by the patroling Ottomans or the resistance, who posed just as much a threat in the dark. It was a worry to Trent and Rose that they could be shot by either side.

Rose stopped. "Trent, we have to rest. I'm so tired and sore. Right now I don't care if I am shot."

"Just a little while longer. It's quiet now, but that only means the two sides are sneaking around, looking for one another. In the dark we'll look like the enemy to either group."

Rose knew Trent was right. She forced herself to move along, even if it was at a limp. They didn't stop again until something alerted Trent. A slight sound of stones tumbling set their hearts to pounding. They each listened and strained to pick out the sound again. They searched the bushes but saw nothing.

"It must have been our own footsteps," Rose whispered, trying to convince herself they were alone, even though, like Trent, she sensed they were not.

They moved along, venturing into darker areas of the mountain. Soon, Trent whispered to Rose, "Keep close to me."

A wave of panic spread over Rose. What would they do? They had no weapons, they couldn't see and there was nowhere to hide. She reached for Trent's hand; it was filled with a rock.

Someone jumped at them from behind. Before Rose could finish her scream, a wide, calloused hand clamped over her mouth and her arms were secured behind her back by a man she could not see. She faced Trent and he too was taken. Another man held a shiny blade to his throat. Rose could see that a flintlock hung from his shoulder.

"Captain Jordan!" the man behind her exclaimed, when he recognized Trent. "What are you doing in the hills? We thought the *Raven* had already set sail." The knife still lay across Trent's throat. The patriot addressed his companion in Greek. "Let him go, Nicholas. He is with us."

Although Trent was released, Rose was still held by the man. She wiggled against his hold. "If she screams, she will bring the Turks," he said to Trent.

"She won't. You can let her go." Trent's hand smoothed over his throat.

"I'm sorry if Nicholas cut you."

"Just checking."

"Why are you in the hills?"

Rose joined Trent. He put his arm around her. "It began as a romantic evening, but I'm afraid your skirmish has rudely put an end to it. We didn't wish to get caught in the crossfire so were trying to find a safe place to stay for the night."

"Yes, the roads are not good now. A wagon of guns from your ship has been discovered. The poor peasant was killed trying to take them further north. It would be better to wait out the night. We will take you to a cave. It is an old tomb, long abandoned, but few know where it is."

Rose and Trent were escorted to the tomb by the resistance fighters. Its opening was overgrown with shrubs and partly obstructed by various-sized rocks that had tumbled down the mountain. They thanked the men, climbed over the rocks and ventured into the dark cave. Rose listened as brush was moved behind them to cover the cave's entrance.

It was so dark in the cave that Rose didn't dare let go of Trent's hand as they made their way by feel. Several times she stumbled over the debris that littered the floor of the cave. Something gave way under her foot. A snap and a crack echoed in the tomb. "What was that?" she asked, slightly alarmed.

"Probably a stick. Be careful, there's a pile of rocks here," Trent cautioned.

Rose imagined all kinds of animals that were hiding in the dark. "Trent," her voice was barely a whisper. "Do you think there are bears in here?"

"There aren't any bears. Bats, but not bears."

Rose listened to the deadly silence after they settled on what felt like a stone bench. Even though it was dark as could be, Rose felt better closing her eyes. There was something disturbing about not being able to see the hand in front of her with her eyes wide open.

The smell of the cave was stale. Odors she couldn't identify lingered on the air, none of them pleasant. She was imagining rats of tremendous size scurrying about when she heard a soft rustling sound. Ghosts were also in her thoughts. She definitely didn't like hiding in a tomb.

"Trent?"

"Yes, Rose."

"Do you think we could make a fire?"

"It's too risky. Just try to sleep, and before you know it, it'll be morning."

"That man said this cave was an old tomb. Do you think there are still . . . Lord, Trent I don't even want to think of it! Maybe not being able to see anything is a blessing."

Trent wrapped both his arms around her and pulled her back to his chest. "Don't worry anymore. These people have been dead for a long time."

"Oh, God," Rose wailed. "This is not what I'd call romantic. I can only imagine what I can't see! I don't hear anymore gunfire. Perhaps the fighting has stopped."

"It'll be safer to travel in the morning."

"Hold me tight, Trent."

Trent held Rose tightly until he felt her muscles relax and her breathing become shallow. He leaned his head against hers and fell asleep.

Waking before Rose, Trent eased her slowly out of his arms. By feel, he found his way to the opening of the cave and pushed aside the brush that concealed its entrance. A faint light penetrated a few feet into the tomb. He stepped out of the cave to check the area. His eyes scanned the mountains that were now backlighted by the rosy blush of dawn. He could see the Acropolis below. The city was quiet. One of a hundred such clashes between the encroaching Turks and the peasants had ended. But this one, however small it was, could implicate him in the distribution of guns. A man had been killed, and a wagon smuggling guns had been discovered. He knew the penalty for helping the resistance: death. It had been foolish to risk all of their lives by delaying the *Raven's* departure. Since Rose had been with him, he had not been able to think rationally. She was turning him into mush!

A shrill scream echoed in the cave, sending Trent running to see what was wrong. His heart leaped into his throat when he thought of Rose in danger. Trent stopped several feet in front of Rose and was amazed at what he saw. Even though he knew the cave was a tomb, he wasn't prepared for the sight before him. Now that morning light had entered the cave, its other occupants were clearly visible. Scattered about the floor in haphazard arrangements were ribs and skulls, long leg bones, vertebrae, and the smaller bones of broken hands and feet. There were shattered urns swept in the corners, and pieces of cloth that still clung to some skeletal remains. The condition of the tomb told that grave robbers had searched for riches without care to the bones of the dead.

"I thought it was sticks and stones I was tripping over last night," Rose screeched. After she had regained some composure, she stepped carefully but quickly over the remains. "And to think we spent the night in here!" Rose shivered at the thought. She looked at Trent accusingly. "Where were you? Can you imagine what it was like to wake up to that sight?"

Trent couldn't help but grin, and then he laughed thinking of it. Rose glared at him. "It's not funny. I'll face a whole army of Turks before I step in *that* cave again," she declared, marching past him.

Trent followed Rose down the side of the mountain. "I'm sorry I laughed," he chuckled. "Rose, slow down before you fall. It's not anything to get huffy about. I didn't know there'd be skeletons in there."

"You knew when they said it was a tomb. I knew! And you left me in there alone."

"Rose, I only just stepped outside for a little while. It was still pretty dark in the cave. I didn't see the skeletons. Besides, you were asleep. I didn't want to wake you. We may have to walk back to the village if our wagon is gone."

"Well, that's just wonderful news. I wish I'd known what business you were in before setting foot on your ship."

Trent had finally caught up with Rose and grabbed her arm. "Now, you don't really mean that." He pulled her to him. For the moment she was silent. "You would have chased me anyway."

Rose stubbornly refused to admit he was right, but when she returned his smile, he knew. "All right, yes. I wanted to know why you left me so suddenly, without a word of goodbye or an explanation of any kind. I thought we shared something special and I couldn't understand why you would leave like that. But I think I know now," she said with a glimmer of light in her eyes.

Trent's brow rose. "Why?"

Rose slipped away from him and continued down the hill. She wasn't going to be the one to tell him he had felt something special, too, and was running away from it. Her voice sailed back at him and there was definitely a smile in it. "I think you'll have to discover that on your own."

They found their donkey right where they'd left him; he was grazing on the grass sprouting up around a block of marble. Rose was thankful they wouldn't have to walk all the way back to the village. Her feet were blistered from climbing all over the mountain in nothing but a pair of thin-soled slippers. She was also starved, and the sooner they got to the village, the sooner she'd have something with which to fill her rumbling stomach. She hoped and prayed that they wouldn't meet up with any soldiers along the way and breathed a great sigh of relief when she saw the silver dome of the church peek up from behind the hillside.

Ramos greeted them, relief beaming on his face. "Thank the stars you're safe. We heard shooting last night and thought . . . Well, here you are, without a scratch. You must be hungry."

"Oh, Ramos, bless you. But I could use more than food. I need somewhere to wash up," Rose exclaimed.

"Of course. What first?"

"I definitely could eat first."

After filling her stomach with bread, fruit, cheese and wine, Rose followed one of the women to a small rocky inlet. The woman held a basket of clothes on her head, obviously taking them to be washed.

Following a rock-strewn path, Rose gingerly stepped down to the beach. Her feet did not tread over soft sand but were pained by thousands of pebbles. Several women were washing clothes, standing knee-deep in the aqua water. Larger rocks at the washing site served as places to spread out the clothing to dry, and smaller ones set in the shallow water made convenient washboards. The women, all in black, reminded Rose of a flock of ravens gathered at the water's edge. They glanced at her without much interest and then went back to their work.

Rose abandoned all modesty and stripped down to her skin. She limped over the stony ground and submerged herself in the warm water of the Aegean Sea. In front of her the sea stretched as far as her eyes could see, rocky islands dotted by gulls looking as though they had been thrown into it by some giant hand. It reminded her of the legend Trent had told her. "It is said that when God created the world, He sifted the earth through a strainer, making one good country after another. When he was done, the rocks fell out, making Greece." Looking out at the rock-strewn sea and then behind her, where the land rose in jagged limestone cliffs, Rose could almost believe that.

Rose basked in gentle golden sunlight, listening to the women chatter as they worked and to the water lapping around the rocks. When she was clean, rested and dry, she dressed and made the steep climb up to the village.

There was a spring in Rose's step when she returned to the village. Thinking of Trent as she walked, she smiled and hummed to herself. Her jolly mood instantly dissipated when she saw Marguerite leaning against the donkey cart and smiling at Trent. Though she told herself Trent couldn't help it if the woman wanted to talk to him, she felt a biting surge of jealousy sting her tolerance.

Hortense saw Rose coming and stepped in her path. "Rose, how refreshed you look."

Rose didn't feel like making idle chatter when Marguerite was so close to Trent. "Yes, the water felt wonderful."

A knowing gleam sparked the madame's eye. "Captain Jordan showed you the Acropolis last night. It must have been very romantic."

"It was." Rose couldn't keep her eyes from returning to Marguerite.

"Well, it will be one of those memories to think about when Captain Jordan's affections cool."

"What do you mean?"

"You can't expect him to always desire you the way he may now. Men are restless creatures. My business depends on that."

Rose felt her blood boil at the madame's insinuations. "Trent is not like that. Last night he asked me to marry him."

Surprise flashed on Hortense's face. "Really?" Both women looked over to Trent and Marguerite. Hortense was skeptical. "He may want you to be his wife, out of a need to own you, but that doesn't mean he will give up women like Marguerite."

"As long as Trent is my husband, he will not have any desire for another woman—I'll see to that myself!"

"You're not married yet," Hortense reminded her. "We'll see just how serious Trent Jordan is about marriage."

Rose stamped off, leaving Hortense grinning with amusement.

Chapter 24

"The church is yours." Hortense's arm made a generous arch over the front of the white building. Rose's eyes followed her hand up to the shiny silver dome, then gazed over to Trent's face and measured his reaction. She thought he had turned a shade paler at the immediate offer, but it could have been the sudden wash of light sweeping over them as the clouds moved away from the sun. Just the same, he didn't jump at the suggestion. Rose felt her heart sink to the pit of her stomach. Could Hortense be right? Was he having doubts already?

"Everyone is here," Ramos added with an unenthusiastic shrug, "and there is still food for the celebration." And then, as though the gist of the conversation just hit him, "Zeus, I cannot believe it. Trent Jordan to become a married man. It is dangerous to visit the Parthenon on a night when there is a full moon. Athena must have put you under a spell." He announced his superstition so seriously that Hortense laughed.

"Well, what will it be? My daughters will make lovely bridesmaids, don't you agree, Rose?"

Rose could just imagine it; the five daughters—

Monique, Mary, Mona, Michelle and Monica—trailing behind her like the vibrant tail of a peacock. Marguerite, of course, would make a splendid maid-of-honor. And the bride herself—ravishing in scarlet. It would certainly be a wedding to tell her grandchildren about—if there *was* a wedding.

Trent clasped his hands behind his back and quickly glanced at Rose. The offer had taken him by surprise. He still hadn't gotten used to the idea of becoming a married man, and he had to admit that the thought of taking the actual step was somewhat frightening. Rose noted Trent's pained expression while he thought over his reply.

"It wouldn't be proper. I haven't asked Rose's aunt permission for her hand. We couldn't possibly be wed before then." Trent chuckled, "I wouldn't want to start off on the wrong foot—the woman's a dragon. We appreciate the offer of the church, but we couldn't think of offending my future family in England. Isn't that right, Rose?"

Rose was thinking so hard she frowned. Since when did Trent worry about propriety and what other people thought? As far as she was concerned, accepting the idea would have solved the problem of her aunt refusing his offer of marriage. She had spent the ride back to the hamlet trying to figure out a way to convince her aunt to let her marry Trent. It seemed that Hortense had the best solution. If they arrived married, there was little her aunt could do about it.

"Rose?" Trent was looking for her agreement.

The three of them were looking at her. "Yes, of course, you're right. It wouldn't be proper to marry without permission," she agreed rather downheartedly. It wouldn't really have been proper to marry without talking to her aunt first, especially considering how she was planning on orchestrating the grand day; but Trent could have at least considered Hortense's idea.

"There you have it in a nutshell." Trent concurred too quickly for Rose's comfort and in such a tone that she dared not disagree.

Rose was afraid disappointment showed too plainly on her face, judging from the way Hortense looked at her. She forced a weak smile to her lips.

"Well then," Ramos said, turning his attention to Trent, "you'll want to be leaving as soon as possible. Hortense and her daughters are ready." Four pairs of eyes looked over to the flamboyant women perched in their wagons with their parasols opened over their heads like bright flowers. The ladies returned their gaze with smiles.

"Pardon us," Ramos said suddenly, hurrying Trent away from them. Rose excused him with a nod. Hortense smiled as though she knew exactly what was in the Greek's head.

It was obvious to Rose that he wanted to talk to Trent alone, either to offer his advice on the affairs of the heart or to discuss some further business with the Filiki Hetairia. Rose didn't like the prospect of either topic. Ramos's glance back at her gave her a clue: it wasn't the freedom of Greece they were discussing, it was a single man's freedom he was trying to save.

"Zeus, what happened?" Ramos asked in a loud whisper. "We discuss a mistress and you propose marriage? Obviously you had a weak moment. It's understandable: the moon, the Parthenon, a beautiful woman—a dangerous concoction to be sure; any man would succumb to it. However, I offer you my help. There may be a way around this without losing the lady. If she sees you as a rebel, a smuggler, a—"

Trent grinned at his friend's upset. "A scoundrel."

"Precisely. And what woman would want someone like that to be the father of her babies?"

"Mary Rose Whitley would. I intend on marrying her and doing it up proper."

"But you don't need to." Ramos was frantic to save his friend from a fate worse than death. "Married, she'll enslave you."

Trent tightened the donkey's hitch. "On the contrary, friend, if I don't marry her, I'll be a slave to her for sure. I would not sleep, eat or breathe for want of her."

Ramos threw up his arms in despair. "Zeus, you've become a poet. I should have warned you about the moonlight in Athens." He leveled his dark eyes on his friend. "Then why don't you marry the girl today if you're so smitten?"

"Her aunt would be convinced I married her godchild out of spite, not love, and her father will be in London intent on seeing his daughter's wedding. I wouldn't want to disappoint my future father-in-law. There you have it . . ."

". . . neatly wrapped in a grape leaf. Be warned: our best laid plans are the ones that go awry." Ramos wrapped his arms around his friend in a warm, backslapping embrace, but this time, instead of suffering through the show of affection, Trent hugged back with ease.

Holding Rose's arm in hers, Hortense proposed her own helpful words of advice. She had seen men come and go without a care for the feelings of the women they left behind. Her girls knew better

298

than to attach their heartstrings to a wanderlust like Trent, and when they did she did her best to sever those strings. Her only loss was Marie. Like Marie, poor Rose, blinded by love, had also chosen the wrong man to fall in love with. Hortense took it upon herself to ease the blow that would inevitably come down on the girl. She put her arm around Rose's shoulders.

"Ma petite, you think you are so in love with this man. Yet he is like so many ships that have sailed in and out of the harbor: you know he will always leave, but you hope he will not. Trent has sailed out of many harbors in his lifetime."

Rose slipped her arm from the well-meaning madame. "Maybe he's decided to weigh anchor."

"Not for more than a minute. Your word 'maybe' says you are not so sure yourself. If he wanted to marry you, he would have, right here, today. He would not wait to ask for permission."

Rose had a sinking feeling Hortense was right. Trent hadn't looked pleased with her suggestion to make the commitment right then. Perhaps he did want to reconsider.

"He said he loved me." She made a weak attempt at trying to convince herself he really meant those words.

"A romantic moment can do that. A man and a woman, alone together in the moonlight. Of course he would say he loved you."

"Of course," Rose agreed faintly. She glanced over her shoulder at Trent. He was intently packing their wagon, obviously more determined to return to London than to waste time in the church. She was such a fool to believe him. Hortense was right: if he intended to marry her at all, he would have done so right then. Trent would have wanted to stand her in front of her aunt as his wife, not battle the stubborn woman for her hand. There was much she had to learn about men. Hortense had been polite to spare her feelings. Hortense hadn't told her outright that Trent had said he loved her just because he wanted her. Rose had been too stricken by the moonlight to see the difference between loving and wanting.

"I don't mean to make you sad," Hortense continued, "just make you wise. Look how Marguerite still smiles. Had she taken Trent seriously, she would have been devastated by your arrival in Piraeus."

Rose's eyes widened. "You mean Trent told her he loved her, too?"

Hortense shrugged and patted Rose's hand. "Men are like that. Don't be too trusting."

"I certainly intend to be more wary, now that I understand what drives him." Rose looked to Trent and felt her head instantly pound. She was not generally prone to headaches, but the man smiling back at her had suddenly brought the worst one on.

Trent wrapped his hands around Rose's waist and lifted her up into the cart. She cursed her emotions for turning her stomach into jelly every time he touched her. A warm heat rushed through her like a field fire, setting her cheeks aflame. The effect he had on her was so obvious she feared it would make her less convincing when she told him that she no longer wished to marry him. It was better to be the one to end it all and keep hold of a thread of pride at the same time. If only she didn't have to sit so blasted close to him. She tried to squeeze herself over to the other side of the wagon

300

so her leg wouldn't rub against his. That was a useless move. He dropped his hand on her thigh and pulled her back over. It was going to be a long, hot, ride back to Piraeus.

Hot as hades for sure, Trent was determined to set her on fire. Born of boredom or mischief, he boldly worked his hand under her skirt. Rose suffered the titillating feel of his calloused hand trail up her calf and to her thigh without the sheerest bit of fabric between them. Before he dared go any further, she clamped her knees together and pressed her hand down over his.

"Good God, Trent, not now."

He leaned over to whisper in her ear. "Why not?"

"Someone might see you." It was a lame excuse, for no one was around for miles and the ladies were a good quarter mile behind them.

"Who's going to see?" He forced his hand over another inch of flesh.

Rose didn't look at him, but she could hear the amusement in his voice. The blood rushed through her veins; her pulse pounded furiously at her temples. "Get your hand off my leg! I'm not like Marguerite." Her voice snapped like a dry twig.

Trent stilled his hand and asked with surprise, "What do you mean by that?"

"I'm not the first you've professed love to."

"I've never . . . What are you hinting at, Rose?"

"I've reconsidered. Marriage is not such a grand idea. In fact, it would be a disaster." She didn't want him to agree with her. She wanted him to dispel all the feelings of doubt that Hortense had sowed inside her. She wanted him to tell her he really did want to wed her, that he intended to do

301

just that when they got back to London, but he didn't.

"Then so be it," he said, then added smugly, "I can have everything I want without marriage."

Hortense was right: he didn't want a wife. He was stalling until they reached London, and when her aunt refused to consent, he would be free to leave her without guilt. Well, she had freed him a little sooner than he'd expected and it was natural that he'd be surprised. It still hurt to have him confirm her suspicions. "If you don't mind, could you remove your hand?"

"Pay attention, Rose. I said I could have everything I want with or without marriage. I just agreed with you that marriage was a bad idea. Until we get back to London, you're all mine. If I fancy to drag you into those bushes over there, I will."

"You have no right." Rose's eyes widened in disbelief. He couldn't be serious. He wouldn't dare do such a thing.

"When you stowed away on my ship, you should have been aware of the consequences to that action."

"I didn't stow—"

"You did. And I have *every* right." He looked into her flaming blue eyes and with cool directness made his intentions clear. "You'll be my willing mistress until we make port. You don't expect me to ignore you just because you've decided you no longer want my attentions?"

"I certainly do. I expect you to be—"

"A gentleman?" Removing his hand, he laughed with mordant humor. "I thought I've already dispelled that myth. Apparently I have not, but I promise you—before our journey ends, there will be no doubt in your mind."

For the rest of the bumpy ride, they had nothing to say to each other—until the soldiers came.

"This country's crawling with Turks," Trent exclaimed when a group of four soldiers on horseback stopped their caravan. "Ramos is right; in six months' time there will be war with the Ottoman Empire."

Rose looked nervously at the men as they dismounted their horses. She felt physically sick when she looked upon the arsenal of weapons that adorned their uniforms. They were dark and lean, their expressions serious. The men approached Trent, ready to strike at the slightest threatening movement.

Trent shrugged off the harsh words the leader directed at him. "What did he say?" Rose whispered."

"I don't know," Trent answered, barely opening his mouth when he spoke.

Rose looked over her shoulder as a soldier rifled through the back of their wagon. He threw up the blankets that covered the bread and cheese Ramos had given them. He removed the tops of the jugs of wine and looked inside. Everything was thrown back, haphazardly. The same was repeated with the three other wagons behind them. Finding nothing, disappointment soured the soldier's expression when he motioned that they could continue.

"They were looking for guns," Rose worried aloud. "Somehow they know guns were smuggled in. That soldier who boarded the *Raven* . . ."

Trent grinned, "You mean the one you walloped?"

"Maybe he saw more than we think. Maybe he

didn't believe the story that he never left Hortense's house that night. Trent, he could suspect you."

"You worry too much." Though Trent sounded positive, he was beginning to doubt Hassan had believed Marguerite's story. And perhaps Marguerite hadn't tried to be too convincing. He was concerned that the wagon of guns discovered north of Piraeus would be traced to the *Raven*. He had to get Rose safely aboard the ship before the country exploded right under their feet.

When at last they arrived in Piraeus, Trent ordered Rose to get aboard the *Raven* and to wait for him in his cabin.

"Aren't you coming along?" she asked, eyeing Hortense's daughters.

"Not yet. I have some business to attend to first."

Rose helped herself down from the wagon and hurried up the gangway to the *Raven*. She turned to see Trent enter Hortense's house with Marguerite.

"That scoundrel," she muttered. "How right Hortense was." Rose marched into Trent's cabin and slammed the door behind her, not giving a fig if it stuck. She threw herself on the bed and, sure she was alone, sobbed the tears she had held in check all the way to Piraeus. Blast, she hadn't meant to fall in love with the devil; *he* was supposed to be the one heartbroken, not *her*.

Not until she quieted down did she feel the presence of someone else in the room. She turned on her side and looked to the foot of the bed. She had to blink away the remainder of her tears before she was actually sure she saw him. When the watery vision cleared, a soldier appeared, leaning against Trent's desk. His arms crossed his chest as he regarded her with curious patience. Seeing the

304

soldier startled her into a round of hiccups.

He straightened and walked around to the foot of the bed. Rose knew he wasn't Greek, and he was too formal looking to be a pirate, so that left one other option. He was a Turkish soldier. From the ornamentation on his clothes and sword, she assumed he held a rank of some importance.

The soldier put his hand in his pocket and withdrew a silk handkerchief, which he gallantly presented to her. She sat up and took it from his outstretched hand, dried her eyes and face and wiped her nose. His brown eyes, darkened even more by the shadow of his brow, were as penetrating as the night. He studied every inch of her while she tried to get her wits about her. She decided not to ask him right off what he was doing there in Trent's cabin, although the thought came to mind as he so rudely let his eyes appraise her. Instead, she matched his perusal almost as boldly. His sharply cut features and thin, humorless mouth gave him a severe look that defied question. Not a strand of his jet-black hair was out of place. Like everything about him, his stance was ramrod straight. It was obvious he was well disciplined and very serious about whatever reason he had for being there. Something about him was disturbingly familiar when she summed up the whole of him. He gave her a minute to get herself together before he cleared his throat.

"I was behind the screen when you came in." He nodded to the corner of the room where the washbasin and commode were located.

"Oh," Rose said faintly, acknowledging his explanation as to why she hadn't seen him. She was certain her face glowed profusely. She had not only disturbed the man during a private moment but had also allowed him to witness her outburst of tears, and considering his whole posture, she did not doubt he would ask a multitude of questions.

"You're the lady who fell into the harbor."

That was it! He was the one who had ordered the crates be opened and searched. Good God, why was he in Trent's cabin?

"You caused quite a commotion on the quay. I'm glad to see you didn't drown."

Though there was a good distance between them, Rose slid back against the headboard of the bed. If he was glad she didn't drown, he had a reason for feeling that way, and she was sure she'd soon be enlightened as to what that reason was.

Chapter 25

If Rose hadn't had enough stress to contend with before, she certainly did now. The headache she hadn't been able to dispel promised to be with her a long time.

The soldier did not waste time getting to the point. "This ship has been watched for activities that would be considered threatening to the Ottoman Empire. I have reason to suspect that the *Raven* has delivered supplies to a group of cowardly insurrectionists hiding in the hills. Therefore, my men and I will remain aboard the vessel until my suspicions have been satisfied. If I am wrong, which I think not, then the delay shall not distress you."

In his firm words, the soldier made it clear she would be considered guilty by association. Despite the panic that gripped her, Rose squared her shoulders and glared at the stoic man.

"I am dismayed that you would make such accusations without proof, and I am certain a complaint will be lodged against you. Now, if you'll give me your name, I'll make a note of it."

The slight smile that crept over the soldier's lips

was like a dark cloud passing over the sun. "Hassan al-Hassan. You're welcome to go to Constantinople and issue your complaint, but until I've satisfied my suspicions, you'll not leave this ship. It will be better for you if you are cooperative."

Rose wondered what exactly he meant by cooperative, but before she had the chance to ask, he outlined everything for her. "There will be no hysterics, such as I've just been witness to. It wouldn't help you. You are to stay in this cabin which will be shared with me. Don't fear, I've no interest in you personally, just your truthful answers to my questions. And you will answer them truthfully. Do you understand?"

"Where is the crew?"

"They are safe."

"And Captain Jordan? What will you do with him?" Her insides twisted waiting for the dreaded answer. Surely it was Trent he'd been waiting for, not her. In her hurry to separate herself from Trent, she had rushed aboard the *Raven* without noticing anything wrong. Trent hadn't followed her immediately. She hoped he would notice something amiss and be forewarned.

"Captain Jordan will be detained below with the others until I am ready to question him."

Rose was appalled. They had unloaded the *Raven* without incident. How could this man keep them prisoner on suspicion alone? But then she was reminded by her captivity that she was not in London and that people did not enjoy the same privileged freedoms everywhere. This was precisely why Trent risked his life smuggling guns.

The soldier locked his hands behind his back and leveled his eyes on her. He was preparing to question her and she knew that only a well-thought-out lie could pass his discerning judgment. She felt her nerves tingle already, just planning how she would sound convincing enough to satisfy him. Nervousness would not do; it would warn him right away that she was not being truthful. She would have to look at him squarely and answer every question sincerely and as vaguely as possible. There was nothing else to do but meet his unsmiling face with unfaltering calm. Not to be disappointed, he began his interrogation.

"What kind of cargo did the *Raven* bring to Piraeus?"

"China."

"And you are returning with . . . ?"

"Tea."

"There is no tea in the hold, only ballast."

"I surely can't tell you why. Captain Jordan said he would be bringing tea back to London. My best guess would be that Greece is not where one would find tea." She smiled pleasantly at his unamused look. "Sorry I'm not much help." It was curious news to her that Trent intended on heading straight for London rather than stop at his usual ports to load the *Raven* with the goods that would make his trip profitable. She thought he must have come to that decision before they left Piraeus for Ramos's village and had had his crew fill the hold with what was needed to steady and balance the *Raven's* empty belly. It made her wonder why he hadn't told her his intentions.

"Where were you today?"

"I can't be much help with that question, either. We visited a hamlet, but for the life of me I can't recall the name." The throbbing pulse at his

309

temple should have warned her not to taunt his temper, but she was so vexed with the nerve he had to board the *Raven* and keep them all prisoner without justification that her resolve to keep calm revolted.

"Why did you jump into the harbor?" he asked, irritation rising in his voice.

Indignant, Rose stood up to answer him. "I did not *jump* into the harbor. Why would I do such a thing? I can't swim. I nearly drowned."

The soldier sighed, disappointed that she was going to be difficult. "I was wondering so myself. Why would a young lady who could not swim jump into water so deep?"

Rose feared he had seen her. Her foolish stunt could have drawn suspicion rather than distract it. She suffered over the thought that she had put Trent's life in danger.

He took a step toward her, closing the gap between them. "That question kept returning to me, over and over again, like a recurring dream. But you say you did not jump?"

"You're mistaken, sir. I did not jump. You may even ask Captain Jordan."

"Oh, I intend to ask him many things that have been puzzling me." His smug grin promised he would. "Just one more question. Are you lovers?"

Rose was taken aback for an instant, and then, out of reflex, she slapped his face. She was not happy about losing control, but the day had strained her composure to its limit and being asked about her personal relationship with Trent when it was at its low ebb was the last straw. By the startled look on his face, she was sure the soldier had not expected the blow. Surprise, however, was replaced by controlled fury, then satisfaction. Rose braced herself for the return blow.

"Good. That knowledge is most helpful. Your close relationship with Captain Jordan should effectively pry the truth from his lips."

The soldier marched to the door and flung it open. Without turning to look at her, he issued a warning. "Be advised, you'll be closely guarded." The door closed and she was left alone.

Trent had lost patience trying to get any information out of Marguerite. She swore through her teeth that she had convinced Hassan he had spent the whole night with her. Trent knew she was lying and was sorely tempted to wring her neck. His hands were ready to squeeze the truth from her when Hortense intervened.

"Captain Jordan!" she screamed, bringing him back to his senses. "You don't want to kill Marguerite." Hortense pulled him from her. "Mon Dieu, this is no good. Leave here while you can. I will deal with her myself."

Trent was reluctant to leave without a confession from Marguerite, but he knew Hortense was right—he had to leave Piraeus soon.

"Marguerite," Trent warned, "you would be wise to board the next vessel out of Greece. Last night a peasant met his death when the Turks uncovered the guns in his wagon. The Filiki Hetairia is looking for the traitor."

Trent felt his stomach lurch when Hassan al-Hassan's men stepped out and showed themselves on the deck of the *Raven*. They were so confident he would return without a threat, knowing that

Rose was on board. He swore under his breath; this was going to be an inconvenience.

With Marguerite's eyes at his back, Trent was escorted to Hassan al-Hassan with a Turkish guard on either side. There wasn't a flicker of worry running through Trent's body. Without solid evidence, which he was sure they did not have, he would be questioned, then warned, and after the annoyance of being detained, he would be free to leave. What Trent didn't know was that this time Hassan had more than suspicion to go on.

"Business or pleasure, Hassan?" Trent asked, grinning at the steadfast soldier.

"I could ask you the same, Captain Jordan."

"You should really get a sense of humor," Trent added while his body was being stripped of its weapons.

Without a smile, al-Hassan pursued his questioning. "What brings you to Piraeus this time?"

"Now, you really don't expect an answer just like that? Not when I haven't seen my crew or the lady who ran aboard not too long ago."

The soldier ignored him. He wasn't ready to bring the girl into the conversation—yet. "I find it curious that you've come all this way to deliver . . . china and are returning with nothing but ballast."

"Not just china—cotton and rum. Had you missed all that? And this time I'm in a hurry to get back to London."

"I suppose it was too optimistic of me to expect the truth from you without some kind of incentive." Al-Hassan nodded to one of his men, who slipped out of the shadows holding the stock of a very familiar looking modified flintlock. Despite his surprise, Trent's expression didn't waver. Al-Hassan took the weapon from the soldier and examined it. "You may be interested in how I acquired this.

"Not everyone in Athens is unhappy with Mahmud's rule. Just the other night I was having an intimate discussion with a mutual friend of ours who has become quite distressed by your activities. Naturally, I offered to put you on the true path. Oh, you must be wondering where this came from." Al-Hassan smoothed his hand over the long barrel. "Our friend was good enough to send me in the right direction, but not soon enough. Only one wagon had not yet disappeared into the hills. Its driver guarded its load with his life. It was a fatal decision. One of my overly zealous men shot him. Had he lived, there were many questions I would have asked him, for instance: where did the guns come from and who were they going to?" Al-Hassan waited for Trent to offer an explanation.

"Why don't you ask your friend?" Trent said with a surly smile that irritated the soldier.

"I really didn't expect this to be easy. I'm glad, in a way, you haven't disappointed me." Al-Hassan's lips twitched, anticipating how willingly the captain would eventually tell him all he wanted to know. "I'm told you have a special passenger on this trip. I believe her name is Rose Whitley."

Trent's muscles tightened against the restraining hands of the two men who held him.

"Don't fear, I'm not interested in her—myself. But there is a Turk I know who would offer a fortune to add a yellow-haired, blue-eyed beauty such as your companion to his harem."

Al-Hassan didn't flinch when Trent pulled his guards with him and came only inches away from

313

his face before he was again restrained. "Touch her, Hassan, and I'll—"

The soldier laughed. "There's not much you'll be able to do from the hold except sit on your ballast." With a motion of his hand he sent Trent down into the bowels of the *Raven* to join his crew.

Al-Hassan returned to Trent's cabin, where he intended to wait for the captain's change of heart. When he eyed Rose from the doorway, he didn't doubt the man would tell him everything. He hoped he wouldn't have to go as far as sending the girl away, but pressure from Sultan Mahmud II to subdue the bands of revolutionists who peppered them with shots from the hills was increasing. The crags and passes had become death traps as the klephts of the Peloponnese continued their deadly harassment. Supplies feeding the peasants with guns and ammunition were coming into port from Europe and the *Raven* had made more than one suspicious trip to Piraeus. The world powers' sympathy was leaning towards Greek independence. He couldn't let the fate of a mere girl exceed the needs of the empire. As much as it nipped at his conscience, he had to use what weapons were at his disposal—the weaknesses of mankind: jealousy, greed and love. Discovering the feelings the two had for each other would indeed be a formidable weapon. Al-Hassan knew he would get what he wanted—eventually.

Rose searched al-Hassan's face and knew he had already met with Trent. There was a small glint of triumph in his eyes that belied the success of his interrogation. She was filled with a sickening feeling that Trent had succumbed to whatever threats the soldier had voiced in order to spare her skin. While al-Hassan was away, she had tortured herself with guilt-ridden thoughts. Her own revolt against her aunt was what led to their capture. If she had not pursued Trent in London and insisted on making him love her for childish revenge, he would be safe. If she had only listened to her aunt from the very start, Trent would be safe.

Looking at al-Hassan suddenly brought tears to her eyes, and despite his warning, she burst into sobbing hysterics. As though looking through the back of a waterfall, she saw his stiff stance waver and the grim line of his mouth soften just slightly.

Al-Hassan stood nearly at attention, suffering through her sorrowful display of misery, trying to determine his best line of action. Didn't he tell her not to try hysterics? He wasn't used to his orders not being obeyed, but this was a westerner and they were as undisciplined as they came. He ran through a gamut of options: he could remind her that he would not tolerate such displays of behavior, or firmly tell her that she was disobeying his orders. He could also let her feel the back of his hand, which would at least startle her into compliance, but raising his hand against anyone weaker than himself would be cowardly. Al-Hassan drew a deep breath and resigned himself to the desk chair. If he could stand it, she had to stop sometime.

Sometime was a long time. Every minute or so al-Hassan looked up from his folded hands at the glistening face of the wailing girl and sighed. He had to wonder who was going through a worse time, Captain Jordan or himself. He pushed back his chair and tried to talk to Rose through her sobs.

"Young lady, I can't sit here any longer and listen to this senseless wailing." Realizing how uncomfortable she had made the soldier, Rose sobbed even more. "I order you to stop this weak display of emotion." Expressing an oath foreign to Rose, al-Hassan stormed from the cabin. Rose's heartache was eased a little by her small victory. At least she didn't have to share the cabin with him.

She walked over to the washstand and splashed her face with cool water. Her thoughts trailed to the soldier. He was a hard figure to look at, but he certainly didn't have the strength to stand a lady's tears for very long. She did carry on terribly, but given the circumstances, she didn't know what else he would have expected.

Her tears came out of guilt, frustration and the terror she felt at the prospect of losing Trent forever. She had never felt so helpless as she did then. There was nothing to do except wait for the soldier's verdict. Someone had to know the danger they were in. She didn't think the soldiers would keep their presence a secret any longer, not now that Trent was a prisoner. Her faith that they would somehow be allowed to return to London held fast to the hope that al-Hassan only had a suspicion that Trent was supplying the revolutionists and that without real evidence he would have to let them go. But she knew he'd do whatever possible to get a confession, and she tried not to upset herself with those possibilities. She took a deep breath and patted her face dry.

Just when she rounded the corner of the screen that sheltered the bathing area, the door opened and she was greeted by al-Hassan's smile.

"I see you're finished with your tantrum. Now we can settle some unfinished business. Don't think to start up again," he warned. "I won't be so tolerant as I was before."

As it was, Rose's stomach hurt from all the crying she'd done earlier, and she felt as wrung out as a washcloth anyway. She sat stiffly in the desk chair and peered at the soldier with hard eyes.

"I can tell you are a sensitive woman." he began in a calm voice, hoping she would not remind him just how sensitive by releasing a new flood of tears. "I know I can count on your good heart to understand the tragic results Captain Jordan's latest cargo has reaped. His shipment of guns to be exact." He watched her eyes brighten and her lips part. "I have a witness and a crate of the so-called English china, so don't waste your breath trying to protect him. He has brought death from England. Without a confession, I will hang him and his crew on this very ship and you, my dear lady, will be forced to watch. Then you will be sent to a friend of mine in Constantinople—you'll never see your home again. However, it need not end this way. If he gives me the names of the murderers in the hills, I will spare his life and yours. You will be free to return to London. Captain Jordan is a stubborn man; it will be up to you to convince him that your lives together are more important than those of murderous outlaws."

That was the gist of it: Trent had committed a criminal act and if she wanted him and his crew to be spared punishment she had to convince him to betray the freedom fighters. It didn't seem to be very much of a choice; either way, whatever Trent decided, lives would be condemned to death. He knew the risks involved and was probably ready for the consequences, only her presence would complicate how he looked at it. She felt sick at the cruel choices the soldier was making him consider. He had backed them into a corner, using the lives of others as weapons they would be forced to turn against themselves. "You are despicable," she hissed. "I wouldn't utter a word to help you. Trent would die before he'd betray a single soul in those hills."

"I've no doubt he'd relinquish his own life—but yours? That's the decision he is faced with this very moment. It is quite his misfortune to have brought you, and I suppose," he added wearily, "it is my good fortune."

Al-Hassan walked over to the door and opened it. His guard entered and pulled Rose up from her seat. It was clear al-Hassan had expected her to refuse his offer and had an alternate plan in mind. "Now," he continued, "it would only be fair if you helped Captain Jordan. After all, he has a very difficult decision to make alone."

Chapter 26

Moonlight filtered down the mizzenmast like a spotlight, illuminating Rose and Trent in a soft, misty haze. Al-Hassan had tied them shoulder to shoulder, anchoring them to the mast. Rose was sure he meant to keep them there until he got exactly what he wanted. And in case it wasn't clear enough, he restated his demands.

Al-Hassan towered over them, looking down his long, straight nose, his hands on his hips and his legs parted to brace his stance against the subtle movement of the deck. Rose refused to look up at him when he talked, knowing it would irritate a soldier issuing orders. Instead, she stared at his impeccably polished black boots and pretended to ignore him. But al-Hassan wasn't about to be ignored. He squatted down in front of her and gripped her chin in his hand. Her eyes were forced to meet his.

"As I told Captain Jordan, I'll wait until sunrise. By then you will have had enough time to decide if you want to spend the rest of your lives together or, in your case, start a new life." Al-Hassan looked burdened with what he thought he had to do, but that didn't make Rose hate him any less.

He left them under the watchful eyes of two guards positioned to make sure the prisoners would be quickly caught if they managed to escape. The possibility of that was slim. The guards had made sure the ropes around Rose's middle were so tight it felt like she'd be cut in two by morning, and the constant friction against her wrists each time she made a move soon became sheer torture. When she dared to look at them with blame, she was suddenly chilled by a kind of fear she had never felt in al-Hassan's presence. The sentries didn't have a single line of compassion in their faces. They didn't speak English like al-Hassan. After appraising their charges, they commented to each other in their own language. Even though she didn't know their words, she did understand the cruel implications of their exchanged sneers and she worried that as soon as al-Hassan was far enough away they might decide to ease their boredom on their helpless prisoners.

For the time, the guards kept their distance and she was thankful for that. Any conversation she had with Trent would be in confidence—if he wanted to talk to her at all. She couldn't blame him if he didn't. By now he was probably regretting not tossing her overboard from the beginning. He probably wished he would have carried through on his threat to let her swim back to England. She didn't know what to say to him except offer an apology for the mess she'd gotten him into. Her throat was too tight to talk and she feared if she said anything at all it would come out in unintelligible sobs. She didn't want to risk making Trent feel sorry for her. No matter what, she knew he wouldn't betray Ramos and her tears would only make it harder for him. She just had to bravely accept the fact that he was going to die—"for inciting a revolution," as her father would say. Well, there wasn't a more noble cause to die for than freedom. She thought of Athena's warriors galloping into battle, their bravery immortalized in the frieze of the Parthenon. Maybe their sacrifice would be remembered as well. She felt a hot tear slip down her cheek. Against all her determined resolve, she was going to cry.

"I didn't expect we were going to be tying the knot so soon," Trent joked as he strained against the rope binding them together.

Rose sniffed back her tears. He found the most damnable time to make a joke. Her bottom, she felt sure was bruised just from sitting in one spot for so long, her wrists hurt terribly, a persistent pain gripped her shoulders and back, and she was ready to cry her eyes out. Through all of this he was making fun of something she certainly didn't see any humor in. By making such a flippant remark, he only assured her further he was not one bit serious about marrying her. Not that, at the present moment, it was even an option to consider. She brought her knees up against her chest and slid them back down again.

"You damn well have a distorted sense of humor, Trent Jordan," she said flatly.

"At the moment, we haven't got much else going for us."

"You're very encouraging." She felt a flood of despair rush over her and the tears well up again. "They're going to hang you and you're making jokes! And it's my fault because I didn't listen to anyone and came charging into your life when you didn't want me. I don't want you to feel responsible for me when it was my own doing that put me on this ship. You should have thrown me into the channel when you had a chance. I've been nothing but trouble for you. Your crew mutinied, I almost got you killed by pirates . . ."

"Rose, my crew didn't really mutiny, and Angel was no more of a danger than a fly to a bull."

"You could have drowned trying to save me when I jumped into the harbor."

"I can swim, Rose."

"I could have pulled you under."

Trent would have hugged her if he could have. "Rose, sweetheart . . ."

"I'm a menace. Now, look at the trouble you're in. That soldier would have never suspected you smuggled guns if I hadn't drawn his attention by jumping . . ." Her eyes darted to the guards. They were gazing at the lights in Hortense's windows. "You see, they probably heard me. I just confessed for you!"

Trent's eyes were also directed to Hortense's brothel. One window in particular interested him. He hoped Hassan was relieving his tension in Marguerite's bed. "You're just a danger to be around, Rose. Hassan should be wary of you," he said, trying to tease a smile to her lips. "Now, as admirable as it is for you to blame yourself for all the—"

"It's true, if I'd only—"

"Rose!" He said in a sharp whisper. "Keep still for a minute. It's not your fault. Marguerite told Hassan about the guns. He was the one who boarded the *Raven* that night. He knew something was up."

Rose stayed quiet for a minute. Marguerite

didn't hate Trent. Rose saw how she looked at him. Marguerite longed for him. Why would she want to see him hang? Then Rose remembered the murderous feelings she had felt when she saw Angel with him. She turned her head to look at Trent. It was the first time she dared since they were bound together. Her heart was gripped with a longing for him the instant their eyes met. "How do you know it was Marguerite?"

Trent nodded to the second-floor window that softly glowed with the light from a lamp turned low. "She's with him now."

Of course. Rose should have realized it sooner. The rose perfume—the same scent that clung on Hassan's clothing the night he boarded the *Raven*. He had been with Marguerite that night, too.

"Rose, how many of Hassan's men did you see on board?"

"Just one below and the two here."

"Good."

Good? Didn't he notice they were trussed up like Christmas geese with not even one man able to help them? Hassan's small band may as well have been a hundred men. Perhaps he thought he could overtake them once they were untied. She only knew she'd be so stiff that she'd be lucky if she could stand.

She bent her knees up to her chest and stretched her legs out again, then wiggled against the ropes. The coarse rope cut into her wrists, forcing a quiet whimper from her lips. She fell back against Trent's warm side. As bleak as it all seemed, it was comforting to feel him so close. She tried not to think of it as their last night together, but the somber thought was persistent. Try as she might, she couldn't share his optimism.

"I would have wanted our last night together to be different," she confessed wistfully, gazing up at the stars that peeked down through the crisscross of rigging that slashed across the heavens.

"It's not the way I would have planned it," he assured her. Then, intrigued, he asked, "How would you have planned it?"

She glanced at him and saw his smile from the corner of her vision. "I suppose it doesn't matter."

"Our fates are sealed," he agreed, smiling. "But if tonight could be changed, you would . . ." He encouraged her to go on as he intently watched a black figure leap over the side of the *Raven*.

"I would take a long, hot bath and I'd make love with you again."

"I thought you didn't want any part of me."

Rose sighed. She couldn't let him hang thinking she didn't love him. "I only said that because I was angry. I really didn't mean it. Actually, I find you very hard to resist." She smiled, knowing at least he would not die with a wounded ego.

"Hmmm, I didn't know that. What exactly do I do to . . ."—he smiled to himself as he watched another dark shadow slip over the side of the rail—". . . to set your heart beating?"

Rose shifted against the restraints and looked up into the stars. Trent didn't have to do anything to get her pulse racing, but there were some things he did . . . well, it wasn't as if he'd ever be able to use his charms on her again. The thought of that made her sad, for she really did like when he . . .

"Well, is there anything special I do to fire you up?"

She smiled and giggled a little. She was surely delirious with grief. "You only have to set those dark eyes of yours on me. When I see the fire

324

burning behind them, there isn't much I could do to resist you even if I tried."

"I didn't know you were that easy," he said with light humor in his voice. "All I have to do is look at you, huh?"

Rose closed her eyes and tried to imagine that the restraints were gone and she was in his protective arms. "Then when you touch me with your wide, strong hands and pull me into your chest and your lips touch mine—well, that's the end, I couldn't resist you if I tried."

"It's smooth sailing from there—so to say."

"Quite." Thinking of him was a wonderful distraction.

"You should have told me all of this sooner, Rose."

"I certainly wouldn't have. I wouldn't admit to anything like that."

"It's customary for the condemned to be given a last request and Hassan is a soldier with some honor. Could I have one more time with you—before I hang."

Hearing him say it like that tore at her heart. She felt tears come to her eyes again.

"Would you promise me that last request?" Trent smiled as another dark shadow slipped onto deck.

"Of course, but I don't see what difference it makes promising you anything now, the way we're tied up."

"But if we weren't tied."

She sighed. "Anything you'd want. It's the least I could do before they ha—"

The sound of two dull thuds and a quick flurry of dark shadows about the deck interrupted her words. She watched their guards fall to the deck in

325

a motionless heap. The shadows silently moved about the ship. Soon more of them rose up like ghosts from the hold. One large shadow turned out to be Ramos, dressed from head to foot in black and soaked to the bone. He dripped over her as he cut the ropes and freed them.

Not a sound was made above a whisper. Rose watched the organized movement with astonishment. It was obviously a well-planned rescue. Ramos let his freedom fighters over the sides of the *Raven,* took the guards and released the crew all in a matter of minutes. The silence was catching; all seemed to know the need for it if they were going to slip from the harbor and into the Aegean Sea to freedom. The crew scurried everywhere, whispering orders usually shouted. The sails were unfurled and softly fell into place. Rose felt the *Raven* push away from its berth and heard the splashes of their rescuers as they jumped back into the harbor to swim to shore.

Trent was up first, a sword thrust in his hand. He reached down and pulled Rose to her feet. "Get ready to make good on that promise." His smile was a wicked one.

She had only admitted how much he excited her since he'd be taking it all to a watery grave. Never did she imagine Ramos and his men were rescuing them—but *he* did! "You knew all along, you scoundrel!"

He handed her into the hold of one of the Greek revolutionists. "Hold her tight," he advised, staring into her hot blue eyes.

"You have no conscience. How could you let me go on admitting those things . . ." She straightened with indignation. "You certainly are no gentleman, Trent Jordan."

He grinned wickedly. "And didn't I promise to prove that to you?" And then to the confused Greek: "Did you ever see such an ungrateful girl? Take her below and lock her in before all her ranting and raving has Hassan running out of Marguerite's room in his altogether."

"You! Next time you can hang . . . lonely."

Trent only laughed at her. "My, you have a hot little temper, which I intend to channel in another direction once we're under way. And, from what you've just admitted, that shouldn't be too difficult, should it?"

Chapter 27

If he thought he was going to get away with it, he was in for a surprise. If his love didn't run deep enough for him to give up his freedom and marry her, then she wasn't going to act as his mistress. Trent would just have to think of her as a passenger.

It would take some firm resolve on her part to resist him, but all she had to do was think of his latest trickery and that would certainly counter all the charm she was sure he'd try to use to get her into his bed again. However, she worried about his oath to prove to her that he wasn't a gentleman. That brought to mind other possibilities. What if he cast his charm to the wind? He could very well force her into his bed. She didn't expect any help from anyone aboard if that should come to be. He was unscrupulous for sure!

A knock on the door warned her someone was about to enter. At first her heart jolted, but then she realized Trent wouldn't knock, he'd just walk in. The door unlocked and a timid boy's head peeked through the crack.

Rose greeted him pleasantly. "Aren't you the

boy Peach found in Piraeus?" He was such a skinny, neglected boy. Rose hoped Bones would fatten him up.

"I've brought water for your bath, miss," Sean announced with a smile, eager to prove what a good cabin boy he could be.

Rose's reply took him by surprise. "Well, you can take it back to the kitchen. Bones can use it for soup."

His eyes widened with disbelief. "I can't do that, miss. The captain ordered it." ·

Rose knew it wasn't fair to put the boy through such agony, but she wasn't about to let Trent have his way. "I'm sorry, you'll just have to bring it back. If it's Captain Jordan you're worried about, I'll explain to him later that I was just too tired for a bath."

The boy stepped all the way into the room, the bucket of water gripped in his hand, the water sloshing over its rim. He was nearly shaking, but he pressed on, determined to please the captain he admired. "The captain said you might refuse a bath."

"Did he, then?"

"Yes, miss, but he said not to listen to you. I really have to fill the tub, miss. If you don't want it, that's between you and the captain."

Trent had sent the youngest of the crew to do this thinking she'd take pity on him—it just wasn't going to work. Rose folded her arms across her chest and glared at the boy.

"Fill this tub, young man, and I will dump every drop of water out onto the floor."

The boy's eyes rounded with surprise. Rose watched his throat move with the dread he swallowed. He recalled Paddy telling how she had

330

almost killed Hassan. He didn't want to test his own luck. If she carried out her threat to spill out all the water, the captain would be furious and he'd be mopping up from dawn to dusk. He backed out of the room, leaving the pail behind.

Rose's moment of triumph was a brief one. She had no sooner sat down on the edge of the bed when the door opened again. Trent's frame filled the doorway, his hands folded across his chest. Rose bolted up from the bed at the sight of him.

"What's this I hear about you badgering a poor boy into defying his captain's orders?" his voice boomed into the room.

Good God, he was handsome as sin standing there in his full arrogance: his hair whipped wild by the wind, his black eyes shadowed by a slight frown, his mouth so seriously set, his chin proud and determined, daring her to refuse the bath in his presence.

She just wouldn't look at him—she couldn't look at him. Her eyes fell to his arms. Tan and muscled, exposed by turned-up sleeves, they rested arrogantly across his broad chest, some of which stood out against the crisp white of his half-buttoned shirt. The strategy didn't do her determination to stand up against him much good. Her gaze dipped lower to his waist, where a wide belt spanned over the top of his narrow hips. Good God, that wasn't any better. She'd have to be staring at his boots to be able to talk to him without losing all her nerve. Then her eyes caught a movement behind his thick thighs. The boy was hiding behind him, another pail in his hand. She gritted her teeth. He was back with the boy to make sure the tub got filled. Her heart thumped against her rib cage and her legs shook beneath her skirt, but still her eyes flashed up to meet his.

"What's this I hear about your threat to flood my cabin?"

She folded her arms over her chest and raised her chin. "I've no intention of bathing here, Captain Jordan."

"If I recall," he said with a smile, "you requested a bath. Fill the tub, boy."

The boy moved from behind his legs, two hands gripped on the pail's handle. "Stop right there," Rose ordered sharply. The boy paused between his captain and Rose. "Captain Jordan is mistaken. I did not order a bath."

Trent's hands rested on his hips, the smile gone and replaced by an angry scowl. He glared at her for an agonizing moment. The poor boy didn't know whether to move forward or back and turned pleading eyes on Rose. Rose didn't notice. She looked right over his head, her eyes locking with Trent's, her face set in a stubborn expression that told him she was not going to soften her stance on the issue.

"Very well," Trent said, in too calm a voice. "If you insist on being so stubborn, I don't have any choice—do I?"

Rose regarded him with a suspicious eye. "I don't see that you do," she said stiffly.

"Well, I'm glad we're in agreement." While she was feeling the issue was settled, he stripped off his shirt and threw it down on the floor at her feet. Rose looked down at it and then back to Trent's face. His smile sent a shiver right through her.

The boy turned to look to his captain and then back to Rose. He certainly wished he were on deck doing anything other than witnessing to the Battle of the Bath, as it would come to be known.

"Fill the tub, boy," Trent ordered again, stepping closer to Rose. This time not a sound came out of Rose's mouth. The boy scurried past her as fast as he could without spilling too much of the precious fresh water. He ran out into the hall and returned with another pail he had set aside the door and quickly poured it into the tub. He moved quickly, his object to get out of the cabin as fast as he could.

Rose backed away from Trent, moving along the bed. Her heart pounded in her chest, blood surged through her veins and pulsed at her temples—she was ready to take flight, only there was nowhere to run. Every step away from him was blocked by something. She hoped to make her way around the room, possibly get the boy between them when he returned with another pail of water, then sail out of the room. Her only thought was to get out of the cabin. She forgot that there was nowhere she could go to completely escape him—until he reminded her of it.

"Where are you planning on running to, Rose? To the upper deck, the galley or perhaps the hold? Are you forgetting you are imprisoned by the bounds of this ship or that any one of my crewmen would swiftly put you in my arms?"

Rose knew he was right. There was no getting away from the devil until they returned to London port. But that certainly didn't mean she couldn't make him miserable in the meantime. She ran for the door, nearly crashing into the boy returning with another pail, and fled up the steps. In her wake, Trent was hollering at the boy for getting in his way. Still, his longer strides brought him up behind her before she could top the stairs. He caught her hips with both hands and pulled her back into him with a thud hard enough to knock the breath from her lungs. He lifted her up and over his shoulder, one hand behind her knees and the other hand resting familiarly on her behind. He ignored her hands flailing at his back and carried her back to his cabin, a pleased grin lighting his face.

Rose's long blond tresses swept over her face, hiding the hot anger ablaze in her eyes and cheeks. Through her swinging hair she could see the astonished boy, his eyes popping and his mouth agape, as she was carted past him and the empty pail clutched in his hand.

"It's all filled, Captain," he said with much relief in his voice.

"Thank you, boy," Trent replied, kicking the door shut behind him.

"Put me down this instant," Rose growled at his back, only to have her request granted all too quickly. Trent put her down—clothes and all— right into the tub of warm water.

While Rose sputtered and cursed him and shook the water from her hands, he pulled up the desk chair and sat at the side of the tub. When she rose to climb out, he pushed her down. "It would be a sin to waste the water," he said with a stern warning that told he wasn't going to let her out of the tub.

"You're a sinful man, Trent Jordan," she swore, taking off her shoes and spilling out the water that filled them. They dropped to the floor with a thud. Under his amused gaze, she peeled off her stockings and tossed them in his lap; next, she wiggled out of the rest of her undergarments and threw them at him. The red silk of her dress floated around her like the tentacles of a jellyfish, shielding the bare skin beneath.

"I can't see that you can bathe properly with your dress on," he commented with a grin.

"You can go to—"

"Now you're not going to start swearing, are you?" There was a warning in his husky voice. Then he added lightly, "You did promise a last request. Anything I wanted, if I recall."

"That was when you were about to be hung!" she snapped. "Unfortunately," she mocked, "you're not going to die. I promised a dying man's request. You tricked me, I might remind you. So I'm taking back that promise."

"We'll see." He grinned too assuredly for her comfort.

Rose turned her back to him and stiffly waited for him to unfasten each of the little buttons that ran down her back. He gathered her mane of hair and threw it over her shoulder, exposing the long row of silk-covered buttons. His fingers began at her shoulder blades, carefully pulling the buttons from their holes. She felt his touch run down her back as little by little her dress was peeled apart, exposing a line of smooth skin. She took a deep breath. He scooped his hands inside the back of her dress, over her ribs and up, filling them with each one of her breasts. His thumbs brushed over her nipples, raising them to hard peaks and sending a bolt of hot fire through her body. The bodice of her dress fell off her shoulders, slipping over his hands and down to float around her waist. Her wet hair clung to her shoulders and licked around the tops of her breasts.

She would resist him; she would not give in to the command his touch signaled. But her body was not as determined as her mind. His lips touched the back of her neck warmly and traveled down the

335

center of her spine, spreading out a charge of hot flashes. His hands squeezed the soft flesh of her breasts, his fingers taunting her nipples and then slipping down her stomach, below the waterline of the tub, down past the swirling red silk to what lay tempting in the depths of the bath. They spread over her stomach, then down further to the part in her legs and between.

Rose was suffused with a heated desire that enticed with its promised pleasure and that cajoled denial to consent. She closed her eyes and listened to the siren's song tempt and draw her into its lusty arms.

She turned and kneeled to face him, the silk still floating around her like the petals of a waterlily, water sliding down her skin in rivulets. She rose from its center into his arms, drawing him to her. He leaned over the tub, grasping her face in his hands, claiming her mouth with his, devouring her with a hungry kiss that left no part of her mouth untouched. His tongue slipped in to caress and play in the moist, warm valleys of her mouth. She joined him—touching, twisting, tasting.

He smelled of salt air and lavender soap. The touch of his hands slipped over her so gently they seemed to float, exploring without resistance each curve and valley over and over again, diving deep into the water, down her thighs and then back up. He pulled her from the water to stand in front of him, the silk now at her knees. He held her at arm's length and appraised her with warm eyes. His hands traveled every inch of her. They slipped down the long curve of her throat, along her collarbones, around her breasts, down the flat plane of her stomach, her hips and buttocks, and over the tops of her thighs. Rose let him explore with his hands and taste with his tongue. She let him spread the heat and fire of his touch until it became an uncontrollable wildfire burning and ravaging wherever the flames licked. He wrapped one arm around her back and held her breasts against his chest. She felt their heartbeats pound together like wild drums. His hand fell between her legs; she parted them and waited for him to slip inside. He stroked and stroked and slipped over the velvet petals of her body. Her mouth hungered over his, taking the passion from his lips and returning it. She throbbed and quivered at the touch that teased and probed and brought her to the edge of insanity. Her fingers twisted in his hair, she moved her hips to take his touch deep inside her, she whispered his name in a ragged breath and begged him to take her.

Trent lifted her from the tub and carried her wet and dripping to his bed. He laid her down across it and stepped out of his breeches. Rose looked at him with glazed eyes. He kneeled over her in proud male glory. She reached to touch him, to run her fingers over the hard shaft and the softer part of him. She bent her knees and called him. With his tongue, he touched the inviting part of her that opened the way to her heart. It slipped between her warm, wet lips, flicking and probing, sucking and tasting. Rose groaned and her body moved verily against the light torture of his tongue.

Sensing the fire would consume her too soon, Trent moved up her body, spreading the heat with a trail of wet kisses that led to her lips. With his chest poised over her, he came down, his shaft pointing to her center, and with a swift, purposeful thrust, he drove into the hot throbbing core of her body.

Their bodies slipped against each other with their movement. Her breasts pushed into his chest, and her hips met his when he pressed her down into the bed and moved over her, demanding and taking as he thrust again and again into the hot, wet heat of her. Rose held him around his neck; his cheek chafed against hers, and his mouth clung to her shoulder, spreading wet kisses along it in a trail over her neck.

Her mind was in a heady spin when he rolled over, pulling her with him and centering her atop his stomach. Her hair fell down over him, and her nipples, hard from his attention, brushed against the soft fur of his chest. He cupped his hands under her buttocks and filled her inside, slowly stroking his throbbing core against the walls that touched him, prolonging the rapture that would take them in its arms. Their mouths touched, tongues licked; their breath mingled in hot whispers.

"There is no other food for my soul than you, Rose. You are my cream and strawberries, the wine that warms me like no other." His mouth caught her tempting breast, drawing its nipple gently between his teeth and then twisting his tongue around it, licking with strokes that spread over her breast. He grabbed the other and continued the sweet caress of his tongue and mouth.

"Oh God, Trent, you are wicked with your taming. Your touch sends a fire sweeping over me and through me. It burns away every breath of protest and tends a craving that grows and grows until I am filled to bursting with it. I could never refuse you. I was a fool to try to," she confessed as the fire blazed around them.

"It only made the taming sweeter." Trent smiled tenderly, crushing her response with the demand of his mouth and the demand of his hips.

Their loving surged from one to the other, erotic pulses throbbing between them, building in the furious rhythm of their movement, beating like the wings of an eagle; faster and faster, higher and higher, together they climbed and reached the plateau. Rose felt the hot wave of love burst in her; it flowed like lava and filled the cavern inside with promise. They lay together happy and breathless, numb with ebbing piquancy.

Rose rested on her side, her back nestled against Trent's stomach. His arm was wrapped around her and his hand gently fondled her breasts. She did not know how long they rested, their bodies molded together, entwined in each other's arms, but she knew it was heaven. She thought of how he had taken what he wanted, knowing in her heart it was what she had wanted too, only she'd been too blind to see it and too foolish to think he would let her resist him. She thought of her dress.

"My dress is ruined," she said, kissing his arm.

He buried his face in her neck and whispered huskily, "I like you better without it."

"You are not a gentleman, Trent Jordan, but I suppose you've proven that already."

"As promised. And, I've proven that you are not a lady. You are a wanton little witch," he teased, nibbling on her earlobe. He pushed his knee between her legs. They parted without her even realizing it until she felt his finger run along the part between them, searching for and finding the bud hidden within the moist folds. He played within her, starting a new desire. Rose felt his longing harden and push against her buttock. She twisted around in his arms and faced him.

"You make me wanton, you scoundrel. Now, let

me up before you're missed and Peach comes looking for you."

"He knows better . . . and besides," he grinned, "I don't think you want me to leave—just yet."

"You—"

He kissed her protests away and rolled on top of her to drive his arousal into the depths of her warm body and join together their undeniable love.

Trent wanted Rose and he wanted no one else to have her as he did. He would marry her in London even if it was under protest. And Stephanie would protest. She wouldn't be receptive to marrying her niece to someone like him when she had a nice titled Englishman already chosen to give Rose respectability and, in a sense, return her to her English family. Her father would be back in London soon after their arrival. He would know that Trent had returned his daughter, unharmed, with sincere intentions of having her as his wife. And that Trent Jordan was an honorable man, not one to marry another man's daughter without consent. Trent never considered the possibility that Roger Whitley might say no.

Chapter 28

Rose was trembling with trepidation as they approached Philip's town house. That her aunt hadn't noticed her absence over the past weeks was too much to hope for. She fervently prayed her father hadn't arrived in London yet. Trent hadn't helped her much with a believable excuse. A swelled door locking her in Trent's cabin was a lame one indeed, even if it was the truth. Even so, that didn't excuse her being there alone in the first place. There was no question she'd be disowned from her English side of the family and shipped back to America as soon as her father arrived.

She looked faintly at the solid oak door of the town house and imagined her aunt would swoon from the shock of seeing her again. She hoped Philip had explained her disappearance. Frowning at that, she wondered exactly what kind of a reason Philip would come up with as to why she was missing. Certainly, he and Mrs. Witherspoon had come to the conclusion that she'd left with Trent.

The voyage back to London had been wonderful, almost making what she had to face worth it all. Trent had allowed her full reign of the *Raven* when the weather was calm, as long as she promised to stay clear of the rail. She promised, but just the same, he kept a watchful eye, and when she wasn't in *his* sight, Peach was always coincidentally nearby. The only member of the crew who avoided her was Sean. When she tried to talk to him, he ran away, casting her a suspicious look. Unlike the other crewmen, he was too young to recognize the way Trent looked at her and the way she couldn't keep her eyes from admiring him.

There was no one aboard who would tell her it was improper or unladylike to so boldly watch a man, so she enjoyed the freedom of laying her eyes on him whenever she pleased. She watched him in the early morning, the sunrise at his back and the dark green sea spread all around him, and in the afternoon, when the wind whipped his black hair wildly over his shoulders. Then in the evening she gazed at him longingly when the dying sun set them both ablaze in warm orange light. Trent looked longingly to her, too, and when she felt the heat of his gaze she retreated to his cabin to wait for him. She wished upon the stars at night, when he wrapped her in his arms and held her close to the warmth of his chest, that the voyage would never end, that they could sail around the world and stay forever in each other's arms. But they *had* returned, and what future lay before her was still uncertain when Trent lifted the brass knocker on Philip's door.

"Are you ready?" he asked before bringing it down on the door, his eyes light.

Rose stiffened against his good humor. He should have been filled with as much dread at facing her aunt as she. After all, it was mostly his

342

fault she'd sailed all the way to Greece. She had asked him to take her back while they were still in the channel and he'd refused. In effect, it was mostly his doing. Still, it wasn't fair to blame him. She had put herself on board the *Raven*, and he had insisted on seeing her safely to Philip's town house. She just wished he weren't so amused by it all.

"Be ready to scoop Aunt Stephanie off the floor when she sees us," Rose warned with a snap to her voice. More to her dismay, he only laughed.

The door finally opened after what seemed like an eternity and, to Rose's relief, it was only Thomas who greeted them.

"Come in, Mr. Jordan," Thomas said formally, ignoring Rose. She didn't hide her pique. "I'll just wait out here," she grumbled, only to have her cowardly self hauled inside by Trent.

The butler showed them to the parlor, where Philip sat in filtered light under a small cloud of smoke that rose from his pipe; his brown head was bent over a newspaper, and a frownline creased his forehead while he read. He posed a very serious picture until he saw them. He bolted from his chair and grasped Trent by the shoulders, eyeing him with a mix of relief and curiosity. "Here you are, unscathed once again," he said lightly. "And Rose . . ." Rose was warned by the mischief weighting his words and the dancing gold lights in his appraising eyes. "You look well. How was the voyage?"

She wasn't going to fall into his trap. A simple answer was all he'd get from her. "It was fine, Philip. Where's Aunt Stephanie?"

But Philip wasn't going to let the details slip

away that easily. He looked from Rose to Trent. "Just fine? I'd rather think it would be—"

"Uneventful," Trent said bluntly, but he couldn't stop the telling grin that slowly curved his lips.

Rose set a frown on them both. "You're both incorrigible!"

"Now that's a familiar word," Philip hailed. "It's all we've been hearing in this household since you took off on the *Raven*. Incorrigible!"

Rose sank into a wing-backed chair. "I hope Aunt Stephanie wasn't too upset." Her eyes swept up the long staircase and she sighed. "I suppose I'll have to face her soon and make amends for my awful behavior."

"She'll probably insist you marry tomorrow," Philip taunted with a twinkle in his eye. "Poor Lord Wesley wasn't completely deterred, you know. He's been away himself, so your escapades aren't known to him."

Rose couldn't help glance at Trent. He remained silent. She rubbed her forehead. "Has Father arrived yet?"

"Yesterday, as a matter of fact."

"Wonderful timing." Rose stood up. "Well, there's no use delaying the inevitable hanging." Her hand was on the banister when Philip called her back.

"Aunt Stephanie's not here. She's back at Briar Hill. Walking about . . . somewhat. The stubborn woman refuses to stay in her wheelchair. Your father's there also. If you prefer a day's rest, we can ride in tomorrow. Trent and I can catch up on old news."

Rose was agreeable to Philip's suggestion. Now that she was sure her father was in England and

344

already knew of her unscheduled voyage, she needed some more time to think. Her head pounded with a tremendous headache and she didn't think matters could get much worse—until later that day.

After Philip and Trent had left her alone in the town house, she soaked in a deep bath until the water turned cold, then dressed in a light-blue gown she found still hanging in the wardrobe. She was snacking on bread and jam and sipping a hot cup of tea in the parlor when the front door slammed open. Startled by the loud bang, Rose nearly spilled her tea in her lap.

Before she could get up and before Thomas could make his announcement, Trent sailed into the room as if on a strong gust of wind. He planted his feet in front of her. Rose looked up into his eyes and found they were as dark and furious as a brewing storm.

"On my knees?" he nearly growled. "Did I ask you proper enough, Rose, to win your wager?"

Rose didn't know why she had thought her bet with Philip would remain a secret, but she had. Trent's knowledge of it caught her off guard, leaving her speechless.

Rose placed her cup and saucer on a small round candlestand. She would have stood up, but that would have brought them face to face and she didn't think she could bear it—as it was, his look nearly singed her despite the distance between them. She had forgotten about the silly wager. She owed him an explanation and Philip a tongue-lashing—at least—for telling him.

She doubted Philip's disclosure was deliberate. She could imagine just how it fell off his lips— laughing and drinking and exchanging tales. She felt her face warm with indignation when she thought of the conversation exchanged over mugs of ale. Rose looked up at Trent with an accusing glare—exactly what had he told Philip about their journey? And hadn't Trent made a similar wager? How dare he burst in and accuse her! She was stewing in her own hot, angry juices when he grabbed her by the shoulders and pulled her up on her feet.

"I want some answers, Rose. Did you mean it when you said you loved me or was it a game all along?"

"Aren't you a hypocrite," she accused, throwing the blame back in his face. "You made a wager yourself—one quite despicable. How does it feel to have the tables turned on you, Trent? What answers do you have for me? Was I just one of your many trollops?" Rose fought back tears as she realized a silly game was threatening to put a wedge between them.

Trent was suddenly quiet. Rose calmed. She was not about to let them both lose.

Letting go of her, Trent admitted quietly, "I didn't mean to hurt you. I never gave it a thought after . . . I wanted you in a different way. Not like you think."

"The wager didn't matter to me in Greece. I wanted you there, in the village. You were the one who had a change of heart. You thought of the excuse not to marry me. I would have married you then, when Hortense offered the church, because I loved you, not because of a wager I wanted to win. I thought you still wanted Marguerite." Rose timidly approached him. She wrapped her arms around his middle and rested her head against his chest. "I love you with all my heart, Trent. I could have lost you to pirates, whores and Turkish soldiers, but I will die if I lose you to something such as stubborn pride."

Trent softened. A reluctant grin crept over his mouth. His arms came around Rose and he held her tight against him. He kissed the top of her head. "I love you, Rose, not Marguerite. When Philip told me of your wager, I was afraid you didn't feel the same way. I thought you had made a fool of me. And," he added sheepishly, "I suppose I would have deserved it after making my own bet with your meddling cousin."

Rose stood on her toes and turned her face up to Trent. His hands held her head firmly; his mouth hungered over hers. Rose molded her body to his and returned his kiss with all the desire that flowed through her. "Will you marry me, Rose?" Trent asked between kisses.

"No one could stop me." Rose frowned after making that proclamation. "Are you going to ask for Aunt Stephanie's approval?"

"And your father's."

Trent was determined to prove he was not the scoundrel Stephanie thought him to be. He was going to go by all the rules this time. Rose wouldn't protest if it was so important to him to prove himself to be a gentleman. Not that it mattered to her. She wouldn't care if he swept her off her feet and carried her away with him.

Rose was happy. Trent had proven he could have had all of her. Rose had proven he would love her enough to marry her. They both had won their wagers and each was happy with the outcome. What her aunt thought didn't matter a fig, but she did want her father to approve of her choice.

The ride to Briar Hill in Philip's carriage was morbidly quiet. Even the weather was an undertaker's holiday. A chilling mist fell from the sky and settled thick in the valleys, covering the rich green of summer with drab gray. Standing like ghosts, trees were draped in the fog that hung in their branches. Rose pulled her cloak around her to keep the damp from penetrating to her bones. The carriage jostled back and forth and was soothing enough, except for her tormented thoughts. Rose dreaded facing her father and aunt.

Philip added to her misery by displaying his own guilt so regally. He was afraid to say a word to her other than what was polite. She missed his teasing and scandalous tales, even if he was dastardly enough to add her to them—they were preferable to his silent gloom. After a while, she couldn't endure the silence any longer.

"Philip, for God's sake, what's wrong?"

"I am sorry I mucked up everything. I had no idea he'd actually—"

"Well, he did," she told him, with a gleam in her eyes.

Philip leaned forward and frowned. "He left ready to strangle you when he heard of the wager. I couldn't believe you actually got him to ask for your hand. I never dreamed when I mentioned the ridiculous wager you made that he had—Why are you smiling?"

"You didn't spoil things. I was going to let you suffer longer, but I can't bear to look at your long face another minute. And, let me remind you, I wasn't the only one who made a wager. It was not right to play with our emotions like we did. We were both guilty and we admitted to it. You . . ."
Rose's mouth spread into a wide smile. "You just

gave us a reason to soothe our hurt, and it was quite lovely."

Philip's laugh exploded into the carriage, releasing all the tension he had felt in the past day. "Dear Lord, Rose. Did he get down on his knees? I just can't imagine Trent actually going through with it, especially knowing Aunt Stephanie would never give her consent."

Rose frowned and turned away, but Philip's humor at his friend's posture did manage to coax a slight smile to her lips. "He did," she said sweetly, and to Trent's defense added, "As regally as any prince of England. You'd do well to take a lesson or two from him."

"And propose? Hells's bells, Rose, I'd never consider changing my ways to be tied to a woman . . . unless," he amended with a tease of a smile, "she's as incorrigible as you. Then maybe the misery might be worth it."

Rose thought of Angelique, the beautiful pirate of the Mediterranean who had men shaking in their boots. "I think I have just the woman for you, Philip. Only it's too bad she's found a poor old soul to wed."

"All the better—she'd make a feisty mistress. You must introduce us."

"Only if I wanted to exact revenge on you, Philip. Her husband will be the earl of Hatfield."

"The man's in his eighties," Philip said incredulously, not giving the invitation he had just received much thought until now.

Rose attempted to sober his mood. "I suppose *he* vowed never to marry, but, you see, some female finally did pirate his heart." She smiled at her private joke.

"And his fortune," he added grimly.

"Not everyone is interested in a fortune, Philip," she told him sharply, wondering if Trent had told him she knew of his recent thievery. "Are you still looking for fortunes, dear cousin," she asked directly. There was enough accusation in her words to startle him back into a solemn mood.

"Whatever do you mean by that?" he asked innocently. She took her father's ring from her reticule and handed it to him. There was nothing he could deny after seeing it. A slow grin curved his lips. Now he was face to face with the little thing who had so neatly toppled him from his horse to pull him into the mire. "I couldn't sell it after knowing it was your father's. I gave it to Trent for safekeeping."

"What were you thinking of, robbing people and—"

Philip's face was serious, and his words were hushed by the velvet interior of the coach. "Freedom, Rose. To end the continuing march of the Ottoman Empire, to save people from tyranny. Freedom is expensive, as well your countrymen know. However," he sighed with regret, "the Liberty Thief has retired. There are enough who want to donate money for the Greek revolution. They took the fun out of playing Robin Hood— until, of course, we stumbled upon you. It took me a week to get the mud out of my ears and even longer before Trent stopped laughing about how you so deliberately dismounted me from my horse. He would not have guessed he'd be the one taking the greatest fall." He smiled, but Rose ignored him.

"Father was ready to see you both hang." Rose held his hand in hers. "Philip, promise me you and Trent will never do this again. Even now, if someone was to discover your past deeds . . ."

"Don't worry, darling, we are officially retired. The Liberty Thief rides no more."

Somewhat satisfied, Rose leaned back against her seat. "Your poor aunt. Shame on you, Philip, for scaring her so."

"Ah, she's recovered—she's not as delicate as you think. Besides, she had her niece's latest exploits to worry her head over," he reminded her.

Rose sank back into the seat. She had actually forgotten about her imminent demise for a few minutes, but now it raced back to her in full force and she groaned with the pain of it. Her father and her aunt together. Well, if there was a silver lining, it was that she'd only have to tell the story once.

Chapter 29

Stephanie's balance faltered and she collapsed against Roger Whitley. Her lashes fluttered over deep-violet eyes; the blue-gray gown she wore rustled into place around her, its color paling her skin. Stephanie's hand rested against her forehead, and her lips twitched with a slight tremble. Looking as distressed as his sister-in-law, Roger fanned her face with his hand and helped her to her chair. Philip simply poured himself another drink from the sideboard, unaffected by his aunt's performance.

Rose stood in front of her father and aunt, her hands clasped in front of her. She was the object of their distress. Rose had wanted to break the news of her travels gradually, gently, as nonchalantly as she could, as if the occurrence of a young woman sailing off to Greece with a rake like Trent were commonplace. Her father thought otherwise. "Come out with it, Rose, and remember who you're talking to," he warned. "Did you willingly leave London with this man?"

"Yes, Father," she admitted without reluctance, without giving thought to an excuse, without lame apologies.

"Why, in heaven's name?" Roger was astonished. His daughter had done some daring things in her life, but this—this was too much to take calmly. "Why, Rose?" he nearly shouted.

Rose was nothing less than distraught. Her father had never raised his voice or hand to her in her life; however, his patience had long been lost when she'd arrived with Philip. He looked tired and worn from the worry she had put him through. There was more gray dulling his brown hair, and lines she hadn't noticed before were etched around his shadowed eyes. She owed him something, not an excuse but a good explanation; yet explaining why was impossible. She couldn't very well tell him she suspected Trent was the Liberty Thief, or that she was compelled to settle a wager between herself and Philip and in the process had fallen in love with Trent. So she admitted to a weakness her father would easily believe, placing all the blame on her shoulders.

"I suppose I was just looking for adventure, Father. A trip to Greece seemed . . . exciting. Mr. Jordan didn't know I was on his ship until it was too late. He had no choice except to take me along."

It was then that her aunt had heard all she could bear and fell against the back of her chair in a near faint. Everyone's attention was drawn by her woeful moan. The poor woman was at the end of her tether.

Once Stephanie had control of her vapors, Roger turned his eyes on Rose—there were more questions he intended on settling. "And where did you stay aboard his ship?"

Rose looked to Philip, who held his tight grin

354

on the rim of his glass. There would be no help coming from him. "In one of the smaller cabins, Father. Mr. Jordan was a complete gentleman." Philip choked on his drink, deepening her distress.

"Are you all right, Philip?" her father asked.

"Yes, quite—just a bad swallow."

Roger turned his attention back to his daughter. "It seems you've upset the whole family in one way or another. I certainly didn't expect anything like this to happen here." Roger addressed his sister-in-law. "Not that I'm blaming you, Stephanie. I know how difficult my daughter can be." He paced between Rose and the sideboard, his hands clasped behind his back and his eyes contemplating the floor. Rose assumed that he was so disgusted with her that he found it unbearable to look at her when he spoke.

"Understandably," Roger went on, "your aunt was indisposed, sick in her bed. For you to take advantage of your guardian like you did is . . . upsetting, to say the least. Never mind how shocking your behavior has been in the past—running off with Mr. Jordan . . ." Roger's hand shot up in frustration.

Making an effort to calm his voice, Roger continued. "You can thank your aunt and Philip for saving your reputation by spreading the word that you'd gone to France with Chloe to meet her husband. So if anyone asks where you've been, you know your reply." He joined Philip at the sideboard and poured himself a full glass of whiskey. Rose heard the glass clink against the neck of the bottle and knew her father's hand was less than steady.

"For heaven's sake, Rose, don't tell anyone

you've been to Greece and back. It's too much to believe—even for you. Adventure indeed! I still suspect we haven't gotten to the bottom of this. I'm going to want to talk to Mr. Jordan to assure his behavior was what it should have been."

"I'm sure it was exactly what we would all expect from a gentleman like Mr. Jordan," Philip said, winking at Rose in a vain effort to pick up her spirit.

"Still, I'd like to speak with him."

Rose didn't share Philip's amusement in the matter. She had never seen her father act so distant before. She was nothing but a disappointment to him. She hadn't lived up to her promise to make him proud. He was supposed to return to a well-bred lady and instead was greeted with the news that she had sailed off with a man he had never met. How would he ever accept Trent? Rose feared that her father would never agree to their marriage. With her aunt's help he had already formed a damning opinion of him. She felt hot pools of tears well up in her eyes. Somehow she had to explain.

"Father, I . . . Philip has known Mr. Jordan for a long time. I'm sure he can vouch for the man's upstanding morals." She looked warily at Philip, who somehow managed to keep the amusement off his face. "It would be an insult to even hint that Mr. Jordan would be anything less than a gentleman."

"Not if his behavior was less than honorable."

"Father, don't you believe me?"

Roger looked at his daughter's sweet face. She could fool anyone with her water-blue eyes. The tears he knew were about to spill down her cheeks pulled at his heart. Not this time, he told himself.

Rose was not going to sob her way out of this one. According to her aunt, Trent Jordan was not known around London for being a gentleman, and it would only be natural for his friend to defend him. "No," Roger said bluntly. "I'll send a missive to Mr. Jordan in the morning. I'll see what he has to say on the matter. And if he has tarnished more than your reputation—you will both be married."

Stephanie gasped.

Rose agonized over her father's threat. If she admitted the truth, that she and Trent had gotten to know each other very well on the long journey, they would be married—married shamefully. She wasn't going to allow their lives to begin that way. Somehow she'd have to prove to her father that Trent was a good man and not the scoundrel her aunt had described.

"Father." Rose took a hesitant step but stopped when he turned his back to her. They had talked long enough on the matter. She could say nothing to convince him to believe her assertion that Trent had acted as a gentleman.

Rose's eyes spilled over with the tears she had tried to hold back. She opened her reticule and pulled out a lace handkerchief. The cloth unfolded. The ring fell out and rolled over the floor, finally settling between her father's feet.

Rose and Philip's eyes followed the gold ring as it traveled over Stephanie's fine carpet. Neither one could take a breath. Both stood still. Rose thought to chase after the ring, but it was too late to do anything but watch her father stoop down and pick it up. He wrapped his fingers around it. Standing up, he held the gold band in the palm of his hand. Rose glanced at Philip. Their eyes met for a second before Stephanie broke the silence.

"Roger, what is that?"

"My ring." Roger looked to his daughter. "The one that was taken from me the night we came here."

"The one the Liberty Thief—"

Roger's eyes did not leave Rose's face. "The same one." Rose looked at the ring. Her father's hand closed around it. "How did you come by it, Rose?"

Rose resisted the temptation to turn to Philip. She struggled with the choice of telling the truth or lying to protect Trent and her cousin.

"Well, Rose? It did fall out of your handkerchief, didn't it?"

"Yes, father."

"How did you come by it, then?" Now leaning on her cane and grasping Harold's arm, Stephanie hobbled over to Roger. She looked down at the ring in his hand.

"I—" Rose stumbled.

Philip rushed over to Rose and put his arm around her shoulder. "Now you've gone and spoiled the surprise."

"I've had my fill of surprises. I surely don't need another one," Roger said.

Philip smiled at Rose. She managed to brave a weak smile, wondering all along what he was up to. "Shall we tell them, Rose dear?"

"I suppose we must now."

"While in London, Rose and I passed by a pawnbrokerage and there, right in the window, was Roger's ring. I wouldn't have known it, of course, but Rose recognized it right off. Isn't that right, Rose."

"I'd recognize your ring anywhere, Father.

When Philip realized it was yours, he insisted on seeing it returned to you."

Roger slipped the ring on his finger. "I certainly am grateful, Philip. This ring was a gift from my wife."

"Think nothing of it. The beggar must have sold it to support his cause."

Rose wanted to collapse into the nearest chair.

"I'd still like to get my hands around that thief's neck," Roger said, thinking back on the scuffle he had had with the brigand.

"You do throw quite a punch for a gentleman on in—" Philip realized his mistake too late.

"How would you know what kind of a punch I—"

Rose rushed in. "I told him, Father. I explained just how gallantly you defended us against the highwaymen."

Roger grinned. "Flattery is not going to save you, darling girl. But thank you."

Rose's face sombered at the reminder that her father was still displeased with her. There wasn't much else she could do other than excuse herself and hope the morning would bring a brighter day. Once her father met and talked to Trent, he would know how much of a gentleman the young man was.

Chapter 30

Knowing Trent had received her father's missive, Rose had waited all morning and a good part of the afternoon for the moment he'd arrive. She was in the east garden when she saw Trent ride up the stone path on the back of a large roan mare. Even though he was still a distance away, Rose knew his form well enough without having to see his face. He rose up from the back of his horse, more a part of the beautiful animal than not. His thick thighs pressed against the horse's lathered side. Horse and rider moved in one fluid motion, combining the power of man and beast as they rode together over the hills and scant valleys between to the manor house. His black hair flew back behind his neck, free of the satin ribbon he usually wore. His face was windburned to a burnished bronze, his expression tightly controlled by the serious set of his jaw.

Rose shifted the basket of flowers she held over her arm and laid her cutting knife on top of their stems. Her heart stopped as soon as she heard the clapping of horses hooves against the stone.

He rode up to the manor, charged emotion

crackling around him. His hair was untamed, hanging loose around his shoulders; his riding coat gaped, exposing a loosely tied cravat and silk shirt. He flung down from his horse, threw its reins into the hands of the groom who had met him, and tossed his riding coat on the steps of the manor. He looked to Rose as though he was prepared to do battle; his eyes flashed like polished steel, and his walk was determined. Rose's legs became as stiff as fence pickets when she regarded him.

With her heart pounding against her chest, Rose ran to Trent and threw her arms around his neck. Her feet flew off the ground with her exuberance. Trent braced his hands around her waist.

"Trent, they're waiting in the library like a firing squad. I'm afraid Aunt Stephanie has Father convinced you are the worst man alive. He wouldn't speak to me at all this morning. All he did was grumble from behind his paper." Rose was close to tears when she thought of how angry her father had been, even after knowing she was safe. She had certainly gone too far this time; there was nothing she could do to soften him.

"I doubt he'll stay angry with you for much longer." Trent wiped a tear from her cheek.

"I returned the ring."

Trent frowned. "You told him?"

"No. Philip made up some story about me seeing it in a pawnbrokerage. So don't mention it. Oh, Trent, I hope he doesn't recognize you from that night on the road."

Trent laughed at her worry. "All he'd have to go on is my laugh."

"Then don't laugh."

362

"I'm not likely to laugh in the face of a firing squad."

Rose forced a smile. "Look at you. Your shirt's unbuttoned, your hair's untidy . . . Looking as you do, Father will never be convinced you're the gentleman Philip and I described."

"Philip said I was a gentleman?"

Rose secured the buttons at his collar and knotted the cravat at his neck. "Yes, Philip. He did try to be helpful by standing up for your impeccable manners."

Trent was thoughtful as Rose fussed with his clothes. "I'll have to remember that. The day may come when Philip needs a similar favor."

Rose walked around him to gather up his unruly hair. "Humph! I'm sure it will. Do you have a hair ribbon?"

"No. This will have to do."

"It won't do," Rose said, looking distressed at the wild array of black hair that swirled to his shoulders. "You look like a pirate. Wait right here." Rose slipped inside the entryway and hailed Harold as he passed her. "Harold, give me your hair ribbon."

"Pardon me, Miss Whitley?" His brows rose in disbelief. He was even further shocked when Rose whipped the black satin ribbon from his hair. "Miss Whitley!"

Rose said a quick thank you as she ran from the house.

"Here we are," Rose exclaimed triumphantly, and then neatly tied back Trent's hair.

Rose held up Trent's frock coat. He slipped his arms into its sleeves and smoothed out the wrinkles with his hand. "Well, how do I look now? Ready to face the executioner?" he teased.

"You look very much the gentleman." Rose beamed over how handsome he looked. "And if Aunt Stephanie—"

Trent kissed her lips closed. "Let me handle Aunt Stephanie."

Rose watched Trent enter the house, and then when a respectable amount of time had passed, she walked into the manor.

She was met in the entranceway by Lizzie, who whispered the news with annoying excitement. "Mr. Jordan's here."

Her hands trembling, Rose replied sharply, "I know that, Lizzie. I saw him ride up." She handed the girl her basket of flowers. "Here, see to these."

Rose peeled off her gloves and pushed her bonnet back. Her hair fell out from under it in a wild array of gold. She continued on to the study, brushing bits of leaves off the front of her dress. Her ears burned to know what was being said behind closed doors, and eavesdropping was not beyond the extent to which she'd go to find out.

The massive library doors were closed, and there was nary a crack between them to let her have a look inside. From the conversation she heard, it was only her father and Trent talking, and she thanked God her aunt was, so far, keeping quiet.

"Miss, what are you doing?" Already as tightly wound as a watch spring, Lizzie's hard whisper made Rose jump to attention.

"Lizzie, don't sneak up on people like that. If I had a weak heart, you would have killed me."

"It isn't—"

"Lizzie, shh!"

The maid set the vase of flowers on the marble table beside the door. "I'll set your evening clothes out, miss," she whispered, and then turned to leave.

Rose called her attention. "Riding habit. I think I'll go riding before supper. I'll be up soon to change."

Rose gave up trying to hear anything through the solid doors and followed Lizzie up the stairs. She ran past her and pulled a green riding habit from the wardrobe. With Lizzie's help, she dressed and was on her way to the stables determined to catch Trent before he left. She would know what her father and Aunt Stephanie said before Trent left Briar Hill.

"Going out alone, miss?" the groom confirmed, a tinge of disapproval in his voice. "It looks like a storm is coming."

"I always go out alone at home. I'm quite capable of handling a horse and I promise to stay close," she said, adding the last part just in case he was tempted to tell her father.

Rose didn't tear off into the rolling hills as she was so tempted to until she knew for sure the groom's eyes had been satisfied that she wasn't going to do any such unladylike thing. She turned her head and looked over her shoulder and, seeing he no longer watched her, gave the horse its lead, tearing up the earth behind her. Her hair whipped at her back freely; the wind rushed past her ears and brushed her face in a soft caress, calming all the tension that had restrained even the slightest smile. Her legs hugged the horse's powerful sides in what she knew was a scandalous riding style. At the top of the hill, she leaned over the mare's neck and gave it an appreciative hug. She dismounted and looked down upon the manor, prepared to wait all day for Trent if she had to.

It felt like an eternity later when Trent emerged from the house.

Upon seeing Rose atop the hill overlooking the manor, Trent galloped over the long stretch of meadow to meet her. He was even taller on the back of his horse, and Rose had to look up to meet his eyes. They were so dark and intense they grabbed her breath and ravaged every part of her they touched. "What did Father say?" her voice trembled slightly.

Trent slowly dismounted, his shoulders and arms taut with the strength harbored within each sinew of muscle. He moved toward her, shed his riding coat and tossed it on the ground. Rose's eyes fell to the jonquil-yellow coat spread at her feet, and her mouth went dry. Trent grabbed her hand and pulled her down on the coat and wrapped her in his arms. They sat together gazing down on the manor, now hidden in the dark shadows cast by a gathering of storm clouds. Trent held Rose's hands in his.

"Your aunt is absolutely against her niece marrying someone like me. She's already filled your father in on my background as a man with an eye for the ladies, and she's warned him that a marriage would never work between us. Your father is uncertain about the whole thing, but he is impressed that I am enough of a gentleman to offer to marry you. He's not convinced love has anything to do with it." Trent confused Rose with a hearty laugh. "He thinks I asked for your hand out of a feeling of obligation—to save your reputation, so to say. Never did I think acting the gentleman would go against me."

"Father said no?"

"Not exactly. He wants to give it more time."

Rose turned around in his arms and faced him. "So Aunt Stephanie can have more time to change his mind? Absolutely not!"

"Rose, be patient," Trent pleaded. "We will be married and with your father's blessing."

A gust of wind tore at Trent's sleeves and whipped around Rose's skirt. The sun was darkened by storm clouds that swiftly rolled across the sky. Leaves turned over, showing their silver backs; the horses whinnied; birds fluttered into the trees; drops fell one by one. Even with the threatening weather, Rose and Trent did not want to part.

As if the power of the encroaching summer storm threw them together, they huddled closer. Rose felt the strength of his arms hold her tightly against him.

"When will I see you again?" Rose asked.

"It will not be long, love."

Rose sank into his eyes, dark as the center of a storm cloud, and let the ravenous demand of his mouth draw her lips to his. The wind rushed against them, blowing gold and black strands of hair together. The rain fell in large, cool drops, pelting their skin and dripping down their faces and into their mouths. The sky turned black; distant thunder rumbled through them.

The beat of the rain quickened with her heartbeat; it drenched Trent's shirt to an almost transparent film that clung to each rounded muscle of his chest and shoulders. His hair fell over his forehead in wet wedges, dripping sweet rain at their ends. The rain fell off his face like a hundred sorrowful tears; they touched Rose and joined with the tears that ran from her eyes. Everything she had loved was cursed by a storm that haunted her life and dreams, and that storm would take Trent, too. Her fingers gripped his arms as though he would be washed away in the rain; she held him close to her heart and felt the warmth of him pierce the cold edging into her.

Trent kissed the drops from her cheeks, sliding his mouth again over hers to taste her sweetness. Rose's fingers pushed into the wet and tangled strands of his hair, pulling him closer, drawing the heat from his body. Rose rested her head on his shoulder and vowed, "If I have to run away with you, I will."

Trent lifted her up. "You'll do no such thing. You'll go back to your father and do as he says." He grabbed the reins of her horse.

"I'll see you safely home," he shouted over the rushing noise of the storm.

"No, Father shouldn't know we've met here," Rose shouted over a long roll of thunder. Trent reluctantly agreed; it would do no good to have her father know they had met secretly. He mounted his horse and turned it away from her. In a matter of seconds, Rose could no longer see Trent; he had been washed away in the sudden deluge of rain.

The stone structure of Briar Hill seemed to disappear into the dark gray of the ground-hugging clouds. A blinding sheet of rain poured from the sky, making finding Briar Hill in the storm a chance of fate. It was only down the hill and over the pasture below, certainly not a distance anyone would expect to get lost in, but her thoughts were distracted and troubled. Rose was anxious to speak with her father and to convince him how much she loved Trent. As stubborn as Trent was to gain approval on his own, Rose was just as determined to convince her father of how genuine their love was.

Wind gusts and rain slashed at her skin, boring through her like a rod of ice. How she longed for Trent's warm embrace. She wished for him to return and take her into his arms again. She shivered and huddled against the onslaught of the relentless storm while her horse plodded over the soggy ground. Leaves and sticks that were picked up in the gusty wind sailed around her. Then, as she began to hope they only had a short way to go before Briar Hill broke out of the dark gray, a sudden gale tossed a heavy branch in her path. It flew up again, startling her mare to rear up on its hind legs. The sudden panic of the horse took Rose off guard, but she managed to keep the reins in her hand. She shouted to her horse over its piercing whinny and the heavy breath of the wind. Her arms clung around its neck when it reared again. Despite her tight hold, the horse threw her off balance and she slipped from the saddle, sliding over its slick sides to the ground.

Chapter 31

Trent was blown into the manor by a storm that practically willed him to stay. It would be next to impossible to find his way back to London on such a night, so he turned his horse around and plowed through wind and rain until he was back at Briar Hill.

Harold braved a gust of wind as he held the door ajar. The skirt of Trent's riding coat whipped around his hips, his hair blew in dark strands around his face, and water ran in rivulets down his boots and puddled on the floor at his feet. Philip stood in the entryway, marveling at Trent's disheveled state. "You look like Hattie's mop when she's done with the floor."

"You don't mind if I help myself to dry clothes?" Trent asked, peeling away his riding coat.

"Not at all," Philip replied, as he showed Trent to his room.

Philip leaned against the bedpost. Trent was changing into a muslin shirt and dry breeches. His hair fell limply around his shoulders as he leaned to set his boots in front of the fire to dry. Trent watched the flames dance around the small logs while the heat warmed his face and drew the cold from his body. He struck the log with an iron poker and looked back at his friend. "Well, what do you have to say for yourself? I can tell you're near bursting with something."

"Just curiosity, old friend. How did it go this afternoon?"

"I fared well enough, with no thanks to your aunt informing Mr. Whitley of my renowned reputation around London. I don't think he is so gullible as to believe me or Rose—or you, for that matter."

Philip looked thoughtful. "Aunt Stephanie can be persuasive when she wants to be. Consider her viewpoint for a moment. She had her heart set on marrying cousin Rose off to Lord Wesley. It's her last chance to put her only sister's daughter back into English society, and now you've come along offering to take her back to the wilds of America."

"She doesn't know that," Trent said defensively. "I never mentioned returning to Virginia—we could stay in London."

"You'd do better to convince her father you'll be returning to America. All he wants is for Rose to be happy."

"Then he should give us his blessing. Rose wouldn't be happy with Lord Wesley, even you know that's a mismatch." The fire flared and Trent's eyes lit up. "Since it looks as though I'll be spending the night, I may as well get to know Rose's father better."

"If Aunt Stephanie doesn't make you sleep in the barn," Philip said with a chuckle as the two men headed for the library.

"Why don't you keep your aunt occupied for the

evening while I put my best foot forward with Mr. Whitley?" Trent countered.

Still deep in his thoughts, Philip continued without acknowledging his friend's suggestion, "What I don't understand is why you just don't marry Rose and sail off on the *Raven*. Why is it so important to get her father's permission? It's not something that you would normally be concerned with." Philip chuckled, "Then again, you haven't been your normal self since you returned from Greece."

"This time is different. It's Rose's life, not just mine, and it'll be my son's life. I will not have my future family hurt by scandal."

When Trent walked into the library with Philip, he was looking forward to waiting out the storm in front of a chill-chasing fire with a soothing drink in his hand. All the arguments for convincing Roger Whitley to bless his intention to marry Rose formed in his head. Upon seeing Roger's face, Trent turned pale. Something was wrong and he knew Rose was in the middle of it. "What is it?" he asked with dread.

"Rose went riding earlier. The groom just found her horse in the courtyard," Roger explained, alarm ringing in his voice.

Trent's heart lurched with fear and blame. He shouldn't have left her in the storm. Even though they weren't far, it had come up with a quick vengeance, tearing limbs from trees and picking up anything else that wasn't securely anchored. If any ill had come to her, it would be his doing. He took the stairs two steps at a time, found his boots and descended just as swiftly. He ran all the way to the stables. Roger and Philip were close behind him.

Trent mounted the bare back of his horse and charged through the shroud of fog and light rain. The three split into different directions and blindly combed the uncertain terrain. They checked every shadow and gray form that emerged in their path. Trent rode to the top of the hill and then spanned out from there, shouting Rose's name every few feet of the way, only to be answered by Philip and Roger's similar cries. A gray mound called his attention and he urged his horse quickly to it. With a sinking heart, he discovered that it was just another group of rocks.

Trent's wet clothes molded to his skin, drawing every breath of warmth from his body. Driven by his determination to find her, he pushed on. When all hope seemed to be lost, another form emerged out of the ground fog. This time, his prayers were answered. He swung down from his horse and kneeled next to Rose. She lay against a rock. Her forehead was cut and bruised but clean of blood from the constant wash of rain. Her clothes were soaked and pasted to her cold skin. Lifting her up to his horse, he held Rose against his chest, desperately trying to renew the warm life within her as he galloped back to the house.

Cradling Rose in his arms, Trent followed Lizzie up the long staircase to Rose's room, where he laid her down before the small fire that had been set to ward away the dampness brought by the storm. He pulled off her wet slippers then peeled off her stockings and proceeded to unfasten her skirt when he heard a shocked cry from behind.

"Trent," Stephanie gasped from the doorway. She was completely aghast that Trent would go so far as to undress her niece, even in his concern.

"Stephanie, now's not the time to start lecturing. Seeing Rose without clothes is not going to shock me. She needs to get out of these wet things quickly and into something warm."

Speechless, Stephanie clamped her mouth shut and looked to her brother-in-law. Her hand gripped the curved handle of her cane.

Roger Whitley's voice sounded from the door. "Mr. Jordan, I thank you for your concern and quick action, but Lizzie here can tend to my daughter." Roger put a gentle hand on Trent's shoulder. "The storm's subsided enough for Philip to ride out for Dr. Wood."

Trent reluctantly left Rose's side, leaving her in the women's care, but not before issuing a parting remark to Stephanie. "You should be off your feet." He followed Roger out of the room, only stepping as far as a few feet from the door.

"They'll call us when she's in dry clothes," Roger assured him when he noted the pained expression on Trent's face. "She'll be fine. Tough as nails, that one. It's only a small bump that's put her out," he said, as much to console his own worry as Trent's. Roger knew it wasn't so much the bump on her head but the ice-cold feel of her skin that worried them the most.

"If she'd come to, we could get something hot in her," Trent said, looking beyond the door, his patience ready to snap. "What's taking them? I've gotten her clothes off in less—" Roger and Trent's eyes met. "I could have, is what I meant to say," Trent amended with a grim smile.

"Whether or not you've undressed my daughter, Mr. Jordan, is hardly of any consequence at this moment. But there will come the time when that

375

issue will need to be addressed with due seriousness." Roger placed his hand on Trent's shoulder. "I am grateful for your genuine concern for Rose. She may very well owe her life to you for finding her."

The men changed into dry clothes and returned to Rose's room. Deciding that they had waited long enough, Roger tapped on the door and pushed it open. Lizzie hurried by them with a bundle of wet clothes in her arms. Stephanie rested in a chair by the bed. Trent frowned. In his view, Rose was too far away from the fire for it to do any good. To Stephanie's shock and Roger's chagrin, he folded Rose up in the blanket and brought her to the fire.

"Roger," Stephanie began to object.

His eye on Trent, Roger interrupted firmly, "Mr. Jordan's as concerned as we are. It's better for her to be closer to the fire." He took his sister-in-law's arm and helped her from the room despite her scalding looks.

"Roger, you don't mean to leave him alone with her? Not after I warned you of his—"

"They were alone to Athens and back. What's he going to do but keep her warm until Dr. Wood gets here?"

Stephanie grumbled all the way to her room. She was sure Rose was so independent because of Roger's permissiveness. "Dr. Wood won't be here for hours—perhaps not until morning. Roger, you and your daughter will be the death of me. I am telling you again, the girl needs a husband, one who can handle her reckless nature before she does herself harm." The gray tendrils on her head trembled with her conviction.

Roger grinned. "I believe you're right, Stephanie." Stephanie looked at him curiously. Now, why after all this time was he so agreeable?

Trent leaned against a trunk he had pulled up to the fire and held Rose in his arms. He kept her close to his body, the comforter wrapped around them both until her cool skin gradually warmed against his. He felt all the life in her: her breath against his arm, the light beat of her heart, the rise and fall of her chest. He stroked the silken strands of her hair and brushed his hand over her cheek. His finger traced the line of her lips and curved around her chin. Looking at the raw bruise marring her forehead made him grimace. His lips brushed a light kiss at her temple.

He kept her close for most of the night, falling in and out of sleep himself until he became so stiff and pained from his position on the floor that he moved to the bed. He took Rose with him. She was warm as toast, her cheeks glowing pink to prove it. His lips brushed against hers. Feeling the barest response to his kiss, his worry was somewhat relieved. Trent tucked her in and threw more wood on the fire.

When Roger peeked in on Rose, he was touched by the sight set before him. Bathed in the yellow glow of firelight, his daughter rested peacefully in her bed. Trent was at her side, slumped over in a chair; he had surrendered to sleep while keeping watch. His head rested on the edge of her pillow; his arm was thrown protectively over her. Roger's throat tightened as he remembered the long vigil he had kept over his ill wife so many years ago. He remembered the love that bound him to Roseanna and the pain of knowing they had come to the end of their lives together.

Trent Jordan loved Rose, *that* Roger had read in his face when Trent carried Rose in from the storm. Trent was afraid of losing her as Roger had been afraid of losing his wife. But Rose was strong, her color had returned, and she slept peacefully knowing Trent was with her. That made the scene different from the one he remembered with sadness. Rose and Trent could begin their lives together.

Roger tapped Trent on the shoulder. Trent woke from his light sleep, looked at Rose and then turned to her father.

"She's going to be all right, thanks to you. I have a feeling you're the first person she'll be asking for in the morning, so may I suggest a few hours sleep in a comfortable bed? You don't want to worry Rose by looking as though you were the one who took the brunt of the storm. Stephanie's had a room prepared for you."

Trent's brow arched, disbelieving Stephanie would be so thoughtful, then Roger gave voice to his suspicion that she'd even stoop to kindness to separate him from her niece.

"She really hoped you'd retire much earlier," Roger said.

Trent looked back on Rose.

Roger sensed his hesitancy. "And there's a matter of importance I wish to discuss with you before Rose wakes."

Rose's hand went to her head, where a slight throbbing pulsed at her temple. Her fingertips checked the area gingerly. There was an obvious bump where her head hurt. She pushed back the blanket with some difficulty, since it was secured under the mattress. Feeling a little dizzy, she stayed on the edge of the bed for a while. She was sitting like that when the door cracked open.

"What are you doing, young lady?" Dr. Wood nearly shouted, straining his old voice to a croaking sound. "Philip tore up the sod to get me and here you are chancing further injury." He then turned and pushed away whoever was behind him and closed the door.

Dr. Wood plopped his black bag on the chair next to the bed. He continued talking as he examined Rose. "You've got the men in this household sick with worry," he said, looking from one eye to the next. "None of them have slept more than an hour. You look better than they do. I told them all no one is coming in here until they've bathed and shaved!" He squinted again at the bruise on her forehead. "And your aunt is going to wring her fingers off. I'll have to leave them all some laudanum."

"Trent—"

"He's the worst one. But I can't blame him much. He's anxious to see how his patient is faring."

"His patient?"

"After finding you, he stayed up half the night keeping the lung fever at bay." Dr. Wood held her hands. "All right, let's see how steady you are on your feet." Rose took cautious steps for his appraisal. "Good, good. Now turn around, back to the bed with you."

There was a knock on the door. Dr. Wood's bushy brows met, and a quirky smile gave his amusement away. "Which one of the three do you think it is?"

Rose hoped it was Trent.

At Dr. Wood's permission, the door opened and then just as quickly closed.

"Father." She held her arms out to him. It was good to see something other than a scowl cross his brow. Roger's smile reached from one side of his face to the other.

"Try to keep her warm and in bed for the day," Dr. Wood ordered as he let himself out.

When Roger looked into his daughter's bright blue eyes and felt the strength in her hug, the guilt he had been suffering suddenly overcame him. "I thought I was going to lose you. If it wasn't for Mr. Jordan . . . Rose, the man is quite affected by you."

Rose smiled. "I know, and I'm quite affected by him."

"Before I left you with your aunt, I said you could choose the man you wished to wed. Is Trent Jordan your choice?"

Rose nodded.

"After last night, I don't doubt his love for you. Of course, he's not your aunt's first choice." Roger became thoughtful. "Your mother and I married for love, and I couldn't fairly expect you not to do the same. We defied all conventions and made some heartbreaking sacrifices through it all. But the love we had weathered through the storm of criticism and rejection by her family. Our lives would have been misery had we bowed to what everyone else wanted for us and not married. I like your Mr. Jordan. I think he has the stamina to put up with you."

"Does that mean you'll give us your blessing?" Rose saw her father's answer twinkle in his eye.

"I've already done so. It was the only way I could

convince him to leave your bedside."

"Oh, thank you, Father. I must get dressed and—"

Roger pulled his daughter back to bed. "Now wait a minute. Dr. Wood said—"

"Oh pooh! I feel fine." Rose thought of her aunt. "What did Aunt Stephanie say?"

"Something about an apple not falling too far from the tree. Me being the tree, I suppose." Roger kissed her forehead. "You get some rest. I'll stop in again later."

Now that Rose was awake and bursting like a flower in full bloom, it was impossible for her to do as she was told and stay in bed. She ventured to the windows, feeling the strength return to her legs with each step. She threw open the drapes. Bright sunshine rushed into the room. Picking up a pillow from the bed and hugging it tightly to her chest, Rose slowly danced around the room. She spun in wide circles across the floor, her hair swinging behind her and the lace hem of her nightgown spinning around her ankles and sweeping the floor as she went.

On his way back to peek in on Rose, Trent stopped in the doorway. He knew she should be in bed, not dancing around the room, but it was hard to pull his eyes from the mesmerizing movement of her body. The light from the window streamed through the fabric of her wrapper, making it appear as translucent as morning mist. Her long legs moved underneath in long, graceful strides. She held a pillow against her cheek, her eyes were closed and her face was lit with happiness. A sweet melody hummed from her throat while her feet graced the floor so lightly he wondered if she was not floating over it.

"May I have this dance?" Rose heard the familiar voice trail across the room. She stopped and, still hugging the pillow against her breast, stared at Trent. He looked as elegant as a prince in Philip's sky-blue frock coat. His fawn breeches appeared as soft as a colt's muzzle. A gold watch and chain draped from the pocket of a brocade waistcoat, and a creamy flounce of silk swathed his neck.

When their eyes met, it was though their hearts touched. Rose laid the pillow on the bed and reached out to him. Their fingers touched, then threaded together. Rose felt the roughness of his hand brush along her palm. Trent slipped his arm around her waist and pulled her to him. He held her so close there was nothing between them except for the warmth of their bodies and the beat of their hearts. Rose felt his every breath in the rise and fall of his chest, and the familiar touch of his hips sent her temperature rising. She lifted up on her toes and kissed the rounded point of his chin. His skin was smooth from a recent shave and smelled of vanilla and spice.

"I would be most pleased to share this dance with such a gentleman as yourself," Rose answered sweetly, pulling out the side of her wrapper as though it was an elegant ball gown.

Trent held Rose at arm's length to admire all of her with loving eyes and then, as if the room were filled with music, led her in a slow and gentle waltz. It was not long before he pulled her back to him again, flattening his hand on her back and then moving it down the length of her spine to rest just above the curve of her derriere. His other hand tilted her chin up, raising her lips up to meet his. His mouth was firm and warm over hers, moving tenderly with controlled passion.

"I'm not going to break in your arms," Rose said when he let his kiss fade from her lips.

"The doctor said—"

"The doctor said," Rose began with a devilish grin, "to stay in bed."

"And rest," Trent finished, not missing her meaning. He lifted her in his arms and put her back to bed.

Trent looked up at Rose while he industriously tucked her in. Her rosy lips were puckered in a pout too tempting for him to refuse.

Rose's eyes glowed with love as she watched Trent fuss over her. Her heart swelled inside her breast. She suddenly wanted to hold him close and feel the beat of his heart against hers.

Trent leaned over Rose and placed his lips on hers. He meant to leave her so she could rest. Rose had other ideas. She wrapped her arms around his neck and succeeded in toppling him onto her. "Rose, if anyone saw us they'd—"

"They'd think we were in love. You've absolutely won Father over and I suspect in time Aunt Stephanie will warm to you. Now stop being such a gentleman and—"

Trent didn't need any more convincing. Once Rose released him, he locked the door and began to shed his coat. "Are you sure you feel strong enough," he asked, still worried.

Rose kneeled on the bed and began to wiggle the buttons from his breeches. There was a sparkle in her eyes. "I intend to prove to you just how well you nursed me back to health."

Trent slipped beside Rose and cradled her in his arms. He nuzzled her neck and nibbled at her earlobe. "How I do love you, Rose. From the first moment I saw you, I knew you were special."

Rose held his head in her hands and sank into the dark depths of his eyes. "I know."

"You do? When did you know that?"

Rose giggled. "There were many times I thought I was sure you loved me, until you did something to make me doubt it. Like running off to Greece and staying away from me like the plague, or flirting with Marguerite."

"I never flirted with Marguerite. That was your jealousy stirring up your imagination. And running away . . . I suppose I was. Feeling myself so affected by a woman was a startling revelation. I wasn't ready for it."

"Are you ready now?" Rose asked in a sultry voice that provoked a low moan of surrender from Trent's throat.

"I'm ready for a lifetime of you, Rosie dear, beginning right now."

A sweet sigh of surrender came from beneath the blanket.